SPRING FORWARD

A MYSTIC CREEK NOVEL

Catherine Anderson

JOVE
New York

A JOVE BOOK
Published by Berkley
An imprint of Penguin Random House LLC
375 Hudson Street, New York, New York 10014

ISBN 9780399586347

First Printing: January 2018

Printed in the United States of America
1 3 5 7 9 10 8 6 4 2

Cover art: background daffodils © Alexander Raths/Shutterstock; heeler pup © Fotolia;
foreground daffodils © Master-L/Shutterstock; grass © antpkr/Shutterstock;
close-up of grass © Ievgenii Meyer/Shutterstock
Cover design by Colleen Reinhart
Book design by Tiffany Estreicher

Sometimes an animal creates spectacular magic in the lives of the people around it and brings the most unlikely of friends together so they can find love where they never expected to find it.

This book is dedicated to a dog named Rip who inspired me to write his story. I'd also like to thank his human mom, Renee Abbe, for all of her wonderful insights to help me portray Rip's loyal nature, his funny quirks, and so many stories about his life. Given that this is a novel, I have fictionalized the scenes that feature Rip, but I've tried to remain true to Rip's personality and bring him to life for you. He is an incredible canine and an unforgettable character.

Much appreciation also goes to my son John for all the evenings he spent helping me to plot this fabulous story.

Prologue

Seven years ago

A cutting Idaho wind, laced with the bawling of cattle, blew across the pasture and whined in Tuck Malloy's ears. Winter would come soon. Squinting, he studied the tops of tall evergreen trees undulating against the horizon. Soon the verdant grassland would turn the color of fresh-baked bread, and the blue of the sky would deepen to rifle-barrel gray. Snow would shroud the land, covering the hills and filling in the gullies. Imagining that biting cold made his arthritic joints pang, an unwelcome reminder that he was seventy-three and not getting any younger.

Tuck sighed, wishing he were anywhere but on his neighbor's, Jared Prince's, land. Unfortunately, there was an unspoken rule among ranchers in this area that a call for help from a fellow cattleman never went unheeded without good reason—and Tuck hadn't had a believable excuse to stay home. He'd grumped to himself as he'd driven here with his horse in the stock trailer, but now, saddled up and ready to go, he'd resigned himself to a long day. He enjoyed working with cattle. He'd focus on that and try not to let Prince get his goat.

Tuck guessed his animosity stemmed from the other man's abusive treatment of his wife before she finally found the courage to leave him. She'd been a scrawny thing, and as timid as an oft-kicked dog. Tuck had seen her sporting bruises too many times to believe she was merely accident-prone. Jared Prince was a woman beater, no two ways around it, and Tuck had no use for men of his ilk.

Cows bellowed as Tuck and other neighboring ranchers edged their horses into the milling herd. Jared hadn't castrated or marked last spring's calves yet. He was a lazy fellow and a procrastinator to boot. The aim today was to get all the postponed work done. Tuck disapproved of Jared's timing. Early castration was less stressful for a calf, and physical recovery was normally faster. It was also easier on the men doing the work when the calves were small.

Tuck pointed his gelding, Bolt, at a calf. His horse was well trained and only needed to be shown which critter he was supposed to single out. Mike Polson, the owner of a ranch a few miles south, manned the gate of the crowding pen. Just as Tuck pushed his first target inside the enclosure, he heard a canine yelping. It was the high-pitched cry of an animal in awful pain.

Tuck turned in the saddle to see whose dog had gotten hurt. His blood heated when he realized it was Jared's female blue heeler. Though her belly was swollen with pregnancy, Jared had chosen to work her today. Apparently, she had done something wrong, because Jared was leaning sideways in the saddle to jolt her with a cattle prod. The poor thing turned onto her back in surrender, giving her owner an opportunity to shock her swollen teats.

It took a great deal to make Tuck see red. Over the years, he'd turned a blind eye to a lot of things that disgusted him, but he couldn't and wouldn't tolerate animal abuse. Without thinking it through, he bumped his heels against Bolt's sides and the astonished horse jumped into a run. Tuck headed straight for Prince, still astride his mount, and leaped from the saddle onto his back. They both plummeted to the ground. Upon impact, Tuck rolled, struggled to his feet, and grabbed the prod that Prince had dropped. Pushing the pronged end against the fly of the other rancher's jeans, he pressed the trigger.

Prince screamed and huddled to protect his groin. Tuck didn't hesitate and shocked him a second time on the back of his neck where bare skin was exposed. All Tuck got were those two chances to give Prince a taste of his own medicine. Then someone grabbed the prod and jerked it from his hand.

"What do you think you're doing?" Polson had abandoned the gate and run over to intervene. "Damn, Tuck. Hotshots are for animals!"

"Not for a pregnant dog that's workin' her heart out. I'd like to shove it up the bastard's ass and light him up like a Christmas tree." Tuck swung out of the man's hold, picked up his Stetson, and strode back to his horse. "Y'all can turn a blind eye if you want. All I care about now is findin' that poor dog and takin' her to my place, where she'll be safe." He scanned the area. The blue heeler was nowhere in sight. "Which way did she go?"

Polson pointed. "Down yonder toward the river."

Tuck mounted his gelding as Prince scrambled to his feet. "That bitch belongs to me!" he yelled, thumping his chest and taking a step toward Tuck. "I already have buyers for her pups. You'll take her over my dead body!"

"That can be arranged," Tuck replied in a level voice. Prince stopped in his tracks. For the first time in his life Tuck felt capable of murder. He turned his horse toward the stream. Then he stopped to drill Prince with a glare. "A piece of advice to you, Jared. When I come back with that dog, stay the hell out of my way."

When Tuck reached the rocky bank of the river, he searched for the blue heeler's tracks. After ten minutes, he felt his pulse slow to a normal rate, but even though his anger had diminished, he didn't regret what he'd done and knew he never would. At least once in every man's life there came a moment when he couldn't stand aside and do nothing.

A picture lingered in his mind of the dog, and the thought of her whelping out here alone made him heartsick. Even if she found shelter, she'd endure a cold night. She'd also have no food, and once her pups were born, she'd be hard-pressed to hunt. It didn't seem fair that such a loyal and hardworking animal should suffer like that, and he hoped he could find her before darkness fell.

He combed the riverbank until dusk. *Tomorrow*, he vowed as he turned back. He'd return at first light to search again, and he wouldn't stop looking until he found her. She had more grit and stamina than a lot of men he knew, and she deserved a better life.

Once his ranch chores were done, Tuck spent nearly every afternoon for almost a month scouring the riverbank for Prince's dog. At the end of each day, he swore it would be the last. Looking this long for an animal that might already be dead was crazy. Only, for reasons beyond him, he couldn't give up the search. She couldn't have traveled far. She'd been about to whelp the morning she ran away. Had she been able to leave her pups long enough to hunt for food? Had she found some shelter to shield herself and the babies from the wind? The questions haunted him and deprived him of sleep at night.

He'd learned from a friend that the blue heeler's name was Molly. He'd called her so many times that he'd grown hoarse. If she heard his voice, would she come to him? She might be so frightened of men that she'd hide instead, and Tuck couldn't say he'd blame her.

The rockiness of the shore made it difficult for him to find tracks, and even when he did come across some in sandy stretches, they were blurred by wind and rain. He couldn't be sure if they'd been left by a dog or a coyote. Was he getting warm, or was he miles away from where Molly had holed up? If her puppies had survived, they'd be almost four weeks old by now. He wondered how many she might have had. Five, maybe six? Even as few as three would have suckled away the nutrients she needed to survive herself.

Toward the end of that last day, Tuck still didn't want to give up, but the weather forecast offered him no choice. About a week ago, it had turned colder, and tonight a foot of snowfall was predicted. He couldn't ride his horse through deep drifts when the ground underneath was so uneven. *Please, God, let me find her.*

He didn't know why it was so important to him to rescue a dog. Maybe it was because he'd failed others so many times that he was loath to do it again. He'd done a poor job of raising his daughter, Lisa, allowing her to grow up expecting her every wish to be granted. Then, despite symptoms he should have recognized, he'd let his wife, Marge, die of cardiac arrest. Only a few years after that, he'd hemmed and hawed around before taking his granddaughter, Crystal, away from her neglectful parents. As a result, the child had been emotionally damaged before he got custody. Just once, he wanted to make a difference. Just once, he wanted to think ahead, react in time to change an outcome, and be able to say, "I did it right this time."

He'd ridden several miles upstream since early afternoon. When he turned around, he knew it would be a long, cold ride back to his stock trailer. He began the trek with a heavy feeling in his chest and the metallic taste of failure on his tongue. He called Molly's name intermittently as he guided the gelding over the rocky ground. About halfway back to his starting point, he spotted what appeared to be a smooth, smallish boulder wedged under a high-water washout in the bank. Only, something about it made him stop and stare. Then he noticed a spot of rusty brown, and his heart started to pound.

"Molly?" he said. "Molly, come here, girl."

Only, the dog didn't move. *If* it was *even a dog.* After searching the woodlands that bordered the stream for so long, his eyes had begun to play tricks on him. He swung off the horse and walked toward the washout. As he drew closer, he could see the breeze furrowing the gray fur along the blue heeler's spine. *Molly.* At long last, he'd found her.

He rested his hand on her back and felt the coldness of death. How many times had he ridden past this spot? Had she been here all along, blocking the opening of the hollow with her body to protect her babies from the cold? A tight, squeezing sensation assailed his throat, and for a moment, he could barely breathe.

"Aw, Molly," he said softly. "I'm sorry, little lady."

Tuck slipped his hand over her body to feel inside the hole for her babies. His fingertips encountered six smaller shapes, all of them pressed against her belly and as cold and stiff as she was. He could only wish that he'd found them sooner.

Just as he started to draw back his hand, he heard an odd sound, and the next instant, it felt as if a dozen needles stabbed his thumb. Startled, he jerked his arm from the hole. The face and front feet of a puppy emerged from between the upper lip of the washout and Molly's body. Shrill barks and growls erupted from its scrawny chest, and then the little thing tumbled over its mother's back and hit the rocks. Tuck had never in his life been so taken aback. Judging by the pup's wobbly legs, it was weak with hunger and hanging on to life by a thread. But it had somehow survived and would have ripped him to shreds if it had had the size and strength.

"I'll be damned. With all that attitude, you're a boy, I bet."

The pup jumped and gave another shrill bark, trying to bite his hand again.

"Well, let 'er rip!" Tuck felt a grin lifting the corners of his mouth. "You tryin' to protect your family, little fella?"

The pup missed his mark, staggered forward, and then collapsed on his side. Concern wiped the smile from Tuck's face. This baby was about to join his littermates on the other side. The thought appalled Tuck. But he had nothing by way of food to keep the pup alive while he made the long ride back to the stock trailer and then drove home.

Tuck pulled Molly from the washout to make sure all the other babies were dead. When he felt confident there was only one to rescue, he rested his hand on the adult blue heeler's head. "You were a good dog, Molly. I'll be back to bury you and your babies, I swear. But right now, I've gotta save your son."

Scooping the puppy up in his hands, Tuck smiled again when the tiny blue heeler found the strength to growl at him. Granted, it was a faint growl, but it gave measure of his mettle. "You've got the heart of a lion," he observed as he opened the front of his sheepskin jacket and tucked the puppy inside his shirt. "If I can save you, you're gonna be one hell of a dog someday."

Holding his left arm across his ribs to keep his new charge held safely against him, Tuck swung back into the saddle and clicked his tongue at the gelding. "Easy does it, Bolt. We're carryin' precious cargo."

Tuck knew it would take at least three hours to get the dog to his ranch. Molly's son wouldn't last that long, not without sustenance and more warmth than Tuck could provide. He tipped his head back, pictured an aerial view of the surrounding terrain, and decided to head for Smokey's Bar. As the crow flies, it was about an hour away. Tuck went there often at night to have a few beers with local ranchers. Most of them had raised puppies on a bottle at some point, and Nora, the owner and operator, kept a fire blazing in the potbelly stove all winter.

He turned Bolt in that direction and settled in for one of the most urgent rides of his life. It seemed like forever before he finally saw lights in the distance. Maybe Nora had a recipe for puppy formula and the ingredients to make some.

Only a few rigs dotted the parking lot, which sported more potholes than gravel. Tuck recognized most of the vehicles and counted their owners as friends. He was glad Prince's red Silverado wasn't there. He was in no mood for a run-in with Jared over ownership of this dog. He cradled the puppy against his chest as he dismounted. The buckskin chuffed and grunted as Tuck flipped the reins over the boardwalk railing.

"I know," Tuck said to Bolt. "Time for your supper. I'll be back out shortly."

His footsteps rang out on the weathered steps. He pushed hard on the door and let the snow-flecked wind at his back help blow him inside. Nora, whose long, straight hair had turned salt-and-pepper, glanced up at the sound of the bell. She wore her usual attire, an oversize T-shirt over faded jeans. An expression of concern moved over her square-shaped face.

"Dear God, Tuck. You got a busted rib? Did Bolt throw you?"

Tuck realized he was still hugging his chest with his left arm. "Hell, no, Bolt didn't throw me. I've got one of Molly's pups inside my shirt."

A broad smile curved Nora's mouth. Mike Polson swiveled on his barstool. "After all this time, you finally found Prince's dog?"

Another rancher, named Dick Schneider, emulated Mike's movement to give Tuck an incredulous look. "Well, Jared will be fit to be tied. All he does is whine about losing the money he'd have made on that litter. Purebreds, and he could've registered all of them."

"I found her, but I was too late. She and the rest of the pups didn't make it." Tuck strode to the bar, reaching inside his jacket. "You got a heatin' pad and a warm blanket, Nora? Even better, if you've got the fixin's for puppy formula, I'll celebrate."

Nora shook her head. "I've got a blanket and heating pad, but I've never made puppy formula."

Glancing down the counter at Polson, Tuck said, "If I remember right, your wife saved a bunch of pups when your Aussie's milk didn't come down. You think she's still got the formula recipe?"

As Tuck withdrew the puppy from inside his jacket, Nora pressed her hands together as if she were praying. A glow touched her skin, blurring the wrinkles that fanned out from her blue eyes. "If that isn't the cutest thing I ever saw!"

Tuck had admired the puppy's gumption earlier, but he hadn't assessed him for cuteness. Turning the little guy to study him, he couldn't help but smile. All babies were cute, he guessed, but this one was downright handsome. Prick ears, outlined in black and furred within with curry, stood up at each side of his head like inverted shovel blades. The white blaze on his forehead veered off-center and ended just above his right brow, which looked as if it had been drawn with a charcoal pencil in a perfect arch. Temple splashes of rust offset his dark eyes. His nose was as brown and shiny as a raisin. Overall, except for more burnished markings on his chest and feet, his coat was the classic blend of gray and white common to blue heelers.

"He's damned near perfect, ain't he?" Murmurs of agreement made Tuck's smile broaden. He told his friends about finding the pup and getting his thumb bitten. "So weak he could barely walk, but he was determined to protect his family. I said, 'Let 'er rip!' So that's what I'm namin' him—Rip."

"You keeping him?" Mike asked. "You haven't had a dog since Tabasco died."

Tuck chuckled. "Nope, and it's high time I change that."

Nora whirled away, calling over her shoulder, "A heating pad and a blanket, coming right up. Mike, call your wife. If Molly and the other pups are dead, that one can't be long for this world. We need puppy formula, fast."

Mike fished his cell phone from his hip pocket. Bruce Smelt grappled for his as well. "Susan made puppy milk last spring. Maybe she saved the recipe."

Tuck swung up on a barstool and slipped Rip back inside his coat until Nora could fetch bedding. When she returned, she made a fluffy pallet on the bar, plugged in the warming device, and rested her palm on it to test the temperature.

"It's ready for him," she said. "Just a gentle warmth."

Tuck laid the puppy on the pad and pulled a corner of the blanket over him. "That'll warm his bones. Poor whippersnapper."

Bruce said, "Susan just texted back. She kept the recipe, and she has the stuff to make a batch. She'll have it here in an hour and a half."

"Good thing," Mike inserted. "My wife can't find her recipe."

Nora slipped her hand under the blanket to touch the animal. "He's painful thin, Tuck. Not much to him but fur and bones. What if he doesn't last until Susan gets here?"

"He's in God's hands, Nora, same as the rest of us. He'll make it or he won't."

Nora nodded. "Gonna break my heart if he dies. He's mighty precious."

Just then Rip pushed his nose from under the blanket and staggered onto the Formica countertop. Nora got tears in her eyes. "He's hungry. If he bit your thumb, he must have teeth. You think he could eat a beef patty if I crumble it up for him?"

"Maybe." Tuck glanced at Mike. "It's blizzardlike out there. I need to get Bolt inside and fork him some hay. While Nora's grillin' a patty, can you watch my dog? I don't wanna take him back out in that bitter cold."

Mike reached over to move the puppy and bedding in front of him. "I'll make sure he doesn't fall. Can't promise he won't cock up his toes from hunger, though."

Tuck nodded and swung off the stool. "Bolt put in a long day." Angling a look at Nora, he added, "I'll catch a ride to my truck and board him here for the night. I'll happily pay."

Nora flapped her hand. "Don't be silly. What's a few flakes of hay between old friends?"

Tuck refastened the front of his jacket. When he reached the porch, the wind cut through the sheepskin and chilled him to the bone. Bolt whickered and chuffed. Tuck could barely see him through the swirling snowflakes.

"Sorry, old friend."

Tuck led his horse to Nora's ramshackle excuse for a barn. Worried about the puppy, he made fast work of unsaddling Bolt, rubbing him down, and putting him up for the night.

"You'll do fine now," he said, reaching over the sagging gate to scratch the horse's poll. "You did me proud today, Bolt. Always do. You're a loyal friend, and that's a fact."

Once outside again, Tuck shuddered as he picked his way back toward the tavern. When he pushed back into the building, snow followed him inside and salted the rough-plank floor. He slapped his coat and stomped his riding boots on the rubber-backed carpet runner. "It's too cold out there for man or beast. Thank you, Nora. Bolt appreciates the accommodations."

Nora's face bore an odd expression. She glanced at Mike. "I'm sorry, Tuck. They don't listen worth a damn."

Tuck stepped over to the bar and saw that Rip had his head stuck into Mike's glass, his little tongue lapping beer at high speed.

"What the hell?" Tuck cried, reaching for his dog. "That stuff ain't good for him! What are you thinkin'?"

Mike lifted a staying hand. "The beef ain't done yet, and beer won't hurt him none. At least it's some nourishment."

Tuck glanced at Nora. "Is beer safe for him?"

She shrugged. "He's a mammal, just like us, and we drink it. Don't see why it'd hurt a dog. I just worry because he's only a baby."

Mike tipped the glass at a sharper angle to give the puppy better access. "He's starvin'. At least it's something on his tummy until the burger's cooked."

Tuck wasn't up-to-date on what was or wasn't good for a dog. But he trusted his friends, who'd both raised litters recently. He also reasoned that beer had to be rich in calories. His three cans a night sure kept his belly riding proud over the top of his belt buckle. The tension in his shoulders relaxed.

"If you're certain it won't hurt him, I reckon it's okay."

"My grandpa gave his border collie a big bowl of home brew every night, and that stuff was strong enough to stand up straight and kick out behind. His dog lived to be seventeen."

Tuck resumed his seat on the barstool. "He's gettin' his nose wet, for sure, and he does seem to like it." Rip kept lapping. Then he suddenly stopped and lay down. Tuck peeked around to see the puppy's face. The tip of his tongue protruded over his bottom teeth, and he had a happy look about him. Tuck couldn't help but smile. "I reckon that'll hold him until the formula arrives."

Just then Nora emerged from the kitchen with a beef patty on a plate. When she put it on the counter and began breaking the meat into small pieces, Rip struggled to his feet and began eating. Nora laughed when the puppy devoured every morsel.

"I think he's going to make it, Tuck. I truly do."

Tuck hoped she was right. At one time his dog Tabasco had been his constant companion, but he'd been gone for almost ten years now. It was time for Tuck to have a new best friend.

Chapter One

Wind whistled into the big black van, whipping Tanner Richards' hair across his forehead as he drove. Squinting at the gravel road through the brown strands drifting over his eyes, he hauled in a deep breath of pine-scented air. Five years ago he'd agonized over his decision to sell his accounting firm and move to Crystal Falls, Oregon. He'd given up a six-figure annual income with no assurance that he could even find a job in this area. Crazy, really. Looking back on it now, though, he was glad that he'd come. Being a deliveryman wasn't as prestigious as working in his former chosen profession, but he made enough money to provide a good life for his kids, and he truly enjoyed the occupation. Having a rural route suited him. He was required to make fewer stops than he would have been in town, which equated to shorter workdays and more time in the evening to be with his children. And he'd made a lot of friends. Folks around here were more congenial than they were in larger towns.

As he rounded a curve in the country road, Tanner saw Tuck Malloy's house. Sadness punched into him. For three years running, he'd often stopped there to visit at the end of his workday, and he'd enjoyed a lot of cold ones on the porch with his elderly friend. Now the windows reflected the darkness of an empty structure. A For Sale sign rode high on the front gate. It had appeared nearly a month ago.

Tanner had considered calling the Realtor to learn what had happened to the property owner after his calls to Tuck went unanswered, but he really didn't want to know. Tuck had been a crusty old codger and eighty years young, as he'd been fond of saying. Unexpected things could happen to people that age. A heart attack, maybe, or a stroke. Tuck liked that piece of ground, and he would never have left voluntarily. He'd said so more than once. Tanner figured the old fellow was dead. Otherwise why would his place be up for sale?

Tanner pulled over and stopped outside the hurricane fence for a moment, a habit he had developed since the home had been vacated. He trailed his gaze over the front porch, now devoid of the comfortable Adirondack chairs where he had once sat with Tuck to chat. Recalling the old man's recalcitrant dog, he smiled. *Rip.* Tanner hoped the blue heeler had found a good home. He'd been a handful and was probably difficult to place.

Damn, he missed them both. With a sigh Tanner eased the van back onto the road. He had only one more delivery before he could call it a day. Maybe he could mow the lawn and do some weeding before his kids got home. Tori, now eight, had dance class after school today, and Michael, eleven and getting gangly, had baseball practice. Since his wife's death, Tanner had been a single dad, and not a day went by that he wasn't grateful for his mom's help. She got his kids off to the bus stop each morning and chauffeured them to most of their activities, which took a huge load of responsibility off his shoulders.

Tanner delivered the last parcel of the day. After he dropped the van off at Courier Express, he needed to pick up some groceries. Milk, for one thing. Tori wouldn't eat breakfast without it. And if he didn't get bread, he'd have no fixings for his lunch tomorrow.

His cell phone, which rode atop a sticky mat on the dash, chimed with a message notification. Tanner grabbed the device and glanced at the screen to make sure the text wasn't from his mother. She never contacted him during work hours unless it was urgent. When he read the name of the sender, his hand froze on the steering wheel. *Tuck Malloy?* He almost went off the road into a ditch. How could that be? The old coot was dead. Wasn't he?

Tanner pulled over onto a wide spot, shifted into PARK, and stared at his phone. The message was definitely from Tuck. They had exchanged cell numbers months ago, and Tuck had occasionally texted to ask Tanner to pick up items he needed from the store. It hadn't been a bother for Tanner. There was a mom-and-pop grocery not that far away, and Tuck's house was on the road he always took back to town.

He swiped the screen. A smile curved his lips as he read the message. *"I fell off the damned porch. Busted my arm, some ribs, and had to get a hip replacement. Now I'm doing time in assisted living, and the bitch that runs the place won't let me have my beer or chew. Can you buy me some of both and sneak it in to me? I'll pay you back."*

Tanner had been picturing the old fart in heaven, sitting on an Adirondack chair with a six-pack of Pabst Blue Ribbon and a spittoon within easy reach. It was unsettling to think someone was dead and then receive a text from him.

He tapped out a response. *"I don't mind bringing you things. My kids have activities this afternoon, so I'm not pressed for time. But I don't want to get in trouble for delivering forbidden substances. My job could be on the line."*

Tuck replied, *"No trouble. Just put it inside a box*

and pretend it's something I ordered. If I get caught, I'll never tell who brought me the stuff. Sorry I can't just call, but these nurses have sharp ears and I got no privacy."

Tanner grinned. He trusted the old man not to reveal his name if it came down to that. And he truly did sympathize with Tuck's feelings of deprivation. Just because a man was eighty shouldn't mean he no longer had a right to indulge his habits. Staying at an assisted living facility was costly, and in Tanner's estimation, the residents should be able to do whatever they liked in their apartments as long as their physicians didn't object.

He texted, *"Do you have your doctor's permission to drink and chew?"*

Tuck replied, *"Well, he ain't said I shouldn't. I been drinking and chewing my whole life. I'm eighty. What can he say, that my pleasures might kill me?"*

Tanner chuckled. He agreed to deliver the requested items and asked Tuck for the address. He was surprised to learn the facility was in Mystic Creek. Tanner didn't cover that area, and it was a thirty-minute drive to get there. He mulled over the fact that he would be driving for more than an hour round-trip in a Courier Express van to run a personal errand. He'd also be using company fuel, which didn't seem right, but he supposed he could top off the tank to make up for that. He could also adjust his time sheet so he wouldn't be paid for an hour he hadn't actually worked.

Whistling tunelessly, Tanner made the drive to Mystic Creek. He hadn't yet gotten over this way. The curvy two-lane highway offered beautiful scenery, tree-covered mountain peaks, craggy buttes, and silvery flashes of a river beyond the stands of ponderosa pine. To his surprise, he saw a turnoff to Crystal Falls—the actual waterfall, not the town—and he made a mental note to bring the kids up sometime to see it. They'd get a kick out of that. Maybe they could spread a blanket on the riverbank and have a picnic.

Once in Mystic Creek, a quaint and well-kept little town, he found a grocery store on East Main called Flagg's Market, where he purchased two six-packs of beer and a whole roll of Copenhagen for his elderly friend. In the van he always carried extra box flats. He assembled a medium-size one, stuck what he now thought of as the contraband into it, and taped the flaps closed. With a ballpoint pen, he wrote Tuck's full name, the address, and the apartment number on a Courier Express mailing slip, which he affixed to the cardboard. *Done.* Now he'd just drive to the facility and make the delivery. The rest would be up to Tuck.

Mystic Creek Retirement Living was in a large brick building with two wings that angled out toward the front parking lot. The back of the facility bordered Mystic Creek, which bubbled and chattered cheerfully between banks lined with greenery, weeping willows, and pines. He suspected the residents spent a lot of time on the rear lawns, enjoying the sounds of rushing water and birdsong. If he were living there, that's what he would do.

Striding across the parking area with the box in his arms, Tanner began to feel nervous. What if someone questioned him? Pausing outside the double glass doors, he took a calming breath and then pushed inside. A middle-aged woman with red hair sat at the front desk. She fixed her friendly-looking blue gaze on Tanner's face and smiled.

"You're new," she observed. "Brian usually delivers our Courier Express packages."

Tanner nodded. "Uh, yeah. Just helping out today.

I've got a package for Tucker Malloy, apartment twenty-three."

She pointed to a wide hallway to the left of the counter. "About halfway down on the right."

Tanner circled her workstation and moved past her. When he reached Tuck's room, he knocked on the door and called, "Delivery. Courier Express."

He heard a shuffling sound, and seconds later, Tuck opened the door, flashing a broad grin. "Come in, come in," he said in a booming voice. "Must be those shoes and pants I ordered."

Tanner winked at his old friend as he made his way through the doorway. As he set the box on the living room floor, he noticed that Tuck held a walking cane in his left hand. After closing the door, he walked with a limp as he crossed the tiny kitchen. Tanner guessed the old fellow's hip still pained him. Otherwise he looked the same, tall and lean with slightly stooped shoulders. His blue eyes held the same merry twinkle. Deep smile creases bracketed his mouth. His hair, still thick, was mostly silver, but a few streaks of brown remained to indicate its original color.

"It's good to see you," Tanner told him. "When your place went up for sale, I tried to call you several times and left you voice mails. Then I couldn't get through anymore. I figured you'd passed away and your phone had been retired to a drawer."

"Hell, no. I'm too ornery to kick the bucket just yet. Not to say it's an outlandish thing for you to think. At eighty, I don't buy green bananas anymore. They're a risky investment."

Tanner laughed. Tuck bent to open the box, plucked a can of beer from one six-pack yoke, and offered it up. With regret, Tanner declined. "I can't stay, Tuck. My kids will be getting home in a couple of hours."

Tuck straightened slowly, as if stiffness had settled into his spine. On his right arm he wore a red elbow-high cast that extended down over the back of his hand to his knuckles and encircled his thumb. "That's a shame. I miss our bullshit sessions."

"Me, too," Tanner confessed. "I'll try to come back for a visit when I have more time." He bent to lift the six-packs from the box. "Where you planning to hide these?"

"In my boots and coat pockets. My beer'll be warm, but that's better'n nothin'."

Tanner carried the twelve-ounce containers to the closet, opened the doors, and began slipping cans into the old man's footwear. Tuck hobbled in with the roll of Copenhagen, which Tanner broke open before stuffing the rounds into shirt and jacket pockets. He couldn't help but grin when everything was hidden. With a wink at Tuck, he whispered, "They'll never know."

"Damn, I hope not," Tuck said. "My Pabst Blue Ribbon helps me relax at night. Without it I toss and turn. When I complain, the damned administrator just scowls at me and says to ask my doctor for sleeping pills. Like that'd be any better for my health? Hell, no. I like my beer."

Tanner stared at him. "What are you going to do with the empties?"

Tuck winked. "They got a resident laundry room down the hall with two tall trash cans. I'll sneak 'em down there and bury 'em real deep under other garbage."

"I see no harm in you enjoying your beer of an evening unless your doctor has forbidden it," Tanner said. "You'd tell me if that were the case. Right?"

"Wouldn't have asked you if he had. I don't have a death wish. I just want my damn beers and chew. The doc knows I have three beers a night and he never said nothin'. Of course, it's a different fella here. Their Dr. Fancy Pants might not make allowances for a man's personal pleasures."

"That sucks." Tanner had never stopped to consider how many liberties people could lose when they grew old. "But it's temporary. Right? Once you've healed, you can live somewhere else again." Tanner remembered the real estate sign on Tuck's front gate. "You *do* get to leave here, I hope."

"The doctors are sayin' that I shouldn't live alone again." He shrugged. "At my age, that's how it goes, with other people decidin' what's best for you."

"I'm sorry to hear you can't live alone anymore." Tanner sincerely meant that. "Maybe you can make arrangements for some kind of in-home care. If you can afford that, of course."

"I'm workin' on it. I got plenty of money saved back, so I had Crystal get me another house here in Mystic Creek. She found a nice little place on ten acres just outside town. It's a short drive from her salon, and she's already livin' there. The house was made over for an old lady in a wheelchair, but she passed away. Crystal thinks it'll suit my needs, and she's willin' to stay there to look after me."

Tanner nodded. "That sounds ideal. Ten acres isn't quite as much land as you had in Crystal Falls, but at least you'll still have elbow room." For most of his life, Tuck had been a rancher. Tanner doubted he would be happy living inside the city limits on a small lot. "You're blessed to have a granddaughter who loves you so much."

"I am, for certain. She's a sweet girl."

"Where's Bolt? At the new place?"

"Nope. Crystal has enough to do without fussin' over

a horse. I had her find a place to board him. When I'm able, I'll bring him home and take care of him."

Tanner walked back into the living room, stabbing his fingers under his belt to neaten the tuck of his brown uniform shirt. "I sure wish I could stay for a while, but I've got to run."

"I understand. It'll soon be suppertime, and you've got kiddos to feed. Next time we'll enjoy a beer together and get caught up. You drive safe on that curlicue highway gettin' home. You're all your kids have left."

Tanner paused at the door. An urge came over him to hug the old fart goodbye. He wasn't sure when he'd come to care so much about Tuck, but after believing him to be dead for nearly a month, he found the feelings were there inside him. The old man had some crazy notions that Tanner didn't agree with, and sometimes he told stories so far-fetched that no sane person could believe them. But he also had a big heart, an indomitable spirit, and a way of looking at life that brought everything into perspective for Tanner sometimes. Still, Tanner wasn't sure the older man would appreciate being hugged.

"I'll be seeing you," he said.

Then he let himself out and softly closed the door.

Crystal Malloy's feet ached as if she'd run barefoot on concrete for eight hours. When she glanced in the styling mirror and saw her reflection, she yearned to wash her long red hair. Pink spray-on highlights had been a poor choice. The clash of color was nauseating, and she looked awful. But she had no time to spare for herself. She hadn't even found time to eat lunch or visit the bathroom.

Prom night. It was normally her favorite spring event,

the school year's grand finale that always filled her salon to the brim with customers. She had girls sitting double in the chairs lining one wall and all four stations were filled with more teenagers. They wanted updos, wash-out streaks, metallic highlights, straight hair, curly hair, or crimped hair. And all of them wanted their makeup done.

The sulfuric smell of permanent-wave solution burned Crystal's nostrils, her skin felt sticky from the clouds of hair spray inside the building, and her nerves were shot. Her technicians had been trained never to overbook appointments, so half these kids must have been walk-ins. With only four stations, how would they get to all of them? There were drawbacks to owning the most popular salon in town.

Relax, she told herself. *Just roll with it. By six thirty, they'll all look gorgeous and be going home to put on their gowns.* Only, she was so tired. It had been a long day, and everything that could go wrong had gone wrong. At noon she'd gotten a call from a neighbor that Rip, her grandfather's dog, was running loose again. In order to find the animal, she'd had to hand over a tint job to Shannon Monroe, a tall, slender brunette who'd had a cancellation and was able to finish the customer's hair. Then, after two hours of driving the gravel roads surrounding Tuck's new house, she had missed two more appointments and she *still* hadn't found the dog. Where was he? Had he been struck by a car? Her grandfather loved that heeler like no tomorrow and would be inconsolable if anything happened to him. Even worse, Rip's escapes were becoming a daily occurrence. How could she make a living when she spent half of what should have been her workdays looking for a runaway canine? Locking him up inside the house was out. He was destructive when he was confined indoors alone.

Glancing around the salon, Crystal remembered a time when this place had been only a dream. Instead of being in a foul mood, she should have felt proud of her accomplishments and thankful that she'd met her goals. The shop was high-end and classy. The hair and nail techs were dressed in designer uniforms. The waiting room was packed with paying customers who hoped to look beautiful when they left. Soft Hawaiian music played on the sound system, enabling people to imagine they were in a tropical paradise. The thought made Crystal smile. Mystic Creek was anything but tropical. City plows sometimes left berms of winter snow in the middle of the street that were higher than her head.

The phone rang just as Crystal had finished applying temporary color to a strand of a girl's blond hair. "I can't get it! Does anyone have a hand free?"

Nadine Judge, a half-Cherokee woman with thick black hair and almond-shaped brown eyes, yelled back, "I'll get it!" Then Crystal heard her say, "I'm sorry. Is this an emergency, Patricia? She's really busy." Then, in a louder voice, she cried, "You've got to take it, Crystal. It's Patricia from the assisted living facility. Tuck has done something wrong, and she's threatening to evict him."

Pain bulleted into Crystal's temples. For a dizzying moment, bright spots danced before her eyes. When her vision cleared, she grabbed a piece of foil, laid a still-wet strand of her young client's lavender hair on it, and said, "Sorry, Megan. I'll be right back."

Crystal walked over to the front desk. Nadine cupped her hand over the mouthpiece and said in a stage whisper, "God, she can't kick him out! You don't even have neighbors near the house who can check on him during the day, and according to what you've said, he's still not steady on his feet."

Crystal didn't need anyone to outline the reasons she couldn't take her grandfather home yet. She tried to smile at Nadine and knew she failed miserably. She took the phone and pressed it to her ear. "This is Crystal."

"Hello, Crystal. This is Patricia Flintlock. *Again*. Your grandfather has really done it this time."

Crystal clenched her teeth and counted to five. She didn't have time to go clear to ten. "Hi, Patricia. I know Tuck is having a hard time adjusting to his new surroundings, but surely he's done nothing so bad that he should be evicted."

"Think again." Patricia didn't handle a position of authority well. As administrator of the assisted living center, she reigned like a female Hitler. "I have rules in this facility, and they're nonnegotiable."

The pain in Crystal's temples stabbed deeper. "What rule has Tuck broken?"

"Make that *rules*. We caught him drinking beer and chewing tobacco in his apartment. I will not countenance drunkenness in my building, and chewing tobacco is messy and thoroughly disgusting. I won't have it, I'm telling you!"

Crystal had to bite her tongue. She'd gone to live with Tuck when she was eleven; she was now thirty-two, and in all those years she'd never seen her grandfather drunk. "How could Tuck get his hands on beer and chew? He can't drive yet, and even if he could, his truck is at the house."

"Well, now," Patricia replied in a snarky tone, "that's a good question, and the only answer I can think of is that *you* brought it to him. I know you're aware of the facility rules. Your flagrant disregard of them is infuriating, to say the least."

Crystal struggled to control her temper. "That's a preposterous accusation. You know Tuck isn't recovered enough to come home. I haven't even found a daytime caregiver for him yet. Why would I take him beer and tobacco when I'm fully aware that you might evict him from the only place he has to stay right now?"

"Another good question. Tuck is new to Mystic Creek. Nobody but you comes to visit him. Do you expect me to believe those substances appeared out of thin air?"

"I expect you to believe me when I tell you straight-out that I did not supply my grandfather with beer and chew."

"You complained early on about the rules here being too strict."

"But I agreed to abide by them," Crystal argued. "And I have. I don't know how Tuck got his hands on beer, but I can assure you I'll find out and it'll never happen again."

"You need to come to the facility. We'll discuss the matter further. Your grandfather is upset and yelling obscenities. If you don't get him calmed down, I'm calling the police."

Crystal scanned the crowded salon. She couldn't leave her techs to deal with all this by themselves. But she knew the facility administrator meant what she said. She'd evict Tuck without hesitation. "It's prom night, Patricia, one of my busiest days of the year. I've got a girl half-finished at my station. I can't drop everything and leave her with only one side of her head streaked."

"We all have our problems. Mine is an angry old man who is disturbing other residents."

Crystal started to reply, but Patricia hung up before

she could. She stared stupidly at the phone and then returned it to the charging base.

"What did Tuck do this time?" Nadine, putting the finishing touches on a girl's layered bob, flashed a worried look over her shoulder. "What'll you do if she kicks him out?"

Crystal jerked off her salon jacket, a dark brown tunic-length garment patterned with palm fronds. "They caught him with beer and chewing tobacco. Patricia says he's yelling obscenities and being disruptive."

"Patricia Flintlock is an uptight pain in the butt," Nadine retorted. "Why can't Tuck have a couple of beers? Better question, what is her definition of an obscenity?"

Crystal tossed the jacket in the laundry basket. "Regardless, I have to drive over there and get Tuck settled down. Then I need to defuse the situation so he doesn't get kicked out." Glancing toward her station, she said, "I'm sorry for abandoning all of you, but I see no way around it."

Jules Wilson, a slightly plump blonde with twinkly blue eyes, said, "I can finish Megan. You have an emergency on your hands. And, Crystal, recommend to Patricia that she come to see me. I'll color her hair and accidently make it green."

Crystal grabbed her purse and left the building. The moment she stepped out onto the back porch, she dragged in a deep breath of fresh air and took a moment to appreciate the sunlight angling through the pine boughs to splash the needle-covered ground with butter yellow. *Everything will be okay,* she assured herself. *Patricia will get over her snit, and Tuck will start behaving himself. All I need is a couple more weeks to make arrangements. Then I'll be able to take care of him.*

* * *

After making the fifteen-minute drive, Crystal reached the assisted living center at five thirty. The sun clung to the horizon in the western sky over snowcapped peaks, and she knew dusk would soon blanket the valley. It had taken Crystal a long while to grow accustomed to the early sunsets that occurred in an area surrounded by mountains. Twilight lasted for hours. But now she appreciated the cool summer evenings and the ever-present breezes.

Dropping her keys into her purse, she slipped out of her Chevy Equinox. Flower-bed tulips had sprung up under the drive-through portico, but the petals hadn't opened yet. Even so, the closed blossoms lent color to the evergreen landscaping.

The sound of Tuck yelling obscenities didn't greet her when she entered the facility. The heels of her shoes clicked against the creamy tile floor as she walked to the front desk. Marsha, a friendly redhead who'd recently divorced her husband, manned the desk for most of the weeknight shifts. She seemed to like her job, but Crystal knew she didn't care for her boss. Marsha was a regular at the salon and complained nonstop about Patricia while her gray roots were touched up.

"The dragon is in her cave," she said. "Enter with caution. She's breathing fire tonight."

Crystal sighed. "Can she really evict an old man who has nowhere else to go?"

Marsha shrugged. "Legally? It beats me. But I wouldn't put it past her. And just so you know, Tuck didn't yell obscenities like she says. He cussed a lot, but he said nothing I haven't said myself many a time. At its worst, I don't think of my language as being obscene."

"I appreciate the information."

Crystal had visited the dragon's cave frequently and needed no direction. She turned to cross the community area, which was also tiled in cream squares, and furnished with brown sofas and chairs. She tapped on the door tagged with a brass plaque that read, ADMINISTRATOR, PATRICIA FLINTLOCK.

"You may enter," the woman called out.

Crystal might have laughed if her mood hadn't been so sour. Did the woman think she was a military commander? She stepped into the office, a small space sparsely appointed with only a desk, two chairs, and a file cabinet. Creamy walls blended with the floor, giving Crystal the feeling she'd just been dunked into a tub of milk.

Patricia's steel gray hair was cut in a jaw-length pageboy and lacquered so heavily that a high wind wouldn't disturb a strand. It looked like a metal helmet sitting on her head. Her unfriendly hazel eyes peered at Crystal through narrowed lids. Her mouth was drawn into a grim line. Her cheeks had lost the war with gravity and slipped downward to give her face a jowly appearance. If she wore a trace of cosmetics, it wasn't apparent.

She straightened the collar of her gray shirtwaist dress. "Please, take a seat."

Thinking the woman would have made a formidable high school principal, Crystal sat down. "I haven't heard a peep coming from Tuck's residence," she observed. "I assume he stopped yelling."

"Only after he called me a power-mongering, menopausal bitch."

Trust Tuck to be accurate as well as profane. Crystal cleared her throat. "He's normally a mellow man. This has been a difficult time for him and has brought a lot of changes into his life."

"We all must adjust to old age and the changes that come with it."

"That doesn't mean all of us can do it gracefully. My grandfather has been independent until now, and suddenly he's surrounded by attendants who monitor his every move and tell him what to do. Surely you can understand that it's difficult for him."

"Where are you going with this?"

Crystal crossed her legs and folded her hands on her lap. "I'm hoping to convince you Tuck deserves another chance. I'll have a talk with him, and I assure you this will never happen again."

Patricia's eyes narrowed even more. "There is the matter of who brought him the forbidden substances. You've yet to name a single person who might have done it, which leaves you as the only suspect."

Crystal's mouth went chalky. "You can't seriously believe I would jeopardize my grandfather's residency here. I have nowhere else to place him within a reasonable driving distance. Round-trips to see him in Crystal Falls would eat up over an hour of each day, not to mention the length of my visits and the cost of gas."

"Until I'm convinced you didn't sneak beer and tobacco into this building, your grandfather's right to be here is in jeopardy."

Crystal knew the woman meant it. Whether it was reasonable or not, she wouldn't hesitate to kick Tuck out. "I'll talk with Tuck. Maybe he'll tell me how he got the stuff."

"Good luck. He won't want to reveal his source. I'm sure he hopes to get more."

Crystal stood and collected her purse. "After my talk with Tuck, I'll be back to discuss this further."

Patricia inclined her head like a queen who'd just

granted a lowly attendant permission to leave. Crystal wished she could put the woman in her place, but for Tuck's sake, she had to keep her mouth shut.

As she passed Marsha's station, the receptionist asked, "Did she breathe fire and singe your eyebrows?"

Crystal winked. "I held her at bay with the fire extinguisher."

She walked down the hall to Tuck's apartment, rapped on the door, and then cracked it open to poke her head inside. "You decent, Tuck? It's me, Crystal."

"At least you gave me a warnin'. Come on in, but don't start yammerin' at me."

Crystal walked through the tiny kitchen into his adjoining living room. Tuck sat in a brown recliner that she'd brought from his home in Crystal Falls. The faux-suede sofa and burl coffee table had also come from there. She set her purse on the glossy wood and folded her arms at her waist.

"When you stand like that, I know I'm in for a scold. But before you start, that woman tells outright lies."

She loved this old man. He had taken her in when her life at home had been miserable beyond bearing, and he'd helped her make a fresh start. In all the years since, he'd never once let her down. No matter what it took, she'd never let him down, either. "She says you called her a power-mongering, menopausal bitch. Was that a lie?"

"Nope. I said that, and I stand behind it. It's the God's honest truth."

A smile tugged at Crystal's lips. With a sigh, she sat near him on the sofa. "Oh, Tuck, what am I going to do with you? Patricia is an extremely unpleasant and rigid person, but in order for you to stay here, we have to get along with her."

"Honey, I don't want to stay here. I'm workin' hard

to get stronger and countin' the days until I can leave. I'm gettin' better every day."

"I know you are. But the doctors want you to remain here for two more months. They say the daily physical therapy sessions are crucial to a full recovery."

"I ain't stayin' in this hellhole that long," Tuck retorted. "I got no privacy or freedom to do as I like."

"I understand, and I'm doing everything I can to get you out of here sooner. I can take you in for physical therapy. We'll make it all work somehow. Just give me a little more time to make arrangements."

"I don't wanna die in this place."

Crystal picked at a fleck of lint on her dark brown slacks. She hated it when Tuck talked about dying. It made her stomach hurt. "I won't let that happen. But you're still not steady on your feet. It's hard for you to get up and down with only one good arm. What if you fell? I can't leave you alone yet."

He sighed. "I think I'd be okay. I ain't some invalid who can't do nothin'."

Searching for words, Crystal smoothed the sofa arm. She couldn't allow Tuck's pride to rule the day. In his younger years, he'd worked from dawn until well after dark, and he'd refused to ask for help unless there'd been no way around it. If she tried to picture a man among men, she saw her grandfather. He would never admit now that he needed supervision. But, regardless, it was her job to see that he got it. "Can you work with me? Give me two more weeks?"

"That ain't so long. I reckon I can stand almost anything for two weeks."

Her shoulders relaxed. "Patricia thinks I brought you the beer and tobacco. If I can't convince her otherwise, she says she'll evict you. Please tell me who brought those things to you."

Tuck shook his head. "I can't do that."

Crystal met his gaze. "I won't get the person in trouble, Tuck. I just need to pacify Patricia by telling her who did it."

He snorted. "It won't be up to you! That woman don't care who she hurts."

Crystal couldn't argue with that point. She'd never met anyone like Patricia Flintlock. "Until I can take you home, you have to cooperate and follow the rules so you can stay here."

"Like I'm five years old? I did nothin' wrong. Drinkin' beer and chewin' snuff ain't a crime. You should've been here! When a nurse saw I had beer in a coffee mug, she acted like Jack the Ripper had invaded the buildin'. Next thing I knew, the alpha bitch came in with two more women, and they started tearin' the place apart. When they came across cans of Pabst Blue Ribbon in my shoes and boots, they acted like they'd found that crack Coca-Cola stuff!"

Crystal's brain snagged on that. Then she realized he was talking about illegal drugs he'd heard about on the news. "I know it can be difficult here," she tried.

"*Difficult?* You ever had someone go through your cupboards and drawers? One gal reached under my mattress and found my *Playboy* magazines!"

"You read *Playboy*?"

"I don't *read* 'em. What man in his right mind *reads* 'em? I buy 'em to look at the girls. And she was gonna throw 'em away! How is that right? I pay for 'em. They're mine."

Crystal held up a hand. "It isn't right, Tuck. This whole mess frustrates me, too. You're entitled to your privacy, even here."

"As far as that goes, I got a right to drink beer and chew snuff if I've a mind."

"Yes, you do. Patricia is unreasonably strict."

"Then get me outta here! It's like doin' time in prison."

Crystal pushed up from the sofa and began to pace. "I will, Tuck. Only two more weeks. That's all I'm asking."

"I'll give you that, but not a day more. Then I'm leavin' whether you like it or not. I'll take care of my own damned self."

"I'll be here to help you pack," she assured him. "And I'll have men hired to move you home. No more rules, Tuck. No more nosy women to violate your rights. But for now, we have to play along and keep peace with Patricia. In order to do that, I need the name of the person who brought you the beer and chew."

"How do you know I didn't just order the stuff?"

"Why didn't you tell me that in the first place?" A wave of relief washed over her. "I can show her the order to prove a third party wasn't involved. That should settle her down."

Crystal grabbed his phone from the arm of his chair. Tuck tried to take it back, but in her eagerness to find the evidence she needed, she avoided his reach. She tapped the screen of the cell and began searching the communication data. She saw nothing to indicate Tuck had ordered anything recently, but she did find a message thread with an individual named Tanner. Her heart sank as she met her grandfather's fiery gaze.

"You didn't order anything."

"Of course not!" Tuck puffed air into his wrinkled cheeks. "You can't order beer and chew online."

Crystal thought a person probably could, but she wasn't about to disabuse her grandfather of that notion. "So this Tanner person brought you the forbidden stuff."

"He's my friend. I promised he wouldn't get in trouble!"

"I have no intention of getting him in trouble. He just did you a favor. He meant no harm." She took a calming breath. "Is that his first or last name? And who is he?"

Tuck sat back in his recliner and clenched his teeth. She knew by his expression that he wouldn't divulge a full name under threat of death. Feeling defeated, she scanned the room. In one corner sat a box. She walked over, lifted it by a flap, and studied the mailing label. "You've had a recent delivery from Courier Express."

"I don't know what you're talkin' about," Tuck said. "That's old, a movin' box you left here."

Crystal had fleetingly hoped her grandfather actually had ordered the contraband, but his quick denial negated that possibility. Otherwise he would have just said the delivery company had brought him his purchases. This definitely wasn't a moving box. She'd long since flattened all of them and stored them in a closet at the farmhouse. "What's your friend's full name, Tuck?"

"I ain't talkin'." Anger flickered in his eyes. "Those bitches can waterboard me, and I still won't sing."

"Fine." She returned the cell phone to the arm of his recliner. "I'll handle it from here."

"How? You don't got his name."

"With a simple phone call to Courier Express, I'll have his name. I can prove to Patricia that I didn't aid and abet you in breaking her stupid rules." She tried to smile. "It'll be better this way, Tuck. You don't have to betray your friend, and I can get the situation under control with Patricia."

"Don't you *dare* do that," Tuck said softly. "If you get Tanner in trouble, I may never forgive you. I mean it."

Crystal collected her purse. "Trust me just a little. I know your friend did nothing wrong, and I'll make sure he doesn't get in trouble. All I want is to pacify Patricia so you don't get evicted before I can take proper care of you."

She turned to leave. Tuck yelled, "Crystal Lynn Malloy, if you tell anyone his name, I'll be mad enough to chew nails and spit out screws! I mean it!"

Chapter Two

At the front desk, Crystal looked up the phone number of Courier Express in Crystal Falls. It wasn't yet six, and she hoped a mail center would have employees still on-site. Employees stayed pretty busy in those places, sorting parcels and loading delivery trucks for the following day. She would do everything she possibly could to protect Tuck's friend, but her number one priority had to be her grandfather's welfare. He was steadier on his feet, but she still couldn't be positive he wouldn't get overbalanced and take another fall. She placed the call. A woman finally answered.

"Hello. My name is Crystal Malloy. One of your drivers delivered a package to my grandfather today, and I need to learn his last name. I believe his first name is Tanner."

The employee said, "Oh, yes, that would be Tanner Richards. He's already left. May I take a message?"

"Oh, uh, no, that's fine. I just wanted his last name. Thank you so much."

Crystal ended the call and squeezed her eyes shut. Opening them, she found Marsha staring at her with an inquiring look. "The Courier Express guy brought the goodies? He was a new face, but he nice."

Crystal nodded. "I'm sure he is."

"Are you going to report him?"

Crystal shook her head. "I only needed his name to

convince Patricia that I played no part in this mess. If Tuck gets kicked out of here, I'm out of good options . . . and so is he."

Marsha rested her bent arms on the edge of the desk. "It was only a few beers and some tobacco. I don't know what that woman's problem is. Most people would just laugh and shrug it off."

"Patricia Flintlock isn't most people."

Crystal retraced her steps to the administrator's door and tapped lightly on the wood.

"You may enter," Patricia called.

Crystal stepped into the office. Patricia didn't appear to have budged since Crystal's departure. It seemed odd that no paperwork lay in front of her. What did she do in here, only fiddle with her pen? "My grandfather refused to give me the man's last name, but I got it anyway. Before I tell you anything more, I want your word that you won't try to get Tuck's friend in trouble."

Patricia shrugged. "You have my word. I won't try to get his friend in trouble."

Some of the tension eased from Crystal's body. She could deal with this woman. Tuck should have trusted her to do that. "There's a box in Tuck's living room, which you must have overlooked. It bears a Courier Express mailing label. I got the deliveryman's first name from Tuck's phone, and I was told his last name when I called the company."

"And?" Patricia pressed. She did not invite Crystal to sit down.

"And what?"

"I'd like his full name."

"I'd greatly appreciate it if you don't pursue this."

"I've already told you I have no intention of pursuing it. What is his name?"

"Tanner Richards," Crystal confessed. "He's a company driver. I'm guessing his regular route is in Crystal Falls and Tuck became friendly with him when he delivered packages to his house there."

Patricia dipped her chin. "I see. I must compliment you on your good detective work. Now all that remains is for you to call Courier Express and file a formal complaint against the individual."

Crystal's heart lurched. "But you just said you had no intention—"

"I don't," Patricia said, cutting her off. "But you must pursue it. In fact, I insist on it. That driver committed a serious infraction by bringing a nicotine product and alcohol to an elderly man living in a facility that allows neither." Patricia's tone and her expression were triumphant.

Crystal gulped. This was getting worse by the minute. "Tuck's doctor in Crystal Falls gave him permission to chew and drink beer. I don't see any point in getting this driver in trouble. He just tried to do something nice for an old man."

"By doing so, he broke the rules of this institution. I'll also point out that birds of a feather flock together. For all I know, you're friendly with Mr. Richards, too. You appear to be defending his breach of our rules, and I find your reluctance to report him extremely telling."

Crystal balled her hands into fists. When she felt certain she had her voice under control, she said, "I've never laid eyes on Tanner Richards. And if I had any intention of covering up for him, I'd do a lot better job! How can you think that of me?"

The other woman placed her pen on the desk pad. "If the shoe fits . . ."

"I— This is really outrageous. I've given you the name of the person who brought the items. If you're determined to get him in trouble, file a complaint, but don't involve me."

Patricia smiled. "Oh, but I *am* involving you. As final proof to me that you had nothing to do with the complete disregard of this facility's rules, you must call Courier Express and file a complaint."

Crystal wanted to reach across the desk and jerk the old biddy's helmet hair out by the roots. Instead she stood, collected her purse, and made for the door. She paused to say, "You deliberately misled me, and I refuse to be a part of this. My first loyalty is to my grandfather."

"Very well. I'll call the police and have him removed from the building immediately."

Crystal whirled to gape at her. "You can't do that!"

"Watch me. A half dozen staff members will testify that he screamed obscenities and actually pushed one of my aides while she was in his bedroom." Patricia picked up the phone. "That qualifies as a physical assault, which will, of course, go in his records." She arched an eyebrow. "That may make it difficult for you to place him elsewhere."

"Was this aide he supposedly pushed the same person who looked under his mattress and found his magazines?"

"What if she was? He had no right to shove her. And, I might add, pornography is not allowed in this building, either."

Crystal couldn't envision Tuck laying a violent hand on a woman. It was far more likely that he'd bumped into her while trying to protect his personal property. "He's eighty years old and recovering from serious injuries. Surely you won't throw him out when you know I have nowhere to take him. That's illegal."

Patricia depressed one button on the phone. "Your

attorney can contact the facility's legal team. By the time you get a suit filed against me, your grandfather will be living elsewhere. Do you know how long it takes just to get a court hearing? Or how dreadfully expensive all the legal fees can be?"

Crystal had been raised by Tuck to believe there was at least some good in everyone. But this woman had a heart wrapped in barbed wire.

Thinking fast, Crystal decided she could make the call later and carefully phrase what she said so Tanner Richards wouldn't be fired. More of a for-your-information call and a request that no more contraband be delivered to her grandfather. "All right. I'll lodge a complaint first thing in the morning."

"You'll do so now and in my presence."

"I beg your pardon?"

"You will make the phone call in my presence, so there's no question in my mind that you've followed through. If you refuse, I can only take it to mean that you knew about the delivery and are trying to protect the perpetrator. In that event, your grandfather must leave the premises immediately, and all his belongings, including furniture, must be off this property by five o'clock tomorrow afternoon."

If Patricia followed through on her threat, it would mean almost certain financial ruin for Crystal. She couldn't work and care for her grandfather at the same time. And there would be complications for Tuck as well. She put out a hand and steadied herself on the wall.

She allowed herself an instant's fantasy of trying to contact an attorney or a governmental advocate for the elderly. But it was after normal business hours. All she could do was leave messages, and she would get no responses until sometime tomorrow. What if the assisted living facilities in Crystal Falls had no openings or refused to take Tuck because Patricia claimed he was violent? Even if she took Tuck home, she couldn't move all his furniture out of here by herself. She needed to find a crew of helpers, and that would take at least a day, if not two. Knowing Patricia, the woman would call a secondhand store and give away anything of Tuck's that remained in the building after five tomorrow afternoon. The burl coffee table had been one of her grandmother's prized possessions, and Tuck's bedroom set was another family heirloom. He'd be heartbroken if he lost all those pieces.

Crystal sat down, uninvited, and endeavored to keep her expression under control as she placed the phone call under the stern eye of the administrator. When the conversation ended, she met Patricia's gaze. "Are you satisfied now? I've jumped through all your hoops and possibly damaged my relationship with my grandfather, not to mention that the driver, who intended to do no harm, may be fired."

"I'm satisfied. For the moment. But don't allow Tuck to pull a shenanigan like this again. I'll boot him out of here so fast, it'll make your head spin."

"I'm sure you will," Crystal replied. She meant it as sarcasm, but a quick glance at Patricia told her the woman had taken it as a well-deserved compliment.

Trembling with anger, Crystal strode from the office. It took a huge effort of will not to slam the door. She needed to tell Tuck what had occurred, but she couldn't do that until she calmed down. Instead she made a bee-line for the front desk.

In a low voice, she told Marsha, "That woman is one of the cruelest people I've ever met."

"She truly is." Marsha glanced toward Patricia's office door. "I really like this job. I'm not required to do much on the evening shift. The pay isn't great, but I do get health care coverage. I really don't want to quit, so instead I pray Patricia will either retire or drop over dead from heart failure." Marsha leaned forward and whispered, "She's skimming off the top. *Stealing* from these old folks. I can't prove it, but I know that it's happening."

Normally Crystal would have been shocked by such a statement, but Patricia incited anger and bitterness in others. She also couldn't discount Marsha's claim that Patricia was embezzling funds, but that was someone else's worry. Crystal's only concern was her grandfather's welfare.

"She says Tuck pushed one of the aides. Do you know if that's true?"

Marsha rolled her eyes. "Tuck would never push a woman. That's probably an exaggerated account of what was actually an accident. He was very upset and trying to stop the aides from taking his stuff and throwing it away."

"Patricia says it will go on his record and make it difficult for me to place him in another facility."

"Dear heaven. Will that woman stop at nothing?"

"I doubt it. She lied and said she wouldn't try to get Tuck's friend in trouble. But after I told her his name, she made *me* file a complaint against him. What if he loses his job?"

Marsha's face took on a worried expression. "Oh, I hope not! It was just beer and chew, and delivered to an old man who's been forced to quit cold turkey. It's not easy to give up chewing tobacco. He's probably craving it something fierce. I quit smoking ten years ago. It was the hardest thing I've ever done. And to this day I want to smoke sometimes."

Crystal had never used tobacco products, so she

hadn't stopped to think of Tuck's physical addiction to Copenhagen. Had he gone through withdrawal symptoms? Was he still suffering from them? Guilt weighed heavily on her mind. Mainly she'd thought about how difficult all of this had been for her. Getting Tuck moved. Cleaning his former residence and sprucing up the paint to get it ready for staging. Dealing with the Realtor. Getting all the paperwork signed to get the house on the market. Chasing after that crazy dog of his. Missing appointments with clients. Watching her income take a downhill slide. But all the while, Tuck had been enduring his own version of hell.

"Oh, Marsha. Is it just as hard to give up chewing tobacco as it is cigarettes?"

"Some people say it's even harder."

Crystal's gaze flicked to the hallway where Tuck's apartment was located. She felt a bit calmer now. She walked to his unit, tapped on the door, and let herself in. He still sat in his recliner. She groped for the words to tell him what had happened. She wanted to explain how Patricia had lied and then forced her to lodge a complaint. The words collected at the base of her throat like popcorn she had swallowed without chewing thoroughly. And in the end, nothing came out the way she wanted.

"You were right, Tuck. I thought I could handle the situation without getting Tanner in trouble, but I couldn't. Patricia made me file a complaint against him."

Her grandfather's blue eyes went stone cold. The lines on his face deepened and suddenly seemed to be set as rigidly as expansion joints in concrete. "Get out," he said, his voice flat. "I don't want to look at you right now."

Crystal's chest constricted. "I didn't want to do it, Tuck."

"But you did. That's all I need to know. Get out."

Tuck had never spoken to her with this hard, unfeeling tone of voice. Until now. Her heart felt as if it cracked in two. Tears filled her eyes.

"Tuck, please. Just listen. She was going to evict you immediately if I didn't do it. I have nowhere to take you. I had no choice. There was nothing else—"

He cut her off, still using that icy tone. "I could have gone to our new place here in Mystic Creek," he said. "I could have slept on the sofa."

"It's a love seat, not even long enough for me."

"I could've stayed there alone while you worked until you could find somebody to help me during the day. I ain't some child that needs a sitter. Get out. I don't want you here right now."

"I just wanted to take care of you, Tuck. I can't move all your stuff by myself. I need a crew of helpers. It takes time to arrange those things, and she said your furniture would have to be out of here by five tomorrow afternoon if I didn't do what she said. She might've given away Grandma's table and the bedroom set! Please, please try to understand just a little."

"Get out," he told her again.

She knew when she looked into his eyes that nothing she said would change his mind.

On the way home, Crystal called the salon. Nadine answered and said all the teenage girls had looked beautiful when they left. Now the techs were nearly finished cleaning up. Nadine had her own set of shop keys. She could make the final rounds and lock up for the night. There was no reason for Crystal to come back.

"So, did you save Tuck from being evicted?" Nadine asked.

Crystal's face burned and felt puffy from crying. All she wanted was to drive home and huddle under the blankets to cry even more. "I'll tell you about it tomorrow," she promised. Then she ended the call.

When she got home, Rip had returned and was waiting outside the yard gate. Crystal wasn't sure how much the final bill for the hurricane fence had been. Tuck had written the check. But she suspected it had been a huge waste of money. Rip was a determined runner, and no physical barrier would ever keep him contained.

"Where have you been all day?" Crystal cried as she exited the vehicle. "Do you know how many hours I spent looking for you? Or how worried I was? What do you do, hide behind bushes when you see my car?"

Rip's tongue lolled from the side of his mouth, streaming drool. His silly grin told her he was completely unrepentant. He was a gorgeous dog with beautiful markings, a perfect blend of gray and white, enhanced by curry markings. He was also one of the smartest creatures she'd ever met. But his quirks and bad habits made it difficult to appreciate his finer points.

Swinging her purse strap onto her shoulder, she walked toward the gate. "I haven't eaten since six this morning because of you."

Rip turned to follow her, staggered, and fell over on his side. Crystal's heart caught and her annoyance fled in a millisecond. "Rip?" She dropped her bag on the gravel and ran to the dog. "What's wrong with you? Are you hurt?"

She squatted down to run her hands over his body. He growled and bared his teeth.

"Stop it. I know you don't like to be touched, but get over it for once." Rip loved other people, the only exception being anyone in uniform, whom he detested.

But he'd always been cantankerous with her. "I'm really not a bad person, you know. If you gave me half a chance, you might even like me."

She palpated each of his legs, searching for wounds or possible fractures. When she found nothing and moved on to his ribs, he snarled and bit her three times on her right forearm. "Darn it!" Crystal sat back on her haunches, which wasn't easy in spike heels. "Look what you did!" Red marks already showed on her skin. "Tuck may call it pinching and make light of it, saying that you never draw blood, but I sure won't. You're mean and impossible no matter how hard I try to make you like me."

Crystal could see nothing wrong with the dog, so she stood and fetched her purse. Lightning flashed, bathing the house and yard in white light. An instant later thunder cracked, so loud it sounded like an explosion. Then the sky split open and started spilling rain, a hard, driving deluge that instantly soaked her hair and shirt.

"Come on," she said to Rip. "You aren't hurt. If you want any dinner, get your ornery butt in the house."

She threw open the gate, half-tempted to close it behind her. The dog's main occupation seemed to be climbing over or under the fence to run away. Maybe she should have made him do the same to get back home. Only, she couldn't quite bring herself to be that mean. He obviously wasn't at the top of his game. Maybe he had run so hard that his legs were giving out on him.

She held the barrier open, squinting against the drops of water that pelted her face like BBs. "Come on, Rip. You can't lie out here in this. Get up. I can't leave you."

It took the dog three tries to regain his feet. Then he staggered over to her and growled. Crystal realized he was demanding a biscuit for allowing her safe passage through the gate. Incredulity washed through her. "You're *kidding*. When you can barely *walk*?"

Even as she spoke, she reached into her purse for a treat and tossed it to him. He let it drop to the ground and didn't bother to pick it up. She stormed across the yard. "Okay, fine. *Whatever.*"

Rip moved across the yard in a crooked line. What on earth was wrong with him? *A head injury.* She hadn't thought of that. Oh, dear God. Tuck was already furious. If his dog got hurt on her watch, he might never forgive her.

She hurried onto the porch, hoping the heeler would follow her. Only, Rip couldn't get up the steps or the wheelchair ramp off to one side. She dropped her purse and went down to help him. That earned her two more bites, this time on her left arm.

"You nasty little monster! I *hate* you."

Rip didn't seem to care what she thought of him. And the feeling was mutual. Crystal hugged his belly to pick him up. He snapped the air and growled, but he couldn't reach her with his teeth. Dear Lord, he was heavy. He didn't look that big, but he was stout. Huffing and puffing, she lugged him indoors and set him on the wood floor. He braced his front legs wide apart to push upright and looked at her as if his world were spinning.

"Oh, Rip." Leaving the door open, Crystal sank to her knees. She couldn't see any obvious injury, but under his thick fur something might be hidden. She tried to run her fingers over his skull, and he snapped at her fingertips. "Stop it, Rip!" She grabbed his muzzle to hold his mouth closed and did a thorough palpation of his head. *Nothing.* "Have you been such a pest that someone threw you meat laced with poison?"

Crystal struggled erect, kicked off her heels, and hurried out onto the porch to grab her purse. Dropping into the chair by the small kitchen desk where her laptop resided, she found her cell phone just as thunder cracked overhead again. She located the number for Cassidy Peck, who worked at the Caring Hands Veterinary Clinic for Jack Palmer, the town's only veterinarian.

"Hi, Crystal. If you're calling to remind me of my appointment, I have it on my calendar."

"Actually, Cassidy, I'm calling to pick your brain. I'm caring for my grandfather's dog, and he's acting weird." Crystal told the younger woman what had happened. "After-hours trips to the vet are expensive. I'll take him in if it's necessary. But I'm hoping to avoid it if I can."

"Of course you are, and I shouldn't make any diagnosis. But friend to friend, I can say it doesn't sound like he's been poisoned." She listed the symptoms.

"No," Crystal agreed, "I'm not seeing any of those things."

"And since there are no visible signs of injury, it could be something else. Exhaustion, possibly, especially if he was at large all day and had no water. Another possibility is that he's fearful of thunder and lightning. A lot of dogs are, and they can grow so frightened they have mild seizures. Sometimes they can't walk until it passes. They drool. Run into walls. It's scary but normally not fatal."

Crystal heard another rumble. "He didn't seem afraid. And the thunderstorm just started."

"Not on our side of town. You said he was gone. Maybe where he was, it had already started. And sometimes it's hard to tell if dogs are frightened. What I would do is give him a small amount of food and a big bowl of fresh water. Then keep a close eye on him. If he gets worse, take him to see Jack. He lives right beside the clinic. Chances are good that Rip will start to get better, though."

Crystal thanked Cassidy for the advice and ended the call. Then she turned on the chair to look at the dog, who had made it to his bed and now sprawled on it, belly up, with all four legs dangling outward from his body.

"You have none of the symptoms Cassidy described, and if you're frightened by the storm, you have an odd way of showing it." Bewildered and worn-out, she slumped against the back of the chair and shivered herself. She was soaked to the skin. Her long hair, which had started to curl from being wet, hung over her breasts like the strands of a dripping mop. "So what *is* wrong with you, Rip?"

Rip was snoring and offered no explanation. Studying him, Crystal decided he was probably suffering from nothing more than exhaustion. He'd been gone for hours, and there was no way of knowing how far his adventures had taken him. He'd probably be fine after a long rest. She'd set her alarm to check on him during the night, and if he got worse, she'd call Jack.

Rain. She heard it hammering on the metal roof. Staggering a little herself, she went to close the front door. Utter exhaustion definitely compromised one's sense of balance. Hunger gnawed at her belly, and she realized she felt weak. Had she had enough water herself today? Probably not. She rinsed out Rip's dishes, refilled them, and set them near his bed.

"Rip? I brought you food and water."

The dog groaned and limply flapped his front paws. She sighed and went in search of something to eat herself. Cooking anything right then loomed as a herculean task. She settled for breakfast cereal—healthy whole-grain flakes that she drowned in sugar and milk, negating any healthful benefit they could possibly offer. After devouring two bowls, she made toast, slathered it with butter, and ate it sitting at Tuck's mahogany dinner table. She still wanted to cry, but she was afraid if she gave in to the impulse it would be hours before she could stop.

She'd grabbed a napkin before sitting down. Pink spots had appeared on the white rectangle of paper. Bewildered, she felt her hair, and her fingers came away with the same color on them. *The spray-on streaks.* In the pouring rain, the color had gone watery. She looked down at her ecru silk blouse. *Spotted with pink.* She examined the beautiful barnwood floor. *Spotted with pink.* She'd have to mop before she went to bed. She couldn't let Tuck's floor get stained. Could *anything* else go wrong today?

She went to turban her hair in a towel. Then she got the wringer bucket, filled it with steaming water, and set to work. When the floor was spotless, she took a shower, washing her hair and then standing in the hot, soothing spray until she felt warm again. Normally she wore silky lingerie, but tonight a long-sleeve flannel nightgown and fluffy slippers sounded cozier. Rain still pelted the metal roof, filling the house with a steady drone of pleasant noise. She wished she could just go to bed, but first she had to find a way to keep Rip at home before she missed so many appointments with clients that she went broke.

She checked on the dog, who hadn't moved, but he seemed to be sleeping peacefully. Then she poured herself a glass of white wine, hoping it would relax her, and descended on her laptop to do some research on dog confinement systems. After a few minutes she found what she believed might be just what she needed, an invisible-fencing kit. The purchaser had to bury wire in shallow trenches all around a property perimeter. *I can do that,* she assured herself. Growing up on an

Idaho ranch, she'd spent plenty of time at the end of a shovel. Once buried, the wire had to be attached to a controller that produced a signal. The setup sounded similar to electric fencing, and she had dealt with her share of that. The dog being contained had to wear a pronged signal collar, which would shock its neck if it got within zapping range. Rip liked to tunnel out under the fence or climb over it. He'd quickly stop trying to do either if he got zinged repeatedly.

Crystal started to order the kit. But then she looked over her shoulder at Rip. While asleep, he looked so darling. How strong were the shocks that came from a collar? Would they be painful? She needed to keep the dog at home, but she couldn't find it in her heart to actually hurt him. Sighing with weariness, she researched shock collars and read that they delivered only gentle correction and offered three signal strengths. The goal, according to the information published, was to train the canine to halt when the collar emitted a warning beep.

That didn't sound inhumane, so she decided on an invisible-fencing kit with a collar strength for a medium-size dog and paid nearly fifty dollars extra for overnight shipping. She doubted her purchase would be processed until morning, but she should receive it the day after tomorrow.

She'd no sooner submitted her order than she heard what sounded like a kitten meowing outside. Following the faint noise, she opened the front door. Wind drove sheets of rain under the veranda overhang. She flipped on the outside light in order to see. Sure enough, a soaking-wet kitten huddled on the doormat.

"Oh, baby." Crystal sank into a crouch to pick up the kitten. All she felt through its sodden fur was a layer of cold skin and fragile bones. "You poor little thing.

Where did you come from? You're barely old enough to be away from your mama."

After closing the door Crystal carried the feline to her bathroom and dried it off. She couldn't tell what color it might have been when its fur was no longer damp. Varying shades of gray? It had a sweet face with a white blaze on the forehead and white dots that reminded her of freckles around the nose. Once back in the kitchen, she held the small creature close against her breasts, hoping to share her warmth as she decided what she could feed it. Since adolescence, she had avoided being a pet owner.

"I'm lousy at nurturing," she told the tiny feline. "So don't think, even for a second, that I'll let you stay here. Rip doesn't like cats, for one thing, and I'm challenged even to keep houseplants alive. In the morning, I'll call the no-kill shelter. They'll take wonderful care of you until you find a forever home." She stepped to a cupboard and searched through the canned goods. "Tuna should be tasty. Right?"

She put a small amount in a bowl and set the kitten down beside it on the plank floor. While the starving creature ate, she warmed some milk and offered that as well. The kitten devoured all the fish and drank the tepid liquid. When Crystal picked the baby back up, she smiled when it snuggled against her.

"Only for tonight," she warned as she moved through the house. After checking on Rip again, whose even snores reassured her, she switched off the lights on the way to her bedroom. As she swept back the covers and climbed beneath them, she said to the kitten, "I may seem like a nice lady, but the truth is, I'm jinxed. Except for Tuck, anything I love always meets a bad end. You'll be much better off with someone else."

The kitten never moved within the protective cup of her hand. It just settled against her and began to purr.

Crystal stared at the shadowy ceiling and listened to the patter of rain on the roof. Her thoughts strayed to her grandfather. For years she had allowed herself to love only him, and even that had been frightening for her at first. He had been her whole world. But over time, he'd started to seem as big as a mountain to her—and just as solid. The unrelenting fear within her had eased away, and she'd come to count on her grandfather to be the only constant in her life. He never got seriously hurt, although she worried that he might. He caught occasional colds but had never grown gravely ill. At some point, she had started to believe that nothing could ever get the better of Tucker Malloy.

Now he faced old age, and Crystal had to accept that not even Tuck could escape the inevitability of death. There was nothing she could do to change that, so instead she just hoped to take fabulous care of him and enjoy every second she could with him until he had to leave her. Tomorrow she would convince him to forgive her. *Somehow. Please, God, somehow.* She'd make him understand that Patricia had deceived her and given her no option but to file a complaint against Tanner Richards. And she'd also ramp up her efforts to find a daytime caregiver so she could bring her grandfather home as soon as possible. Crystal or the caregiver could transport him to his physical therapy sessions. Under his own roof Tuck could drink as many beers a day as he liked, chew and spit to his heart's content, and enjoy home-cooked meals.

On those thoughts, she rode the wave into slumber.

The bright sunshine made the wet pavement sparkle as Tanner drove to work early the next morning. He found Prime Country on Sirius XM and blasted the music through the speakers of his truck to vibrate the cab.

Singing along with the honeyed voice of a famous country singer was one of his favorite ways to start the day.

Once he reached Courier Express he parked in his usual spot, grabbed his uniform jacket in case it started to rain again, and ran toward the building. He entered by a side door, planning to reorganize the parcels already stowed inside his assigned van. People on the night shift tried to do it for him, but nobody knew Tanner's route as well as he did. He liked the boxes to be in order for the roads he took, early deliveries on top, late-afternoon ones at the bottom. Nothing irritated him more than to find a package at the end of the day that should have been dropped off at the beginning of his shift.

When he reached the vehicle, he jumped in the back and found Brian Redmond inside. "Hey, Tanner." Heavier set and slightly shorter than Tanner, Brian was a nice guy and always friendly, but this morning his smile seemed off. "I, um— The super told me to cover your route today."

"Why? I didn't call in sick."

Brian ran a hand over his brown buzz cut. "I, um— He wants to see you. I don't know why."

"Okay."

Obviously, something was up, but Tanner wasn't worried. He did his job well. He rarely missed a day. His ranking on good public relations couldn't be better, not because he was nicer or liked his job better than anyone else, but because he truly enjoyed chatting with the people on his route. They counted him as a friend, and he felt the same way about them. Promotion? A raise? Maybe. He sure could deal with that.

He swung out the back of the van, weaved between other loaded vehicles parked on the concrete floor, and pushed through a personnel door that led to the front cubicles. He knew the way to the supervisor's office. He went there every six months for his job performance interviews, which were always positive meetings, and it had been the supervisor who had promoted Tanner to the rural route, a cherry assignment that Tanner had wished for long before he'd been given the opportunity to take it.

He tapped on the door before opening it. "Hey, Mac. Brian says you want to see me."

"Tanner." Mac didn't smile as he motioned toward the chair in front of his desk. "Have a seat."

It was then that Tanner knew he was in trouble. Mac seldom looked like a storm cloud about to rain all over someone. "So, what's up?" Tanner asked.

Mac tugged a paper from a pile on the blotter. A stocky man with a belly that strained the buttons of his dress shirt, he scanned some notes. "The night-shift super left this report for me," he explained. "Do you know a man named Tucker Malloy?"

Tanner's heart sank. "Yes, he's a good friend."

"A very *old* friend, actually. As in elderly." Mac glanced up to meet Tanner's gaze. "An old friend in assisted living who is presently under a doctor's care. You allegedly delivered beer and chewing tobacco to his apartment. That's against the assisted living facility's rules. The old fellow may be evicted because of it." Mac's blue eyes sharpened. "I try to be a fair boss, Tanner. I'd like to hear your side of the story before I decide on any punitive measures."

Tanner couldn't think of anything to say. "I'm guilty as charged, Mac. Like I said, we're good friends. He asked me to do him a favor, and I couldn't say no."

Removing his glasses, Mac rubbed the bridge of his nose. "For the love of God, what were you thinking? You're one of my best drivers. Am I correct in assuming that you used the company vehicle to do him this favor?"

"Yes." Tanner quickly added, "But I topped off the van's tank with gas, putting in way more than I used."

"I know. I had Brian check the gauge." Mac slipped his glasses back on and stared at Tanner as if he hoped the picture might change if he looked at it long enough. "And I suspect you figured the extra you spent on gas would make up for the wear and tear on the tires and the vehicle itself." He dropped the sheet of paper. "I know you're honest. You'd never take advantage of the company. But, damn it, that's not the point. You drove our vehicle outside your assigned area. You purchased goods for an old man that were forbidden to him. You disregarded all the insurance liabilities that the company might have faced if the van were involved in an accident. What the hell were you thinking?"

Tanner slumped in the chair. Everything Mac said was dead-on accurate. "That my friend missed his cans of beer in the evening, that they'd taken away his Copenhagen, and that he felt like a prisoner. He wasn't asking for a lot, nothing that he didn't enjoy at home on a daily basis. I felt really bad for him, Mac."

"Did you stop to consider that an old man who has broken his arm and undergone hip-replacement surgery might be taking heavy-duty pain medications?"

"Yes. Tuck may be eighty, but he's still as sharp as a tack. He wouldn't mix alcohol with pain meds. And I did ask him if drinking and chewing were things his doctor still allowed."

"Not good enough," Mac said. "I'm really sorry, Tanner, but I can't let this slide. If I do, next thing I know, somebody will drive a company vehicle to Reno."

Tanner nodded. "No need to be sorry." Nausea rolled through his stomach. What would he say to his kids? "I knew better, Mac, but I did it anyway. I've put you in an uncomfortable position. I deserve to be fired."

"You *do* deserve that," Mac agreed, "but this is your first violation, and you're too good a driver for me to just let you go. I gave you one of the cushiest assignments I had available here when I put you on the Crystal Falls rural route. I did that because you're a single father, and it allowed you to spend more time with your kids at night."

Heartened to hear that he wouldn't be let go, Tanner nodded. "I appreciated that, Mac."

"Yeah, well, now I have to demote you. Brian gets the cushy route for at least the next year. I'm assigning you to his rural route in Mystic Creek. You'll still finish your deliveries earlier than you would in town, but the hour of driving there and back each day will pretty much cancel that out. If you keep your nose clean for twelve months, you can have the Crystal Falls route back."

Tanner stood up. "I'm sorry for disappointing you."

Flapping his hand, Mac said, "Ah, hell. If you'd used your own vehicle and helped out the old man when you were off duty, I would've had a good laugh. Probably would have done it myself. Just don't involve the company again when you're playing Good Samaritan, or I'll have no choice but to can you."

Tanner collected his personal things from the van he normally drove and climbed inside a similar vehicle that he'd probably be driving for the foreseeable future. He put a spare uniform he liked to carry on a shelf behind the driver's seat. He pressed the sticky pad for his cell phone on the dash. Then he stared at the parcels. There was no point in trying to organize them. He'd driven in Mystic Creek only once, and that had been yesterday. Recalling how nerve-racking the first day on a new route could be, he knew he'd be using GPS almost constantly. Getting to know all the dogs along a route would also be challenging. *I'm such a dipshit,* he told himself. *I had the easiest route in Crystal Falls, and I blew it to do a favor for a friend.* Tanner could only hope that Tuck had been able to enjoy at least one beer. Otherwise Tanner had just gotten himself demoted for nothing.

After slumping down in the driver's seat, he started the van engine, adjusted the mirrors, and drove from the warehouse, braced for a long day of confusion, countless U-turns, and getting lost. In his experience, country roads were the worst. GPS was a fabulous invention, but in rural areas it could go wonky.

He wasn't looking forward to the rest of the day. What the hell might go wrong next?

Chapter Three

"What do you mean, you don't have room?" Crystal tightened her grip on the salon phone.

The volunteer at the Mystic Creek No-Kill Shelter sounded anything but encouraging, and the conversation wasn't going well. So many people had crowded into the shop that Crystal could barely hear over the drone of voices. Nadine had just returned from Jake 'n' Bake across the street, and the techs were arguing good-naturedly over the cream-cheese-and-strawberry bagel that Nadine had ordered for her own breakfast. Unfortunately, it smelled so divine that everybody wanted one.

With a giggle, Nadine curled her arms around the bag. "No! I brought you your orders. If you want one of these, go buy one."

Crystal pressed her thumb over the opening of her free ear, hoping to block out the noise. "But I can't keep a kitten," she told the shelter volunteer. "Surely there's a way around this."

The bell above the salon door jingled, and she looked up to see Ma Thomas walk in. She wore a wildflower-print bolero over a rose pink top, and her short blond hair shone like polished brass. Crystal waved hello. Ma approached the front desk and told Nadine she needed to make an appointment with Crystal for a cut and style.

Refocusing on what the volunteer was saying, Crystal

replied, "But he's just an itty-bitty baby and won't take up much room. I honestly can't keep him. I just *can't*."

"I'm sorry to hear that," the woman countered. "We're filled to the limit. Can you give the kitten a home for only a couple of weeks? He'll be easy to care for. In that amount of time we'll re-home some animals and make room for new ones."

Crystal shook her head. "You don't understand. It's not the time involved to care for a cat that prevents me from giving it a temporary home. I'm just unsuitable. Every time I take charge of an animal, something awful happens." *And if I keep him for two weeks, I'll fall in love with him. No way! It's too heartbreaking.* "For the kitten's safety, you absolutely *must* take him."

"We would if we could, but we're limited by law to a certain number of animals, and all our foster families are full up. There is a Humane Society shelter in Crystal Falls, though. They do their best there to re-home the strays."

Crystal knew that. She had spent a few months working in a salon in Crystal Falls. When she'd been in Idaho and barely managing to make ends meet, she'd started looking for an area where there might be more of a demand for cosmetologists. The name of the town, Crystal Falls, had spoken to her because it was so similar to her own, and she'd ended up moving there. "As I recall, that place isn't a no-kill shelter."

"It tries to be, but that's where most of the strays picked up by law enforcement are taken, and when the building gets above maximum occupancy, some of the animals must be euthanized to make room for more."

Crystal leaned an elbow on the counter. "That's horrible. I can't take a kitten there. In three days, he could be put down."

"I know it's brutal," the volunteer agreed. "All that saves this facility from doing the same thing is that we're not contractually obligated to the county to accept more strays when our occupancy is maxed out."

Crystal understood how difficult it must have been when animal shelters got full, which led her to wonder whether the kitten at her house had been dropped off by a harried owner who couldn't find any safe place to take it. She didn't approve of abandoning animals. It was heartless.

"Okay," she said. "I'll give the kitten temporary shelter, but only on the condition that you call me the moment you have an opening."

"I'll put your name at the top of our waiting list."

A waiting list? Her heart broke for the poor animals with nowhere to go. They were probably in more urgent need of help than her kitten. *No, not my kitten. I can't start thinking that way. I won't love it. I won't give it a name. I won't hold it. I can pretend he isn't there for two weeks.* "Thank you so much for your help."

When the conversation ended, Crystal raised her voice and said, "Anybody in here want a darling kitten, or know of anyone who might want one?"

A chorus of "No" was the response.

"I really need some help with this, ladies. I can't have a kitten."

Ma Thomas, who was now looking at a display of hair mousse, glanced over her shoulder. "Why can't you, dear? You live on a lovely little farm now, not in the upstairs flat. That's a perfect place to have a cat."

Perfect for someone else, maybe, Crystal thought. But it wouldn't be perfect for her. She would start to love that kitten. She just knew she would. And right after she invested all of her heart into it, something terrible would happen. When she was younger, she had been foolish enough to let herself love a puppy and a horse. She'd lost both of them.

Crystal went to her station to sweep up hair clippings from the last styling session. As she stared down at the black bristles of the broom moving over the laminated plank floor, her mind took her back in time to when she was only eleven years old. She stood over an open grave, staring down at a small cherrywood casket. The sky above her was leaden with approaching rain. The moist Washington breeze sliced through her wool coat and made her bones feel cold. But no matter how badly she shivered, she knew she would never feel as cold as her little sister—until she died herself.

"Crystal! Crystal?"

Jerking back to reality, Crystal stared stupidly at Jules, who'd been waving a hand in front of her face. "What? I'm sorry. I zoned out for a second."

"I've misplaced my perm rollers. Can I borrow yours?"

"Uh . . . sure. Help yourself."

Crystal resumed her task, sweeping with more vigor than necessary. She should never let herself think about that day. *Never.* She could cry until she felt sick. She could bleed inside where nobody else could see. She could even wish she were dead herself. But nothing would ever bring Mary Ann back. Nothing.

Tanner dialed Tuck's number during his midmorning coffee break, which consisted of sipping hot java from a thermos cup while he sat in the parked van along a gravel road. When a workingman was raising children, he didn't stop at a café and spend money on coffee. He also packed a lunch even though he made sure his kids got to eat cafeteria food, which was a whole lot better than his cold sandwiches.

Tuck answered on the fourth ring. "Tanner. Saw it was you on my phone. I'm so sorry about what happened, son. All I can say is, I didn't do it."

Tanner already knew that. Tuck would never betray a friend. "I just called to make sure you're all right and didn't get in serious trouble when they caught you. I heard you could be evicted."

"I didn't get that lucky. But forget about me. You've got two kids to support. Did you lose your job?"

"No. I only have to drive a different route for a while. And I'm glad you got to stay in your apartment."

"If I got evicted, I'd jump for joy on my one good leg. I hate this damned place." He sighed. "My granddaughter filed the complaint, and now we ain't speakin'. I'm real pissed off at her."

Tanner stared out the windshield. "Yesterday you called her a sweet girl. Don't damage the relationship on my account."

"I won't. But she stepped over a bunch of lines last night, and I ain't of a mind to forgive her too fast. Grabbed my cell phone and invaded my privacy, like as if I'm a teenage boy and she bought the damned thing for me. I'll be hanged. I been payin' my own way for sixty-six freakin' years."

Tanner tried to imagine how furious he would be if that happened to him. He valued his privacy and would be beside himself if someone read his phone records, personal texts, and email messages.

"It wasn't a fun time," Tuck went on. "The hell bitch that runs this joint brought in a crew of women to ransack my place. Lordy! They even found my damned rubbers and almost threw 'em away. I threatened to call the cops and charge 'em with theft."

Tanner nearly choked on his coffee. "Rubbers? You mean prophylactics?"

"Call 'em any fancy name you want, they're still just rubbers."

Tanner barely managed to turn a whoop of laughter into a strangled cough. He cleared his throat and grinned. "Tuck, maybe I don't want to know, but what the hell do you need rubbers for?"

"What the hell do you think I need 'em for? I always keep some on hand. You just never know when you might need one. This place is spillin' over with single women. Ain't you ever heard of safe sex? If you haven't, get your ass over here, and I'll educate you over a cold one."

This time the laugh got out before Tanner could stop it. This old man was good for him. "They took all your beer."

"Sure as shit. I'm countin' on you to bring me more."

"Oh, no, not me. I didn't get fired, but I'm demoted for a year, stuck with the rural route in Mystic Creek."

"Aw, damn." Tuck heaved a disgruntled sigh, which created a whoosh of static that hissed against Tanner's eardrum. "There went gettin' home early to spend time with your kiddos. I'm sorry, son. I shouldn't have asked you."

"It's my own fault. Don't blame yourself." Tanner took a cautious sip of coffee. "Next time you're thirsty and needing a chew, I'll tell you to wait until I'm off work and driving my own vehicle."

Tuck laughed. "You're a true friend. I can count the ones I've had in my lifetime on the fingers of one hand, so consider yourself special."

"Well, don't count me as being so special that you ruin things between you and your granddaughter." In actuality, Tanner wished he had Crystal Malloy sitting on the collapsible bench of a dunking tank. He'd thrown countless baseballs with his son and developed a good enough arm to almost drown her. "She's your only family. It's not worth it."

"Don't worry," Tuck replied. "I'll forgive her in time. She got pushed into doing it by the woman who runs this outfit. I gotta tell you, that old bitch is scary. She got her bluff in on Crystal, anyhow, and that don't happen often. My granddaughter is a spitfire redhead, and most times she don't take shit off nobody."

Tanner washed the bitterness he felt toward Crystal off his tongue with another swallow of coffee.

Then Tuck added, "She's worried about me. Where will she take me if I get kicked out? How will she care for me when she's got to work? And I think my damned dog is runnin' her ragged when she's supposed to be at the salon. But knowin' all that ain't enough to get me over feelin' mad at her."

Tanner recalled watching Tuck struggle yesterday to walk across a room, and a sick feeling settled in his stomach for the second time that day. The old man was prideful, and he wouldn't admit he was finished until his last ounce of strength was gone. As much as Tanner wanted to hold a grudge against Crystal Malloy, he could understand how protective she must have felt of her grandfather right now.

Tuck continued talking. "She seems to think I've reached an age where she's gotta mother me. I see some battles between us on the road ahead. I surely do."

Tanner did, too. He stared out the windshield again, trying to picture Crystal Malloy. A female version of Tuck with red hair sprang into his mind. Not an attractive picture.

He rolled down his window and tossed out the remainder of the coffee. "I need to roll, Tuck. My coffee break's over. Working this area with another hour of driving tacked onto my day means getting home later.

I need to finish my route as fast as I can so I can have some free time with my kids tonight."

"I know. And I'm almighty sorry that you got turned in. I promised that wouldn't happen."

"I'll be by to see you as soon as I can. We'll drink coffee and have a bullshit session."

Crystal normally loved lunchtime at the salon. Most of the local restaurants and cafés delivered, and each of the gals ordered different food so everyone could share and enjoy a smorgasbord. Today they'd gone with a Mexican theme—always a favorite, not so much because of the menu, but because the owners of the town's two Mexican places were both handsome bachelors under forty. Joe Paisley was tall with dark hair and dreamy brown eyes. He was also nice, which made him difficult to resist. José Hayden, about Joe's age at thirty-four, had his Latina mother's black hair, café au lait skin, and a muscular build that made a woman look twice.

Right now, though, Crystal had other things on her mind besides men or food. She was still edgy about Tuck being angry with her, so instead of dishing up a plate, she nibbled on corn chips at the front desk while she ordered salon supplies. Every few minutes she allowed herself to surface long enough to absorb some of the girl talk being exchanged over the heads of female clients in varying stages of procedures. Even the two older women who'd come in for shampoos and cuts were laughing at all the nonsense.

One of them said, "I've never understood what any woman can find attractive about a man's butt."

"Oh, honey," Jules said with a grin. "Start looking at the guys in tight jeans. You'll finally get it."

Crystal blocked out the chatter, trying to remember which styling gel she'd run low on. Her attention was snagged when Nadine said, "All joking aside, I heard something scary at the Pill Minder this morning. Mystic Creek has a peeping tom who has stepped up his game to burglary. He steals ladies' underthings."

Crystal snapped to full attention at the word *burglary*. "You're kidding," she said. "I've lived here for ages, and it's always been safe."

"I have it on good authority," Nadine assured her.

"I heard about it, too," Shannon confirmed. "At first he only peered in windows at the golf course, but now he's entering houses and branching out into other areas of town. Wendy Edwards actually saw him once. She came out of the master bath wearing a short nightie, and he was standing outside her patio door, bold as brass. It scared the dickens out of her. She guessed him to be around forty-five. Brown hair. Stocky build. And she told me she thinks he's been in their house during the day. She and John golf a lot, and until now they've never bothered with locking their doors. She's missing lingerie. At first she thought she'd just misplaced things."

"That is just too weird." Shannon held up a section of her client's hair and snipped the strands. "Guys who do stuff like that give me the creeps."

Crystal got up and tossed what was left of her chips into a trash receptacle. "For once I'm glad I have Rip living with me."

"Yeah, right," Jules said with a laugh. "Like he's ever home to protect you. He's such a nonpresence, none of us have ever met him. Besides, Sheriff Lang is on it, I'm sure. He and his deputies will nail the guy."

"Maybe. But I find it odd that Wendy didn't recognize the man." Crystal hung her salon jacket on a wall hook and grabbed her purse. "Mystic Creek is so small that I rarely see an unfamiliar face."

"Maybe he's an outsider, someone who drives here to live out his sick fantasies," Shannon said. "He'd be less likely to be identified in a town where nobody knows him."

Crystal sighed. "Well, ladies, enjoy scaring one another senseless. My advice is to start locking your doors. I'm out of here for the rest of my lunch hour. I have to buy stuff for the kitten and run home. If Rip has gotten out of the yard again and I get arrested for animal abuse, pool your funds and bail me out."

A chorus of comments followed her from the building. "Oh, you're such a meanie." "Don't you hurt Tuck's dog!" "The only thing I've ever seen you harm was a spider, and afterward you felt bad."

Crystal headed for the market, propelled her shopping cart through the aisles at breakneck speed, and headed for home. As she jammed on the brakes outside the fence, she didn't see Rip in the yard, but sometimes he found a patch of shade and took a nap. The canine had seemed perfectly healthy this morning, which had been a huge relief. After collecting bags from the trunk of her car, she walked to the gate with both arms loaded. With a twist of her hips, she managed to get the fingers of one hand under the flip-up latch.

Just then Rip bounded up, stopped at the opposite side of the chain-link fence, and bared his teeth at her. Crystal groaned. "Come on, Rip. Not now, when I've got groceries to carry. Give me a break."

But the dog continued to snarl. Muttering under her breath, Crystal deposited her purchases on the ground and returned to the car to get dog biscuits from the storage bin on the inside of the driver's door. "You're a royal pain in the neck," she told the heeler as she retraced her steps. "Why Tuck allowed you to do this, I'll never know."

She gave the dog one treat and then stuffed all but three of the others in the front pocket of her brown slacks. After she picked up the bags again, Rip allowed her safe passage through the gate, but when she reached the porch, she had to toss him another bribe in order to ascend the steps. At the door, she proffered yet another biscuit and then struggled to turn the knob to get inside.

Rip followed her in, his nails clacking on the plank floor. As she deposited the bulging plastic bags on the kitchen counter, she said, "I should order you a second shock collar controlled by remote. Oh, yeah, bad news for you, but I know about those gadgets now. Instead of bribing my way into the yard, I could just push a button and zing the orneriness right out of you. Now that I've come to think of it, Rip, your reign of terror could be short-lived." She opened a bag of kitten kibble. Then she washed the newly purchased cat dish. "No more biting only me and Tuck while you act all sweet and nice to strangers. No more terrorizing the postman or law officers, either. You could become a perfect gentleman." The kitten came bounding into the kitchen. All the hair along Rip's spine bristled. "Don't you dare!" Crystal warned. "If you so much as snap at that baby, I'll beat you with a ball bat!"

Crystal didn't own a ball bat, but the threat seemed to work. Rip only growled as the kitten trotted over to her.

"You met No Name this morning before I put you outside," Crystal reminded the dog. "Nothing has changed except that he'll be staying longer than I thought. And make no mistake: I like him a lot better than I do you. So be nice."

With an expression of disgust, Rip went to lie on his bed while Crystal fed the feline and familiarized him with his freshly filled litter box, which she placed in the laundry room. When she returned to the kitchen, she found Rip polishing off the kitten kibble that had been left in the bowl.

"You see?" Crystal said to the dog. "There are perks to having a cat in the house. Just don't get used to it. He's staying here only two weeks."

She finished putting away her purchases, then shut the kitten in the laundry room with his litter box, food, and water. She wanted to make sure Rip didn't somehow gain entrance to the house and harm the little guy while she was gone. As she moved back into the living area, she dug in her pocket for more dog biscuits and whistled for Rip. She gave him a treat before she opened the door, then again as she left the porch, and yet again before she went out the gate.

"For once, Rip, do me a huge favor and stay in the yard. I really need to work, and it won't hurt you to take a day off from running amok." She turned to make sure the latch caught. "And hello. I buy your kibble. The money I make should matter to you. What if I run short and can't buy you food?"

Rip dropped to his belly and angled a paw over his eyes as he emitted a mournful whine.

"What's that mean?" Crystal tipped her head to stare at him. "Sometimes I get the eerie feeling you understand everything I say."

Crystal finished her last client at five and drove to the assisted living center, torn between wanting to speed and to drive as slowly as possible. She dreaded facing Tuck, but she'd learned years ago that he admired bravery and had little use for cowards. Luckily, a parking space was available near the main door. Her feet ached from wearing three-inch heels, but when she was at the salon or running errands in town, she tried to look fashionable. She told herself it was good for business, but there was a sad broken child buried inside her, too, and the only way Crystal knew to keep her hidden was to dress so flashy that people never looked too deeply beneath the surface. Instead they beheld Crystal Malloy, a tall, confident redhead who embraced bold fashion as if her life were an open book.

She pushed through the double glass doors of the facility. It was Thursday, so Marsha, who had seniority and didn't work weekends, was manning the front desk. Crystal had never visited late enough yet to know exactly when her shift ended, but it began at three.

"Hey, you," Crystal called out as she moved across the vestibule. "How has everything gone for Tuck today?"

Marsha shrugged. "He hasn't left his room, not even for meals. The aides took trays to his apartment. Even right after his surgery, he always went to the dining room."

Crystal released a taut breath. Then she forced a smile. "He's mad at me, Marsha. Or maybe I should say disappointed in me, because I betrayed his friend."

"The fire-breathing dragon gave you no choice. She backed you into a corner."

Crystal set her purse on the elevated countertop and folded her arms on the faux-granite surface. "I need some help. I've been trying to find an in-home caregiver for Tuck, but my sources aren't panning out. I've researched temp services. They're too expensive. Newspaper ads offer me very few leads. Craigslist is a disaster. I'm afraid I'll hire a murderer." She spread her hands. "Tuck doesn't need a trained nurse, only someone who can keep him company, cook a little, and tidy up."

Marsha brightened. "I know someone." Then her smile vanished. "No, she wouldn't work. She's got a new baby."

Crystal sighed. "Tuck likes babies, but I don't think a young mother would be ideal. I need someone I can depend on five days a week, no matter what."

"I'll keep an ear out for you." Marsha leaned forward. "The dragon is smiling today. Whenever she does that, I know she's scored a satisfying victory."

Remembering how she had allowed herself to be pushed around by Patricia last night, Crystal cringed. "She definitely won the round last night, but only because she had me over a barrel."

Marsha caught her bottom lip between her teeth. Then she said, "I don't start my shift until late afternoon. I'd be happy to stay with Tuck at the house until you find someone permanent. From almost three until you get home from the salon, he would have to be alone, but he wouldn't the rest of the time." She shrugged. "And I'm cheap. I get ten an hour here. I wouldn't expect more from you."

Crystal felt as if a thousand pounds had been lifted from her shoulders. She trusted Marsha. "Oh, wow, that's a fabulous solution! I could schedule my clients and leave most of my late afternoons free. Are you sure you really want to do this?"

"If I weren't sure, I wouldn't have offered."

Crystal felt like skipping, she was so happy. But instead of going straight to Tuck's suite, she went out onto the back deck, found an unoccupied corner, and dialed a number on her phone. It was a call that she'd been wanting to make ever since last night.

When she was patched through to the individual she wanted to speak with, she said, "This is Crystal Malloy, the woman who called in last night. I want to withdraw my complaint against Tanner Richards."

Dusk had descended by the time Tanner parked in the driveway of his suburban home. It wasn't a fancy house, more homey and utilitarian, but the ranch-style rambler suited his family's needs. After buying it, he had updated the kitchen and three bathrooms, painted it inside and out, and put in all new flooring. Each of his kids had a separate bedroom, he had the master suite, and the fourth room was used as a study, which had a futon for a guest bed, no television allowed. He and the kids each had a desk in there with a computer. He'd set up a small table where the three of them could play board games. Beanbag chairs provided lounging spots.

No lights shone from inside. He texted his mom to let her know he was home, and then just sat in the truck to unwind after his stressful day. Guilt weighed on his chest like a boulder. Because he'd made one bad decision, both Tori and Michael would suffer. Tanner wouldn't get home early enough to throw balls with his son every evening. Bike rides with Tori, one of her favorite activities with Daddy, might become only weekend treats. Dinner would reach the table later, and the domino effect would leave less time afterward for kitchen cleanup, study time, movie or reading time, and baths. He was the only parent his kids had, and he should have made them his first priority.

He glimpsed their approach in the rearview mirror. They always took a shortcut from his mother's place one block over and walked between two houses to reach the sidewalk across the street from their home. Michael had taken after Carolyn with his midnight blue eyes and shiny hair the color of coffee beans. Tori had Tanner's coloring, her eyes sky blue and her curls resembling a swirl of melted milk chocolate and butterscotch. Today they both wore jeans, Michael's topped by a University of Oregon T-shirt, Tori's by a sleeveless pink thing with ruffles around the armholes and elastic gathers over the midriff.

He exited the truck. Tori squealed when she saw him. He yelled, "Look both ways!"

Her head swiveled back and forth, flinging her curly locks over her tiny shoulders. Then she raced across the ribbon of asphalt bracketed by parked cars. Tanner squatted down to catch her when she threw herself into his arms. Her small book bag, clutched in one hand, whacked him on the ear. He buried his face in her hair and breathed in her scent: little-girl sweetness laced with traces of bubble-bath soap, tearless shampoo, and cafeteria aromas.

Tanner growled ferociously. "I smell nacho-cheese corn chips, and that makes me hungry!"

Tori giggled and squirmed in his embrace. Tanner released her and stood to loop his arm over Michael's shoulders. The youth stiffened, resisting the hug. He kept telling Tanner he was getting too old for mushy stuff. "How was school, sport?"

"Boring. I can't wait for summer."

Tanner nodded, thinking of yet another count against him. Over summer break, his kids would see a lot less of him than they would if he hadn't gotten in trouble. "I need to tell you both something."

Michael's gaze sharpened on Tanner's face. "I just saw Nana, so I know she's okay. Is it Grandma or Grandpa Hampton?"

It saddened Tanner that his son's first thought was that someone he loved had died or been hurt. But he guessed that was to be expected. Michael was five when his mother's car collided head-on with an eighteen-wheeler truck, and he still remembered how things changed after her death.

"It's nothing like that," Tanner assured the boy.

"But I can tell by your voice that it's something pretty bad."

Tanner led the way to the front porch, low profile with only two steps. Each of the kids took a seat beside him, Michael retying his Nike running shoe before settling and Tori fussing with her bag to make it balance on the lower step.

"I lost my route in Crystal Falls," Tanner said. He'd never been good at small talk. "I did something wrong and could have lost my job, but instead of firing me, my super gave me the rural route in Mystic Creek for a year."

Michael looked startled, then curious. Tori was still messing with her book bag. "What did you do wrong?"

Tanner studied the palms of his hands. He had no idea why. He didn't know the meaning of one line from another, except for his life line, which had a wide break in the middle just above where it began the gradual curve downward to the base of his thumb. He'd often wondered if that meant he'd have two lives: the one he'd had with Carolyn and another with someone else. So far he'd met no one who'd interested him enough to draw him into a serious relationship. Probably a good thing. His kids came first. They always would.

"I broke the rules to do a favor for an old man who's a friend of mine," he settled for saying.

"Why was that breaking the rules?" Tori finally got her lopsided bag balanced and frowned up at him. "You and Nana say we should always be nice to old people."

"True, and I hope you always will be, but sometimes you need to wait until you're off work to do nice things, and I didn't do that. When we're on a job, we're being paid to do only what our employer expects us to. We should save personal errands for later." Tanner saw no point in giving his kids the details. It was enough to let them know he'd made a mistake and what the ramifications would be. He hoped his confession would be a good learning experience for them, an example of the consequences that could result from one bad decision. "My punishment is to drive an hour longer each day back and forth to work. That means I'll be at home with you a whole hour less every night for a year."

Tori's already large eyes went rounder. "Will I miss you a lot, Daddy?"

Michael said, "Don't be dumb, Tori. We'll still see him all the time."

Tanner intervened before more shots were fired. "It isn't a dumb question, Michael. Tori may miss me, and you may as well. I won't have as much time at night to do fun things with each of you." He leveled his gaze on Michael and then looked out over the yard. "The way it's been, I could mow the lawn and tidy the flower beds and still have time to do fun stuff. Now that may change quite a lot."

"That sucks. My friend Bobby over on Nana's street can't help me with my pitching arm."

Tanner stood. "I'm sorry, Michael. I'll throw balls with you as much as I can. But right now, it's time for me to start dinner while you do homework."

"We already did it at Nana's," Michael said.

"Fine. You two can watch something educational on TV while I cook."

"I got five happy faces on my paper today!" Tori cried.

"Good for you," Tanner told her.

Once inside, Tanner ignored the socks Michael had

left on the living room floor last night and the pajamas Tori had shed in the hallway that morning. He'd tidy up after he got the kids tucked in for the night. He opened the fridge and studied the contents, a nightly pastime. He could never think what to make for dinner. Carolyn had always planned ahead.

Hands planted on her narrow hips, Tori joined him in staring at the fridge shelves. Then she frowned up at him. "Daddy, the play is tomorrow. Where's my wolf costume?"

Tanner stared down at his daughter, sensing a mini disaster in the making. "Your *what*?"

"My wolf costume. You remember. Wolves are wild dogs, and that's what Mrs. Walker said I could be, because I really like dogs."

Tanner vaguely remembered Tori talking about a play. The school was doing a wildlife-awareness month. But he had no recollection of seeing a note that Tori needed a wolf outfit. He had assumed that any necessary attire would be provided by the school. "You need a costume *tomorrow*?"

The dreaded reply came, accompanied by tears springing to Tori's eyes. "Yes. I'm supposed to take it to school in the morning."

Tanner had no clue how to create a wolf costume. He closed the refrigerator, decided fast food was on the menu for dinner, and did the only thing a smart man could in emergencies like this.

He called his mother.

Chapter Four

Armed with a map and struggling to wake up, Tanner penciled in his route the next morning, numbered the roads he had highlighted, and then organized the parcels in his truck accordingly. Since he had decided to work the south section of his route first, anything to be delivered at the north end had to be at the bottom of the stacks.

As he drove the road toward Mystic Creek a few minutes later, he rolled the van window down to enjoy the sun-scented morning air, even though it was still chilly in the mountains. Right after the turnoff to the waterfall, Tanner's cell phone chirped on the dashboard. He saw a wide spot where he could pull over and answer.

It was his supervisor. "Hey, I didn't have time to find you before you left the building. That Malloy woman called in yesterday and withdrew her complaint against you. It won't change the outcome for you, but I thought you should know."

Crystal had dropped her complaint? Tanner was mystified. "I wonder why she did that."

"Beats me. Maybe a change of heart."

"Well, it was a nice gesture. Thanks for letting me know."

After the call ended Tanner resumed driving the curvy mountain road. What had prompted Crystal to withdraw the grievance? Maybe, he decided, Tuck had raised so much sand, she'd felt pressured into it. Or maybe she realized three months without one's simple pleasures was a long time to an old man who considered green bananas to be a risky investment. Every day was a gift to someone like Tuck, and sometimes tomorrow never came.

Tanner had learned that the hard way. The day before Carolyn was killed was their wedding anniversary. Both of them had had busy careers, so they'd decided not to celebrate on the actual date in favor of waiting until the following day, a Friday. Carolyn had arranged for a sitter. Tanner had gotten reservations at a five-star restaurant. They had planned to end their evening at a swank hotel, making love and lying in each other's arms. Instead Carolyn had ended up lying on a stainless-steel slab at the morgue.

If Tanner could avoid it, he no longer put off things for tomorrow. He knew now that a man's whole world could change in a blink and there were no second chances.

Crystal got up earlier than usual so she would have time to visit Tuck before heading for the salon. She was hoping a night's sleep might see him relent a bit, but experience told her that probably wouldn't happen. Experience won. Tuck just glared at her when she entered his apartment. For so long Crystal had counted on him to love her no matter what. Dealing with his anger was a new experience for her.

"How are you, Tuck?" Her voice was high-pitched. No answer.

"How was dinner last night?" She glanced at her watch to see if he'd already eaten breakfast. "And how was the food this morning?"

She expected more silence, but Tuck exploded. It was so sudden and loud that she actually dropped her purse and had to pick it back up.

"Dinner last night sucked!" he roared. "I ain't had proper food since I been in this jail. The only time they cook *decent* is on Sunday when most folks' families come to visit. The rest of the time, breakfast is plastic, lunch is plastic, and so is dinner. Fake eggs. Turkey bacon. Sugar-free and fat-free yogurt. Artificially sweetened syrup. Soggy cereal that tastes like cardboard. We get watered-down juice only at breakfast. *God forbid* that we might get a sugar rush and kill ourselves!"

"What do you want?" Crystal tried. "I could bring you food, and then you could—"

"Just shut up!"

Shock rooted Crystal's feet to the carpeting. Tuck had never spoken to her this way.

Anger glittered like ice in the depths of his blue eyes. "I don't want you bringin' me nothin' right now. You betrayed my only true friend in Oregon. His wife's dead, and he's raisin' two kids alone. He got taken off the Crystal Falls rural route and reassigned to drive over here! So he'll get a lot less time with his children at night. And you grabbed my cell phone, damn it! Did it make you feel powerful to hold it out of my reach while you looked at my personal stuff? Was it satisfyin' to best me, just because you could?"

Crystal's heart jerked. She had grabbed Tuck's phone, but she'd never meant to make him think it was a power play. "No!" she cried. "I didn't mean it that way."

"How else did you mean it? It's *my* phone, and the stuff on it is *private*."

"Oh, Tuck. All I wanted was to find your order for

the beer and chew! I never intended to invade your privacy."

"So why did you do it, then? There was a time when I was way stronger than you. Did I ever once treat you like your feelin's didn't matter to me?"

"No," Crystal admitted, her throat aching with an urge to sob. "Never even once, Tuck."

"When you was a teenage girl with secrets you didn't want me to know about, did I ever once snoop in your room? Or ever once pick up another phone in the house to listen in when you talked to a friend?"

"No." She flung out her hands in a helpless gesture.

"I'm a broken old man now. My strength is pert near gone. But that don't give you no right to snoop on my phone and then rat out my friend. No right!"

Every word he spoke cut into Crystal like a machete. "I'm sorry, Tuck. What can I do to earn your forgiveness? Maybe I handled everything wrong, but my heart was in the right place. I only wanted to protect you and take care of you. I love you."

"Maybe I don't wanna be protected. Maybe I don't wanna be taken care of. Maybe all I want is to be treated with respect. You need to think on that, long and hard, and until you have, stay away from me. I can't bear to look at you!"

Memories crashed over her like brutal ocean waves. *"Murderer! I'll never forgive you. I can't even bear to look at you!"* She could almost hear her mother screaming those words. And her father, yelling at her to stay in her room so he didn't have to see her and be reminded of the horrible thing she'd done. For months, Crystal had felt unwelcome and completely unloved in her own home. Then Tuck had come to take her away to his ranch. Tuck, who'd told her she had done nothing wrong. Tuck, who had helped her heal and given her unconditional love. Tuck, who'd never yelled at her.

Until now. And suddenly Crystal realized that she'd never really healed. Tuck's love had been a protective bandage over the wounds deep within her, and now he had ripped it away. Her body felt paralyzed and ice-cold. Pressure built inside her chest.

She retreated a step, and then her feet seemed to move of their own accord to carry her backward. At the doorway leading out to the hall, she swung around, grappled with the knob, and finally escaped.

Tuck yelled after her, "Crystal! Wait! Don't go! I got somethin' more I need to say!"

Crystal had heard enough. More than enough. She needed to be alone until she could shove away the old memories and try to sort out the mess she'd created with her grandfather.

She rushed from the building, her stomach roiling. Would he ever forgive her? She'd meant to tell him all the many reasons she was sorry for how she'd handled Patricia. She'd hoped to tell him that she'd withdrawn her complaint against Tanner Richards. She had wanted so badly to mend fences with him. She needed to be in his good graces again. Needed to know that he still loved her and that nothing she ever did would make him stop. He was the only family she had.

But he hadn't given her a chance to say much of anything. She'd had no idea how dearly Tuck treasured Tanner's friendship—or how much he cared about the younger man's kids. She also hadn't known two motherless children would suffer if she filed a complaint. And, oh, God, what had she been thinking when she'd taken his cell phone and held it beyond his reach?

She had wanted Tuck to talk to her again. Now she almost wished he'd clung to his angry silence. She felt as if he'd flailed her with a whip. Outside her car, the nausea struck with more vengeance. She ran to the edge of the parking lot, doubled over, and purged her stomach.

By the time Crystal reached the salon, the nausea had subsided a little, replaced by an awful headache. She had an appointment with Ma Thomas, so nicknamed because she signed documents with only her first two initials, M for Mary and A for Alice. At some point in time, someone had started calling her Ma, and the handle had stuck. Crystal just hoped her hands would stop shaking so she could cut the woman's hair properly. Ma was one of her favorite clients.

"A little shorter this time," Ma told her after she got settled in the styling chair. "Summer is right around the corner, and a shorter cut will be cooler if the air conditioner at my shop goes on the blink again."

"Oh, let's hope not," Crystal said, trying to sound normal. It was difficult to make her mind focus. "How much shorter? I'm thinking about an inch. I can always take off more if it doesn't suit you, but I can't glue it back on."

"Smart thinking." Ma smiled as Crystal began cutting. Then her expression became pensive. "What's wrong, honey? You're as pale as milk."

"I'm fine, Ma. Just feeling a little off this morning."

"Have you and Tuck patched things up yet?"

The question slammed into Crystal's stomach, which already ached. She couldn't believe how quickly gossip traveled in this town. Only her techs knew firsthand about the spat she'd had with Tuck, but somehow word had spread.

Ma was one of the few individuals Crystal didn't mind knowing her personal business. She was a delightful lady, one of the community's beloved matriarchs.

Back when Crystal had lived in the flat above the salon, she had eaten frequently at the Cauldron and gotten to know Ma there. Despite their age difference, they'd become friends.

"No, I'm afraid not," she confessed. "I saw him this morning, and he's still very angry with me." She stepped over to draw the privacy curtain, which she seldom used. In a lower voice, she said, "I don't know if he'll ever forgive me." Her voice went thin and squeaky on those last words. "And he's all I have left."

Following Crystal's lead, Ma spoke softly, too. "Oh, honey, he hasn't stopped loving you. He's just mad. He'll come around soon." A tiny frown pleated her forehead. "I have a possibly difficult question for you. Do you feel you were within your rights to side against your grandfather with the administrator of the living center?"

"I didn't side against him. Patricia forced me to file the complaint. If I didn't, she said she'd evict him. And she *lied*, but that's a long story. He's in no condition to stay alone at my place. I doubt he could even cook or make a sandwich without getting the lining of his cast wet." She paused with the scissors hovering above strands of Ma's blond hair. "That isn't all Tuck's mad at me about, though. I grabbed his cell phone and looked at all his calls, messages, and emails to find out who brought him the contraband. And then I found the Courier Express box. The rest was pretty simple detective work."

"You searched his phone?"

Ma's tone held a note of censure, and Crystal met her gaze in the mirror. "Normally I'd never do that," she explained. "It just sort of happened. I didn't mean to invade his privacy. He led me to think he ordered the stuff, and I hoped to find a copy of the invoice so I could derail Patricia. I couldn't just let him be kicked out on the street when I had no other place to take him."

"No wonder Tuck is in a snit. He realizes you still don't understand his side of it."

"Oh, I understand. He skinned me alive with words this morning, so I totally understand now. I invaded his privacy. I used my youth and agility to outmaneuver him when I grabbed his phone and he tried to take it back. He reminded me of when he was the strong one and I was only a little girl. He never once used his physical advantage against me. He never once invaded my privacy." Tears burned like acid in her eyes. "When I grabbed his phone, I *did* invade his. I had no right to do that. Then, using the information I found, I ratted out his friend and caused trouble for him at work. I was wrong, Ma, so very wrong. But no matter what I say, Tuck refuses to forgive me. I love him so much. I want to make things right between us again. Only, saying I'm sorry doesn't seem to be enough."

"Did you say all that to him?"

"No, not all of it. Hardly any of it. I didn't get a chance. He's been so angry that he doesn't let me say a whole lot, and I get tongue-tied. If I say something, it's usually the *wrong* thing. I wish I could go back and do everything differently. I wouldn't touch his phone. And I would defy Patricia Flintlock and tell her to shove all her rules where they'd never again see sunlight. I'd just pack up some of Tuck's clothes and take him home. Give him my bed. Reschedule appointments to take time off from work to care for him. I *would*. I *swear*. He's the most important thing in the world to me."

Ma reached back to pat Crystal's arm. "I think he knows that, but maybe, in order to get over his anger, he needs to hear you say all this to *him*."

"He won't listen."

"Don't give him a choice." Ma stared at her half-shorn locks. "Finish my hair. Your hands are shaking, so if it's not right, I'll come back for a redo, no charge. While you're working, let me tell you *my* story. I didn't stand up to Patricia Flintlock, either, until it was almost too late. So I probably understand what went on better than anyone else can."

"You've dealt with her?"

She grimaced. "No, I failed to deal with her. And to this day, I still feel guilty about that."

Crystal nodded. "She's impossible, isn't she?"

"She's puredee old mean. That's what she is."

Trying to keep her hands steady, Crystal resumed her work with the scissors while her friend talked.

"My husband, Bob, died of cancer," she began. "He passed away before you opened the salon here, so you never met him. But he was a kind and wonderful man. About six months before he died, he grew very weak. He could no longer move from his wheelchair to the commode, or to his recliner, or into bed. He also became incontinent. Even reduced to little more than skin and bones, he was too big a man for me to lift, and I decided I had no choice but to put him in assisted living. They have a patient hoist there, and the attendants work together to transfer residents. I thought it would be a good place for him. Only it wasn't. Before I made the decision to take him there, I didn't know Patricia or how vicious she can be.

"Bob loved his whiskey. It was his preferred pain-killer and tranquilizer, and at home I always kept his glass full. The doctor authorized it. He said my husband should be allowed to escape the pain and anxiety in whatever way worked best for him. There was no concern about Bob developing health problems if he overindulged. He was already dying, so depriving him of anything that made his final days more bearable would have been ridiculous."

Crystal ran her hands through her friend's hair, checking for evenness. "Oh, Ma, that must have been so horrible for you." She couldn't imagine watching Tuck, sick and in pain, losing ground. "I'm so sorry."

"It was far more horrible for Bob. When I got him into the assisted living center, my job became so much easier, and I knew he was kept cleaner and more comfortable. Soiled bedding was quickly changed. He got sponge baths right away if he had an accident. But when Patricia found out his medication of choice was alcohol, she went ballistic and threatened to evict him. My only alternative was to get his liquor out of there, or I would have had only twenty-four hours to take him somewhere else."

Crystal cringed. "Did you do it? Take his liquor away, I mean."

"Yes. The situation seemed impossible to me. I couldn't afford to hire in-home attendants. A simple patient lift cost a fortune and our insurance wouldn't cover it. There was no other assisted living facility here in town, and I liked spending days and evenings with him. I knew that if I transferred him to another place in Crystal Falls, the driving distance would shorten the time I could be with him. It's a long, icy drive in the winter, and I knew storms might sometimes prevent me from making the trip at all."

"So you caved, just like I did, or sort of, anyway."

"Yes, I caved. I took the liquor home. Bob was miserable. The doctor prescribed pain medication and tranquilizers for him, but they made him sick to his stomach. I toughed it out for a month—or maybe I should say I made Bob tough it out. At some point during that time he started refusing to take the medication. In the end I decided to take him home. We had some savings, not much, but some. I bought a lift, and I hired help, and he could have all the whiskey he wanted during the last month of his life. He was at peace. He died with a glass of booze on the bedside table."

"You did the right thing," Crystal said softly.

"Yes. I was not only broke, but in debt by the time it was over. The cost of in-home care was astronomical. All my credit cards were maxed, and I'd gotten new ones so I could max them out, too. But none of that mattered, not really. My only regret was that I didn't get him out of there sooner. Why didn't I try to hide his whiskey? Why didn't I hire a lawyer and battle it out with Patricia? I don't think she can legally evict people without more notice. And technically, Bob rented his apartment, so what he did inside those walls should have been nobody's business as long as his doctor was on board. By the time I found the courage to do what needed doing, Bob had been miserable for a whole month, and he didn't have that much time left."

Tuck was eighty. He didn't have that much time left, either. The thought made Crystal's legs go weak. "I hear what you're saying, but how can I win a battle against Patricia Flintlock?"

"At least the situation is temporary, Crystal. It won't be that long before your grandfather can go home. Until then, do your best to outsmart the witch. Show your grandfather that you're on his side."

"By breaking her stupid rules? She'll retaliate."

"Not if she doesn't know." Ma grinned. "You're a bright young woman. You can find ways to work around her."

"She may evict him if we get caught."

"Possibly. Get a lawyer. I highly recommend Ramsey

or Sullivan in town. Both of them are good advocates for the elderly. Get one of them on retainer so he'll be ready to go to bat for your grandfather at the drop of a hat. And remember something. The concept of assisted living came into being so that oldsters can have a home away from home where they can live much as they always have. Do you think Patricia is allowing Tuck to do that? Do you think his habits would bother other residents? It isn't cheap to stay there. Do you feel that he's happy or getting his money's worth?"

Crystal's answer to all of Ma's questions was a resounding no, and the older woman had given her a lot to think about. Just then her phone rang. When she grabbed it off her station cabinet, she saw that it was Tuck calling her. She dropped the phone as if it burned her. If he yelled at her again, she'd totally lose it. And she was in a public place. Her brain froze when he raised his voice to her in anger, probably because he'd never done it while she was growing up. The next time they spoke, she needed to have rehearsed her lines so many times she wouldn't flounder. *Only, what if he's calling about something urgent?* She nixed that thought. Someone at the facility would call if Tuck needed her.

Tanner had forgotten what it was like to memorize a new delivery route. Mystic Creek was particularly challenging because it was surrounded by curvy, unpaved roads. It was also difficult to read the addresses of houses that sat way back on parcels of land. Some homeowners had house numbers on reflective green signs at the end of the driveway. Others didn't. *Is that the right house?* He'd asked himself that question at least a hundred times already, and his workday wasn't even half over. He was behind schedule and had a headache. His little girl was performing in the school play that night. He couldn't miss seeing that. His mom planned to go early so she could paint black circles around Tori's eyes, a dot on the end of her nose, and whiskers on her cheeks. She was even taking the glue gun in case the costume they had created last night needed repairs.

Tanner finally found the house he'd been looking for and pulled up in front of a hurricane fence. In a hurry, he didn't bother to read the name of the recipient as he lugged the large parcel to a chain-link gate that bore a long note in a sheet protector. *Dog instructions.* People always seemed to think their dogs had special quirks that no other canine possessed. Well, Tanner knew the drill and carried three biscuits in his uniform pocket, one to bribe his way in, another to afford him safe passage to the porch, and a final offering to exit the yard safely. He'd only ever met one dog that demanded four biscuits. That had been Rip, Tuck's blue heeler, who went ballistic over Tanner's uniform and calmed down only after Tanner mollified him with treats.

Tanner saw no dog and hurried through the gate, latching it behind him. *No hassle with this delivery,* he thought. But when he was halfway to the porch, he heard a low growl. He turned to see a familiar-looking blue heeler. *Nah,* he assured himself. *It can't be Rip. God forbid, because I'm carrying only three biscuits, and that damned dog can count.* He shrugged the suspicion off. Most blue heelers looked alike.

Tanner doled out the first biscuit. Then he gave the dog a second one to gain the porch. He knew he was in trouble when he tried to descend the steps. The dog lunged at him, snarled, and bared its teeth.

"Rip?" Tanner stared at the dog. "Please tell me it's not you."

But the dog was telling him just the opposite. Tanner

glanced at the last biscuit in his hand. If this was Rip, Tanner would need another one to get safely out the gate. With Rip, it was either four biscuits or bloodletting. Well, Tuck swore the dog didn't *really* bite. He only pinched with his front teeth. Tanner didn't find that difference very comforting.

He stood on the bottom stair and slowly eased one foot toward the ground. The cattle dog lunged at his leg. Tanner jerked his boot back onto the step. "Damn it. Just my luck. You *are* Rip. That means I'm in deep shit." He couldn't *believe* this was Tuck's place. Correction. He knew Tuck had purchased a mini farm somewhere outside the Mystic Creek city limits and that his granddaughter was living there with Tuck's dog. But how likely was it that this was the house and that Crystal had ordered something to be delivered the second day of his new assignment? Pretty damned likely, he decided. It was a small town.

Tanner clenched the one remaining biscuit in his fist and tried to think of a plan, until his sweaty palm started to soften the crusty bone-shaped treat. He studied the dog. The trick would be to outsmart Rip. *That shouldn't be hard to do,* Tanner decided. Man against dog. His IQ had to be much higher.

"Okay," he said in a friendly voice. "I know you remember me, and somewhere along the way, we became pals. Remember that, Rip?" He paused as if he expected a response, and felt like an idiot. "Right. You don't talk. So, do you see the biscuit?" Tanner waggled it in the air well above the dog's leaping reach. "Yum. It'll be so good. And I'm going to give it to you with one little catch. Are you ready?" He did a figure eight with the biscuit. Rip bounced around with a greedy expression on his face. "I'm going to throw it. And when you run to get it, I'm going to haul ass for that gate. It's only about five feet tall. I'm a lot taller than you, and I can vault over it. So, here you go!"

Tanner threw the biscuit, and while Rip tore after it, Tanner burst into a run, covering four feet with his starting leap. *The gate.* It was only ten yards away. He could make it. He took long strides and pumped his arms for speed. No worries. He'd been a champion runner in track. Only, something collided with his knee. He felt sharp teeth graze his calf. The next second he was jumping around the yard with Rip attached to his pant leg. He tried to shake the dog loose, but within an instant, he wasn't sure who was shaking whom.

"Son of a bitch! You little *bastard.*" Tanner headed back for the porch, dragging the dog along with him, his right leg weighted down behind him. As he gained the steps, he felt his pant leg rip just above the knee, and then in a frenzy, Rip shook it ferociously to pull it off over Tanner's boot. Score for man, zero. Score for canine, one. Huffing for breath, Tanner sank onto the porch steps. As long as he didn't leave this spot, he knew he was safe. Rip knew the rules of the game. *He should,* Tanner thought. *He created it.*

Tanner stared at his van. His cell phone was inside, perched on the sticky pad he kept on the dash. Oh, how Tanner wished he had carried the communication device with him. He could call for help. The county sheriff's office would work. Or to keep Rip off the cop radar, he could call Tuck, who would notify Crystal. But as it stood, Tanner was stuck.

Rip kept guard at the bottom of the steps. A look of sheer canine delight shone on his face. Tanner had gotten to know the dog while visiting Tuck. He knew Rip wasn't inherently vicious. He just had quirks, one of which was a hatred of uniforms. This was a game to the heeler, nothing more. A stranger in civilian clothes could enter the yard without a challenge.

"Okay," Tanner said. "Here's the deal. My little girl, Tori, has a play tonight. I'm running late, and I don't want to miss her performance. I know you like to charge a toll for safe passage, but I'm out of biscuits. So what else would you accept as payment?"

The blue heeler ducked his head, grabbed the torn-off part of Tanner's uniform pants, and gave it a vicious shake. An idea began to germinate in Tanner's brain and he smiled.

"You want to tear apart every uniform you see. Don't you? I don't think it's so much the people wearing them that you detest. What if I gave you my shirt to destroy? Would that entertain you long enough for me to make a run for it?"

Rip knew when he was being spoken to, and he barked. The dog's intelligence unnerved Tanner a bit. He decided to think through his tactical maneuvers before he settled on a plan. It was expensive to replace a uniform shirt. Maybe he'd be smarter to sacrifice the already-destroyed pants. On the other hand, the front door was only a few feet behind where he sat. Could he reach it, let himself in, slam it closed, and then find a phone?

Only, what if there was no phone? Tanner knew Tuck would insist on having a landline when and if he got to come home, but Crystal was far younger and a member of the cellular-communication age. Tanner paid for a landline because he had kids, but she was single. She probably hadn't coughed up the bucks for a wired phone. Most people her age—and his—figured it was a waste of money. Still, since it was Tuck's house, she might have sprung for a landline.

He measured the distance to the door. Definitely a

possibility. Only, he didn't have Tuck's cell number memorized, and he doubted there was a phone book inside. If there was a computer in the house, he could look up the assisted living facility and contact Tuck that way. He could also call information or 911. But he hated to get Rip branded as a biter. Tuck loved the dog. At eighty, the old man didn't have a whole lot left that he cared about. His Idaho ranchland was long gone. His former life in Crystal Falls had ended. All he really cared about now was his granddaughter, his horse, and that dog. Tanner didn't want to disappoint Tori by missing her play, but he guessed she would survive if he couldn't get there.

Not that he was surrendering yet. Surely, he could outsmart a dog. Rip guarded the steps. Maybe if Tanner slipped off the side of the porch, the blue heeler wouldn't get upset, because he was unaccustomed to people going that way. He tried that tactic, and Rip plunged into the flower garden to nip at his remaining pant leg. He shot back onto the porch.

After collapsing on the top step again, he thought about making a dash for the front door. Only what if there was no landline? He decided there probably wasn't and studied his brown pants. *Already ruined.* He'd never be able to wear them again, so they'd be the better choice. If he pulled his belt from the loops, wadded the trousers into a tight ball, and used all his strength, how far would he be able to throw them? He concluded that he'd never know the answer until he gave them a toss.

The nearest neighboring house was about a quarter mile away. Tanner doubted that anyone would be watching Tuck's place. Feeling ridiculous, he worked the uniform pants off over his work boots. He fastened the belt around his waist, not because it now held anything up, but because he'd paid fifty bucks for it and knew Rip would chew on it if he got half a chance.

He rolled the ruined britches into the tightest ball he could; then he teased Rip with it until the blue heeler grew excited and became focused solely on getting it. Tanner stood, planted his feet on two different steps, and assumed a pitching stance. He needed to put all his strength into this and send the garment flying far enough that Rip would have a lot of ground to cover in order to double back to the gate.

"One!" Rip yipped in excitement. "Two!" Rip growled. *"Three!"* Tanner threw the wadded pants. "Go get 'em, Rip!"

The dog darted after the brown missile. Tanner charged toward the gate. He was almost there. So close. Maybe only five feet to go. Then Rip sprang into his path, teeth bared, saliva hanging in frothy white strings from his jowls. *Shit.* Tanner wore no pants now, only his boxers. This time Rip might bite his legs, not uniform cloth.

Tanner grabbed the front of his shirt with both fists. Buttons went flying as he jerked off the garment. He dangled it in front of Rip as he walked backward toward the porch. "Here you go. Look at the shirt, Rip. Stay focused. You'll have so much more fun with it. Legs are boring."

Just as Tanner reached his destination, Rip lunged, grabbed the shirt, and yanked it from his hand. Tanner sank onto the top step again, only this time he was naked except for his belt, boxers, and boots. He glanced down and saw that he was wearing the boxers that Tori had gotten him for Christmas.

Shit. They had puppies all over them. What would Crystal think when she saw them? And she would see them. He was stuck where he sat. No more brilliant plans for escape came to him. He'd still be here when she got home.

And he'd be naked. Well, *almost* naked. But he was close enough to the mark to score in a game of horseshoes.

Chapter Five

On the way home Crystal almost drove to the assisted living center to talk with Tuck again. She ached inside and wanted nothing more than to make peace with him. But although she regretted everything she'd done and was sorry for a dozen different reasons, she wasn't a person who was quick on her feet, especially not when someone was angry with her. If he started to yell at her again, she'd never be able to apologize coherently. She'd just flub it all up—*again*.

The invisible-fencing kit was scheduled to arrive today. Her evening would be well spent at the end of a shovel. She did her best thinking while she worked at a mindless chore. Tension would ooze out of her with the sweat that seeped from her pores. It always had. Hopefully she'd be able to analyze everything, consider all the different ways that she'd transgressed against her grandfather, how she'd made him feel, and be fully prepared to talk to him in the morning.

When she reached the farm, she saw a Courier Express van outside the gate. As she parked her vehicle, she stared at a nearly nude man sitting on the steps. Until that instant, she'd believed that she'd never met Tanner Richards, who, she now knew, had been assigned the Mystic Creek rural route. *Oh, dear God. He's the deliveryman I met at the medical supply store right after Tuck got hurt.* She recalled that meeting in vivid detail. A beautiful little girl had been with him. And, as embarrassing as it had been at the time, Crystal had been bowled over by him. It wasn't often that she met a man so attractive that just meeting his gaze made her skin tingle with awareness.

Staring at him through the sun-washed windshield, she still thought he was a hunk. Especially without clothes. His shoulders, arms, and chest were well padded with muscle—not like a weight lifter's, but more the physique of a man who labored for a living. She guessed that delivering heavy parcels kept a guy in superb condition.

No, she told herself, *this isn't really happening.* She was imagining things. Maybe he was there. . . . Okay, she'd accept that . . . but almost naked? No way. She struggled to collect her thoughts. *Why* was he nearly naked? She tried to push the likely answer straight out of her mind. Only, it barged in anyway. *Rip. He must have caused this!* She wasn't sure exactly how, but she knew the dog was behind the odd situation. What would she say? How would she apologize? Why hadn't he read the letter she'd posted on the gate? Rip turned into Attila the Hun when he encountered someone in a uniform.

Her mouth went dry, and her palms got sweaty. She cut the car engine, grabbed her handbag, and climbed out. A breeze scented with pine and spring grass played with her long hair. She thought about calling out a friendly hello. Except that would have been stupid. No one who'd been stuck for God knew how long on someone's porch, with the added frustration of not being dressed, was interested in a polite exchange. He wore only a belt, boxers and boots. And he looked as if he'd been sitting there for a long while, possibly hours. He'd clearly encountered Rip in terrorist mode and lost the battle.

"I can see you didn't read the dog instructions," she yelled out in greeting, and immediately wished she'd said something else. But she hadn't, and now all she could think to do was run with it. "Why on earth didn't you?" She pointed at a gnarly old oak that stood like a sentry just outside the fence. "I have a sealed bag of dog biscuits in a knothole of that tree for anyone who needs them." She paused, hoping he'd say something, but he didn't. That unnerved her. She tried again.

"I've heard of men saying, 'Come naked and bring beer,' but I've never known a man who reversed the roles. And where's the beer?" She'd meant that as a joke, but he didn't laugh. Why did she always say the most inappropriate thing possible when she was upset or nervous? It was like some kind of social-gaffe disease. He'd gotten in trouble for taking Tuck beer. Now he would think she was jabbing him about it. She pretended to clean a blackboard with an invisible eraser. "Nix that. I know Rip, and I'm very sorry. He's a sweet dog. Well, I've seen him be sweet to other people. But he's seldom nice to me, and I think you must have arrived in a uniform. Did he tear it off you?"

He studied her with sky blue eyes that made her feel as if the thoughts racing through her brain were words on a computer screen that he could read. "I didn't look at the note because it's a new route for me, and I was running late. I've also been a deliveryman for years, and I know the drill with dogs. Three biscuits was all I'd ever needed."

"Except with Rip."

"Yeah, except with Rip. But how was I supposed to know he lives here?"

Crystal took a step forward. "By reading the note on the gate printed in large block letters?"

He shrugged. "You wrote a whole book, and I was in a hurry." His gaze moved slowly over her. "So, your name is Crystal Malloy. I regretted that I never thought to ask your name when my daughter and I met you."

Crystal's stomach tightened. "You remember that?"

"Oh, yeah. You were wonderful with my daughter. She still talks about the pretty lady with long red hair. And she hasn't let my mother cut hers since. I think she wants straight hair like yours, though, and hers is curly."

Most men she'd met would have been mortified to be caught in his state of undress, but he seemed to be comfortable in mostly only his skin. And with a second downward sweep of her gaze, she could understand why. He had a gorgeous body. Six-pack abs. Well-muscled legs. His skin was caramel brown, but just under the sag of his boxers at the back of his upraised thighs, she saw two tan lines that melded into paler flesh, lightly furred with hair that matched the dark swath of curls that arrowed down from his chest. She pictured him working in his yard wearing only shorts that rode high on his legs. How did his female neighbors manage not to stare out their windows?

She scanned the area for Rip. "Where is the little monster?"

"Under the porch, tearing my uniform shirt to shreds. He can make sure from there that I stay put while he lies in the shade."

Crystal fished in her purse for dog biscuits. She wasn't foolish enough to think she could go through the gate without Rip demanding a payment.

"You're kidding," Tanner remarked. "He bites you if you don't give him toll cookies? Sorry. Tuck calls them that. But he also told me that he's Rip's chosen one, the only person, except for someone in a uniform, who has to play the game."

Crystal opened the gate. Rip came racing out from under the porch. She bent to give him a treat. "That was true before Tuck fell off the porch at his house in Crystal Falls. After that, I became more than just a cook and housekeeper. Rip and I live together now, and I've become another chosen one. Tuck says I should feel honored." She shrugged. "Rip has never really liked me, so I don't feel privileged. Mostly only put-upon."

"Rip is probably jealous of you. He knows Tuck loves you, and he doesn't want to share him with you."

Crystal had never considered it that way. *Jealous?* She scratched the dog behind his ears. Rip growled. A smile curved her lips and caught her by surprise. She knew the heeler loved getting scratches, and he allowed her to administer them, but he couldn't resist letting her know he didn't like her while he accepted the petting. "Jealousy. That makes sense. Only, how do I overcome that?"

Despite the electrical charge she felt in the air between her and Tanner Richards, she found it easy to talk to him.

He shrugged. "Rip is just Rip. There's no understanding him. Sometimes I think he's brain damaged. I've never met another dog like him."

As Crystal crossed the yard, she fished in her purse for another biscuit, knowing that she would have to bribe Rip again in order to reach the porch. "Neither have I. How long have you been trapped here?"

"I got here about noon."

It was six in the evening. Crystal's breathing hitched. "Oh, my God. Six hours?"

"Six hours and a sunburn. The sun finally sank low enough behind the house that the veranda overhang is casting shade. Fortunately, with my skin, I'll tan and not blister."

Crystal gave Rip another biscuit for the privilege of trespassing on the bottom step. "I am *so* sorry, Tanner." A tight feeling seized hold of her throat. "For everything! For Rip's behavior, of course. But I also got you in trouble at work by filing that complaint. I wish I could undo that. Tuck says the route change means you can't spend as much time with your kids. I never intended to hurt you or your children."

He propped his thick forearms on his upraised knees and let his big hands dangle. "I know. I've talked with Tuck. He says you got railroaded into filing a complaint by the facility administrator."

Crystal blinked. She almost said, "Run that by me again?" If Tuck truly believed Patricia had forced her hand, why on earth was he so furious with her? Her heart sank as the answer came to her. Her grandfather was angry, not because of how everything had boomeranged that night, but because she had betrayed *him* by refusing to accept his decision to give Patricia no information and grabbing his phone to take the choice away from him. Oh, how she regretted that moment. She took a deep breath and slowly released it.

"You okay?" Tanner asked.

Crystal shook her head. "No, not really. I think I've destroyed my relationship with my grandfather, and I love him more than anyone or anything." She couldn't think why she would bare her feelings like this to a stranger. "Sorry. More than you need to know. It's my problem."

"You haven't destroyed the relationship. Tuck's just pissed, and, knowing Tuck, he's teaching you a lesson you'll never forget."

Crystal nodded. If that was Tuck's aim, he'd already been successful. Just then she noticed that Tanner's boxers had puppy faces all over them. She was no expert on men's underwear, but shorts with a puppy pattern were definitely a first.

He caught her sidelong look. "A Christmas gift from my daughter. Since no one can see them under my clothing, I try to wear them once a week and make sure I tell Tori when I do. She wants a puppy in the worst way, and this was her idea of a frequent reminder."

"Do you live where she can't have a dog?"

"No, but my mom is helping raise my kids, and until Tori is old enough, a dog would be just one more thing for my mom to take care of. I think she's doing enough."

Crystal stared down at Rip, who lay in wait. He knew she would try to go inside the house sooner or later, and he didn't want to miss an opportunity to demand another treat.

"It's thoughtful of you to think of your mom's workload, but Tori may not be able to understand your reasoning."

"Nope. She thinks she's old enough. But she's still forgetful. Tuck says I should get her a dog, that it will teach her responsibility. But I'm not sure she's ready yet."

Crystal hadn't been ready even at the age of twelve. She would never forget that, and thinking of it now made her heart squeeze. "You know Tuck well."

"Pretty well. He's a rusty old nail, but I've grown very fond of him."

"'A rusty old nail.'" She couldn't help but smile. "That describes Tuck so perfectly."

"Do you call him Tuck?" At her nod, he asked, "How did that come about?"

"When I was little and he came to visit, I loved for

him to tuck me in at night. My father called him Tuck, and when I learned to talk, I'd tug on his jeans and say, 'Tuck,' when it was my bedtime. It somehow stuck."

Tanner couldn't believe he was sitting on a porch almost naked with one of the most beautiful women he'd ever seen. Since that day outside the medical supply store, he'd thought of this lady often. If not for Tori, maybe he would have forgotten that chance encounter, but his daughter frequently mentioned the pretty woman with the red hair, refreshing his memory again and again. A dozen times, at least, he'd wished that he'd asked for her name and phone number. Why, he didn't know. He'd judged her to be way out of his league when he first clapped eyes on her, and seeing her again only drove that home to him a second time. Tall, slender, and stunning, she was what many men might call a traffic stopper. Tanner with his okay looks and mediocre job was so outclassed, it wasn't funny.

"Well," he said, pushing to his feet, "would you mind getting me a dog biscuit so I can finally head home? I'll miss my daughter's play, but maybe I can get there in time to take everyone out for a celebratory dinner."

"What will you be celebrating?"

Tanner scratched behind his ear, a nervous habit of his. And Crystal Malloy definitely jangled his nerves. She wore high heels—really tall, skinny heels. Choosing footwear like that for work when she probably spent hours a day on her feet struck him as being nuts. But he couldn't argue with the result: a fashion statement that was totally classy. "We'll make toasts to Tori for her stellar performance."

"But how can you know it's stellar if you can't watch the play?"

The question told Tanner she hadn't been around kids very much. "All performances by eight-year-old girls are stellar. Even if she forgets her lines or gets stage fright, we'll make a big deal about how wonderful she was. My mom will take video clips. She always does. I'll watch them over dinner. Tori's playing a wolf. It's wildlife-awareness month at her school."

"Since she loves dogs, she'll probably knock 'em dead," she observed with a smile.

"Oh, yeah. She sounded pretty ferocious at breakfast as she practiced her wolf noises. We can say she was the best growler ever."

She dug in the pocket of her brown slacks and handed him a treat. As he took it, their fingers touched, and he could have sworn he felt the jolt clear to his elbow. Her eyes widened, a telltale sign that she'd felt it, too.

"I'm so sorry Rip made you miss your daughter's play." Her regretful expression sharpened. "Will you get in trouble for not finishing your deliveries today?"

Tanner hadn't considered Mac's reaction until now. "Probably not. My boss is an okay guy. And almost every delivery person has a horror story to tell about a dog."

"Good. If your coworkers have had problems with dogs, your boss should be predisposed to understand."

She kicked off her shoes and pushed erect. Standing one step up, she was almost at his eye level. At six five, he could be no more than seven inches taller. He thought her height was sexy, a woman he could kiss without getting a crick in his back.

Handing Rip the biscuit, he turned to leave. "Be seeing you, I guess. If you're like Tuck, you shop online a lot."

"Not really, and thank goodness. This order cost me two hundred and fifty dollars."

"Whoa. What did you buy?"

"An invisible-fencing kit to keep Rip in the yard." She gestured at the sprawling chain-link fence. "Tuck paid thousands for that blasted thing, but Rip always figures out a way under it or over it, whichever suits his purposes at the time."

Tanner's heart caught. The way she'd emphasized the price of her online purchase, he suspected the outlay had hurt her financially. He understood the difficulties of living from payday to payday. Well, he had the proceeds from the sale of his accounting firm and his former home and from Carolyn's life insurance policy in the bank. But he tried never to touch that money. Someday his kids would need a large portion of it for their college educations.

"Can you upgrade the collar that comes with the kit?"

She frowned. "Why would I need to do that? The product description said the collar that comes with it will do the trick."

"Rip isn't just any dog." Tanner could only hope she had spent enough to get a really good waterproof collar. "Just do a little research before you install it. Make sure the controller will work with any brand of collar. Otherwise return it and upgrade."

He studied her face. She had gorgeous eyes, hazel that could look green or brown, depending on how the sunlight touched them. Carolyn's had been a striking dark blue, but Crystal's were no less captivating. A stab of guilt got him in the gut. He decided to pretend he hadn't felt it. He'd been alone for a long time, and Carolyn wouldn't have wanted him to ignore other women for the rest of his life.

"Do you know something I don't?" Crystal asked. "About Rip and electronic collars, I mean."

Tanner didn't feel comfortable discussing Rip's downfalls. If Tuck hadn't told Crystal about the electronic-collar saga, he must have had his reasons. "Only that you may need a collar for a Great Dane or Saint Bernard that can't swim. I noticed a pond out back."

"A collar for dogs that huge would be too strong. Rip's not even a full-fledged medium-size dog."

Oh, boy. She was in for some unpleasant surprises. "Just make sure the controller will pair with all brands of collars. That's my advice, anyway." Tanner crossed the grass. When he'd almost reached the gate, Rip blocked him and growled. "Are you kidding me? I paid you to get off the porch earlier, and I just gave you the gate bribe." He glanced over his shoulder. "Does he demand five biscuits now?"

Crystal walked barefoot across the grass to reach him. She held a bone up between her thumb and forefinger. "He probably lost count because so much time has passed. I can give you this one, but then I won't have one to get inside the house."

Tanner couldn't help it; he started to laugh. When his amusement abated, he said, "He never loses count. He's *cheating*!"

She smiled. "Maybe. But whether he's just confused or deliberately cheating, I'll have no bribe if I give you this biscuit. Will you please get me more out of the tree? Otherwise I'll be stuck out here."

"I've got a whole box of treats in the van." He plucked the biscuit from her hand and gave it to Rip before leaving the yard. Then he got three more bones out of his vehicle and offered them to Crystal over the fence. "Extra ones, just in case he gets confused again."

She took the cookies. "Thank you, Tanner."

Once inside the van, Tanner leaned his head out the window. "Hey, Crystal! My boss told me you withdrew your complaint against me. Just want to say I appreciate that."

She smiled, looking pleased. He wondered if she knew how lovely she was with her long red hair drifting like silk ribbons on the breeze and her bare feet gleaming like polished ivory against the grass.

"I hope you get your old route back!"

That wouldn't happen, but Tanner didn't want to tell her that. He believed she truly did regret his demotion. He had no wish to make her feel worse. Surprise tingled deep in his midsection. He wasn't sure where his bitterness had gone, only that it had left him.

He went to the back of the vehicle to change into his extra uniform. What had happened today was a perfect example of why he carried spare clothing. A delivery person needed to be prepared for almost anything. Being stranded half naked on a porch had come at him from out of left field, for sure. Only, it had ended nicely. He'd encountered Tori's beautiful lady with the long red hair again . . . and now he finally knew her name. That was even more exciting than grabbing the bottle of water he always carried with him and feeling the trickle of it going down his parched throat.

Mystified by Tanner's warning about making sure the controller she'd ordered could pair with any collar, Crystal collected her parcel and purse, paid Rip his fee for allowing her to enter the house, and carefully opened the package. She didn't want to damage the box, in case she had to return it.

To her delight, the item information said that other collars could be used with the controller. She put the pairing directions in a safe place and rested the new dog collar in its charging base. Then she went to her bedroom to change into clothes suitable for outdoor work—jeans, an old T-shirt, and scuffed riding boots she'd once worn on Tuck's ranch. With her pants pockets filled with dog biscuits and her cell phone in a case clipped to her waistband, she fed the kitten and then took Rip outside with her.

It was a gorgeous spring evening with a cool breeze blowing down from the surrounding mountains. She set herself to the task of digging, pleased to find that the soil, recently loosened by the fence builder, was easy to turn.

At around eight, she had almost finished trenching the fence perimeter. She couldn't believe how quickly she'd done the work. If she'd had to break hard ground, it would have taken her at least two evenings. Admiring the straight lines that she'd created, she frowned when her phone rang. Glancing at the screen, she saw that it was Tuck calling again. Her stomach clenched with dread. She needed more time to think before she talked to him. And while she'd been digging, she'd gotten an idea, which she couldn't explain to her grandfather over the phone. Besides, it needed to be a surprise. She returned the device to its case.

Just keep digging, she told herself. *Work out all the details for tomorrow so you can charm his socks off.* A moment later she regretted her decision to ponder her plan, because her thoughts drifted to Tanner Richards, a person she'd believed she would never see again. If anything, he was even handsomer than she remembered from their first encounter. And kind. Not in a suave, flirtatious way, but genuine and warm, which she found attractive. Refreshing, too. She didn't normally find it easy to talk with good-looking men, at least not at first.

As she turned the last shovelful of dirt, she sighed.

"Tomorrow I'll lay the wire," she told Rip, who reclined behind her. "And you'll finally have a fence that keeps you at home. Won't that be lovely?"

The dog growled and put a paw over his eyes.

"Okay. So it's the worst news you've heard in forever," she said with a laugh. "But I think it's *wonderful*. Now it's time to go inside and have dinner. I'm going to celebrate with heated soup and a crusty chunk of sourdough bread. Maybe, as a special treat, you can have some of the kitten's tuna over your food. Does that sound good?"

Rip unveiled his eyes and barked with excitement.

The local Italian place was a favorite with Tanner's family. The ambience was nice enough for a special night out, and the menu prices were easy on the wallet. Tanner always ordered the seven-layer lasagna. Tori, princess for an evening, loved the beef ravioli. His mom, Libby, enjoyed the chicken piccata over angel-hair pasta, and Michael could shovel down an extra-large serving of spaghetti and meatballs with amazing speed. The establishment also served fresh bread and specially seasoned dunking oil, which was delicious. Even Tori, still finicky about her food at eight, liked the bread-dunking activity.

Tanner smiled as he watched the videos Libby had taken of Tori's performance. The little girl looked darling in her wolf costume, and Tanner could hear adults in the audience laughing when she growled, barked, and snarled. A credible wolf howl was the finale.

"Was I good, Daddy?"

"You were phenomenal!" Tanner returned his mother's phone and hugged his daughter. "The best wolf *ever*."

Tori beamed with pleasure. "I didn't forget my words, either. My teacher was proud of me."

Over the top of the child's head, Tanner met his mom's gaze and winked. "I'm very proud of you, too. I'm sorry I couldn't be there."

Libby looked weary as she wound pasta around her fork. Tanner worried about the workload he had thrust upon her since Carolyn's death, and he often mentioned hiring a sitter for the kids. But his mom insisted that she didn't want her grandchildren left with a stranger. She felt it was important for them to be with someone who loved them. Tanner suspected she secretly yearned for the freedom she had envisioned for herself when she left southern Oregon and moved to Crystal Falls after his dad died. But life had dealt her this hand of cards instead. Unless he hired a sitter, she wouldn't be able to pursue her own interests until Tori turned twelve and was mature enough to be alone.

"I'm so sorry I missed the play, Mom. Have I thanked you for getting there early and everything?"

Libby smiled. "Only about ten times. And you're welcome. I enjoyed myself."

"Tell me the dog story again!" Tori demanded around a cheekful of ravioli. "About how he ripped your pant leg off and how you tried to trick him with your uniform."

"No talking with your mouth full," Tanner reminded her. "Are you sure you want to hear about the dog again?" The child had giggled so hard during the first telling that she'd almost wet her pants. "Okay," he relented. "But only if you eat while I tell the story. It's way past your bedtime."

"Especially the part about you on the steps in only your puppy boxers when the beautiful lady got home!"

Tanner began the tale again, only to be interrupted multiple times with questions, mostly about Rip. What kind of dog is he? What does he look like? How long did you have to stay on the porch? He used his phone to look up images of blue heelers and showed Tori a picture of a dog that greatly resembled Rip.

"Oh, Daddy, he's so pretty. When I get a puppy of my own, I want one just like him!"

Tanner, recalling how beautiful Crystal had looked, was jerked back to the moment by his daughter's observation. *Never a blue heeler,* he thought. Maybe all of them weren't quirky like Rip, but Tanner didn't want to take the gamble. Rip was smart, but he used his intelligence only for his own benefit. Tanner had learned one thing. He'd never try distracting the dog again. Rip had a one-track mind.

Then an evil thought occurred to him. Crystal was an incredibly gorgeous woman. If Tanner wanted to get better acquainted with her, all he had to do was pretend Rip had gotten the better of him and trapped him on the porch again. A smile played on his mouth. The dog couldn't narc on him. As smart as Rip might be, he couldn't talk.

Tuck was upset. He'd called his granddaughter twice today, and she hadn't telephoned him back. *Just deserts,* he guessed. He'd known this morning by her stricken expression that he'd gone too far and said too much. *Unreasonable* described his behavior. Yes, she'd screwed up by grabbing his phone and holding it beyond his reach. And, yes, he'd had good reason to be furious. But at some point when a person has apologized repeatedly and sought forgiveness, only a mean old asshole refused to grant it.

Tuck had wanted to tell her that as she ran out the door that morning. He guessed she thought he'd only wanted to yell at her some more. He'd wanted to kick himself ever since, but that was a feat he couldn't accomplish without two strong legs. She'd return tomorrow. She always came. Crystal was nothing if not loyal and caring. He had a bad feeling that he'd come close to breaking her heart. He knew that girl better than anyone. Exactly what filled her with joy, and what filled her with pain.

Tears pooled in his eyes, and that was the last straw. He'd be damned if he would sit here and blubber. Maybe somebody in this joint was still awake and in the community area. A good-looking woman, he hoped. Someone who didn't have pink or blue hair. *Please, God.* He needed some stimulating conversation to take his mind off his problems.

As Tuck spilled from the hallway into the spacious front area of the building, he saw three old men at a table playing cards. Not poker with any money at stake— he knew that for a fact. The administrator didn't allow gambling of any kind. Tuck's question was, "Why play poker, then?" He hadn't introduced himself to any of the men here. They were more crippled up than he was, and probably wanted to talk about their daily bowel movements. *Not my idea of good conversation.*

Then he saw her, sitting alone on a sofa at the far end of the common area. And it wasn't the first time that he'd been tempted to stare. In his mind, he had dubbed her the "Mystery Lady." Dark hair crowned her small head. It had to be dyed, of course. Few women reached her age without some snow on the roof. But he appreciated a gal who hadn't surrendered to the ravages of time. In his books that meant she still wanted to look nice and be noticed. Well, he'd noticed.

She always kept to herself, finding places to sit well away from everyone else. And she dressed as if she worked in an office where she'd be dealing with the public. Creased slacks or formfitting skirts with a matching jacket over a pretty blouse. She also wore flashy jewelry. Her fingers were loaded with chunks of glittery ice, which he knew couldn't be real diamonds. *Hell, no.* In this place, all your valuables were taken from you unless you could afford to pay for your rent and services rendered without eventual help from Uncle Sam. If you couldn't, you had to disclose all your assets. Then the facility started spending you down. That's what they called it, *spending you down.* In truth it was just robbery with a fancy name—well, in his opinion, anyway. Only, the people who ran these old-folk homes didn't think of it as theft. The residents had crossed the finish line, and overcharging them for every little thing spent them down faster. Everything they'd worked for all their lives was up for grabs, and most of them didn't care. All that mattered to them now was being comfortable until they cocked up their toes, and after all their money was gone, Medicare would pay their bills.

Still watching the Mystery Lady, Tuck shuffled to a halt, wishing he hadn't brought his cane. How could a man look sexy with a cane? Now that he was partially recovered from his hip-replacement surgery, he used it mainly for stability, not support.

He decided to angle the cane over his shoulder, all jaunty like Fred Astaire in *Top Hat.* The Mystery Lady caught the movement and glanced up. She had the prettiest brown eyes he'd ever seen. Tuck gave her a broad smile and sat at the opposite end of the sofa from her. He saw her stiffen. Clearly trying to ignore him, she resumed reading whatever was attached to the clipboard she held. He took the opportunity to study her delicate profile. She had dark, arched eyebrows; long, sooty lashes; a dainty nose; and a softly pointed chin. And even from where he sat, he could smell her perfume, a light, flowery scent. She wore a suit the color of bittersweet chocolate chips, a blouse that put him in mind of eggshells, and suede heels that matched her outfit. Every time she moved her fingers, her rings flashed, making him wonder if they might be real after all. He noticed that her fingernails were shell pink with white tips.

"So, how is your evenin' goin'?" It wasn't his cleverest line, but a man had to break the ice somehow.

She gave him a smoldering look. "Until a moment ago, it was lovely."

Tuck took the jab with a smile. "Mine is suddenly lookin' up."

Her full mouth drew into a thin line, deepening the age wrinkles around her lips. "Get lost."

"I can't. Not yet, anyway. Give me a few more years, and I may be able to get lost every time I turn around."

She almost smiled—just a little tug at the corners of her lips. "Can't you see I'm busy?"

"There's always tomorrow." He glanced at the card players. "In this joint, all we have is time. Time to sit. Time to read. Time to watch TV. Whatever you're doin', it can't be all that important."

"Actually, it's very important."

"More important than makin' a new friend?"

She sighed and lowered the clipboard to her lap. "I don't visit the community area to make friends. Staying in my apartment gets old."

"I know the feelin'. And I don't come out here to make friends, either."

She gave him a curious look. "So why are you bothering me?"

"Because you look interestin', like somebody who

might talk about somethin' besides how many glasses of prune juice she's gotta drink a day to stay reg'lar."

She chuckled, a delicate little sound that suited her. "I have to give you high marks for creativity. I've never heard that line before."

"Not a line, darlin', just the truth. The lady with blue hair has a problem with constipation."

She laughed again. "Where are you from?"

"Texas originally. Spent most of my life ranchin' in Idaho."

"You haven't lost the drawl."

"Never tried. Comin' from Texas ain't nothin' to be ashamed of. Where you from?"

"Alaska. Grew up in Ketchikan. Lived in other parts of Alaska later and spent time in the Lower Forty-eight as well."

Tuck nodded. Then he sighed and said, "My name's Tucker Malloy. I go by Tuck."

"I know. You're the only rabble-rouser in residence here and a main topic of conversation."

Tuck laughed. "It don't take much rabble-rousin' here to get a reputation." He arched an eyebrow. "You got a name?"

"Essie Maxwell Childers." She glanced at his arm brace. "What on earth happened to you?"

"Fell off my porch. Busted my arm, my hip, and a couple of ribs. I'll be right as rain in a couple more months."

"Steep steps?"

"Hell, yes. Do I look fragile as blown glass to you?"

"As tough as saddle leather, actually."

Tuck struggled to get back up and had to use his cane for leverage. "It's been a pleasure, Essie. Tomorrow if you're not too busy, maybe we can shoot the breeze a little more."

To Tuck's surprise she nodded and said, "I'll look forward to it."

As Tuck walked away, he tried not to smile. For the first time since being imprisoned in this place, he felt glad that he'd be here one more day.

Chapter Six

The next morning when Tuck went to the dining hall, he spotted Essie sitting at a corner table all alone. She had her head bent over what looked like a business ledger, and he figured that she'd probably tell him to get lost again, but he'd never been a man who was easily discouraged. And he saw no reason to change his ways.

She glanced up when he pulled out a chair. "Not now, Tuck. I work in the mornings."

None of the residents here work, Tuck thought. They were all retired and standing over a grave with one foot on an oil spill. "Sorry. Dementia still hasn't set in, and I can't get lost yet."

Around them, other residents stirred their coffee, creating a musical ping that came from all directions. A few people conversed, their voices a low drone. Essie closed the ledger and thrust it into a black leather briefcase. He got the impression that she didn't want him to see what she'd been working on.

Elbow braced on the table, she clicked the top of her ballpoint pen. "You're screwing up my schedule."

For an instant, he wondered if *she* might have early-stage dementia. Another old gal in this place had once been an ambassador or some damned thing, and every evening she dressed up and held court at what she believed was a state dinner. She rapped on her water glass to get everybody's attention before she gave a speech. Nobody paid her any mind. Most of the old people here were willing to live and let live, and if the woman wanted to believe she was still someone important, it was no skin off their noses. Was Essie living in the past, too? Working at a job she no longer had? The thought troubled him.

"What are you orderin' for breakfast?" he asked. There were no menus, so it was a loaded question.

She twisted her lips. "A croissant with two pats of butter, fresh sliced strawberries sprinkled lightly with granulated sugar and drizzled with cream, a poached egg with a runny yolk, and two slices of extra-crisp bacon."

Tuck laughed. As his mirth subsided, he said, "I'll have what you're havin'."

She sighed. "Wouldn't it be lovely? *Real* bacon. *Real* sugar."

Tuck decided she must have been firmly rooted in reality. At least she realized the food at this facility was awful. "It sure would. I'm cravin' real bacon, and I fantasize about a perfectly broiled steak with straight horse-radish, a loaded baked potato, crusty rolls, lots of butter, and a salad—a *real* salad with stuff besides lettuce in it. Oh, and I can't forget a glass of good red wine."

Her eyes went dreamy. "The location of this place suits my purposes, but little else does. I'd love to have a small dog, but pets aren't allowed."

"I'd like a beer, but that ain't allowed, either. And I have a dog, but that bitch who runs this place won't even let him come for visits."

"Patricia has too many rules."

"You can say that again."

She took a sip of her coffee. "What I wouldn't give for real coffee with breakfast. I managed to get a cup of the caffeinated before it ran out, but it's weak, nothing more than colored water. If I want good coffee, I make it in my apartment."

"Caffeine can speed up our heart rates." Tuck knew for a fact that an increased pulse wouldn't kill him. His heart was racing right now from making eye contact with his breakfast companion. "How old are you, Essie?"

"Never ask a woman her age unless you want her to lie." Then with a slight shrug, she said, "Seventy-eight. A *young* seventy-eight. I've worked hard to stay in shape. Why in the hell don't they have a gym in this dump?"

"A gym? I kept in shape doin' physical work. If I'm gonna dream, why in hell don't they have a bar?"

Essie chuckled. "I'm with you there, only it should be a cocktail lounge. I like a little class with my highballs." She panned the area with her dark gaze. "I should buy this place and expand it. Turn it into a swank community for retirees."

Tuck expected her to add, "Just kidding," but she didn't. He was back to worrying about her mental state again. "Essie, improvements like that would cost a bloody fortune."

"I know, but what the hell? I'm loaded. And I like the isolated location here. If I lived closer to a hub, my kids would bug me all the time. Since I'm staying, I may as well jazz it up."

A kitchen assistant rolled a cart into the dining room and began slapping down bowls of oatmeal and small pitchers of skim milk. Another person followed with a second cart, laden with bowls of canned fruit swimming in sugarless juice, stacks of sawdust toast, and bottles of spray butter, which had zero calories in one squirt. Tuck still had an image of crisp bacon at the forefront of his mind.

Essie dimpled a cheek at him. "I'm definitely looking into buying this place," she told him. "Imagine a huge indoor pool. A gym with Jacuzzis to loosen up in after a workout. A steam room would be fabulous. And this place definitely needs a therapy pool."

Tuck couldn't stop himself from asking, "Essie, are you firin' on all your cylinders?"

She chortled with laughter. "What do you think?"

Hearing her talk about spending millions of dollars she probably didn't have, Tuck wasn't sure how to answer that question. So he said nothing.

After they ate, they went their separate ways, Tuck to a physical therapy session, followed by watching television programs that bored him while he wondered what Essie was doing. Working, she'd tell him, but at what? Seventy-eight-year-old women in assisted living centers didn't normally still have jobs.

At lunch hour, Tuck returned to the dining room. Again Essie sat at a table alone, this time near the windows that overlooked Mystic Creek. In Tuck's opinion, the view was one of the finest features of the whole place. She beckoned him over to join her. He hesitated. As much as he liked the lady, he was starting to worry that she was a few cards shy of having a full deck, and he couldn't have a romantic relationship with a woman who lived in a fantasy world.

"Hi," she said as he sat across from her. "What color of gelatin do you think they'll serve today? I'll bet ten on green. We had red yesterday, and I think I'm seeing a pattern emerge."

Tuck wondered if she could afford to lose ten bucks. Changing the subject, he asked, "How long you been here?"

"Just over six months."

When their meal arrived, Tuck nearly groaned.

Sloppy joes again, and they were always the sorriest he'd ever eaten. The meat goop was served over the same sawdust bread they'd had for breakfast, with canned green beans as the vegetable. "Can't they afford buns?"

Amusement sparkled in her dark eyes. "Let's duck out of here and go to my place. For lunch, I'll serve you one of the best Black Angus steaks you've ever eaten."

His stomach clenched. No question about it, she was off her rocker. "What about your work?"

"I got it wrapped up this morning. For today, at least."

Tuck preferred going hungry over eating the crap on his plate, so he struggled up from his chair, offered Essie his uninjured arm, and walked with her to her suite, which was off a hallway at the other end of the building from his. At her door, she plucked a key from her blazer pocket to let them in.

Tuck stopped in the kitchen to stare. Half of her living room area, no larger than his own, had been converted into an office. The other side had a cozy arrangement of furniture: a cushiony pinkish sofa and one recliner.

"What the hell? You've even got a printer and a landline."

"Necessary. I still run all my businesses. If I decide to buy this place, I'll take the apartment next to this one, knock out some walls, and have much nicer and roomier accommodations. I may do that throughout the building and add on to each wing. Did you know they have sixty acres here? All along the creek, over four miles of water frontage. This could be a first-class operation if somebody invested some money in it."

Tuck studied her, trying to decide whether she was tracking or off somewhere in la-la land. "Essie, pardon the hell out of me for sayin' this, but in order to change this place to that degree, a person would have to have *millions*."

"Your point being?" She arched an eyebrow. Then she started to giggle, holding a slender, veiny hand over her heart. "Oh, dear God, you think I'm like our ambassador. The lady who gives speeches at dinner."

Tuck felt heat rise up his neck. "Well, from my perspective, Essie, nobody rollin' in dough would choose to live here."

She shook her head as she walked to the refrigerator, which Tuck noticed was close to full-size, unlike his tiny one. The cupboards above it had been removed to make room for it. How in the hell, with Patricia the Horrible governing the place, had Essie gotten away with that? Her posterior poked up as she collected cartons from a bottom drawer. She had a very nice backside. "Long story, Tuck. I'm the mother of two grown children who are selfish, lazy, and greedy. Mystic Creek is off the beaten path. They can't take a direct flight into Crystal Falls. They have to fly in from Portland on a puddle jumper. Then they have to rent a car and drive here to see me. When I found this place, I knew their laziness would limit their visits." She straightened with her hands full and bumped the fridge door closed with her hip. "Enough about me. I'll get our gourmet lunch heated up."

"Gourmet? For real?"

She laughed again. "Haven't you noticed? I don't often dine with everyone else. Like you, I can't stomach the food. So I order special things. Otherwise I'd go nuts staying here."

"I thought you just had a tray brought to your rooms."

"Nope." She put something in the microwave on low and turned to smile at him. "Since it's only lunch, and the steaks are large, I hope you don't mind sharing.

Potatoes au gratin come with it." She indicated a cushion on the sofa. "Have a seat. Mine is a long story, and it may go down better with a snifter of brandy." She stepped over to a drawer in her office, felt under the small desk for something, and her hand reappeared holding a key. She said, "Get something that locks, Tuck. A piece of furniture, preferably, not a little box. Patricia thinks she has absolute control here, but she can't lawfully pry open a locked drawer and ruin your furniture."

Tuck stared at the bottle of brandy she lifted out. *Good stuff.* She stepped into the kitchen and withdrew two snifters from a cupboard. After pouring a generous measure into each glass, she capped the bottle and walked to the sofa, offering him his drink before she sat beside him. Tuck admired the graceful way she moved. She cupped her hands around the bowl of crystal to warm the liquor.

"Don't you wanna lock your door?"

She huffed. "If anyone enters this apartment without knocking and getting my permission, I call my team of lawyers. Patricia and I have gone a few rounds in the boxing ring already, and she knows not to mess with me anymore. It looks bad when the facility attorneys get called in, discover that the administrator doesn't have a leg to stand on, and then still charge the corporation for their services. I think Patricia is afraid she'll lose her position if it happens again. She'd have to feel very confident to cross me."

A team of lawyers. Tuck mentally circled that and realized he was starting to believe she wasn't fantasizing. He sipped the brandy. "Nice and smooth."

"I grew up poor, Tuck, and I clawed my way up to a better life. A much better life, and I enjoy my little pleasures." The timer went off. She swirled her brandy, smiling slightly. "And since our lunch is ready and we don't know each other well yet, I'll leave it at that for now."

Tuck wanted to hear more. This woman fascinated him. She went to divide their meal into two servings, returned to hand him his plate along with eating implements and a napkin, then returned to the kitchen for her own portion.

Tuck moaned when he tasted the steak. She smiled and said, "You see? You can choose a loaded baked potato if you like. It comes ready for the oven or microwave, and the toppings come in separate containers. Patricia doesn't rule the world here after all."

Tuck ate every morsel of his meal. After rinsing their plates, Essie walked him to the door, put one hand on the knob, and lifted her other to touch his cheek. "I tried my best to run you off last night. I'm glad now that you didn't let me."

Tuck recognized an invitation when he got one. He bent his head and lightly pressed his lips to hers. *Holy shit.* He felt as if he'd just touched a bare wire with two-twenty surging through it. When he drew back, her sooty lashes rested on her cheeks and a smile curved her mouth. She fluttered her eyes open to gaze up at him.

"I've always thought Texans were sexy. Now I know why. Dinner in tonight? I've got chicken Parmesan and chicken cordon bleu—your choice."

"I don't want to eat all your special food."

Her dimple flashed. "There's more where that came from. I just order online, and it comes in a day."

Tuck wanted to kiss her again. He hadn't felt that kind of zap from a woman since Marge died. "We're on. I'll go for the cordon bleu."

Crystal timed her arrival at the facility for after three, when Marsha would be manning the front desk. She trusted the older woman to keep her mouth shut. Lugging in loaded plastic grocery bags, she winked at her friend.

"Just some special treats for Tuck," she chirped. To herself, she thought, *And if Patricia finds them, I now have an attorney on retainer.*

She knocked on Tuck's door, then pushed it open. "You decent? It's just me."

"Come on in," he said. "Been tryin' to call you. Is your phone broke?"

Crystal gulped down her anxiety. This might be her last chance to set things right with her grandfather. At least he was speaking in a normal tone of voice today. "Nope. I didn't want to talk on the phone. Sometimes, Tuck, my words fail me, so I think I need to show you how sorry I am."

She plopped the bags on his kitchen counter, and the half-gallon glass bottle of bourbon clinked. She retraced her footsteps to lock the door just in case Patricia's minions tried to invade Tuck's inner sanctum again. Then she began unloading the sacks.

"Only saying I was sorry—well, that didn't work. Today I'm going to make up for what I did. It shouldn't have been Tanner who brought you the items you were missing. It should have been me. And in case Patricia discovers this and tries to kick you out before I'm ready to take care of you, I've hired an attorney who's prepared to take her on."

Crystal nearly parted company with her skin when she turned to find her grandfather standing right behind her. He had tears in his eyes. "Yesterday mornin' I didn't try to call you back so I could yell at you again. I wanted to apologize and accept your apology to me. I shouldn't've said all that stuff."

Crystal felt frozen. She loved this man so deeply she

couldn't begin to tell him how much. And she was afraid to try. But then his strong arms were around her, his cast poking against her shoulder blade, and her world came right again. She felt happy. So *happy*.

"I'm sorry I said such nasty things," he mumbled. "I didn't mean a word of it. You just hurt my pride, grabbin' my phone like that. I realized how old and helpless I really am. That don't sit well."

Crystal clung to him. "Oh, Tuck, I was so wrong to do that. I'll never do anything like that again, I swear. Please forgive me."

"Already done, sweet girl. I should have accepted your apology right away."

Tuck wasn't into prolonged displays of affection, so he relaxed his embrace and stepped back to look at her purchases on the counter. He said, "Booze? Be still, my heart. But what the freakin' hell is the tea for?"

Crystal wiped tears from her cheeks, and they were quickly replaced by more. "Camouflage. Iced tea isn't illegal. I also got real sugar, so you can try your best to kill yourself with a carb rush."

Tuck laughed. Then he looped his good arm around her shoulders and gave her a jostle. "Tea as a mixer? Yuck. But damned if I won't take it and say howdy. Only how'll I hide the whiskey bottle?"

"I'm sorry it's not beer, Tuck." Crystal reached into another bag and withdrew a gallon pitcher, a clear plastic one with a pink drop-in lid. "And here is your whiskey container. The color of straight whiskey is a lot like the color of iced tea. If the facility police look in your fridge, all they'll see is that. Put a few tea bags in to make it look real. When I leave, I'll take the evidence with me."

Tuck started to laugh. "You're right. Who can object to tea?"

Crystal could not remember ever feeling so relieved. She had regained Tuck's approval, and at that moment, nothing mattered more to her. If he got caught and was evicted, she'd figure out what to do. Her business wasn't as important as her grandfather. If caring for him plunged her into bankruptcy, she could start over again, rising from the ashes like a phoenix. When she said her final farewell to this man, she wanted to know that she'd been as much of a rock for him as he'd been for her.

Their roles had reversed. As she looked up at his face, lined like a road map with signs of age, the realization settled like a rock in the pit of her stomach. He wasn't the strong one now. He could no longer withstand a hard gale. She needed to be the tree that propped him up. And she would be, because he had once been her tree, the only support she'd had.

"Copenhagen?" He grabbed the roll, broke it open, and left the kitchen, speaking over his shoulder. "I'll keep out one can and hide all the others. I can't wait to have a pinch."

Tuck returned a moment later and got a plastic cup from the cupboard. He stuffed a crumpled section of paper towel into the bottom. "My version of a spittoon. Not much chance an aide won't notice it, though."

"If you chew only in here," Crystal said, "I don't think Patricia can actually evict you. But until I hear back from the attorney and know for sure, try to keep the cup out of sight."

After rinsing the pitcher, she poured the half gallon of whiskey into it and added three tea bags. Then she got two glasses from the cupboard, measured out two fingers for each of them, and handed him his.

"Cheers, Tuck. Since we're making up after our first big fight, let's take it straight."

He clicked his tumbler against hers. "To us, baby girl. We'll always be a team."

Crystal winced, but only inwardly. She'd forgotten for a brief time that she and Tuck had joined forces long ago, and stepping away from that now might mean the destruction of them both. Without her, he could no longer make it, and whether she liked to admit it or not, she'd been leaning on him since she was eleven years old.

They sat in his living room to sip the whiskey. Crystal told him Marsha had offered to hire on as his caregiver until nearly three every afternoon. "Her job here is easy. She mostly sits. And now that she's divorced, she has no one at home. She says she'll be happy with ten dollars an hour. That's really reasonable."

Tuck nodded. "Yep, and she's a nice gal. That's a plus." He shrugged. "But there's no hurry. I'm likin' it here a little better, all of a sudden like."

Crystal nearly dropped her drink. The amber liquid lurched, and she managed to right the glass just in time. "*What* did you say?"

Tuck winked at her. "I met someone interestin', and she orders special dinners. I figure I can afford to do that, too. And—well, I don't know. I'm just not champin' at the bit like I was to get out of this joint."

Crystal mulled that over. "When did you meet this lady?"

"Last night. She's a corker, and I really like her. I'm havin' dinner at her place. And she keeps fine brandy under lock and key. The lady knows how to live it up. Maybe after I start orderin' my own stuff, I'll have you both over for dinner some night."

"That would be fun. I'd enjoy meeting her." Crystal went on to tell him about Tanner's harrowing experience with Rip. Tuck laughed and slapped his knee. "It wasn't funny," Crystal said. "He got sunburned sitting on the porch half naked for six hours, and he missed his little girl's play."

Tuck's smile faded. "Damned dog. Tanner's a dotin' father. He couldn't have been happy about missin' Tori's performance."

"I'm sure he wasn't. I withdrew my complaint against him, by the way. I don't think it made much of a difference, but I'm hoping he may eventually get his Crystal Falls route back."

"If he doesn't, he doesn't. Everything happens for a reason."

Crystal didn't share that opinion. The way she saw it, life was a crapshoot.

"I hired Pete Ramsey to be your legal advocate," she told him. "As long as you're here, I'll keep him on retainer. He's double-checking the Oregon statutes, but basically he says Patricia needs a reality check. He sees no reason why Rip can't come for visits on a leash and be turned loose in your room. He's going to call the doctor you've been assigned here and ask him to write a prescription for dog visits."

"You think the doctor'll do that?"

"You love Rip, and you miss him. Patricia says other residents have pet allergies, but is that true? And if so, Rip passing through the building on a leash shouldn't make anyone have a reaction. I'm going to speak with Patricia about it before I leave today." Crystal paused. "Pete also plans to speak with the doctor about your beer and chew. He says you aren't the first resident who has had problems with Patricia. He's heard she sings a different tune when a lawyer gets involved. Oregon doesn't ban the use of alcohol in assisted living facilities. Some places don't allow it in the common areas, because of liability risks, but a facility can't legally forbid a resident to imbibe inside a private apartment *unless* your use of alcohol somehow infringes upon the rights of others or affects your need for personal care. Say beer gives you diarrhea, and you can't clean yourself up. That requires more work from the facility staff. In that event, your bill for care goes up, or you have to give up the beer, your choice." She gestured around her. "Pete says this is your home, just like if you lived in a house. You're entitled to your privacy and to enjoy your personal pleasures within the confines of this apartment."

"So why didn't you bring me beer?"

Crystal grinned. "I'm waiting for a prescription, just in case Pete's wrong. Same goes for hiding the whiskey and chew. Be sneaky for a couple more days."

Tuck chuckled. "Uh-oh, Red, your Irish is showin'. You remind me of your grandma. Patricia might regret messin' with you."

"Yes, she may." Aiming to keep the conversation light, she added, "If Rip gets to visit, we'll have to hold on to him when a nurse comes in with your meds. You told me once that he went crazy at a vet's office when he saw people in scrubs. He must think they're uniforms."

Tuck guffawed. "Did I ever tell you how much he hates stethoscopes?"

Crystal had heard the story so many times that she'd lost count, but she settled back, happy to listen to Tuck tell it one more time.

Minutes later Crystal didn't bother to knock on Patricia's office door. She just walked in and sat in the visitor chair. The administrator wore a dark blue dress this afternoon, but otherwise she looked the same, her expression stony, not a hair out of place. She met Crystal's gaze with unflinching animosity.

"I've hired Pete Ramsey to be my grandfather's legal advocate," Crystal told her. "In the future he will be here on a moment's notice, night or day, if Tuck is treated unfairly. He's also contacting Tuck's doctor here about writing a script for dog visits and Tuck's personal pleasures, namely three cans of beer a night and Copenhagen. Not that Tuck needs a script for the latter items. But I've requested them just in case you ever dare to invade my grandfather's apartment again. Tuck is over twenty-one years of age, and neither substance is illegal for an adult to use in Oregon." Relaxing in the chair—or pretending to, anyway—Crystal crossed her legs. She studied the other woman, half expecting steam to come out her ears. "Have you ever heard the expression that a man's home is his castle? Well, Tuck pays rent for his apartment, and Pete says your rules don't apply to what Tuck does in the privacy of his own residence."

Patricia flattened her hands on the desk blotter and rose halfway from her chair. "How *dare* you challenge my authority?"

Crystal swung her foot and smiled. "What do you plan to do, Patricia? Attack me? Sue me? Throw my grandfather out on the street? I allowed you to bully me the other night. It won't happen again." She lowered her foot to the floor and leaned forward on the chair, keeping her gaze locked with the other woman's. "I am Tuck's only next of kin. He's estranged from my mother, his only child. That means I'm the person who has to stand up for him. Now that I've hired an attorney, do you *really* want to tangle with me?" Crystal paused for effect. "I'm ready for a fight. The next time *anyone* goes into my grandfather's apartment and rifles through his personal effects, all hell is going to break loose. In case you've forgotten, he is a human being who has civil rights granted to him by our constitution and protected by our laws."

"You're going to regret this."

"Maybe," Crystal conceded, "but probably not. The attorney is going to send me copies of any prescriptions the physician writes for my grandfather. You are the facility administrator. I will continue to respect your authority, insofar as it goes, and I will ask Tuck to do the same. But you are not entitled to deny Tuck anything that a medical professional prescribes for him, and unless he somehow disturbs the peace, you are not entitled to say what he can or cannot do in his apartment."

"Watch me."

Crystal stood. "Oh, I will be watching, Patricia. Tuck may be old, but he's still an individual with personal rights. If you deny him those, it will be interesting to see how it plays out in court."

"You can't afford a long court battle!" Patricia cried.

"Can't I? The last time I checked my account balances, I had plenty of money, and you may be forgetting that Tuck sold a large cattle ranch in Idaho. He'll help me financially. So it may be more appropriate to wonder if *you* can afford a long court battle. Especially if you lose. We'll be asking for our attorney fees to be paid . . . in full."

Crystal left the office, resisting the urge to slam the door.

Once again wearing jeans, boots, and a T-shirt, Crystal shoveled turned earth over the wire she had laid along the perimeter of Tuck's property. Rip's collar was charged, and he'd gotten home from one of his adventures over two hours ago, staggering through the open gate to collapse on the grass and sleep. He had awakened only minutes ago and looked more like himself. The ravages of exhaustion had lost their hold. In a short while, she would put the collar on him, stand back, send him warning beeps with the remote when he got too close to the fence, and then hopefully be able to congratulate herself as the victor in this battle.

Just as she finished covering the wire, she heard a vehicle park outside the fence. She looked up from her work to see a Courier Express van. Tanner piled out through the open side door and lifted a hand to her in greeting.

"What are you doing here?" she called. "I didn't order anything." What a stupid thing to say to a man she couldn't stop fantasizing about. "Not that you aren't welcome to stop by. You're Tuck's friend. By extension, I guess that means you're mine, too."

Tanner had a wide, easy grin that flashed white teeth and creased his lean cheeks. He held up his other hand to show her that he carried several toll cookies for Rip. Striding toward the gate with a masculine shift of his hips, he yelled back, "I couldn't resist stopping by to see how the invisible fence is coming along. Thought I might help with the digging."

Crystal leaned the shovel against the fence and tucked her doffed work gloves into the waistband of her jeans. "I just finished burying the wire, but thank you for offering. Now all that's left is to connect the wire to the controller in the pump house, put the collar on Rip, and see how it works."

Tanner, already through the gate, bent to give Rip a biscuit and then a friendly scratch behind the ears. Then he grinned and sauntered toward Crystal. It was nice to see him again, she realized. Even though he made her skin tingle when he looked at her, she also felt oddly relaxed. How could a guy electrify the air around a woman and send out tranquilizing vibes as well?

"I can hardly wait." He looked down at Rip, who bounced around his legs, acting completely reenergized now that he had rested. "Maybe an invisible fence will finally work on him."

Crystal wondered at that comment. "Has Rip worn an electronic collar prior to this?"

Tanner gifted her with another grin. "Unfair question. Just hook up the wire and get the collar on him, and let's see how it goes."

Crystal hurried out to the pump house. After connecting the perimeter wiring to the controller, she entered the house by the back door, grabbed Rip's new collar and the remote control, then emerged onto the front veranda. When Rip ran up the steps snarling, she greeted him with a biscuit, and while he ate it, she fastened the collar around his neck. He'd lost his old one during one of his great escapes. Tuck insisted on collars being loose so the dog wouldn't choke to death if he got hung up on something.

Holding the remote, Crystal joined Tanner on the lawn. "The instructions call this the training period." She showed him the remote. "See the button that says TONE? I'm supposed to watch Rip, and when he goes too close to the fence, I have to tell him *no* and give him a warning. It says it can take several times for the dog to realize he'll receive correction from the collar if he doesn't heed that sound."

"Uh-huh." Tanner's tone was dubious. She shot him a sharp look. He shrugged. "Don't mind me. I just can't see Rip being that easily defeated."

"So he *has* worn an electronic collar before," she said.

"A few. Tuck finally gave up."

Crystal's stomach knotted. Had she just wasted a

large amount of money? *No,* she decided. The cost of the fencing kit alone was telling. She'd paid for good quality, and that would prevail in the end. "Tuck's a rusty old nail, remember. A Depression baby raised by parents who reused tinfoil. If he can spend less, he always does. Me, I'm different. I go for at least medium grade, sometimes top-of-the-line. I'd rather buy something that will do the job the first time."

Rip trotted away to christen a rosebush that now had spring buds. Both Crystal and Tanner turned to watch him. He angled away from the bush toward one of the metal fence posts. When he got about ten feet from the barrier, Crystal said, "No!" in a firm voice. Then she pressed the TONE button.

Rip turned to look straight at her. She could have sworn that he grinned. Then he dashed around the corner of the house.

"The pond!" Tanner sprang into a run. "Damn it. He hasn't changed one iota." Crystal had long legs, but Tanner outdistanced her with little effort. When she drew up beside him at the back corner of the house, he said, "Well, *shit!*"

She followed his gaze to see Rip take a flying leap into the pond. He pushed into deeper water until he was in up to his chin and then turned to look at Crystal. She saw that victorious grin on his face again.

"What happens if I correct him with the remote while he's in water?" she asked Tanner. "It's an electric shock of sorts. Won't it sizzle him?"

Tanner shook his head. Placing his hands on his narrow hips, he said, "Zap the little bastard. High range."

"I thought you didn't have a dog. How do you know so much about electronic collars?"

"Tuck." He glanced down at her. "Have you given him a jolt yet?"

Crystal adjusted to the highest frequency and pressed the CORRECTION button. Rip continued to grin at her. Anger surfaced within her. The dog was mocking her. She held her thumb down on the control. *Nothing.* Rip just stood in the water and watched her.

"He drowned it," Tanner said.

"He drowned what?"

"The battery. Water ruins most of them."

"But it's water-resistant!"

"Not waterproof, though. *Water-resistant* only means that the battery can tolerate small amounts of water, like rain or wet grass. *Waterproof* means that a battery will still work when submerged in water. That kind is a lot more expensive, though, and you may as well cough up big bucks to get the best of the best, because the less costly ones aren't always one-hundred-percent waterproof."

Crystal stared at her grandfather's dog. "He knows, doesn't he? He beat me at the game, and he's having a good chuckle. Why didn't you tell me to get a waterproof collar?"

"Because most fence kits I've seen don't come with them. I think you've got to spring for a waterproof collar, no matter what. I *did* tell you to get a collar strong enough for a Great Dane or Saint Bernard that can't swim, though. Remember that?" Slanting sunlight played on his honey-streaked hair as he studied her. "Please tell me that you at least made sure the controller will pair with a different collar."

"I did make sure of that," she conceded. "I just wish you'd told me about the waterproof thing. Now it'll take two more days to get a collar that'll keep that darned dog at home."

Tanner started to laugh. Crystal could see nothing funny about the situation. When he quieted, she sent him a serious look. "How many collars has Rip destroyed?"

Hands still riding his hips, he turned to face her. "It doesn't feel right to tell you things about Rip that Tuck didn't share with you."

"Oh, for heaven's sake! It's a *dog*, and I'm in charge of caring for him. I need to know what I'm up against."

Tanner scuffed at the lawn with the sole of his boot. "I'd say he's gone through a half dozen, but he didn't destroy all of them. He just learned that the shocking signal on a collar only lasts for thirty seconds. It's a safety feature in case a dog gets trapped in a signal zone and can't get away from it."

Crystal nodded. "I read about that."

"So Rip learned to hang on for thirty seconds. I've seen him challenge Tuck's invisible fence to dig out, yelping at the shocks until they stopped. Then off he went. Tuck couldn't keep him home, either."

Crystal sank to the grass and sat cross-legged. "So I just spent nearly three hundred dollars for nothing."

Chapter Seven

Tanner shifted beside Crystal on the grass, his arms propped on his bent knees. After a moment's silence, laden with the tension he could feel emanating from her, he said, "I don't think you totally wasted your money. Honestly, I don't. Tuck would never listen to me about getting a collar suited for a larger dog."

"That seems cruel. Rip isn't that big, and no matter how much the manufacturers talk around it, a dog still gets shocked."

Tanner stared at the blue heeler, who was finally out of the pond. "Rip sees himself as being as big as Godzilla. He's got an overabundance of feisty attitude. You fight fire with fire."

Rip raced up to them just then and shook his body, drenching both of them with dog-scented pond water. Crystal shrieked. Tanner swore.

All Rip did was grin. Until he ran. Straight for the fence.

"Rip, *no!*" Crystal yelled.

The dog launched himself at the wire, hooked his paws through the links, and climbed over the barrier. Once on the other side, he whipped around to give Crystal a tongue-lolling look that said more loudly than words that he'd just bested her again. Then he dipped his head, bounced around in a jubilant dance, and took off running.

"Not this time!" she cried as she ran toward her car.

She was inside the vehicle with the engine started before she registered that Tanner was in the passenger seat. "What are you doing? This may take hours. What about your kids?"

"It's Friday. They're staying overnight with friends. Step on it! He went that way." He flung out his arm to gesture, smacked it against the window, and yelped in surprise.

Crystal floored the accelerator in REVERSE, braked to shift into DRIVE, and then wrenched the wheel in the direction of Tanner's pointing finger. Foot slammed down on the pedal, she sent the Equinox into several tail whips along the curvy road.

"Do you see him?" she shouted. Tanner had the window down and his head stuck out.

"Nope!" he shouted. "Damned dog. He couldn't have outrun us. He's got to be hiding in the grass."

Crystal backed off the gas. Outside of town, hobby farms sprawled at each side of the byway, and there were countless fields where a dog could hide. She saw a pull-off that sported a giant oak. She parked under its outstretched limbs, brilliant green with spring leaves.

"He's gone. *Again.* I'm so sick of this. I can't count the hours I've spent driving these stupid roads."

"I'm sorry." Tanner looked over at her, his blue eyes gleaming in the fading light like aquamarine gemstones. "I should have told you about the collar thing."

She folded her arms over the steering wheel. "Actually, Tuck should have told me. I can't understand why he didn't."

Tanner sighed, and she felt the release of his warm breath on her arm where it rested on the steering wheel. That made her acutely aware of how close he was. The breadth of his shoulders inched over on each side of the seat, which he hadn't adjusted for comfort. His long legs, folded sharply at the knees, pressed against the glove compartment. She studied his sharply carved features and felt a zing of arousal deep in her belly. She'd been attracted to other men in the past. But with Tanner it felt different, desire spreading from her core to tingle through her extremities and over her skin. She swore she could feel heat emanating from his rangy body, and she lowered her window because he suddenly seemed to be using more than his share of the oxygen.

"Tuck loves that dog," he told her. "He makes excuses and puts up with his behavior. I'm not sure why he didn't tell you Rip is death on electronic collars, but I'm guessing it's kind of like when I overlook or don't want to tell people about the things my kids do wrong. We're proud of them. Who wants to focus on their faults?"

Tanner's words gave Crystal a glimpse into his heart and told her more about him than he could possibly realize. How deeply he loved his children. How guarded he might be in order to protect them. She also understood her grandfather's adoration of Rip a little better—how he turned a blind eye to the dog's faults, laughed at his antics, and rarely admitted anything the blue heeler did was wrong.

"Thank you for that, Tanner."

He looked bemused. "For what?"

"For your insight. Half the time I want to wring Rip's neck and I wonder why Tuck puts up with him. You just put it all into perspective for me. Tuck loves that dog as if he's a child."

He chuckled. "You just got that?"

"I always got it, in a way, but I could never completely understand it. Rip doesn't try to be lovable. In fact, I think he's on a mission to make me despise him. But

Tuck adores him. Tuck accepts him unconditionally, just like he accepts me."

He flashed one of those irresistible grins at her. "Right now, we need to accept that he's a pain in the ass, and that we have to find him. And with me along, at least you'll have an engaging companion while you drive the roads tonight."

Tuck stepped carefully as he walked from his apartment to Essie's for dinner. The two glasses of iced tea he carried were well laced with something more potent. With one arm in a cast and still limping from the soreness in his hip, he had a devil of a time not sloshing liquid over the edge of either glass. If Patricia showed up and got a whiff of the contents, he would damn well baptize her with whiskey.

He bumped Essie's door with the toe of his boot. When she answered the summons, his breath caught in his throat. Over a silky-looking undershirt, she wore a sheer nylon top with a solid gold, black, and red pattern that tantalized him with glimpses of her figure. The V-neck plunged to the cleavage of her breasts. Gathered at the waist, it flared out over her hips. Flowing sleeves revealed the outline of her arms. She looked beautiful and sexy.

"I didn't dress up" was all he could think to say.

Her mouth curved in a smile. "Blue chambray shirts with a Western cut always look nice with jeans." She glanced at the glasses he carried. "And you brought drinks!"

He stepped inside, and she closed the door. "Spiked iced tea. My granddaughter brought me some bourbon and Copenhagen this afternoon."

"You chew?"

"Yep. If that's a problem, I won't do it around you, but I ain't quittin' ever again."

She laughed. "Just rinse your mouth before you kiss me." She accepted the glass he offered and took a taste. "Mmm. I've never tried tea as a mixer. It's refreshing."

Delicious smells wafted to his nostrils, but the scent intoxicating him most was that of her flowery perfume. She led him to her living area, sat on the sofa, and patted a cushion beside her. He glimpsed a twinkle of mischief in her dark eyes as he sat down. "Do I make you nervous, Tuck?"

"I almost swallowed my tongue when you opened the door."

"I'm glad you didn't. I'm hoping for a deep kiss before the evening ends."

Tuck had never been one to hide his thoughts. "Last night you wanted no part of my company, and now, in less than twenty-four hours, you're hopin' I'll kiss you. It's like you shifted out of PARK into OVERDRIVE."

"Last night I didn't know you and didn't think I'd like you. Now I know a little about you, and I like what I see." She took another taste of her drink. "I don't play games, Tuck. Never have, never will. And I've always enjoyed sex. I'm seventy-eight, and my time left for physical pleasure may be short. Why go slow when OVERDRIVE will get us there faster?"

He chuckled. The mixed drink warmed him and relaxed his muscles. Or maybe it was the woman beside him that made him feel so good. "You speak your mind. I admire that. Tell me more about yourself, Essie Maxwell Childers."

"It's not an easy story to tell. I'm not sure where to start."

"At the beginnin'."

She settled back against the cushions. Her dark hair glistened in the light cast by a floor lamp sitting between the sofa and recliner. "I grew up poor. Most people don't know what real poverty is."

"I do. My folks was poorer than church mice."

"Mine, too. My father was a drunk who bothered to work only when he ran out of booze. Mama kept chickens and sold eggs. We could eat a hen only after it stopped laying, so mostly we ate eggs, when we had them. I took my first lover at fourteen and used a vinegar-soaked sponge for birth control."

"Uh-oh."

She nodded. "I was foolish, but it worked. He was a town boy whose folks ran a bait shop. He slipped me money every time we had sex, and I took it without hesitation, not learning until years later that some people would have said I was prostituting myself. At the time I didn't even know what a prostitute was. I did know there was never enough food on the table for my eight younger siblings, six boys and two girls. If a guy I liked gave me money, I took it and said thank you." She glanced up and met his gaze. "Do you still admire me, Tuck?"

"More an' more by the second. Not many girls would worry about feedin' the younger kids in their family."

"Folks said I'd never amount to much. I set out to prove them wrong. I got a special driver's license that same year, which enabled me to chauffeur my younger siblings to school in a rattletrap car wired together with coat hangers. Our attendance went up along with our grades. I bought gas with my boyfriend money. That's how I thought of it, boyfriend money, as if it were an allowance."

"Are you ashamed of takin' money for sex?"

"No, but I'm well aware some people would look down on me if they knew."

"That's their problem. The first time you did what came natural, an' the boy gave you money afterward. It must have seemed like a windfall to a girl who went hungry a lot."

She smiled. "It was only five bucks. I spent it on two loaves of bread and a jar of peanut butter. Some baloney, too. That kept our bellies full for one day and part of the next." A distant expression came over her face. "It's amazing how much food nine kids can eat. I don't know what my parents were thinking to have so many babies. Daddy was well educated but never did anything with it. Mama used to say he was lazier than an overweight basset hound. As close as I can figure, he bothered himself to do only three things: drink, have sex, and beat on his family. By age sixteen I felt nothing but disgust for him and my mother. She accepted the physical abuse as if it were her due. Maybe she was raised that way and never knew any different, but I was too young back then to wonder about that. She let him take the egg money for booze, and that was all we had for groceries, so hunger was a frequent visitor. She never once defended us when he used us as punching bags."

Tuck toyed with a curl at her temple. "I'm real sorry to hear that. At least my father was kind. In that way, I was lucky, I reckon."

"Very lucky. One afternoon I bought my little sister a pair of shoes, and Daddy realized I was somehow making money. He tried to take away from me what I had left. I clocked him alongside the head with a cast-iron skillet. Knocked him out cold. Mama thought I'd killed him. After that I made him nervous, so he left me alone and stopped pounding on the younger kids."

"Good for you. He had that comin', and a hell of a lot more."

She shrugged. "The boyfriend money kept coming, Tuck. I won't pretty it up for you. And at some point, I realized it was wrong." She met his gaze. "I kept on doing it, anyway. Maybe I was pretty. Maybe I wasn't. I only know the high school boys didn't lose interest. Could be they heard that I could be had for a price, and they didn't blink when I raised it from five to twenty. Later I asked for thirty. What began innocently became a business.

"I saved every dime I could. Shortly after turning eighteen, I had enough money to buy a decent car. Decent by my standards, anyway. With dependable transportation, I landed a job at the bait shop owned by my first boyfriend's parents. Except for what I spent on my siblings, I saved all my wages along with the money I got from admiring fishermen. By then I knew people called me a whore. I didn't care. No matter what I had to do, I wanted to move up in the world. And I did."

"Do you think I'll judge you for that, Essie? Sounds to me like you used your assets to survive."

"At that point, it became more than mere survival. I used my assets to get rich. Eventually, I bought the bait shop. With the proceeds from my first year in business, I built a small marina. The following year, I enlarged it and leased out boat slips. The year after that I bought a seaworthy vessel, hired a fisherman to captain it, and started a charter service, using the money I made from that to cover the boat payments. The next year, I got another vessel. Well-heeled men paid top dollar to go out to catch a big one. When the charter boats returned, I was nice to the gentlemen, and they were nice to me. So nice that I bought my first house at twenty-four and made a home for my brothers and sisters. My parents acted almost glad to see them leave. The six boys were old enough by then to get after-school jobs, and they helped with expenses. That enabled me to continue saving money for future business ventures. When the boys graduated from high school, I paid for their college tuition, and I did the same for my sisters when it was their turn. In the meanwhile I invested in gold-mining operations and became a wealthy woman in my own right. I no longer needed to be nice to any man."

"Wow. Hats off to you, Essie. You proved everyone wrong and made something of yourself."

She took a swallow of tea. "Yes, but telling you the truth about how I did it wasn't easy. I guess I am ashamed in a way. But if I could go back and change it, I wouldn't."

"You weren't the only one who benefited."

"True. Two of my brothers and one of my sisters didn't amount to much, but the others made the most of the opportunities I gave them and are successful individuals now."

"Where would they be if you hadn't done what you did?"

"In Ketchikan. Not that there's anything wrong with the place. But they probably wouldn't have a pot to piss in, and neither would I." She dimpled a cheek at him. "I'd rather be rich. They say money can't buy happiness, but it sure makes life easier." She gulped more tea, which told Tuck it truly had been hard for her to tell him about her past. "I was thirty-five before I finally met Jake Childers. He knew I had taken money for sex in my younger years. I told him flat-out before we were intimate. He didn't hold it against me. Jake had never married, either. He'd made wise financial investments and had an impressive portfolio. We had two children together, Garth and Rebecca. We gave them everything they wanted, which proved to be a mistake. They grew to be self-centered, spoiled, and ungrateful."

"Even with good parentin', kids can turn out that way," Tuck mused.

"Voice of experience talking?"

"Oh, yeah. But that's a story for later. I want to hear the rest of yours."

She sighed. "It's a difficult one to tell. That's why I plowed through the first part so fast. To let you know who I really am." She took a deep breath. "Jake was ten years older than me. He keeled over dead with a heart attack twenty years ago, leaving me a widow at fifty-eight. Seven years later, Garth and Rebecca tried to put me in a care facility and get me deemed legally incompetent. Until then, I intended to leave them all the businesses when I retired. Now I may leave every dime of their inheritance to charity or my siblings."

Tuck laughed and laid his arm over her shoulders.

"Though they failed in their first attempt, I knew it was only a matter of time before they would figure out a way to institutionalize me and get their hands on my money. So I hired professionals to make sure that never happened. Once I felt protected, I lived on the Oregon coast. I soon realized I was too close to Portland, which made it easy for them to visit. It may sound awful, but when they're around I feel as if I'm swimming with sharks. I decided to find someplace more remote, and I began searching for a retirement community where I thought I'd be content. When I finally found this place, I was delighted. Mystic Creek is so isolated that Garth and Rebecca seldom come to visit, and I like it that way. They don't really love me. It's all about the money. Their displays of fake affection make me sick to my stomach."

She released a taut breath. "That's pretty much it as

far as my personal history goes. Health-wise, I've been lucky. My knees bother me a little, and I'm not as active as I used to be. But mentally I'm still as sharp as a filleting knife." She gestured toward her office. "I spend most of each morning at my desk, running my businesses. I truly am loaded. If that bothers you, say so now."

He bent to kiss her dark hair. "It doesn't. Maybe I'll marry you for your money."

She laughed and leaned her head against his shoulder. "Whew! I'm out of breath from talking so fast. But now you know everything, even the ugly parts."

"I think you're amazin'. Do you ever go back to Ketchikan and thumb your nose at the people who said you'd never amount to nothin'?"

"They're mostly all dead now. I went back to bury each of my parents. Afterward I left as fast as my feet could carry me."

"How much time before our dinner's done?"

She glanced at her watch. "Fifteen minutes."

"That'll give me time to tell my story. It won't be as interestin', though." He finished off his tea. "No yawnin' allowed."

She got up and carried their glasses to the kitchen. When she resumed her seat, Tuck settled back to tell her that he'd been born in Texas and raised on a cattle ranch. "When I was thirteen there came a drought and my folks lost pert' near everything. A few months later I quit school and started searchin' for work to help my dad keep the land. I had to go a far piece. The ranches near ours couldn't afford help. For a spell, I worked in Oklahoma for a farmer who gave me room and board. I sent all my wages home. But my parents lost the place anyhow and moved to Houston, where Dad got a factory job.

"I can't rightly recall how I ended up in Idaho, but

I'd been savin' my money as I drifted, and I found a piece of land I could afford. After buying it, I spent every dime I had left on cows and a horse. Had to live in a shack with no plumbin' for about two years before I could start buildin' a house. Along about then I met Marge. I knew I'd found the woman of my dreams when she didn't turn up her nose at my livin' conditions. Instead she rolled up her sleeves and worked beside me.

"After we got hitched, we expected to have babies, but she didn't get pregnant. Right about the time we gave up on havin' kids, we found out our daughter, Lisa, was on the way. That little girl was the center of our world, and there wasn't nothin' she wanted that she didn't get if we could afford it. She grew up spoilt. I see that now, but you can't go back and fix your mistakes."

"No, you can't." Her expression turned wistful. "If only."

"Yep, if only. Lisa hated the ranch. She hated that we was poor. We wasn't really. Poor, I mean. We just wasn't rich enough to afford all the stuff she wanted. Fancy clothes. A new car, not a used one. One time she harped at me for months to buy her a sixty-thousand-dollar racehorse. Hello? She never rode the horses we already had."

Essie laughed.

"Long story short, when she left for college she was gone for good. She came home to visit only once, to show off her new boyfriend, Randall Jenkins. He'd just graduated from college and was a computer programmer. He asked me to take him huntin'. Then he almost pissed himself when I handed him a rifle. I wasn't impressed. But it was Lisa's choice to make, and she made it.

"They got married real fast. To this day I think Lisa thought he was her ticket to the good life. They got a nice enough house on a small acreage in Washington. Gave me and Marge two beautiful granddaughters, Crystal, the older one, and Mary Ann three years later. Crystal was about nine when Marge up and died on me. Near killed me to lose her. Heart attack, just like your Jake. Lookin' back I realized she'd had symptoms, but I didn't pick up on 'em. I wished I had."

"We all do that, Tuck. Want to kick ourselves, blame ourselves."

"I reckon so. I mourned hard, but life went on. Two years later I took Crystal away from her parents, and from then on she lived with me. Havin' to look after her helped me get over losin' Marge. In a way, it saved my life."

"Were Crystal's parents abusive to her?"

"Yep." Tuck felt as if his engine had just stalled. "I wanna tell you everything about me, Essie, but I don't feel right tellin' you everything about Crystal. Those things are for her to tell, and she may never do that."

"I'm satisfied with hearing your story. I don't need to know hers."

"They're kinda tied together, but thank you for understandin'. She has a painful past, and if I told you about it, she'd feel like I betrayed her."

"Does she ever see her parents now—or her younger sister?"

"No. After I took her to Idaho with me, her folks never even called to check on her. When I filed for custody, they were notified, but they didn't contest it. When Crystal turned eighteen, she changed her last name to Malloy. Maybe she'll get in touch with her parents someday, but I doubt it. And I definitely won't. My daughter didn't just burn her bridges with me; she blew them to smithereens."

"It's heartbreaking to cut ties with our children."

Essie had tears in her eyes when she looked up at him. "But it hurts even worse when they do it for us."

Silence fell between them.

Finally, Essie asked, "So, tell me, Tuck. Have you been with any other women since Marge died?"

He shook his head. "By the time I'd healed enough to even think about it, I had Crystal. Raisin' her by myself took most of my time, and I didn't feel right about addin' a woman into the mix. After Crystal grew up and came here to start her own business, I just never met a gal who caught my eye. Ranchin' is a lonely life. You don't meet a lot of new folks. How about you? Been with anybody since Jake?"

"No. I didn't think I'd ever meet another man who'd interest me."

Tuck couldn't help but smile. "Until you met me?"

She nodded. "It's funny how life goes sometimes. You think it's over, only it isn't." She glanced at her watch again. "Oh! Dinner should ready."

While she took the food out of the oven, Tuck set up two TV trays and put place settings on each of them. She poured them each a glass of white wine, and then they filled their plates.

After they sat down to eat, Tuck took a sip of the wine and moaned. "Oh, lawsy, that tastes good." He moaned again when he tasted the chicken. "Before I leave, write down where you get this food. I'm gonna order some."

After eating and tidying up the kitchen, Tuck kissed her good night at the door, a deep, slow exploration of her mouth that tantalized him and made her slender body tremble. He wanted to take her to the bedroom and do far more, but he held his need of her in check. They'd met only last night. He didn't want to rush her.

* * *

Rip didn't come home until three in the morning, and he was staggering again. Crystal laid it down to exhaustion. It had been his second run of the day. After letting him in the house, she lay awake in bed unable to sleep, her thoughts on Tanner. When they were together, did he feel the same level of attraction she did? Wondering whether a man was as interested in her as she was in him was a new experience for her. In the past, she had been more inclined to just go with the flow.

The kitten jumped on Crystal's bed. Determined not to let herself love him, she turned over. Not taking the hint, he curled up on her pillow and snuggled against the back of her head. The sound of his purring finally lulled her to sleep.

Crystal's alarm jerked her awake at five. She got up, feeling exhausted and decidedly unenthusiastic about the workday ahead. The strong coffee she poured into a travel mug and drank as she drove to the salon didn't help much. Nadine was the only tech there when Crystal entered the building.

"I hope you got more rest than I did," Crystal said as she grabbed a salon jacket.

"Nope. I went on a date and didn't get much sleep. He took me to Peck's Red Rooster. Fabulous dinner! Then we took in a movie at Mystic Players. Afterward we went barhopping. Landed last at the Witch's Brew over on Dew Drop Lane. You been there?"

"No." Crystal rarely went to drinking establishments. "I'll have drinks at home sometimes, but I try not to drive if I've had more than one. That kind of ruins barhopping for me."

"We have some nice bars in town, but the Witch's

Brew isn't one of them. I'm not sure I'll go there again. JJ, the old guy who owns the place, isn't big on cleaning. People throw peanut shells on the floor. I swear he sweeps them up only once a week, if that often. And the crowd is kind of seedy."

"I'll be sure never to go there, then."

"There was one notable thing. Some stupid man had his dog sitting at the bar. On a stool, as if he were human. And he bought the poor thing a beer. Then someone else did."

"That's *terrible!*" Crystal cried. "Did you call the sheriff's department? That's animal abuse!"

Nadine shrugged. "I almost did. But a night in jail can't cure stupid. He'd just get out of the clink and take his dog back there again. The other men thought it was funny to get the poor thing drunk."

Crystal shuddered. "If I had been there, I would have called the law."

"I won't be going back," Nadine said. "Not my kind of place. But if it happens that I ever do, and that jerk is in there again, I'll call the sheriff for you."

Crystal's seven o'clock walked in just then. As Crystal got the woman settled in the chair, Nadine began organizing her station and setting up for her first appointment. "I really liked the guy I went out with. He's tall, dark, and gorgeous. Name's John. He owns Beer, Wine, and Smokes. I didn't think he'd be my type, maybe because he sells cigarettes. But he's really awesome. Not so sure he felt the same way about me, though."

Crystal fastened a cape around her client's neck. "I've met a guy who makes the air feel electrified around me. Have you ever felt that way?"

"Oh, yeah, but only once, more's the pity. Apparently, I wasn't wired to give him the same charge."

Crystal's client interjected, "Don't settle for only zing. After a couple years, the excitement wears off."

Crystal nodded in agreement, but the advice would go unheeded. She always ended relationships long before boredom set in.

Now that Tuck knew Essie truly did work all morning, he decided to leave her alone until afternoon. Only now that he'd gotten a taste of socializing, he missed talking to someone over breakfast. He saw an old fellow sitting alone at a table and asked if he'd mind company. His name was Burt, and he welcomed the opportunity to chat. Tuck learned he'd been a farmer and had now taken up fishing. After breakfast Tuck grabbed a lawn chair and followed him out to his fishing spot along the creek.

Burt was a talker. "Farming is a lonely job," he said over his shoulder as he cast his line. "I seldom had anybody to talk to unless I talked to myself."

Tuck understood Burt in a way other men might not. "I was a cattle rancher. Not many people to talk to in that profession, either. But cows make good listeners."

Burt guffawed. "Yep. I had a few. Also had goats, sheep, and chickens."

"No horse?"

"No need. Only had a small chunk of land. Got around on a quad."

"Married?"

"For fifty-five years. Her name was Sarah. Loved her to pieces, but she up and died on me. Diabetes got her. Developed a sore on her foot that wouldn't heal. It turned to an ulcer and became infected. They wanted to take the foot off. She refused. Then they wanted to take the leg off at the knee. She refused. At some point, the infection got into her bloodstream. She died within twenty-four hours."

Tuck was glad Marge had just keeled over. At least she hadn't died inch by inch. "I'm sorry, Burt. That was a hard way for her to go."

"I'd like to die in my sleep, given my druthers. But most of us don't get off that easy."

"No, I guess not." Tuck recalled how Marge had been riding a horse beside him, talking and laughing until suddenly her face had twisted and she'd grabbed her left shoulder. The next instant, she pitched sideways off her mount and was dead before she hit the ground. "A heart attack ain't so bad." He remembered the grimace of pain on Marge's face. "Might hurt like no tomorrow for a second, but at least it's quick for most people. That's how my wife went. Fine one second and gone the next."

"God bless her." Burt reeled in and cast his line again. "Had to be awful for you. No time to prepare yourself."

Tuck would never forget how he'd felt when he gathered Marge into his arms and realized she was gone. "It was like someone turned off the light switch. Didn't seem fair to me at the time, but I'm glad she didn't linger like your Sarah."

Burt glanced over his shoulder. "Did you just spit?"

Tuck wiped the corner of his mouth. "You object to a man chewin'?"

"Hell, no. I'd love to have a pinch. But it's against the rules. Flintlock will kick your ass to the curb if she catches you."

Tuck reached into his pocket and handed his new friend the can. "Help yourself. I won't rat you out. Hell, just keep it if you want. My granddaughter will buy me more."

Burt reeled in, laid his pole on the grass, and sat beside Tuck on the ground. He stared at the silver lid of the snuff can as if it were a wonder of the world. "Holy shit. I haven't had a chew in two years. It might make me sick."

Tuck laughed. "Trust me. I went without it for a year once, and when I started up again, it tasted like an old friend."

Burt opened the round and bent his head to pull in the scent. "Oh, man," he said. "I love that smell."

"Are you gonna stick a wad in your cheek or just admire it all day?" Tuck asked.

"If I do, I'll be right back where I started, wanting more. Hard habit to give up. It about killed me when I came here and had to go without."

Tuck knew how that felt. "My granddaughter can keep you supplied. Just be careful and don't spit in front of the staff."

Burt started to get a pinch. Then his shoulders slumped. "This is the only place I have to live. Kids all left. Farming wasn't for them. They're married. Have jobs and children. No extra bedrooms. If I get kicked out, they'll have to move me to another facility, and they'll be pissed at me. They have their own lives to live. That's what they say, that they have their own lives."

Tuck stared off at the opposite side of the creek. The forest looked so beautiful and peaceful. But in reality, he and Burt were in jail. "Do they come to see you often?"

"Hell, no. At first they tried. But they live in big cities. It's a long drive. The first year my son came to get me for Christmas. But last year he didn't. I'm like an old pair of shoes sitting at the back of a closet, Tuck. I'm cared for here. I get my three squares a day. When

I start messing my pants, my kids won't have to deal with me. I can't say I blame them for wanting it that way."

Tuck nodded. "Didn't used to be this way. The oldsters stayed on the land. The youngsters took over the work while Mom and Dad sat on the porch. Shucked the corn. Snapped the peas. Helped with household chores as best they could. They got to die at home."

Burt sighed. "Those days are gone, I'm afraid."

Tuck studied the water, flecked with froth as it moved downstream. He watched one white spot, following it with his gaze until it collided with a large rock and broke apart, becoming nothing. He guessed that was how life went. The current pushed forward, and the old people separated off and drifted, doing nothing much until they struck something that obliterated them.

"Don't give up the things that make you happy, Burt. My granddaughter hired me a lawyer. He represents old people and fights for their rights. Have a chew. You know you want one. And I'll get you the lawyer's name and phone number. We may be old, but that don't mean we have to do without our simple pleasures."

"I can't afford a lawyer."

The way Tuck saw it, Burt couldn't afford *not* to have one. "Just havin' him on retainer might be all that it'll take. Once Flintlock knows you've got an attorney, she may ignore it if you break her silly rules."

"How much is a retainer fee?"

"Not sure. But they leave you over a hundred a month from your social security check for incidentals. If you ain't chewin' or drinkin', what the hell have you spent it on?"

"Haven't. Well, I've spent some of it on incidentals. But mostly I just write a check to cash and stuff the money in a sock. I'm afraid to let my checking account get over a certain amount. Patricia might spend me down again. She has a lot of ways to do that. All of a sudden she says you need this or that, and she charges a fortune. Pretty soon, you're broke again. A sock is safer than a bank. She can't see how much you got."

"How much do you got?"

"I stopped counting. A couple grand, maybe."

"That should be enough for a retainer."

Burt nodded and put a pinch of tobacco in his cheek. Tuck told him to keep the can. "Let me know when you're runnin' low, and my granddaughter'll get you more. You'll have to pay her back, of course."

"Of course."

"How long's it been since you had a drink?" Tuck asked.

"Ever since I came here."

"You want one?"

Burt turned at the waist to fix Tuck with a questioning look. "Does a monkey want a banana?"

"You got any health problems makin' it unsafe for you?"

"I have a heart condition, but before I moved here, my doctor said a glass of red wine a day might actually help, not hurt."

Tuck grinned. "Stop by my apartment. I got a jug."

"Of what?"

"Bourbon."

"Holy shit." Burt struggled to his feet, collected his fishing pole, and said, "Lead the way."

As Tuck walked up the bank, he realized he'd just made another friend. Maybe living here could be interesting after all.

Chapter Eight

The kitten, whom Crystal had still resisted naming, was waiting by the door when she got home Saturday evening. He didn't seem to know he was a temporary guest, because he tried to climb up her pant leg and purred madly when she detached him. She opened a can of cat food and laughed as he attacked it, giving forth miniature growls as he wolfed it down.

Rip was gone again. She tried not to grow angry. She kept his bowl filled with food and made sure he always had fresh water. When he was home, she even talked to him and tried her best to pet him. Sometimes he let her; other times he didn't. But the way she saw it, she offered him all that most dogs wanted or needed. So why did he constantly run away? Last night before going to bed, she had ordered a waterproof collar. Not one for a huge dog, as Tanner had suggested. She couldn't bring herself to do anything that might hurt him. But at least Rip wouldn't be able to drown it.

So, he's gone again. Fine. The new collar will arrive on Monday. I'll charge it that night, and Rip won't be able to destroy the battery when I put it on him Tuesday morning. His days of running away are over. Feeling determined *and* justified, she changed out of her work slacks, threw on a brightly patterned sundress, and slipped her feet into red sandals. She couldn't survive even five more minutes wearing heels. She found the kitten sleeping off his dinner on Tuck's faux suede love seat. He appeared to be sound asleep, but she felt it would be unkind to leave again without telling him goodbye. He might wake up and wonder where she was.

She settled her fingertips atop his fluffy fur. He blinked awake and stretched. Then he meowed, focusing sleepy eyes on her face. Crystal couldn't help but smile. "I'm leaving again, No Name. It must seem to you that I'm always gone, but I want to take some treats to my grandpa so he knows I'm thinking of him. When I get home, I'll give you a really special treat, canned *salmon*. Yum, right?"

The kitten sprang to his feet and arched his back. Crystal knew she shouldn't pet him, but he was only a baby and probably still missing his mama.

"You are too cute," she told him as she ran her nails along his spine. He seemed to enjoy that, dropping at the front and lifting his rump, asking for a scratch at the base of his tail. Her heart melted. Then she straightened and turned away, determined not to let her guard down. He was a kitten she couldn't love and didn't want. Forgetting that, even for a second, wasn't a good choice for her. And it definitely wasn't a good one for him. Anytime she'd loved anything, it hadn't ended well. "I'll be back," she called over her shoulder.

The drive to Tuck's facility was short. But to Crystal, exhausted from lack of sleep and working all day, the winding roads outside Mystic Creek seemed endlessly long. She felt drowsy as she guided her car into a parking slot.

Marsha didn't work on Saturdays. A young blonde named Sedona manned the front desk. Crystal waved hello as she cut across to the hall leading to Tuck's apartment. At his door, she hesitated. She heard voices inside. Deciding Tuck was probably talking to a nurse, she poked her head inside and said, "It's me! Okay if I come in?"

"Go ahead, honey."

Crystal was surprised to see Tuck had company. An old man in a tan fishing jacket sat on the sofa. At his feet lay a fishing pole and a tackle box. His gray hair was mostly covered by a hat that matched his coat, and fishing hooks with lures and flies dangled from around the brim.

"This is my friend Burt," Tuck said. "I invited him over for a glass of iced tea. We was just talkin' about startin' a poker night. You think you could bring me my foldin' chairs?"

Crystal stowed the baked goods in the cupboard and set her purse on the drop-leaf table that stood against the left wall. With the leaves up, it would seat four, a perfect size for playing cards. "I'd be glad to bring them, Tuck, but I thought you refused to play poker if you can't bet."

"We'll play in my apartment where the battle-ax has no say-so."

"We *hope* she has no say-so," Crystal corrected. "Pete Ramsey is still checking into that. And playing for money—well, I know it's fun, but most of the people here don't have very much."

"Penny ante would be just as exciting," Burt inserted. "Nobody loses a lot."

Tuck nodded in agreement.

"I'll bring you the folding chairs tomorrow if you don't mind waiting," Crystal said. "I'd bring them tonight, but I'm really tired and fading fast."

Tuck frowned. "Why did you even come, then? I would have been happy with a phone call."

"I have bear claws and maple bars from the Jake 'n' Bake. I wanted you to have them for breakfast."

Burt sat straighter. "Maple bars? I'm your best friend. Right, Tuck?"

Tuck laughed. "Only if she brought me two."

On the drive home, Crystal fantasized about a long, hot bath to soothe her aching legs. Maybe wearing heels all day was a bad idea. Perhaps it came from spending so much time at the retirement center, but she felt old tonight—as if she'd blinked her eyes and aged ten years.

She parked in front of the fence. Staring at the house, she realized she felt empty. More to the point, her life felt empty. Maybe living here in Tuck's home had shifted her priorities somehow, because it hit her like a bullet between the eyes that she had nothing—no husband, no home mortgage, and no kids. Rip and the kitten didn't belong to her. She didn't even have a boyfriend, and if she did, she wouldn't allow the relationship to grow serious. She didn't do serious and never would. Only how would that work in the end? In Tuck's old age, he had her to care about him. But who would be there for her when she was eighty?

Her cell phone rang, and she jumped with a start. She fished in her purse for the device, saw an unfamiliar number on the screen, almost didn't answer, but finally took the call.

"Hi, it's Tanner."

The deep resonance of his voice ran through her like warm honey. "Hi. How did you get my number?" *Why did I ask him that?* "I don't mean that I mind you having it, or anything."

"I asked Tuck. I'm calling to see if you'd like to do something tonight. Dinner out. Maybe watch a flick afterward. Both my kids are at another sleepover. My mom went out with a girlfriend. I have the whole evening free, which doesn't happen often. In fact, it happens so rarely I feel lost."

Crystal didn't feel quite as tired or lonely as she had a moment ago. "Your town or mine?"

"Since I suspect you worked today, I'll drive there. Afterward I won't be as drowsy."

"Dressy or casual?"

"My wallet can cover only casual."

She appreciated his honesty. She'd dated too many men who pretended to be rolling in dough and actually weren't. "That's good. I won't have to wear heels."

"Absolutely not. Go for comfort."

"Time?"

"About thirty minutes, if that works for you."

"Awesome."

Crystal had just ended the call when her phone rang again. She saw that it was Peter Ramsey, Tuck's new attorney. "Hello?"

"Hi, Crystal. It's Pete, and I've got some good news. Oregon law *definitely* allows alcohol consumption in assisted living facilities. Some places refuse to serve it due to risks and liabilities, and Ms. Flintlock may be within her rights to ban drinking in any public area. But Tuck has a right to keep alcohol in his private residence and have drinks if he pleases. In Oregon's description of resident law for facilities, it says a person is free 'to exercise individual rights that do not infringe upon the rights or safety of others.' Flintlock is overstepping her bounds by trying to control what he does inside his apartment. The facility physician emailed me two scripts—one for the dog to visit if kept on a leash in all community areas, and another allowing Tuck to drink alcohol and have chewing tobacco. If he spits on the community floor, he's done. If he gets drunk and causes trouble, he's done. But otherwise he can do whatever he wants in his apartment."

Crystal relaxed against the car seat. "Wow, I'm impressed! I didn't know attorneys worked on Saturdays."

He chuckled. "Normally I don't. But this case caught my attention. My uncle is of an age to start thinking about assisted living."

"I'm very grateful. Can you forward me copies of those scripts?"

"I already did. But I don't think you'll need them. I called Ms. Flintlock and told her Tuck now has orders from his doctor to drink, chew, and spend time with his dog. She's an old witch, isn't she? *Not* happy. I couldn't see her expression, but I heard the fury in her voice. If she retaliates against Tuck in any way, call me. It's against the law for her to do that, and I won't hesitate to slap her with a lawsuit."

Tanner arrived five minutes early. Crystal's stomach jumped with nervousness when she opened the door. The man was handsome in a uniform, but he was downright gorgeous in a short-sleeved shirt and khaki slacks. She stepped back to invite him inside. He scanned the kitchen and living area with those incredibly blue eyes.

"Wow. It's awesome in here. I expected it to be dated. Instead it's cute-quaint but all new. Is *cute-quaint* even a proper description?"

Crystal held up her hands. "I hired decorators. *Cute-quaint* works for me." She turned a full circle, trying to see the house through his eyes. "It *is* cute and quaint. I can't take credit, though. The prior owners remodeled it."

He stepped farther into the living room. "I like that

they stuck with the farmhouse theme and didn't try to modernize it too much."

"Me, too. But it does have all the conveniences. They just did everything tastefully, getting fixtures and appliances that reflect another era."

Tanner focused on Rip, who'd come home minutes earlier, staggered to his bed, and now slept sprawled on his back. "What's up with him?" He held up a dog biscuit. "I came armed."

"No need in regular clothes. It's your uniform he hates. As for what's up with him, I think he's suffering from exhaustion. He ran off again. Gone half the day. When he does that, he sleeps for hours to recover."

The kitten emerged from Crystal's bedroom and proceeded to rub against Tanner's ankles. "Who's this?" He picked up the feline and studied his face. "Please tell me you named him Freckles."

Crystal laughed. "I haven't named him. As soon as the shelter has room, he'll go there to find a forever home."

"You don't like cats?"

"I don't dislike them. I'm just not cut out to be a pet owner."

"Hmm. How is Rip handling his presence? Tuck told me he hates cats."

"At first I worried Rip might hurt him. But he seems to have grudgingly accepted him. I don't need to keep them separated, anyway, which makes it easier."

Tanner cupped the kitten against his shirt. "So what do you call him? Kitty?"

"Mostly No Name." It was her way of reminding herself the cat wouldn't be staying. "A permanent name should be chosen by his forever person."

She grabbed her purse from the table. Tanner glanced

at her bare arms. "Do you have a wrap? It'll get cool if a breeze comes up."

"You're right. I wasn't thinking." Crystal hurried to her room, opened the closet, and grabbed a white shawl. As she returned to the front of the house, she said, "All ready. But I do have a request that may change our plans for the evening just a little."

"What's that?"

"I'd like to stop by Flagg's Market and buy Tuck some contraband, two six-packs of beer and another roll of Copenhagen. He made a new friend and I don't want Tuck to run out. It won't cut into our evening too much if I stop by to deliver it. If you don't mind, that is."

"The last time I took Tuck beer and chew, I almost got fired."

She couldn't contain a startled laugh. "You won't get in trouble this time." She reached into her purse and withdrew a folded email printout. Handing it over, she said, "Prescriptions from the facility physician for substances deemed by Patricia Flintlock to be forbidden."

Tanner shuffled through the scripts; then he held Crystal's gaze. Her attraction to him sizzled just beneath her skin. "How did you pull this off? And will the administrator take this lying down?"

It took her a moment to find her voice. "Patricia has no choice but to allow it. I hired Tuck an attorney, who contacted the facility physician and asked for the prescriptions. He says Tuck can do whatever he pleases in the privacy of his apartment. Oregon law."

Tanner's bronzed face creased into a broad grin that crinkled the corners of his eyes. "You're amazing, and Tuck is lucky to have you. I wasn't stuck on watching a movie, anyway. Let's go shopping, make a delivery, and then get something to eat."

*   *   *

Tanner drove a Chevrolet extended-cab pickup with after-factory running boards that allowed Crystal to climb inside with little effort. The interior, boasting buttery leather seats and dash contours, was as comfortable as her car, but it was peppered with kid paraphernalia. Tanner bent to grab a little girl's shoe from the floorboard and threw it on the backseat. A boy's baseball mitt followed.

"Sorry. I should have tidied up before you got in."

Crystal realized he was nervous. That warmed her heart. Maybe that meant she wasn't alone in feeling the buzz of attraction between them.

"Don't fuss," she said. "Tuck says my car looks like a moving van. I travel prepared for anything. If I go somewhere dressed up, I can be ready for a mountain hike in five minutes flat. I can also give emergency haircuts."

He sighed. "I'm really not a messy person. It's just that my kids shed, kind of like dogs. Snack wrappers. Hair clips. Dolls. Soccer cleats. Fast-food bags." He sent her a sideways glance. "Mostly I cook. But sometimes on Saturdays when I'm juggling dance recitals or dental appointments with baseball games, I take the easy way out."

"Please, just relax. I didn't bring my white gloves."

He leaned his head back against the rectangular rest, sighed, and stared at the ceiling. "I'm really blowing this. I'm sorry. I haven't been on a date since I lost my wife."

Crystal's heart squeezed. He was so handsome. She found it difficult to see him as an ordinary guy who felt unsure of himself.

"You must miss her horribly." The moment she said it, she wished she hadn't. "I'm sorry. That was a stupid thing to say. Of course you do."

"Not so much anymore." He keyed the ignition, and the truck engine rumbled. "Strike that. Of course I miss her, but it no longer casts a shadow over my world. It's been over six years. I still think of her. But at some point, you start to heal from the pain. My life with her ended abruptly, and I'm ready now to start a new one. Does that make any sense?"

"Absolute sense." Crystal understood better than he knew. When you lost someone, the memory of that person remained with you, but the pain did eventually lessen and fade. For most people, anyway. Crystal's pain and sense of loss seemed to be stuck to her heart with superglue. "I'm glad you've healed enough to move on."

"Forward," he corrected. "To me, 'moving on' implies that I'm leaving my memories of her behind."

The trip to the market went quickly, and in what seemed like no time at all, Tanner parked his truck in front of the facility. "So, should we keep the beer and chew hidden in bags?" he asked.

"No. Don't misunderstand. I dislike confrontation and try to avoid it, so the coward in me wants to hide everything. But another part of me knows Patricia thrives on confrontation. Sooner or later, she'll find out, and I don't want Tuck to deal with her alone. She is one nasty piece of work."

Tanner opened the rear door on the driver's side and drew the beer and tobacco from the sacks. Standing at his elbow, Crystal said, "I'll carry one six-pack, or everything if you prefer. I know you may feel nervous."

He flashed her a crooked grin. "Actually, no. I'm off duty and driving my own rig, and nothing we're taking inside is illegal."

Crystal did feel nervous. She wanted to believe Patricia would simply accept that she'd lost this round, but judging by past experience, she knew that was wishful thinking.

"Maybe she won't be here this late," Tanner suggested.

"Patricia seems to be married to her job. If I come in the evening, she's here. If I come early in the morning, she's here. I'm starting to think she may live at the facility. Maybe that's one of her job perks, free room and board."

Crystal's prediction proved to be accurate. When she and Tanner walked into the building, Patricia Flintlock stood at the front desk. Apparently, she had been haranguing Sedona. When she noticed what Crystal and Tanner were carrying, she broke off midsentence and flushed the color of a red poppy. Turning toward them, she stiffened her shoulders.

"Get that *out* of my building."

Crystal braced herself for battle. "Actually, Patricia, this is merely passing through the community area, where you have jurisdiction, to my grandfather's private residence, where, according to Oregon law, he is entitled to exercise his individual rights."

"I said get it *out*!" she yelled.

"Make me." The instant those words passed Crystal's lips, she felt like a four-year-old. It was a childish thing for one adult to say to another one. "Please, call the cops. While you do that, I'll call Tuck's attorney. We'll see how far your authority here extends."

Patricia covered the distance between them with long, angry strides. She was a large woman with a strong build, but Crystal was tall enough to look down at her and refused to feel intimidated. "Get out!" the older woman cried. "You are henceforth banned from this facility!"

At any other time, Crystal might have let the woman bully her into leaving. But she was here for Tuck, and for Tuck, she would stay. The receptionist, now behind Patricia, was looking at Crystal with astonished respect. Crystal could have sworn the younger woman winked.

"Um, I don't think so. Oregon law also protects Tuck's right to have visitors of his choosing. Unless I do something wrong—like deface property, use illegal substances, disturb the peace, or something else frowned upon in any regular neighborhood—you can't curtail my visits here. My grandfather pays rent for his apartment, and therefore it is regarded by the state as his private residence."

"You *are* disturbing the peace!" Patricia accused.

"No," Crystal replied. "I haven't even raised my voice. You have."

The administrator was still flushed. For an instant Crystal feared she might keel over from the heart attack Marsha had wished upon her. "This isn't over," she cried. "I'm calling the facility legal team. Your grandfather will be out on the street as of tomorrow."

Crystal handed Tanner the six-pack of beer she carried and put her hands on her hips. Meeting the administrator's gaze, she said, "That isn't going to happen, either. It's illegal. Without due process and warning, you can't evict an old man. If you try, I'll sue you and the corporation you work for, and trust me, Ms. Flintlock, I'll win."

"You're going to regret this."

"Make *me* regret it all you like. I'm young, and I can handle it. But don't make the mistake of retaliating against my grandfather. That, too, is against the law."

Patricia pivoted on the heel of her sturdy black pump and started to walk away. Crystal decided to lob a parting shot. "Oh, I almost forgot. Tomorrow I'll be bringing Tuck's dog to see him. He'll be leashed in all community areas, and I'll hurry him into Tuck's apartment. Tuck has a prescription from the physician for daily visits."

Patricia's shoes skidded on the slick tile as she braked to a stop. She turned and fixed Crystal with a fiery gaze. "As I said, I'm going to call the legal team. We shall see, Ms. Malloy. We shall see."

Crystal wagged her fingertips at the woman in farewell. "Yes, we shall. It may be pertinent for me to mention at this point that I've been going over Tuck's charges here. Twenty-five dollars for a tiny packet of cotton swabs strikes me as being exorbitant. Nineteen ninety-nine for a twelve count of Band-Aids also seems abnormally high. I'm wondering who gets that profit. Need I say more?"

Patricia's high color drained by several hues. She pivoted and hurried away.

Tanner, still standing beside her, said, "I thought she might try to deck you."

"Oh, well—thank you for staying close to protect me."

He emitted a low laugh. "Actually, I felt pretty confident that you could take her on. Good job, Crystal. She's rather scary."

As praise went, it wasn't too flowery. But Crystal felt proud of herself anyway. She hadn't let Tuck down this time, and now she knew Marsha was right. Patricia Flintlock was overcharging these elderly people to skim money from the government.

"Pabst Blue Ribbon!" Tuck shouted when he saw the beer. "I'm surprised you remember, Crystal. That it's my favorite, I mean." He struggled up from his recliner and limped toward the kitchen. Laying his fingers against a can, he said in a softer, almost prayerful tone, "And it's *cold*. I gotta call Burt."

Crystal smiled. "I take it Burt enjoys having a cold one."

"What workin' man don't?" Tuck greeted Tanner and shook his hand. "Aren't you already in enough trouble?"

Tanner chuckled. "It's fine. I'm off the clock and driving my own pickup."

Tuck pulled his cell phone from his shirt pocket, punched in a number, and a second later said, "Burt, this is Tuck. I got cold beer. Come on over. Bring a friend if you want."

The Mystic Creek Park lay in deepening shadow, with tall pine trees throwing dark outlines over the freshly mown grass. The smell of recently shorn blades rising from the sun-warmed earth held promise of summer days to come. Crystal and Tanner sat at a weathered wood picnic table with white sacks anchored down with take-out cartons. They'd gone for simple and ordered hamburgers and fries. Tanner had stopped at Flagg's Market again to grab a bottle of wine. On his belt he carried an all-purpose tool that he'd thought featured a corkscrew, but it didn't, so he'd dug the cork out with a tiny knife. They'd poured their vino into waxed soda cups and now sipped around bobbing bits of bottle stopper.

Enjoying the cool breeze but grateful for the shawl Tanner had suggested she bring, Crystal couldn't remember a time when she'd enjoyed an evening with a man so much. Tanner had an easy, relaxed way about him. Maybe it came from being a single dad. He had learned to take everything in stride, could make the most of a moment, and didn't seem too hooked on everything being perfect.

And yet it was.

He took a huge bite of his burger, pocketed it in his cheek, and said, "What? You're looking at me funny."

"I'm sorry. I was just thinking how down-to-earth you are."

"Oh." He swallowed. "Sorry. I know this isn't the kind of dinner date most women imagine."

"No! It *is*, Tanner. Lots of men get it all wrong. Wine her, dine her, impress her. It gets so *boring*. All that tension? I dislike dating because of it. It gives me a nervous stomach. Men trying so hard, and me feeling bad when I know right away he isn't my type. Him blowing money he can't afford and refusing to let me help pay. I want to say, 'Can you just be *you*? Can you stop trying to be suave and talk about something *real*?'"

He laughed. "Here's real. I'm worried about Michael. He's staying all night with a friend. Other boys are there. The parents are supposedly supervising. But *are* they? He's eleven, almost twelve. He constantly reminds me of that *almost*. He's trying to tell me he's *almost* a teenager, and that I'm way too strict." He wiped the corner of his mouth with a napkin he kept tucked in his fist to keep it from blowing away. "But he *isn't* grown up yet. He's still only a boy. I worry. So many kids get messed up at his age."

Crystal understood. Most of the kids she saw in her salon were growing up surrounded by small-town wholesomeness, but there were a few who seemed to have taken a wrong turn. A good deal larger than Mystic Creek, Crystal Falls was still a small community, though. The people there were community minded, cared about their neighbors, and offered the youth plenty of checks and balances. "I think the most important thing is to provide Michael with a loving home environment and sterling values. If he makes a mistake, he'll know you're there to help him."

He nodded. "He's a good kid. Pulls good grades. Respectful. I don't really think he'll ever do anything nuts, but I accept that it could happen. I try to spend a lot of time with him, keep him active in sports, and be a good parent at night. You know. Talking over dinner. Helping with homework. Family time after that. Listening to him when he talks. But it's scary. Parents have such a small percentage of a day to be with their children. Teachers and other kids are influencing them most of the time."

"True, but you're the one who taught him values. I think that sticks. As a teenager, I'd start to do something I knew I shouldn't, and I'd hear Tuck's voice whisper inside my head." She smiled. "I didn't always listen, but my relationship with my grandfather kept me mostly out of trouble."

A grin creased his cheek. "You're right. No matter where Michael goes, he'll have a little bit of home with him. Thanks for the reminder. I feel better. On to lighter topics. I didn't mean to go all serious on you."

"I don't mind serious, and I enjoy conversations that aren't predictable."

Crystal peered into her wine, saw a tiny bug, and fished it out with her finger. Watching her, Tanner said, "You deserve a better night out than this."

"I suggested the park, and there's no such thing as better than this. At least not for me. I grew up in simple surroundings." She rubbed the bug off her fingertip onto the rough table plank. "I spent my girlhood on a ranch. People tend to glamorize ranch life if they've never lived on one. A ranch does have pastoral views. Tuck's house was really nice. He made sure my wardrobe was as good as any other girl's. But there's another side to ranching that's far from glamorous. In spring the mud was ankle-deep, and it was commonplace to have calves in our bathroom, which served as a steam room for babies with pneumonia. In the summer, do you think bugs never got in the milk as I carried it from the barn to the house? Tuck always said, 'Just some added protein,' and plucked them out." She took a sip of her wine and smiled at him. "And hello. That bug in my wine died happy."

He threw back his head and laughed. "I like you. You're refreshing."

"I like you, too." And as she said that, Crystal feared she might like him too much.

After eating their dinner and stowing their trash, they walked onto the natural bridge. It was a huge archway of rock, tunneled by rushing water over the centuries. A sense of timelessness settled over Crystal. How many people had fallen in love with each other standing right where she and Tanner stood now?

"I don't suppose you've heard the legend about this place."

He shook his head.

"There are several different slants, all on a similar theme. When two people stand together along Mystic Creek, they are destined to fall in love."

He shuffled his feet as if to run for his life, which made her laugh. "We could still take in a film," he suggested.

"Or just enjoy a lovely evening walk along the creek."

He took her by the hand, adjusted his stride to match hers, and said, "Deer."

Crystal scanned the area. On the far side of the stream, she saw a doe with a brand-new spotted fawn. "Oh, how beautiful is that?"

She glanced up and realized Tanner was gazing straight at her. "Pretty damned beautiful."

Chapter Nine

Essie stopped at the front desk to ask Sedona, the gum-chewing blonde, if she could have Tuck's apartment number. The girl glanced at a chart and said, "Twenty-three. But if Flintlock asks, you never got it from me." She resumed doodling on a notepad.

"No worries." Smiling, Essie made her way down the hall and tapped on Tuck's door before she heard voices coming from inside. He had a guest, and she was interrupting. For all she knew, it could have been another woman. He was so damned handsome. She considered running but doubted her rickety knees were up to the task.

He opened the door. His craggy face creased in a broad grin. "Essie! Come in. We're playin' poker. I was about to deal another hand."

"Oh, I'm sorry. I didn't mean to interrupt."

"You're not interruptin'. Come join us."

He closed the door behind her and turned the lock. In a conspiratorial voice, he said, "To keep the wardens out. Burt and I are havin' a beer."

So that was his name. Essie had seen Burt from a distance as he stood along the creek angling for trout. He pushed up from the drop-leaf table, grinned at her, and stretched out a hand as Tuck made the introductions. "Now it's going to get interesting. Three players keep the cards flowing better."

Essie saw only two chairs, and she truly didn't wish

to interrupt them. But Tuck insisted on making her a glass of his special iced tea, Burt went to the community area to borrow a third chair, and before Essie knew quite how it happened, she was holding four aces.

"Sorry, gentlemen. Let this be a lesson to you both. Never invite an old cardsharp like me to play poker with you." She pushed a pile of chips to the center of the table. They weren't playing for money. Tuck said he needed to get rolls of pennies from the bank first so everyone could afford to buy in. "Call or fold."

She caught Tuck studying her face. She got the feeling those blue eyes probed every nuance of her expression. Fortunately, she wasn't bluffing, and she sensed that he knew it. "I fold," he said.

Burt followed his lead, and Essie showed her cards. Both men burst out laughing.

The next time she glanced at her watch, two hours had passed. She couldn't remember the last time she'd had such fun. They'd talked and laughed and bluffed as if they'd played together for years. Burt got up to leave, enveloped her hand in his big paw, and told her he hoped she'd come back and play again.

Tuck insisted on walking her back to her apartment. She knew it wasn't because he was worried she'd get lost or set upon, but it gave her a good feeling. She wasn't used to feeling protected. Jake had been gone so long it seemed like a lifetime. Tuck dropped a chaste kiss on her cheek outside her door.

Lifting his head, he said, "You think she sits in her office and watches all of us on camera?"

She rested her shoulder blades against the wood panel and smiled up at him. "I'm sure they have surveillance in all the common areas."

"Just bothers me to think someone can watch us kiss."

Essie toyed with his shirt buttons. "There are no cameras in our apartments."

"True, an' I'll keep that in mind for later."

Though she knew it was bold, Essie asked, "How much later?"

He pressed his lips to her forehead. "I'll leave that for you to decide."

Before entering her residence, Essie watched him walk away. Then she went inside and kicked off her pumps, pleased that her feet still didn't pain her when she went barefoot. No matter how old she grew, the young girl she'd once been still dwelled within her, and during her youth, wearing her one pair of shoes all the time had made them wear out faster. She still liked to go without footwear. It took her back in time, reminded her where she'd come from, and kept her humble.

Without turning on a light, she sat in her recliner and stared into the shadows of the living room. She'd never expected to fall in love again so late in life. But she was enchanted by Tucker Malloy. Funny, that. He was nothing like Jake, whom she'd once loved with every fiber of her being. Suave, sophisticated, and wealthy, Jake had shown her the world of the rich, yet he'd never lightened his grip on the harsh realities of poverty, which he'd experienced as a boy. They'd been a good match, she and Jake, each of them wanting to carve their own niche in the upper echelons of society. But they'd never lost touch with where they'd come from. They had understood each other—and admired each other. After Jake died, she figured that was it for her. A woman only met so many men who were perfect for her.

But now she'd stumbled upon Tuck. He was a diamond in the rough, and at this stage of his life, no amount of grinding and polishing would ever change him. His lack of secondary education was audible in his speech. The rigors of his profession, pitting himself against cattle and the elements on a daily basis, had been carved on every plane of his face. But he was a good man with a sincerity about him that charmed her—and seduced her. She doubted she'd ever meet another man who spoke to her on so many levels.

So what am I waiting for? At her age, leaping into a relationship was easy. Her assets were protected. It wasn't necessary for her to find a man who'd be a wonderful father or pass on good genetics to her children. She had no need of someone accomplished in ballroom dancing or the social graces. All she wanted now was someone she could talk to, someone who could make her laugh, someone who made her feel desirable again. Was any woman ever so old that she no longer cared about being beautiful? Or too old to yearn to feel strong arms around her and experience physical pleasure?

Sighing, Essie stood to get herself a glass of water with psyllium powder mixed in. As she sat back down to drink it in the shadows, she thought of Tuck again and decided her use of fiber to stay regular should remain her secret. He might dump her if she started mentioning stuff like that. As she drank toward the bottom of the glass, she decided to give their relationship some time before she told him she was ready for intimacy. But not too much time. The clock was ticking. They had a finite number of tomorrows awaiting them, and if things proved to be delightful between them, she would regret every single day she wasted.

Sunday evenings were Crystal's favorite time. The salon was closed and she could relax without feeling guilty or jumping whenever her phone rang. It was her day, whether she spent it in a rush of activity or, more rarely, just doing nothing. At day's end, she could enjoy a long, hot bath. Lounge on the couch afterward in her nightclothes. Sometimes she would read. Other times she would watch something on television. She never knew exactly what Sunday might bring, and for her the lack of structure was just what she needed to regroup. And the evening—well, that was her reward of the week.

So what was she doing out here in the dark, driving the roads to look for a stupid dog? This was *her* night, damn it. "Well, guess what, Rip. Searching for you is getting old."

She pulled over to turn around, remembering the tears she'd seen in her grandfather's eyes earlier that day when he'd finally gotten to see his dog after such a long separation. Her heart squeezed and she felt awful for even *thinking* about going home. If something happened to Rip, Tuck would mourn until he died.

Her cell phone rang. As she dug through her purse, she said, "Please be a neighbor who's seen him. Please, please, *please*." Instead she saw Tanner's name on the screen. After their date last night, she'd added him as a contact. "Hello."

"Uh-oh, you sound stressed. That's not good on a Sunday evening."

His voice curled around her, and she smiled. "Rip's gone again."

"And you're out looking for him."

"Yes. Darned dog. He's blowing my one night a week that I set aside for relaxation. I wish I could just not care. But Tuck loves him."

"And so do you. Grudgingly, maybe, but you do."

"No. I'm not a pet person." She winced at how heartless that made her sound. "I mean, well, I like animals. I think they're cute, and I understand how important having a pet is to a lot of people. It's just never worked out well for me, and I finally gave up on the idea."

"I get it. You work long hours, too, just like me. It's hard to do justice to a pet when you're gone all the time."

Crystal was glad she'd talked her way out of that one. Then she wondered why it mattered. She was attracted to Tanner. She figured most women would have been. If their relationship progressed and they eventually made love, she felt certain she would enjoy being with him. But she had a feeling Tanner was looking for a lasting relationship—and she wasn't. Not now, not ever.

"So . . . how was your Sunday?" she asked.

"Busy. I took the kids for a bike ride. Tossed a ball with Michael. Helped Tori decorate her dollhouse. Cooked three times. Cleaned the kitchen three times. Did laundry. Vacuumed and dusted. I never got around to mopping. It'll keep until one night next week."

Her mouth curved in a smile. "Good grief. Just listening makes me tired."

"I called just to say hi. I wanted to hear your voice."

Crystal cut the car engine and stared out the windshield into country darkness, so much blacker than that in town. In his tone, she heard a lot of things she didn't wish to acknowledge. If Tanner felt physically attracted to her, she was fine with it. But she detected something more in his voice, a growing affection for her. And she wasn't okay with that. He was a great guy, possibly one of the nicest she'd ever met. He'd also lost his wife, had endured more than his fair share of pain, and was trying to raise two kids alone. The last thing he needed was for a woman to toy with his feelings.

"Tanner, there's something you should know about me."

"I'm all ears."

That made her smile again, and she wondered if she was nuts for thinking about putting a halt to this before it even began. "I, um—I can't think how to put this. I just think you should know that I'm not looking for a permanent relationship."

He chuckled. "Well, that's good to know. I'm not sure I'm looking for one, either. Probably not, if I'm smart. I've got young kids. Bringing a woman into the picture might cause problems. Maybe not. But the possibility shouldn't be ignored."

She released a taut breath. "So we're on the same page."

"For now. If I start to feel differently, I'll let you know. I just enjoy your company. I find you attractive. I'd like to see where that takes us."

That sounded safe. Harmless. As long as he walked into it with his eyes wide-open, he couldn't get hurt, and she didn't have to feel as if she were treading on eggshells around him. "I'm good with that."

"I remember you saying that the new electronic collar for Rip is due in tomorrow. That got me thinking. If I stop by your salon with it first thing in the morning, you could charge the collar all day and be ready for the trial run when you get home. I could come by. I'd like to be there to see how it works on him."

Crystal grinned. "You make me smile, Tanner Richards. I thought you were going to ask me out again, and instead we're making a dog-watching date."

He chuckled. "Hey, at least it'll be different."

"True. And undoubtedly exciting. Rip's middle name is Unpredictable. Should I pick up some takeout so we can make it another dinner date?"

He sighed. "I'd love that, but I won't have enough time. You told me something I need to know about you. One thing you need to know about me is my life is scheduled mostly around my kids and my responsibility to them."

"I understand. Monday is a school night."

"Yeah, and nearly every moment has to be structured in order to get them bathed and into bed for a good rest. I wish I had more free time, but that isn't my reality."

"I'm good with that. I go to bed early on weeknights, too."

When Crystal got home, Rip was still gone. She checked the time and decided she had to find some balance in her relationship with the dog. She'd just driven around for over three hours looking for him. If something happened to him, she'd be able to look Tuck straight in the eye and say she'd done everything possible to keep him safe. She would also feel confident of that in her heart. It was after ten. She had to be up at five. Even now she wouldn't get her recommended eight hours.

No hot bath. No lounging. No reading or television. She stripped off, dropped a silky camisole over her head, and crawled into bed. Even with No Name hogging part of her pillow, she fell asleep almost the instant she closed her eyes.

Then a sound woke her up. Rip was home and scratching at the door. Glancing at the digital clock on her nightstand, she saw that it was once again three in the morning. She stumbled through the dark house, caught her little toe on a dining chair, and hopped around on one foot grunting until the pain subsided a little. Then she limped to the door. Flipping on the porch light, she opened the portal and glared down at her grandfather's dog. He wore what she'd come to think of as his exhausted grin, his lips parted, his tongue lolling out one side and dripping drool, and his eyes looking slightly unfocused.

"Where have you been?" she asked.

Rip tripped on the threshold, caught his balance, and staggered right past her to his bed, where he did a half roll in midair to land on his back atop the cushion.

"It's three in the morning, Rip! *Three*. I feel like I'm married to a drunk who never comes home until the bars close. Only, guess what. I can't divorce you."

Crystal hoped she could get back to sleep. She turned off the porch light, hobbled back to her room, and crawled under the covers. She catnapped until her alarm went off at five, and she felt exhausted when she got up to start the day.

How many times could a person explain how she had sprained or broken her little toe? Crystal hadn't been able to stuff her right foot into a pair of heels that morning. Instead she'd chosen an old pair of shoes made of soft leather with well-cushioned soles. Even so, she still limped, and everyone noticed.

"Oh, how did you hurt your foot?" Or "Wow, that's quite a limp you've got. What happened?" Each time Crystal replied, she vowed never to walk through the house again without turning on lights.

By midmorning she had almost given up on Tanner arriving with Rip's new collar. It felt strange to be watching for him. Every time she glimpsed a black vehicle through the shop windows, her heart leaped. It took her back in time to her high school years when she'd crushed on a boy and walked the halls during lunch hour, hoping to see him. Only, she was no longer a teenager, and it was crazy to feel this way about a guy. Unfortunately, her brain didn't seem to be listening.

At a quarter after ten, she saw the Courier Express van pull over at the curb in front of the salon. When Tanner emerged carrying a small package, he looked so good that her knees felt weak.

"Be still, my heart. He's new on this route," Nadine said. "Nice step up from Brian. Eye candy."

"Oh, he *is* yummy," someone else said.

Crystal wanted to say, "No, he's *mine*," but she had no claim on Tanner Richards. Women could flirt with him, and if he wanted to, he could flirt back. That was the way she wanted it. Right? So why did she feel possessive of him?

He flashed that fabulous grin as he opened the door. "Delivery for Crystal Malloy."

She hobbled over to take the package. Bending his head slightly, he asked, "What happened to your foot?"

"Rip finally came home," she told him, and then repeated the response she'd now memorized.

Tanner winced. "Maybe you should get the toe X-rayed."

Crystal didn't think there was a lot to be done for a sprained or broken toe. "See you around six?" she asked.

He nodded. "I'll be looking forward to it."

Crystal half expected Rip to be away gallivanting again and be a no-show for his own collar party, but when she parked in front of the house that evening, she saw the dog sitting beside Tanner on the front steps. It reminded her of the day Tanner had waited in almost the same spot, wearing only his belt, boots, and puppy boxers. This time, he was smiling, though. And dressed.

As she climbed from her car, she smoothed her

blouse and brushed at her slacks, wanting to look her best. Only *why*? It was a question she couldn't answer. Yes, she liked men. And, yes, she enjoyed sex. Well, with the right person, she did. But she wasn't in the market for anything more. If Tanner liked what he saw, fine. If he didn't, she'd be okay with that, too. Only for reasons beyond her, she wasn't sure she really would be okay if he decided he wasn't interested in her. Something within her had altered. She'd finally met a guy who made her wish she had more to offer than a fling.

"I see that frown," he called. "Did you forget I'd be here?"

Crystal made a conscious effort to stop scowling. "No. Long day. I'm glad you came. You can celebrate with me when Rip finally meets his match."

"You're not limping. The toe must be better."

"Still tender, but better, yes."

Crystal gave the dog a treat as she entered the yard. Not so long ago, she'd often forgotten and been pinched for the infraction. Now giving Rip biscuits had become second nature. She held up the box that Tanner had delivered that morning. "I got the collar charged, so it's ready to go. Let me go get it paired with the controller. I'll be right back."

"Mind if I come along?"

"No, not at all."

As they circled the house and crossed the lawn, their arms brushed, and Crystal felt that jolt of awareness again. His blue gaze flicked toward her and arced like the deep aqua at the base of a blowtorch. She'd never felt this way with anyone. And judging by his startled expression, she was pretty sure he hadn't, either, at least not recently. Even Rip seemed to notice. Following them from a few paces back, he braced his front feet in the grass and barked.

Tanner glanced at the dog. Then he came to a halt. "Okay, I know I should let it pass, but I've got to ask if you felt that."

Crystal's throat went tight, and bubbles of sensation bounced just above the V of her collarbone like bingo balls in a blowing machine. Her whole body tingled. Deep in the core of her, she ached with yearning. If her foot still ached, she couldn't feel it.

"I— *Yes*," she managed.

"Good." He thrust his large, burnished fingers through his honey-streaked brown hair and huffed as if he'd been holding his breath. "I think."

And then for no reason at all they both began to laugh. In an odd way it was cathartic. When their mirth abated, the tension between them had eased.

"Collar," he reminded her.

Crystal lifted her hand to stare at the circle of woven nylon with a black box attached. She'd forgotten she held it, even forgotten why they had walked out here. Turning toward the pump house, she said, "It'll only take a moment to pair it with the controller."

He stood just outside the shed. The control box and the collar beeped as they matched signals. She felt Tanner's presence behind her. She couldn't help but think that their bodies had just undergone a human version of pairing. The thought unnerved her. Most of her life she'd prided herself on her self-control. Allowing herself to be attracted to a man had been a conscious decision, and now it suddenly wasn't. Did Tanner feel as rattled as she did?

As she left the shed, he took the collar from her. Their fingertips touched, and she felt another zing of sensation. His gaze met hers, and she knew he'd felt it, too. Only this time he said nothing.

"Come here, Rip." He bent over to adjust the size of

the nylon band to fit the dog's neck. Then he snapped the clasp. "There. Ready for showtime."

Studiously trying not to look at each other, they both stared at Rip. The blue heeler seemed to understand he was supposed to do something, but he clearly didn't know what.

"Okay. We should ignore him," Tanner suggested. "He knows something's up."

Crystal nodded in agreement, but she didn't know if she could behave normally. Her physical reaction to Tanner had scrambled her nerves. Her heart was pounding, and her skin still tingled. Nothing about this was business as usual for her. She wasn't sure she liked it.

They walked toward the front of the house, this time keeping a distance between them. Rip seemed relieved. He dashed around their moving legs, cutting a figure eight. Then he got too close to the fence and yelped.

Crystal clenched her hands into fists. "That hurt him. I *hate* this."

"It's only a little zap. Don't be too hard on yourself."

In unison they turned to watch the dog race toward the pond. Leaping from the bank, Rip went airborne for an instant and then cut the water's surface with a huge splash.

"He's trying to drown it," Tanner observed. "I hope you got a good one."

Crystal hoped so, too. She'd paid nearly three hundred, but high cost didn't *always* mean fine quality. "We'll see."

Face dripping water, Rip surfaced and grinned at her. She understood that look. The dog thought he'd won again. Only this time when he left the pond and ran close to the fence, he yelped, circled away, and stopped in his tracks, his expression bewildered. Then it turned calculating.

"He's plotting," she said. "I can see the wheels in his brain turning."

Tanner folded his arms. "This is when we'll see if you got a collar with strong enough correction."

Rip made a U-turn and ran toward the fence. He yelped when he entered the signal zone, but this time instead of racing away, he kept going, leaped up to hook his paws through the chain links, and started to climb, yipping intermittently until he found purchase on the top crossbar. He sat there for a moment.

"The safety just kicked in," Tanner said. "The signal isn't strong enough. Not enough to discourage him, anyway. He knows that the collars stop correcting him in thirty seconds. It's a safety feature in case a dog gets trapped in a signal zone."

Crystal watched as her grandfather's dog leaped to the ground on the other side of the chain-link fence. She turned to Tanner. "Dogs have no concept of time. Rip doesn't know the difference between thirty seconds and eight hours."

"True. But he's learned that the collar cuts off and he can withstand the correction until it does. It's not about him comprehending time the same way we do. It's about him knowing that he can outlast the collar."

Crystal forgot all about her physical attraction to Tanner. As she watched Rip tear toward an adjacent field and disappear into tall grass, she wanted to scream. "Now what?" She sent the question skyward. She didn't expect Tanner to answer it. "He's got to be kept home. He's making me miss work, plus he's disappearing at night and not coming back until three in the morning.

I'm losing sleep! And I can't afford to buy any more collars that don't work."

He rested his hands on his hips. "I know you don't want to do it, but like I said before, a collar for a much bigger dog may be the only solution."

"That would be cruel."

"Yeah, maybe. You going after him?"

"It's pointless. He hides. I can never find him."

"I guess you have to weigh things out and decide what's best for Rip. You could drive a spike in the ground and chain him."

"I hate seeing dogs chained. They get tangled. Can't reach their water. That's cruel, too."

They stood in silence for a moment. Then he said, "I wish this collar had been a success."

She nodded. "Thanks for the moral support."

"I'd love to stay longer, but Michael's at practice. I'd like to catch the end of it if I can. Watch him throw. Give him some pointers."

"I understand. It's important for you to be there."

He strode toward the gate. Even as upset as she was about Rip being gone again, she admired the masculine grace of his movements. At the door of the van, he sent her a long look. "Weigh your options. Maybe discuss it with Tuck and get his opinion. He doesn't want Rip running at large. It's dangerous."

Crystal knew that. When Rip was gone at night, she could barely sleep for worrying about all the horrible things that might happen to him.

"Bye, Tanner."

He raised a hand, climbed into the vehicle, and drove away.

Instead of searching for Rip again, Crystal decided to visit Tuck and have a heart-to-heart with him. Nobody understood Rip better. Maybe he'd share some ideas with her about how to keep the blue heeler at home.

When Crystal reached the center, Tuck wasn't in his apartment. She looked for him in the community areas but didn't see him. He wasn't out back fishing, either. This was a first. Now both Rip *and* her grandfather were missing. She walked to the front desk, where Marsha sat reading a book. Light from the setting sun slanted in through the dining hall windows to shimmer on her red hair.

"Do you know where Tuck is?"

Marsha lifted her gaze. "If I tell you where he is, then Patricia will know that I know, and I'm not supposed to know." She tilted her head. "Did that make any sense?" She sighed. "If I pretend not to notice, then I don't have to tell on him. Understand? And I really, *really* don't want to tell on him."

Crystal wondered what on earth Tuck was doing wrong now. "Okay. Tell me where he is, and I'll never tell anyone that you told." She wasn't sure if that string of words made any more sense than Marsha's had. "I really need to talk to him."

Barely above a whisper, Marsha said, "He's with his girlfriend."

"His *what*?"

Marsha leaned closer. "His friend Essie. I think they've got a thing going."

Crystal wasn't excited about her grandfather engaging in an end-of-life romance, but she wasn't against it, either. "Don't tell me *that's* against the rules, too."

With a sigh, Marsha said, "'Fraid so."

"I don't get it. If they like each other, what's the problem?"

"Ask Patricia. She has it in her brain that the elderly are incapable of making wise choices for themselves."

Crystal couldn't believe this. "But, Marsha, Oregon law protects their right to have visitors of their choosing. What they do behind closed doors is nobody's business but theirs."

"She can't stop them from visiting each other, but she'll blow a gasket if there's physical intimacy."

"Do you honestly think Tuck can still—well, you know, *do* that?"

Marsha rolled a pen back and forth under the flat of her hand. "Maybe. I don't know. My husband couldn't at fifty-nine without ED medication. But every man may be different."

Crystal suddenly wanted a drink. *Make that a double.* "What's Essie's apartment number?"

The older woman cleared her throat. "Sixty-nine. Sorry. I know it's a bad omen."

Crystal felt a flush crawl up her neck as she crossed the expansive tile floor. Essie lived in the wing opposite Tuck's. She walked nearly to the end of the hall before she reached the old lady's apartment. Imagining the two of them together—and what they might be doing—she knocked louder than necessary and hoped Essie answered the door fully clothed.

But *of course* she would, Crystal assured herself. Tuck was eighty. Men his age who'd recently undergone a hip-replacement surgery and still wore a cast for a broken arm couldn't engage in sex. It was like— *Yuck!* She didn't want to think about her grandfather doing things like that.

Essie opened the door wearing a navy blue pantsuit. Her dark hair was perfectly coiffed. She wore pink lipstick that hadn't been smudged. Crystal released a breath, so relieved that her voice sounded squeaky. "Hello. I'm Tuck's granddaughter."

A smile touched Essie's unkissed mouth. "Ah, Crystal. I've seen you from a distance. Please, come in."

Crystal took in the older woman's apartment as she crossed the small kitchen. The office reflected the tidy nature of its user, and the living area was neat as well. Essie had comfortable mauve furniture dotted with small throw pillows. Feminine, but not overdone. Tuck, in a plaid shirt, faded jeans, and Romeo slippers, didn't look out of place sitting on the sofa. On one knee, he balanced a snifter of what Crystal surmised was brandy.

"Hi, sweetheart. We just finished dinner. I didn't expect to see you this late."

Essie offered Crystal a seat, and she perched beside her grandfather. Tuck made informal introductions. When Essie had relaxed in the recliner, Crystal said, "Tuck, I need to talk to you about Rip. I can't keep him at home."

Crystal recounted what had been happening with the dog as quickly as possible. "I've spent over six hundred dollars on electronic collars. I drive the roads trying to find him at all hours of the day and night. Sometimes he doesn't come home until three in the morning."

Essie broke in. "I had a dog like that once, a terrier. We lived on a golf course, so invisible fencing was our only option. Jake hired a company to install it, and Blinky—that was the dog's name—kept challenging the perimeter. Got loose. Raided trash cans. Stole golf balls off the fairway."

Tuck set aside his brandy and sat forward. "So what did you do?"

Essie lifted her brows. "We called the fence company. The man ordered a super-strong signal collar. In short, Tuck, from that point forward, we shocked the crap out of Blinky, and he finally stayed home."

"That seems cruel," Tuck said, echoing Crystal's reaction.

"Depends on how you look at it, I guess." Essie lifted her narrow shoulders. "I could list a dozen horrid things that can happen to a dog when it's running loose. Sometimes an owner must choose the lesser of two evils."

Chapter Ten

"Now what, Richards?"

The question had stayed with Tanner all day as he drove his route on autopilot. He'd even delivered a package to the wrong address and had to go back and get it. But he couldn't concentrate. How the hell should he move forward in his relationship with Crystal?

As he worked, he was acutely aware of the gentle warmth of the sunlight, the musical birdsong, and the faint scent of wildflowers drifting on the breeze. Spring was a perfect time of year to fall in love, the season of new life and beginnings. Only, Crystal had made it clear she wasn't looking for marriage or even anything long-term.

He wanted to be fine with that. He had two kids and lived thirty minutes away in Crystal Falls. He owned a home there. Eventually, when he got his former delivery route back, he'd have the perfect job there again. Did he really want to move and jerk his kids out of the familiar world he and his mom had created for them? Maybe, if the children fell in love with Mystic Creek, he would consider it. But that was a big *if.* On the flip side, Crystal had a business here, and though they hadn't talked about it, he knew how many hours a person had to invest in an enterprise to make it a thriving operation. She'd be crazy to pull up stakes now. If she even could. Tuck owned a home in the area. As nice as the house was, it might not sell quickly. It wasn't exactly near the middle of town.

Tanner had always considered himself to be a modern-day guy. Open-minded. A liberal thinker in many ways, conservative in others, the kind of man who could live and let live and go with the flow. He made no moral judgments against people who engaged in sex outside of marriage. If people chose to live together without any official commitment, legal or spiritual, he had no problem with that, either. In fact, he'd always thought he could go for an arrangement like that himself if he didn't have kids.

But now that he'd looked a little deeper within himself, he knew he'd never be truly happy in a relationship that had no chance of going anywhere. What should he do with that recently acquired knowledge? He guessed there were men who could float along with a woman indefinitely, but he wasn't one of them. If he hadn't realized it before because it had never come up, he sure as hell knew it now.

So should he end things with Crystal? His mind rebelled at the thought. There was something really special about her. He felt it every time he was with her. And how did a guy end something with a woman when nothing had even *started* yet? Talk about putting the cart before the horse.

As he drove around one curve in the road past a field of placidly grazing Angus, and then eased the van into another sharp bend, he started to feel as if his thoughts were like the road. Hairpin turns of mental activity.

Toward the end of his shift, he pulled onto a shoulder by a line of mailboxes and rested his elbows on the steering wheel, propping his chin on his fists. Maybe he was a slow thinker, but he'd decided he couldn't just walk away from Crystal. He could settle for only attraction, friendship, and possibly a physical relationship for a while. Maybe she'd start to like him as much as he did her. Maybe she would even change her mind and decide she wanted a permanent relationship. And if that never came about, he'd tell her then that he needed something more.

After his last stop, he drove to Crystal's house. Actually, it was Tuck's property, but as long as the old man lived elsewhere, Tanner found it confusing to designate both places as his residences. He parked outside the hurricane fence, searched for Rip, jotted a note to Crystal, and hopped out of the van to slip it into the knothole of the oak tree.

As he walked back to the vehicle, he scanned the yard again and still saw no sign of the dog. The heeler was obviously at large again. Sooner or later, something bad would happen. People drove fast on these country roads, and Rip might get run over. Chasing livestock was a shooting offense in this area. Tanner didn't think Rip, raised on a ranch, was that dumb, but there was always a possibility. And what if the dog was making a pest of himself and some neighbor tossed him poison?

Tanner understood Crystal's reluctance to order a correction collar not meant for a dog Rip's size. Tuck had felt the same way when he lived in Crystal Falls. At some point, though, one of them would have to take the steps necessary to control the animal before he met a terrible end. Nothing else had worked. Getting shocked beat the hell out of being dead.

Crystal squinted against a glare of sunlight coming through the street window as she crimped a piece of foil over a strip of Megan's blond hair. Postprom, the girl had become a fan of wash-out streaks, and today she wanted red. Her mother sold real estate and apparently did well, because Megan was in here regularly and the services she wanted weren't cheap. Some girls did wash-out highlights at home with Kool-Aid. Crystal personally thought Megan was naturally pretty and needed no enhancements, but it wasn't her place to advise the teenager on her appearance.

A text notification chimed on Crystal's cell. Her hands in dye-stained gloves, she made a mental note to read the message as soon as she washed up. A few seconds later Nadine came in from the street, her arms encircling several white bags bearing the Jake 'n' Bake logo. Delicious scents accompanied her entrance.

"Uh-oh!" Shannon cried. "I smell something evil. My nose tells me doughnuts."

Nadine laughed. "Yes, the increasing waistlines are on me today."

"Who can I blame my saddlebags on?" Jules asked.

"Crystal. I can tell by looking at her that she hasn't been eating her share, which means you probably took up the slack."

Standing at the sink toward the back, Crystal smiled as she washed her hands and dried them. "I have broad shoulders. Go ahead and blame me." She drew her phone from its case and thumbed the screen. She saw that the incoming message was from Tanner. It read, *"Left you a message in the oak tree."*

Who could figure out men? Why did he bother with an actual note when he could have just texted her? On the other hand, it gave her something to look forward to when she got home, so she wouldn't overthink it. One eye on the wall clock, which heralded the approach of closing time, she returned to her station to check Megan's color. *Perfect.* Now she could do a quick style, run Megan's mother's credit card, and be finished for the day.

The instant the last customer and the other staff had left, Crystal dropped into a chair and wiggled her toes with a sigh of relief. The little one still felt tender, but the more sensible shoes had protected it from constant pressure. She felt tired, which she always did after a long day, but her legs didn't ache the way they normally did. *Maybe*, she thought, *I should stop wearing heels. Shorter wedge soles might deliver almost the same look and be just as comfortable as these old things I'm wearing.* Since Shannon had vacuumed the salon before leaving, all Crystal had to do was shut off the lights and lock the doors. She took care of it quickly and hurried out to the parking lot.

Gulping in the fresh air, a welcome change after breathing chemical fumes all day, she rolled the windows of the Equinox down for the drive home. She wanted to feel the spring breeze on her face. It had been a gorgeous day, and though it had cooled off slightly, it still wasn't frigid enough to give her a chill.

She scanned for Rip as soon as home came into view, but even after she parked and turned off the engine, she saw no dog. Her stomach knotted. Maybe Essie and Tanner both had it right, and it was time for Crystal to control the blue heeler with the lesser of two evils. She would talk to Tuck again, she guessed. Rip wasn't her dog, and it should be his owner who made decisions in regards to his welfare. Or was she just avoiding making the choice? Pushing it off on Tuck seemed wimpy. Then again, if she made the wrong call, Tuck might grow angry with her again, and she didn't want that.

She was almost to the gate when she remembered the message Tanner had left for her in the tree. Grinning, she made her way to the gnarly old oak.

The note was written on plain white paper, a torn-off piece with a jagged edge. It read, *"I just wanted to tell you how much I enjoyed being with you at the park and that I hope we can do something together again soon. It looks like you-know-who is gone again. I don't see him, anyway. Please get some rest tonight. An hour of driving the roads is more than most people would do. Put your feet up. Have a glass of wine. Hugs, Tanner."*

She smiled and pressed the note over her heart. In this modern day of electronic communication, leaving notes in a tree seemed silly. But it was also sweet and old-fashioned, romantic in a way that text messages weren't. She held the paper out again to study his masculine scrawl, which made the missive seem more personal. She touched a fingertip to his name. Caught by the breeze, the paper fluttered against her nail.

After entering the house, she gave No Name his hello scratches. She knew she was walking a fine line with the kitten, trying to hold back her feelings while still giving him the attention all babies needed. It wasn't easy not to love a creature so fluffy and cute. The kitten had no such reservations. He immediately began to ascend her pant leg and purred madly when she detached him. She distracted him with canned tuna while she looked for some paper to answer Tanner's note.

She pulled out Tuck's desk chair and nibbled at the tip of her pen. After a moment's thought, she wrote, *"Dear Tanner: I loved getting your note. It's more personal than a text. I enjoyed being with you, too, and I'll look forward to next time. Rip is still gone. I'll limit the time I search for him tonight. I truly do need some rest. I hope you have a fabulous evening with your kids. Hugs, Crystal."* She thought about stamping it with a lipstick kiss. But that would have been too corny. Maybe later, if he ever actually kissed her, she'd do that.

She carried the message to the tree and put it in the burl hole. As she turned back toward the house, Rip suddenly appeared in front of her. She started to scold him, but then it occurred to her that might have been one reason he kept running away, because every time he saw her she grumped at him.

Cupping her hands over her bent knees, she said his name and made gushy sounds. "How are you, sweet one? Have you had a good day?" She reached out to give him scratches behind the ears. He growled at her and bared his teeth. "Okay, fine." She straightened and studied him through narrowed eyes. "At least you're not falling over from exhaustion this time, and maybe I can try buying your love with food tonight. First, however, I need dog treats from the car so I can make my way into the house."

The next afternoon when Tanner stopped by Crystal's to leave a note in the tree for her, he found one that she'd left for him. He smiled as he read it. In the note he'd just left her, he'd asked her out on a date Friday night. His mom had agreed to watch the kids in exchange for getting a Saturday night free so she could socialize with friends. Sometimes she got stuck with Tori on weekend nights when Tanner was busy with one of Michael's activities. Normally, Tanner didn't leave Tori with her the whole evening, but he'd been guilty of picking the child up too late for Libby to make plans.

As Tanner headed north on Huckleberry, he felt a stab of guilt for burdening his mother. He knew she loved his children, and whenever he talked about hiring a sitter, she said no. But still. Libby was young enough to enjoy an active social life. Hell, she might even remarry if she had the time to date. Tanner couldn't easily afford to pay a sitter's wages, but in order to set his mom free, he could figure out a way.

He had just turned onto Dew Drop Lane, which lay

two roads north of the Mystic Creek town center, when he saw Rip running alongside the road. Tanner braked and pulled over.

"Rip!" he yelled as he leaped from the van.

If Rip heard Tanner, he paid him no mind. Tanner frowned. Was it Rip? Even as the crow flies, it was quite a distance to Crystal's house, a good mile and a half. Blue heelers were a popular breed with farmers and ranchers, and they tended to look alike. He could see the animal only from behind.

"Rip!" he hollered again.

The canine wheeled around and appeared to almost lose its balance. Then it ran across the bar ditch and disappeared into a field. Tanner shrugged it off as a case of mistaken identity and continued his route. Later as he drove back along the lane to Huckleberry, he noticed a seedy-looking tavern off to the right with a shingle, hanging crookedly from a porch overhang, that read WITCH'S BREW. Parched with thirst, Tanner decided a cola over ice sounded irresistible. He rarely bought coffee or other refreshments and he deserved a treat. He could get it in a to-go cup. He pulled over into the rutted gravel parking lot. Several older-model cars and pickups were parked in front of the establishment, which Tanner suspected was pretty much a dive. The odor of fried food and smoke canted from a ventilation shaft on the shake roof.

He had one foot on the running board of the van when he spotted, on the tavern porch with two men, the dog he'd seen earlier. Not Rip, then. The men entered the building, followed closely by the heeler. Something in the way the animal moved caught his attention, though. If that wasn't Rip, it was his twin brother.

A bad feeling slipped under Tanner's ribs. Way back before Tuck got hurt, he'd referred to Rip as his drinking buddy a few times. Tanner hadn't taken the old man seriously. He knew how much Tuck loved the dog, and everyone knew alcohol was bad for canines. Right? The feeling in Tanner's middle grew weightier. Just because *he* knew something didn't necessarily mean it was common knowledge. Tanner felt certain Tuck would never deliberately do anything to harm Rip, but what if he didn't know any better?

Tanner stared out the dusty windshield. He distinctly recalled Crystal saying that Rip often didn't get home until three in the morning. In Oregon, all bars had to be closed by two thirty. Last call was normally around two. If a dog left the Witch's Brew at last call, it could cover the distance to Crystal's place in an hour. The timing was right.

"Shit." Tanner wanted to shove his suspicions aside. But he couldn't do that. *"Damn!"*

He strode over the graveled ground to the steps at one end of the ramshackle porch, took them in two jumps, and thumped his way along the rickety boardwalk to the double doors. As he stepped inside, shadows obscured his vision. He waited a second for his eyes to adjust.

The bar looked like any other Tanner had seen, but even in the dim lighting he could tell the wall hangings were yellowed and covered with dust. The floor was buried under a thick layer of peanut shells. An old man stood behind the serving bench. He wore a checkered shirt smeared with ketchup across the front. All the hair once atop his head seemed to have traveled south, leaving him with a white beard, bushy sideburns, wild eyebrows, and a ring of gray just above the nape of his neck.

"Wantin' a cold one?" he asked Tanner. "I imagine it gets hot in them Courier Express rigs. Prob'ly no air conditioner."

Tanner approached the bar and swung onto a stool. "I need to wet my whistle. Do you serve cola?"

The bartender laughed. "Not happily. That shit'll rust your pipes."

Tanner slipped a fiver from his wallet and laid it on the counter. "I just dropped in to see if you've seen a dog around here."

Someone at the other end of the bar snorted. The bartender apparently saw no humor in the question and said, "Just ran out the back door. Maybe he heard you on the porch. You the owner of that little son bitch?"

Tanner's stomach clenched. "No, but it may belong to my friend. I know it's a blue heeler, but does it have any special markings?"

"Not that I've noticed. And if your friend owns the little bastard, he owes me money. Son bitch kept sneaking into my beer cooler and making free with my Pabst Blue Ribbon. Punctured the cans with a canine tooth and sucked 'em dry. One evenin' he went through a half rack. I have to lock my cooler door now so I don't go broke."

Pabst Blue Ribbon. It was Tuck's preferred brand. Maybe over time it had become Rip's as well. Tanner hadn't wanted to believe Tuck gave his dog beer. But no matter how he circled the facts he'd gathered so far, his suspicions seemed to be correct.

"If I leave you my cell number, will you call me if the dog comes back?"

The bartender shook his head. "Nope. He's gotten to be popular with my customers, kinda like a mascot. The boys buy his rounds now, so his drinkin' habit isn't on me. If I call you, I have a feelin' we won't be seein' no more of the dog."

Tanner tried for patience. "What you don't seem to understand, sir, is that beer is poisonous to dogs."

A fat guy who sat at the curved corner of the bar with a ball cap pulled low over his scraggly blond hair took exception to that. "Bullshit! He's guzzled a shit-load of beer at this bar. Ain't hurt him none yet."

Another man of equal bulk shoved back his barstool and stood up. Tanner knew he could hold his own against any one fellow in the building, possibly against two, but the last thing he needed was to get arrested during his shift for engaging in a barroom brawl. Mac would fire him for sure. Tanner stood and held up his hands. "I didn't come here for trouble, boys. Like I said, I think the dog belongs to my friend. I'm just trying to look out for it."

"Well," the big guy said, "look out for it on the road. We watch each other's backs in this place, and Guzzler is our friend. We cover him for a few beers when he pushes through the doors. We're just being friendly, and now you're saying we're poisoning him. Next thing we know, you'll have PETA breathing down our necks for animal abuse."

"I didn't come here for trouble, either, Bobby," another man said. "Just leave it alone. If I go home with another shiner, Cheryl will divorce me."

The bartender sent his regular customers a warning glare. "No more fightin' in my joint. Last time you threw barstools through my windows, and not a damned one of you coughed up a dime to pay for damages."

"You got insurance!" Bobby cried.

"With a high deductible." The bartender stretched out a beefy arm. As Tanner shook hands with him, the older man said, "I don't answer to sir. Name's JJ. There's no way of knowin' if Guzzler is your friend's pet. And I ain't the dog police. You wanna park out there and watch for him, have at it. But I won't turn the little beggar in, not to you or anybody. Unless, of course, he gets in my cooler again and shaves twenty bucks off my day's profit by guzzlin' my PBR. Then I might call the law, or shoot him, one."

"My name is Tanner Richards, JJ, and please, no matter what, don't shoot the dog. I'll personally cover any losses you have incurred because of him."

JJ's eyes narrowed. "A hundred would make us even."

A hundred? Tanner drew out his wallet. How much beer could a dog possibly consume? He laid three twenties and a ten spot on the counter. "That's all I've got on me. I'll bring the other thirty tomorrow." He met the bartender's calculating gaze. "My friend's old, and it'd break his heart if anything happened to that heeler. The dog's name is Rip. He has a home, and he's deeply loved." Tanner grabbed a pen from his shirt pocket to dash down his name and number on a bar napkin. "Please, just call me."

As Tanner left the tavern he saw JJ toss the napkin in the trash. Once in the vehicle again, Tanner scanned the immediate area for Rip. Why he bothered, he didn't know. If Rip had caught his scent or seen him pass by one of the windows, he was too smart to hang around. Tanner tried to think what he should do. He could go straight to Tuck, but he didn't want to upset his elderly friend, and he'd also be circumventing Crystal's authority as Rip's caregiver. She deserved to be the first to know what Tanner suspected, and she could decide how to handle the situation.

Rip continued to escape from the fenced acreage for the rest of the week, and Crystal was once again pacing the floors on Friday night when Tanner showed up for their date. He arrived carrying two bottles of wine in the crook of one arm, and a six-pack of PBR was clutched in his other hand.

"I'm wearing clothes this time," he said when she opened the door, "but I did bring the beer. PBR just in case it's your favorite, too."

As worried as she was about her grandfather's missing dog, Crystal laughed and opened the door wider. "Just my luck to get the beer and not the naked guy."

He walked past her to place his burden on Tuck's table. "Dinner's in my pickup. I, um, had some unexpected expenses this week, so I cooked. We'll need to reheat the meatballs. Extra-large Italian ones that simmered all day in homemade sauce. We'll have to cook the pasta. It's never as good heated up. I brought grated Parmesan and crusty bread, already buttered, that I hope we can brown in your oven. And a green salad I made from scratch." He gave her a sheepish look. "I'm sorry, Crystal. A man appreciates it when a woman's a cheap date, but I know the same isn't true in reverse."

She'd dressed up, and so had he. He wore gray slacks and a black sport jacket over a pressed pinstripe shirt with an Ivy League collar. All she could think to say was "Does this mean I can take off the high heels? My little toe is killing me."

He laughed and turned to regard her shoes. "Please, take them off. They're sexy, I have to admit, but they're a little much for a casual dinner at home."

Crystal stowed the beer in the fridge while he ran back out to his truck for dinner. She set the red wine on the counter, opened one bottle to let it breathe, and was barefoot by the time he reappeared. He came up beside her to place their dinner on the bar. Then, without trying to pretend he wasn't, he took in her little black dress with spaghetti straps, his gaze lingering everywhere that made a woman feel desirable.

"You're beautiful."

The compliment touched her. Being tall and slender

with bright red hair and a face that didn't make babies cry, she knew she was striking. But *beautiful*? She had a miniature version of Tuck's sharply bridged nose; her grandmother's complexion, given to freckles; and hazel eyes that could look green one moment and brown the next. But nothing about her was spectacular. And on top of that, she didn't have big boobs.

"Thank you." She couldn't think of a better way to respond. "Beer or wine?"

"Wine. Believe it or not, I sprang for some nice merlot."

From the cupboard Crystal drew goblets, wide-mouthed with large bowls for a red. After she poured and offered him a glass, he rolled the goblet between his palms and stared through its curvature. "Nice legs." Then he settled a twinkling blue gaze on her and said, "Yours, not the wine's. Although it has nice legs, too."

He drew off his jacket and tossed it over the back of the chair that had brutalized her toe. Then he plugged in the Crock-Pot, found a large spoon to turn the sauce and meatballs, and joined her on the sofa. "I hope you like my recipe for Italian meatballs. I got it at an amazing Chicago restaurant. Little hole-in-the-wall place, tucked in between a bunch of small stores and delis. The owner jotted it down for me, and I've been making it ever since." He kissed the tips of his fingers. "The secret is in the spices and simmering the sauce for hours. What a nice man. He and his wife didn't offer a wide menu, but every dish was superb."

"What were you doing in Chicago?" Tuck had taken Crystal to Jamaica once when she was a teen, Hawaii another time, but otherwise she hadn't traveled much. "I've never been there."

"Business trip," he said. "Before Carolyn died, I owned a large accounting firm." He grinned at her.

"Large for southern Oregon, anyway. I had some important clients." He sighed. "Those were the days. Plenty of money. Tailored suits. BMWs. A gorgeous house. And then Carolyn's fancy little car went under a semitruck."

She wasn't sure how to respond. "I'm so sorry."

"Yeah." He turned his wine and gazed into the burgundy depths. "But I grew as a person. I realized I couldn't be a good father when I was stretched so thin professionally. I sold my firm and downsized so I could focus on my kids. I don't look back with any regrets. I think I made the right choice."

"I'm sure you did."

"Except that I'm broke." He winked at her. "Not really, of course, but living on a budget. Life is strange. Back then I worried about where to get my suits made. Now I worry about which baseball cleats will support my son's feet, give him good traction, and wear the longest."

Crystal nodded. In simple ways, Tanner was trying to convey to her who he was: no longer a successful businessman, but a single dad juggling expenses to provide his kids with the best life he could.

He reached over and touched his glass against hers. "No sailing on a catamaran with me. It's rowing all the way upstream."

A few minutes later Crystal helped him finish preparing dinner and was impressed by how easily they worked in tandem. "Hey, we may not be on a catamaran, but we sail right along in a kitchen."

He laughed and held a spoon to her lips. "The sauce. Don't be nice. Tell me the truth."

Crystal closed her eyes as she savored the taste. "Oh, my *goodness*. *That* is amazing."

When they sat down to eat, Crystal decided dinner was beyond fabulous. The meatballs practically melted in her mouth. The sauce had a perfect blend of spices and just a touch of sweetness that held at bay the acidic taste she disliked in many marinara sauces. "Oh, Tanner. I want this recipe. *Please?*"

"Sorry. It's a family recipe. Top secret."

"*Nuh-uh!* You said it came from Chicago."

"I lied. My last name, Richards, is an Americanized version of Riccardo."

Crystal studied his handsome face. "Your eyes are turning brown."

He burst out laughing. "Of course I'll share the recipe with you."

Together they tidied the kitchen and packed up all his dishes. After refilling their wineglasses, they headed toward the love seat. Once reclined beside each other, they leaned back and elevated their feet on her coffee table.

"Where's Rip?" he asked.

"Gone again. I know it's mean of me, but I think he particularly enjoys interrupting my sleep on Friday night. Saturday is my longest day."

"Crystal, I need to tell you something about Rip."

She felt the sudden tension in him. "Okay, go ahead."

He sighed. "I don't think Rip's deliberately trying to make you lose sleep tonight. A lot of people have Saturdays off and party until the bars close on Friday nights."

Crystal stared at him. "What does that have to do with Rip?"

"I think he may be at a bar."

Tanner wished, not for the first time, that he knew how to ease his way into difficult conversations. Crystal looked like someone who'd just been shocked with a stun gun, her eyes wide with startled incredulity, her lips slightly parted, and no discernible expression on the rest of her face.

"Pardon me?" she finally said. "Run that by me again."

Tanner launched into an account of seeing a blue heeler he believed to be Rip running along the shoulder of Dew Drop Lane. "I went inside the Witch's Brew to inquire about the dog. Back when Tuck still lived in Crystal Falls, he referred to Rip as his drinking buddy a few times when I stopped to chat with him."

"He's only joking when he says that! Tuck would *never* give that dog beer. I'm offended that you're suggesting he would."

"I'm not trying to offend anybody. But listen. Tuck was a rancher. He lived out in the back of beyond. He's told me stories about going to some bar called Smokey's, if I remember right. Before Tuck got hurt, he took Rip everywhere with him. Do you honestly think he never took Rip to Smokey's?"

"It's a country bar. Of course he may have taken Rip there. But that doesn't mean he ever let Rip have beer. The lady who owns the place is a nice woman, an animal lover. I've known her over half my life. Nora would never allow Tuck or anyone else to give a dog alcohol."

"Last call for drinks in Oregon bars is around two o'clock. If Rip leaves the Witch's Brew when the drinks stop flowing, he could get back home in an hour. You've told me he gets back here at around three. Do the math."

Crystal pushed to her feet and raked a slender hand through her long hair. Tanner had been hoping that he might get a chance to run his fingers through it tonight. But now she was pissed. "There could be other explanations."

"Sure, there could. But I think we need to check this out." He glanced at his watch. "It's still fairly early. I could visit the bar to see if Rip is there."

"If I agreed to let you do that, I'd be accepting your slant on everything—namely that my grandfather, a wonderful man who's never been cruel to an animal his entire life, has abused his dog!" Ice coated her every word.

Tanner sat forward on the cushion and put his wineglass on the coffee table. "Okay. It's still early enough for Tuck to be awake. How about we drive to the center and just ask him if he ever let Rip taste beer?" He held her gaze. "Asking him that isn't the same as asking if he let Rip drink a whole beer or even part of one. You're taking this all wrong. I'm not saying I think Tuck deliberately did something to hurt his dog. What I'm saying is that Tuck may not *know* beer is bad for Rip."

"How could he *not* know? I know it. You know it. Nadine knows it." An odd expression crept over her face. "Oh, my God, Nadine. She went barhopping last Friday night and they ended the evening at the Witch's Brew. She told me about some crazy guy who had his dog sitting at the bar as if it were a human, and men were buying it beer."

Tanner swallowed. "Was Rip gone last Friday night?"

Her arm jerked and she slopped wine over the edge of her glass onto the floor. "Damn it." She hurried to the kitchen to get a wet cloth. "That'll stain the wood."

Tanner waited until she'd cleaned up the mess. Then he repeated the question. She remained hunkered down, supporting her posterior on the heels of her bare feet. "Yes," she admitted.

"Did he come home around three?"

She bent her head so her hair formed a long curtain at each side of her face. "Yes. Are you satisfied? *Yes.*"

"Please don't make me the bad guy in this, Crystal. You know how fond I am of your grandfather. He's a great guy. All I'm saying is, he's old. What's common knowledge to people of our generation may not be common knowledge to everyone in his. Maybe Tuck has no idea beer is bad for dogs. I'll bet if we took a survey, some people, regardless of age, would know and some people wouldn't."

She finally lifted her head. "You're right. I need to talk with Tuck."

"You mind if I go along?"

She sighed and finally smiled. "No, of course not."

Chapter Eleven

They decided to take Crystal's car. She was so upset that Tanner drove, and she said not a word. Tanner suspected that they were each occupied with their own thoughts.

The first thing they saw when they entered the retirement center was the large form of Patricia Flintlock at the front desk, looming over Marsha and chewing her out about something. When the old biddy saw Crystal, her mouth drew into a tight line.

"You're arriving rather late for a visit," she said.

"It's only eight," Crystal reminded her, her voice cool but polite.

"Be gone by ten." Her tone was the same as she might have used to order a stray dog away from a trash can.

Tanner didn't know if he wanted Crystal to stand her ground or run like a scalded cat. She was already upset, and another round of verbal sparring would only unsettle her more.

"I'm sorry?" Crystal said. "Your rules say visiting hours in the community areas end at ten, but Tuck and any other resident can have guests later than that in an apartment. Someone can even stay all night."

"I've changed the rules."

Crystal straightened her shoulders. Tanner felt proud

of her, although when he considered that, it seemed silly. He'd played no part in raising Crystal to become a strong woman who would dig in and fight for her grandfather's rights. Yet he still wanted to pat her on the back. She'd make a wonderful mother, the kind who would go to bat for her kids without hesitation.

"If so, I haven't seen that in writing. You can change the rules anytime you wish as long as you abide by Oregon law," Crystal replied. "Shall I call Tuck's attorney to see if you've a right to change the in-apartment visiting hours?"

Patricia pivoted on her heel and all but stomped away. Tanner suspected the woman was trying to look regal, but instead she came off as pathetic. He whispered to Crystal, "What's she do, swallow an ugly pill every morning?"

Crystal grimaced. "Maybe she was just born with a nasty disposition. The corporation that owns this facility should screen their employees better."

They walked up the hall to Tuck's apartment. Crystal tapped on the door, then cracked it open. "You at home, Tuck?"

"Sure am," the old man called back. "Come on in."

When they stepped inside, Tanner was surprised to see a woman sitting beside Tuck on the brown sofa. She was a pretty lady with dark hair and brown eyes. Tanner thought she exuded elegance in a black skirt and a jacket over a red blouse. A gold necklace twinkled where it draped down from under her collar. Diamonds flashed on her fingers.

"Essie, this is our friend Tanner Richards," Crystal said. "Tanner, this is Essie, Tuck's new friend."

Essie stood to shake Tanner's hand. Despite the ravages of arthritis in her knuckles, she had a firm grip.

The thought flitted through his mind that she'd be a force to be reckoned with in a board meeting.

"I'm pleased to make your acquaintance, Tanner. My last name is Maxwell Childers. Unhyphenated. When Crystal and I were introduced, I don't think Tuck told her my surname."

Tanner liked this woman. She had a direct, no-nonsense air, and she possessed a commanding presence.

"Have a seat, you two." Tuck didn't stand, and Tanner didn't blame him. The up-and-down business probably bothered his hip. "It's good to see you both. Would you like a drink? Crystal knows where everything is."

Tanner decided that accepting a beer might assist Crystal in easing her way into a conversation with her grandfather about the same beverage. Crystal went to the kitchen area and returned with two glasses, one for him and one for herself. He grabbed a chair from under the table and dragged it over the carpet. Crystal took the recliner so the four of them could sit in a semi-circle.

She tugged at her dress hem as she sat down. Then she tasted the lager. "Mmm, good," she said before glancing over at Tanner. "Tuck used to let me have sips when I was growing up. I developed a liking for it."

"I like it, too."

Crystal smiled at her grandfather. "Did you ever let Rip have tastes of your PBR, Tuck?"

The old man got an odd look on his face. "Why do you ask?"

Crystal met her grandfather's gaze. "Why are you evading the question?"

"Yes," Tuck admitted. "I've let him taste it."

"How often?" Crystal pressed.

"Pretty often. He likes it and I feel guilty if I don't give him some."

She closed her eyes for a moment. As her lashes lifted, she said, "Oh, Tuck. Didn't anyone ever tell you that alcohol is bad for dogs?"

"Alcohol, maybe. But beer and wine won't hurt them. Rip's livin' proof."

The color drained from Crystal's face. "Beer and wine are alcoholic."

"I know, but not like hard liquor."

Essie touched Tuck's shirtsleeve. "It's *all* bad for dogs, Tuck. Especially beer, I believe. I think I heard or read that hops are poisonous to them."

Tuck looked genuinely appalled. "You sure? But Rip's been drinkin' beer since he was a puppy. It's never hurt him a bit."

Crystal set her glass on the small end table. "Oh, Tuck. How much did you let Rip drink?"

"Never more than two."

"Two beers, one after another?" Crystal's voice rang with dismay. "Dear Lord, it's a wonder he's not dead."

Tuck's expression grew defiant. "Don't go makin' a big deal out of nothin'. It never hurt him, I'm tellin' you. I was alone after you left. Rip was my drinkin' buddy and kept me company in the evenin'."

"I know how much you love him, Tuck," Crystal said softly. "And I know you'd never deliberately hurt Rip. But you should have at *least* asked a vet if it was okay."

Tuck looked at Essie. "Is it really bad for dogs?" He gave Essie a brief account of how he'd rescued Rip and taken him to Smokey's to get him warm and feed him something. "An old friend of mine gave that puppy beer while I was outside takin' care of my horse. The other ranchers in the bar said it wouldn't hurt him none, that they'd known dogs that drank beer and wine every day and lived to ripe old ages. I've always believed that the beer Rip got that night might've saved his life."

Essie shifted on the cushion. Tanner wondered if she felt uncomfortable. "I'm afraid they were wrong, Tuck. Alcohol is bad for dogs."

"But *why*? We're all mammals, and humans drink it."

Essie patted Tuck's hand. "I'm not sure of the scientific reasons. And I can see your point. We are all mammals. Perhaps it's because dogs are, for the most part, littler than we are, and what seems like a small amount of alcohol to us is a huge amount for them."

Crystal inserted, "I'm not sure of the reasons, either, Tuck, but—"

"Well," Tuck said, cutting across her, "if you don't know, then *why* are you here ridin' my ass about it?"

"I'm here because Tanner has cause to believe Rip is at a bar right now."

Tanner wanted to shift on his chair like Essie just had. There was a shrill edge in Crystal's voice.

"What?" Tuck looked amazed. "Why would Rip go to a bar without me?"

"To get his beer fix, possibly?" Crystal replied. "I can't believe you weren't aware that beer is bad for dogs. How can anyone live in our modern-day world without ever hearing that?"

Tanner knew Crystal regretted those words as soon as she uttered them. She visibly winced.

"I'm sorry. That didn't come out right, Tuck. I'm not saying that you're not telling the truth. It's just incredible that . . ." Her voice trailed off, and she sent Tanner a pleading look.

"It's just that we're younger," Tanner inserted. "We're on the Internet. We're always looking stuff up. What seems like common knowledge to us apparently isn't common knowledge to everyone."

Tuck sighed and ran a hand over his gray hair.

"Maybe Rip's just lucky. Beer and wine have never made him the least bit sick."

"So far as you know," Essie said. "Blood tests may reveal physical ramifications that aren't obvious."

Crystal took several large swallows from her glass. Tanner realized he'd set his on the table behind him and forgotten all about it. "Did you take Rip to Smokey's and let him drink at the bar?" she asked her grandfather.

Tuck hunched his shoulders. "Now you're makin' me feel like a good-for-nothin' person."

With a sigh, Crystal shook her head. "I'm not trying to make you feel bad, Tuck. I'm just trying to understand our dog. *Your* dog, I mean."

Tanner knew that was a Freudian slip if ever he'd heard one. For reasons he couldn't understand, Crystal didn't want to love Rip or the kitten. She acted as if the thought of loving something frightened her. He didn't get it. She obviously cared about her grandfather's dog. No one else in the room was as upset about Rip drinking beer as she was.

"Yes," Tuck admitted. "I let him drink beer at Smokey's. He sat at the bar. I didn't even have to lift him onto a stool. He jumped up by himself. And he learned real quick how to drink from a glass. Held it between his paws and tipped it toward him when his tongue couldn't reach."

Crystal met Tanner's gaze. Then she looked at Tuck. "It'll be okay," she told her grandfather.

"'Course it'll be okay. Beer don't hurt Rip, I'm tellin' you. Not even Nora got upset when I let him drink with us at Smokey's. And she's a stand-up gal when it comes to animals. You know that. She'd have cracked one of us men over the head with a bottle if she'd thought we was hurtin' that dog."

* * *

After leaving the facility, Tanner drove back to Crystal's to see if Rip had come home. He didn't want to make an unnecessary trip to the Witch's Brew, especially not with Crystal accompanying him. It was a seedy establishment. JJ seemed like a nice enough fellow, but his patrons were lowlifes. If they'd thrown barstools through JJ's windows, they were also scrappers who enjoyed a fight. Tanner didn't want Crystal anywhere near that place, particularly not when she was upset and worried about Rip. If she found the dog drinking alcohol, she might go ballistic.

As luck had it, the dog was sitting on the front porch when Tanner pulled in. The car's headlights washed over the front of the house, illuminating Rip for an instant.

"He's home," Crystal noted. "Now what? If he's been at the bar drinking beer, should I take him to see Jack Palmer? I'm sure he'd meet me at the clinic."

Tanner opened the driver's door, and the dome light came on, revealing the pallor of her face. She adamantly refused to admit that she loved Rip, but the actual truth was obvious. "I think he's done just fine thus far without going to see a vet, so I believe it's safe not to take him in tonight. It's after hours, it'll be far more expensive than a daytime visit, and he'll wake up tomorrow with nothing worse than a slight hangover."

"What if he has liver damage?"

"Then he does, and it won't get any worse overnight. Jack can check for that tomorrow." He reached into the door well for dog treats. "What's done is done. You can't turn back the clock."

After they exited the vehicle, Tanner met her at the front of the car, took her arm, and guided her toward the gate. Rip came to meet them. Tanner, being out of uniform, didn't have to pay a toll to get in the yard, but he handed Crystal a biscuit so she could.

"Well," he said, "you look none the worse for having another adventure, Rip." The dog bounced around Tanner's legs, apparently fine, but Tanner noticed that his coordination was a little off. "And I think it's safe to say you got your nose wet." He sent Crystal a questioning look. "I wonder why he's home so soon. The Witch's Brew will be open for hours yet."

"Maybe that isn't where Rip has been going," Crystal suggested, her tone hopeful.

Drawing his phone from his pocket, Tanner searched online for the bar's phone number and called the place.

JJ answered, his voice a boom of sound. "*Huh-low!* This is JJ."

"Hi, JJ. This is Tanner Richards, the Courier Express driver who came in earlier this week to ask about the blue heeler."

"I remember you, but I ain't got time to talk. Had a kitchen fire."

"Uh-oh. Sorry to hear that."

"Not too bad, but a lot of cleanup. Smoke was so thick I had to close early."

Tanner ended the conversation and told Crystal about the kitchen fire. "That's why Rip's home early. The party ended."

At the porch, Rip received another treat, and yet another before they entered the house. *Crazy dog.*

Crystal flung her shawl over a chair. She stared down at Rip with a look of utter helplessness. "I don't know what to do."

Tanner curled an arm around her shoulders. Her bare skin felt icy beneath his palm. "I think the most important thing you can do for Rip right now is to buy a collar with enough strength to keep him at home. If he's drinking beer, it's going to harm him sooner or later. Tuck doesn't really get that, but you and I do."

She nodded. "It just seems so cruel to shock him to a point that it hurts."

Tanner caught her chin on his bent finger and lifted her face. "Did Tuck have a dog on his ranch when you lived with him?"

"Yes, Tabasco." She smiled slightly. "He was a great dog, half Australian shepherd and as sharp as a tack."

"Did Tabasco ever get shocked by an electric fence?"

"Most dogs that are around electric fencing get shocked occasionally. So do humans."

"Was Tabasco seriously hurt when he got shocked?"

"No, but he cried. It really does hurt."

He led her over to the kitchen desk and eased her down on the chair. "I know. I've gotten shocked a couple of times myself. It's unpleasant." He drew a dining room chair over to sit beside her. "My point is that Tabasco didn't die from getting zapped by an electric fence, and the biggest, strongest electronic collar can't be any worse than the current running through livestock wire. It's to keep cows and horses in, Crystal. Compared to a dog, they're huge animals."

"Yes." She sounded as if she felt numb. "I get what you're saying."

"Do you? You have to get this situation into the proper perspective. Every time Rip gets out and runs loose, he's in danger. He could be struck by a car. Would it be humane to let that happen? He could be shot by a rancher if he appears to be chasing livestock. Would that be humane? Death from poisoning is horrible as well. You have it in your power to prevent any of that from happening." When she still didn't look convinced, he added, "If Rip continues to get out of the yard, think of all the puppies he may sire. It's awful to let puppies be born into a world where they may not find homes."

"What?" She looked so dismayed that Tanner knew he'd just waylaid her. "Puppies? What are you saying?"

He got a sick feeling in the pit of his stomach. She didn't know, he realized. How she'd never noticed that Rip was still packing, he had no idea.

"Crystal, Tuck never got Rip neutered."

She scrunched her shoulders, made fists on her lap, and leaned forward as if violent cramps had just assailed her stomach. "What?" She practically shouted the question. "Why on earth *not*?"

"I can only tell you what Tuck told me. What kind of a friend takes his best buddy to the vet and has his balls cut off? No more sex, ever. All his testosterone *gone*. I tried to tell Tuck that Rip's propensity for getting loose made him a poor candidate for being left intact, but you know how Tuck can be when he has his mind set."

"Oh, dear God." Crystal leaped up and walked over to where Rip slept on his bed, belly up and legs sprawled. "How did I never notice that he has *balls*? I mean, hello. He shows them off every time he sleeps." She lifted her hands in a gesture of appeal and turned to look at Tanner. "I suppose I just assumed he was neutered. What was Tuck *thinking*? How many times has Rip escaped when he smelled a female dog in heat?"

Tanner couldn't think of a thing to say in Tuck's defense except, "He's an old man, Crystal. He has funny ideas."

"Funny? Unwanted puppies are *not* funny! I'm taking Rip to the vet tomorrow, all right, and I'm making an appointment to get him fixed!"

Tanner sighed. "I don't want to see you destroy your

relationship with your grandfather over neutering his dog. Rip is a purebred. Lots of people keep a good stud intact."

"There are many people out there that disapprove of breeding even purebred dogs. They feel that everyone should adopt a dog from a shelter and stop adding to the canine population."

"I'm not saying I disagree with that school of thought," Tanner told her. "This isn't about you or me, though. It's about Tuck and *his* school of thought. Keeping Rip intact is accompanied by a responsibility to make sure he's always kept at home." He lifted his hands. "Until Tuck comes around to the idea that Rip should be fixed, how can you make sure Rip never has an opportunity to impregnate a female?"

"A strong collar, one that will carry such a wallop that Rip can't withstand the shocks for thirty seconds in order to defeat it." She marched back over to the desk and sat down. "I should have listened to you from the start. A strong shock won't really harm Rip. Not any more than making a connection with an electric fence would. I'm sure he's lived through that and also developed a healthy respect for live wires." She moved her computer mouse to bring up a Google search. "I want a correction collar strong enough to stop a mastiff."

After the collars were ordered, Crystal sat on the sofa beside Tanner again. She felt drained, and her thoughts were muddled by stress. He poured them each a goblet of red wine. It seemed like a small eternity had passed since they had enjoyed dinner.

They talked for a while about Rip's future. Crystal needed to have Jack Palmer examine the dog and run blood work. Until the new collars came, she would take Rip outside only when he was leashed.

Crystal began to feel better. Tanner had helped her to verbally outline a plan. She was taking control. Rip would never be able to run away again.

"I can barely wait until Tuesday morning when the new collars are charged," she told him.

Tanner turned his glass, studying the purplish red liquid as it swirled across the sides. "I can deliver the collars to the salon on Monday morning, just like I did this week. That way you can get one of them charged, and you can put it in him Monday night. I'll come over and help."

"I've learned never to leave Rip in the house while I'm gone. Except for when he sleeps, he likes to be outside. He gets destructive if I leave him alone. Separation anxiety, maybe."

"The laundry room, then. Lock him in there. If he does damage, I can repair it."

She sighed. "I feel better. Thank you for talking about everything with me."

"You're more than welcome."

He shifted to turn toward her and set his goblet on the table. Then he pried hers from her grasp. She knew by the intent expression on his face that he intended to kiss her. She wasn't surprised. Their evening together had started out on a lovely note. The meal had been superb. Even though a lot of upsets had occurred since then, it seemed right to end the night with a romantic gesture. She had only one concern.

"Tanner, if we do this— Well, I think you know how attracted I am to you."

"No more than I am to you."

"What if things get out of hand?"

He smiled down at her and then slipped his fingers into her hair. Feeling the heat of his palm against her scalp was almost her undoing. She didn't know how a simple touch could seem so incredibly sexy, but it did. "Then I'll be a very happy man," he whispered.

He bent his head. She felt his breath waft over her lips, which she parted slightly in anticipation. *And welcome.* Then he slanted his mouth over hers. He took control, tracing her lips with the tip of his tongue and then delving deeper. She moaned in pleasure. She felt as if bubbles were bouncing in her chest again. Her breathing became quick and shallow. Her body felt electrified. She wrapped both arms around his neck, pressed herself against him, and kissed him back with urgent need, demand, and an underlying feeling of awe. Never had she felt like this with a man.

He broke contact to catch her bottom lip lightly between his teeth, a teasing titillation that made her wish he were giving other parts of her body the same attention. Her nipples went rock-hard and ached as his chest grazed their tips.

"Aw, Crystal," he murmured huskily. "I knew it would be like this. I just never thought I'd be lucky enough—" He broke off to trail tantalizing kisses across her cheek and then that sensitive place below her earlobe. Every erogenous zone in her body felt as if it had ignited. "Dear God, you are so sweet," he whispered, his voice deep and husky with desire.

Crystal felt as if she'd been caught in a whirlwind—a leaf helplessly drawn into a cyclonic spiral, too light to be anchored by gravity, too insubstantial to resist the pull.

And then, as if some invisible hand had jerked Tanner away from her, he was gone. She blinked, so confused and dizzy headed that she couldn't figure out what had happened.

"Rip! Damn it, dog!"

Crystal sprang to her feet, and saw Rip charging toward his bed with his jaws clamped over the mouth of Tanner's wineglass. She couldn't believe her eyes. For one thing, it was a wide goblet, but the dog had somehow managed to grab it. Just as he reached his bed, he tipped his head back and his whole body jerked as he swallowed. Tanner was hot on Rip's heels, but by the time he reached the cushion, Rip had downed all the wine and released the goblet, which rolled on the wood floor.

Crystal ran over. "What on *earth*?"

"He stole my wine." Tanner's hair stuck up in all directions, and his shirt was partially unbuttoned. "He *stole* it. I can't believe how fast he moved!" He planted his hands on his hips. "Damn it. Talk about a rude interruption. I think the little bastard watched us and chose his moment."

Just then Rip lunged off the bed, cutting a generous berth around them as he ran back for the couch.

"Rip!" Crystal shrieked.

"Rip!" Tanner bellowed.

But the dog kept going. With the agility common in cattle dogs, he leaped up onto the coffee table, pushed his mouth over the top of Crystal's goblet, jumped to the floor, and ran with his head tilted back, gulping down the merlot as he darted this way and that to avoid their reaching hands. When the wine was gone, he dropped the glass, looked up at Crystal with that up-yours grin that she'd come to know so well, and belched. A huge, long, disrespectful expulsion that she felt certain had her name on it somewhere.

"*Why* does he hate me so much?" She knew it was bad timing for the question. "I try so hard to make him like me. Nothing works. It's like he has a vendetta against me."

Tanner sighed. He still looked disheveled, and Crystal could only wonder if she had messed up his hair and nearly stripped his shirt off him. She couldn't remember doing that.

"I think we have a greater worry," he said, his voice deep and edged with masculine frustration.

"What's that?"

"I'm afraid Rip's an alcoholic."

"Can dogs actually become alcoholics?"

He shrugged. "If Tuck were here, he'd say, 'They're mammals, ain't they?'"

Sitting on the couch again, Crystal fixed her gaze on a stool under the lip of the breakfast bar. She didn't know what Tanner was staring at. She knew only that Rip had destroyed their romantic moment with such force that her desire felt as if it had been obliterated by a bomb. She had a feeling Tanner had lost his enthusiasm as well. Rip had ruined their entire evening.

"What do you do if a dog is an alcoholic?" she whispered.

Tanner started buttoning his shirt. "Beats the hell out of me. I don't think a twelve-step program will work. Counseling, maybe? Shit. I can't believe I said that. Enforced abstinence is the only solution. If I'm right about alcohol addiction, maybe Jack can give him medication of some kind."

"I can't believe he drank our wine."

"We have another bottle."

She sighed. "No, I'm fine. Let's save it for next time."

He turned to look at her. "Will we have a next time,

Crystal? I blew the first half of the evening by telling you my suspicions about Rip. Rip blew the last half. I'm not clear on why you'd even want to see me again after two miserable dates in a row."

"The first date was *not* miserable. I had a great time. And it's not your fault that Tuck let Rip drink. That's on Tuck."

"True, but I still feel lousy about it. We didn't have much of a date."

"Please, don't. Feel lousy, I mean." She reached over to smooth his hair. It resisted her fingertips and poked back up. Maybe her hands had been damp when she ran them through it. He looked as if he'd stuck his finger in a light socket. Somehow, though, he was still too handsome for words. "That kiss was pretty darned great in my books. An *almost* thing, a promise of things to come."

He sighed. "Thanks for saying that. I agree that the *almost* part was pretty awesome. If it hadn't been for the damned dog, it would have been fabulous."

Crystal glanced over her shoulder at Rip. He was passed out on his bed again, belly turned up to the ceiling. At least now she knew his stumbling and ensuing crashes weren't due to exhaustion. The poor dog had been drunk. She felt angry with her grandfather all over again. "He's oblivious. I'm sorry he interrupted us."

Crystal got up and went to her computer. "I'm looking up things to watch for in dogs that consume alcohol."

Tanner followed her across the room and leaned over her shoulder. When she'd found a list of symptoms, she and Tanner adjourned to where the dog bed lay. Crystal hunkered down. "Well, he doesn't feel cold, so he doesn't have hypothermia."

"No vomiting, either," Tanner observed. "Or excessive drooling. I honestly think he's just going to sleep it off and be fine."

"Me, too," she said.

He checked the time and stood. "It's late. I should head home. My mom's keeping the kids all night, but they'll hit the deck early."

Crystal retrieved his jacket from where he'd hung it over a chair. She whisked her hand over the fabric, trying to get rid of the dog and cat hair that had stuck to it.

"It'll be fine." He took the garment. "I'll use a lint roller on it in the morning."

Crystal looked into his eyes. She thought she heard him swear under his breath. The next instant, he dropped the blazer, scooped her up in his arms, and carried her to the bedroom. She wondered how he knew which one was hers, but the thought skittered through her mind so fast it didn't stick. As if in a dream, she felt herself land softly on the mattress. Then she heard the door close. In the moonlight seeping through the windows, she saw Tanner stripping off his shirt. Then he joined her on the bed, his body creating a canopy of masculine hardness and heat over hers.

"Are you okay with this? Please say you're okay with this."

Crystal had those bubbles bouncing at the base of her throat again, and she couldn't speak. Instead she pulled his head down so she could kiss him. And just as had happened earlier, the moment their mouths made contact, she forgot everything but the man who held her in his arms.

Moonlight and shadows, heavy breathing and light touches, skin going moist with the heat of desire. Crystal didn't know where her clothing had gone, and she didn't care. His hands, strong yet gentle, grazed over her body, teasing her nerve endings, making her shiver with delight, and pushing her closer to a moment of urgent need she wouldn't be able to deny. His mouth followed the same path, exploring and seeming to savor the taste of her. In return, she ran the tip of her tongue along the column of his throat, across his chest, and over his muscled shoulder, tracing the shape that quivered with each lick.

He drew away and then returned to her. Dimly, she registered that he had slipped on protection. He whispered her name as he pushed cautiously inside of her, and she felt the walls of her femininity clench to embrace him. He groaned at the sensation. She murmured half-formed words as electrical bursts of delight streamed into her lower abdomen like the brilliant trails of fireworks going off in a dark sky.

Afterward they lay exhausted with their heads on the same pillow, their limbs intertwined. She loved the way he held her, his embrace firm but not crushing, one hand splayed over her spine, the other over her hip. She felt cherished.

"That was incredible." His voice vibrated through her, deep and raspy. "I've never felt that way with anyone."

"Me, either. It was fabulous."

He made no offer to move. After her past encounters with men, which had been few, the partings had been matter-of-fact and sometimes hasty. Grabbing for clothing. Tidying up. Saying awkward farewells. With Tanner it still seemed special and beautiful.

"You mind if I crash here tonight? I'd like to stay with you. Hold you for a while."

She smiled against the hollow of his shoulder. No one had ever asked to stay and hold her. "I'd like that," she whispered. "But what about your kids?"

"I'll get up early. Mom will give them breakfast."

With a sigh of contentment, she settled against him, feeling boneless. He stroked her hair, caressed her thigh, and pressed a kiss to her forehead.

"Sweet dreams," he whispered.

Crystal felt certain that nothing could be sweeter than the dream she'd just experienced.

Chapter Twelve

Tanner awakened sometime in the middle of the night and made love to Crystal again. She responded with eagerness and let him know what she liked with small sounds of pleasure. She communicated with him in an open, unabashed way no other woman ever had, and for him, that heightened the enjoyment. He could lose himself in the act of loving her and think of little else.

The second time was as perfect for him as the first, and he knew she felt the same way, because afterward she said, "Dear heaven, I wish you didn't have to leave. What a weekend we could have."

Unfortunately, he had no choice. He had kids at home, and as tempting as staying longer was, he couldn't expect his mother to look after them all day. She'd be worn-out by evening and unable to enjoy her night out with friends.

"You have to work," he reminded her.

"Oh, yeah, that. Sooner or later, I need to take a vacation. I used to go to Idaho and visit Tuck. Now I have no idea where to go."

"Tahiti? Fiji? Go in the winter to escape our bad weather."

"Can I pack you in my suitcase?"

He laughed. "I'd be over the weight limit, and you'd have to pay extra."

"Yes, but you'd be worth it."

He set his cell phone alarm for six, drew Crystal back into his arms, and stroked her hair until both of them drifted off to sleep.

Toward dawn Tanner jerked awake to find Crystal gone. He climbed out of bed, pulled on his slacks, and searched for his shirt. Finally, he decided to look for her without it. He found her sitting on the floor beside Rip's bed. The dog still slept, his belly up, legs sprawled outward. In the faint light coming from the brightening horizon outside the front windows, he could see an introspective expression on her face. The mystery of his missing shirt was solved. She had slipped it on, and he doubted she wore anything else.

In that moment she looked so young to him. She jumped with a start when he crouched, twisted at the waist, and sat beside her with his back to the wall.

"I didn't hear you coming," she said.

"No shoes." He drew up his knees to create a perch for his arms. "Why are you out here? I hope it's nothing I said or did."

"*No.* Everything was wonderful. I'm just—oh, I don't know—doing a little soul-searching."

"Why? What about?"

"Rip. How I've bungled it while caring for him. I can't get it right even when I don't let myself love something."

Tanner's stomach tightened. He had a feeling that Crystal had waded into dark emotional water, and he wasn't sure how to draw her back to the shallows. "Well, from where I'm standing you've done a great job caring for him."

"He's been running away to drink beer at a tavern and coming home drunk. He could have cirrhosis of the liver, which could kill him."

"That wouldn't be your fault." No Name climbed onto his lap. He swept his hand down the kitten's spine. "You've had Rip for only a couple of months, and Tuck had him for more than seven years."

"Yes, but at least Tuck limited how much beer he got. I didn't even know Rip was drinking any. Thinking back, I wonder why, when I first noticed him staggering, I didn't realize he was drunk. It scares me now to think Rip could have gotten really sick any one of those nights and died while I was asleep."

"But he didn't," Tanner pointed out. "And now you're taking control of the situation. You shouldn't blame yourself for not addressing a problem you didn't know existed."

She leaned her head back against the wall with an audible thump. "You're right. I'll remind myself of that if we learn he's got health issues."

"Crystal, remind yourself even if he doesn't. I get the feeling you may blame yourself for things that aren't even really your fault."

After Tanner left, Crystal moved the kitten's dishes and litter box into the full bathroom that adjoined her bedroom and got ready for work. Then she found Rip's leash, a blue-and-white nylon rope with a handgrip loop at one end and a metal clasp at the other. Since Rip had lost his regular collar, she thrust the clip through the loop, creating a circle, and tightened the slack around the blue heeler's neck. Armed with biscuits, she took the dog for a walk around the property. When he had relieved himself, she paid him his toll to reenter the house and then put him in the laundry room with his bed, food, and a large bowl of water.

Rip started to bark when she closed the interior door. Crystal steeled herself against the frantic note she heard in the sounds. She couldn't miss any more appointments today than she'd already handed off to other technicians. She'd spent nearly four hundred dollars on purchasing dog collars last night, and no money tree grew in the backyard.

"Rip!" She spoke to the animal through the wood panel. "Listen to me. Okay? I'll come back in only a while to take you to the vet, and when we're done there, we'll go for a nice, long walk. Don't feel scared. Just take another nap, and I'll be here before you know it."

The dog began scratching at the door. Crystal almost relented. It was hard to go when she knew he might feel frightened. Taking her emotions in hand, she gave No Name a farewell scratch on his head, grabbed her purse, and practically ran from the house.

When Crystal reached the salon, it was nearly seven, her first client was waiting, and she had no time to even walk across the street for a breakfast burrito from the Jake 'n' Bake. She finished three styling jobs in quick succession, glanced at her appointment book, and saw that her next customer was Blackie, who owned the pawnshop. She knew him well from when she'd dined often at the Cauldron. He was a nice older guy whom she guessed to be in his mid-fifties, with black hair, deep blue eyes, and a stocky build he kept trim with regular exercise.

Just as she envisioned him, the bell above the door jangled and he entered the shop. He flashed her an easy grin that made her wonder why he couldn't find some nice woman his age who would appreciate him.

"Hi, stranger," she said as she unfolded a cape and fastened it around his neck.

"Not my fault we're strangers! I still eat regularly at the Cauldron, but I never see you there now."

"Busy." She gave him a brief rundown on Rip and his penchant for running away. "During my breaks, I'm busy hunting for that silly dog."

"Well, I hope the new collar does the trick. With him getting out all the time, it's a headache for you and dangerous for him."

The man had no idea just *how* dangerous it was for Rip. Blackie's hair rarely took much time, and she finished the job quickly. As she ran his credit card, she asked Shannon and Nadine if they were sure they could cover her clients while she took Rip to see the vet. They both assured her that they foresaw no difficulties.

The drive back to the farmhouse gave Crystal a short break, allowing her to relax and take a few deep breaths. She dreaded the vet appointment, mostly because of the stories Tuck had told her about Rip's behavior in clinics. In order to prevent any problems, she'd cautioned the vet and technicians to keep stethoscopes out of sight, and not to wear scrubs, which the dog recognized as uniforms.

She froze when she entered the laundry room to let the dog out. An exterior door that opened onto the backyard bore deep claw marks, the interior door was just as damaged, and Rip had attacked a wicker clothes hamper, dragging all the soiled garments out to tear them with his teeth. The dark brown slacks she'd worn to the salon yesterday had gaping holes in them.

"Oh, Rip."

The heeler lay down and put his paws over his eyes. He was clearly trying to tell her he was sorry, and she didn't have the heart to scold him.

"What's done is done," she settled for saying. "Tanner said he'd help with repairs, and I'm sure Tuck won't mind paying to replace both doors."

She collected Rip's leash, got it tightened around his neck, took him for a walk around the yard, and then led him to her car, feeding him biscuits along the way so he wouldn't pinch her. Once he had received his treat inside the vehicle, he lolled his tongue and sat straight on the passenger seat to see where they were going.

"You'll like Jack Palmer," she assured the dog. "I've only met him once, but people in Mystic Creek speak highly of him."

Rip barked and sent her one of those grins. With a start, she realized she was becoming fond of them—and of the dog. Maybe Tanner had it right, and she loved Rip in her way. The thought alarmed her.

Once at the clinic, Crystal kept a firm grip on Rip's leash. Technicians and assistants in scrubs appeared at the other end of the waiting area, and the dog snarled each time he saw them. Cassidy Peck, a pretty brunette, came out front in her street clothes, crouched down to let Rip smell the back of her hand, and began petting him before she addressed Crystal.

"Sorry. I needed to focus on Rip first. Animals who hate scrubs are often animals that have had bad clinic experiences." Her blue eyes twinkled as she met Crystal's gaze. "How are you?"

"Good," Crystal told her. "Nervous, actually. I've never taken Rip to a vet, and my grandfather's stories about his past behaviors in a clinic have me on edge."

Cassidy stood. "Come on back. You'll be in room three." As Crystal followed her up the left hallway, she spoke over her shoulder. "It's not uncommon for dogs to hate scrubs and stethoscopes, you know. To them, they must look scary."

Crystal doubted that most dogs grabbed the stethoscopes and jumped off examining tables to hide under chairs while tearing the devices apart. "Do most dogs swallow the bell and need an emergency procedure to prevent a bowel blockage?"

"Um, no." Cassidy laughed as she ushered Crystal and the heeler into the examining room. "Jack's been warned. He'll keep the stethoscope out of sight, and he won't wear scrubs." She bent to lift Rip onto the table. "You're a nice boy. Yes, you are."

"He snarls and tries to bite when I pick him up," Crystal observed. "Aren't I blessed? Half the time I can't even pet him. Our friend Tanner says Rip may feel jealous of me, because he senses that my grandfather loves me."

Cassidy gave Rip a scratch behind his ears. "That could be. Some dogs are possessive." She smiled and turned toward the door. "Jack'll be right with you."

Crystal stood at the table, watching Rip to make sure he didn't fall off. "Is that the deal, Rip? That you're jealous?"

The door opened just then and Jack Palmer entered. Crystal had met him at Taffeta Brown and Barney Sterling's wedding. He looked to be in his mid-thirties and was a handsome man, tallish with light brown hair and friendly gray eyes. He wore hiking boots, jeans, and a blue Western shirt with the sleeves rolled back. Beneath the front button placket was a large lump. She suspected that his stethoscope caused the bulge.

"Hi, Crystal." He approached the table, greeted Rip, let the dog get his scent, and then began petting him while he spoke with her. "Did any wires get crossed, or am I correct in believing you told the receptionist that this fellow has a drinking problem?"

"I know it's clear off the charts. But, yes, that is what I told her."

"Not as far off the charts as you might think," he replied. "One of my clients lost her husband a couple of years ago, and last week when she brought her Chesapeake in, a blood test revealed that he had severe cirrhosis of the liver."

Crystal's stomach lurched. "Oh, God."

"Vodka and orange juice, two or three drinks a night. And I think she mixes them strong. Her dog took her husband's place as her drinking partner." Jack was already checking Rip's gums, teeth, and ears. "Can you keep his attention while I listen to his heart and belly activity?"

Crystal did her best to keep the dog's gaze on her by drawing a biscuit from her pocket and showing it to him. Only when Jack had stowed the stethoscope back inside his shirt did she give the blue heeler the treat.

"He seems perfectly healthy," Jack told her. "No detectable stiffness in his joints, no obvious jaundice, no buildup of fluid in the abdominal area, and his gums are pink. I'll take some blood and run a panel on him for any indications of trouble that aren't always obvious during an exam."

"I feel so *awful* about this. I had no idea Rip was regularly given beer."

"It happens," Jack replied. "We'll talk in my office. Let me get Cassidy in here to help with the blood draw first."

Again Cassidy appeared in street clothes and had no stethoscope around her neck. After helping Jack draw blood, she praised Rip for being such a good boy and gave him a treat from a cookie jar. Jack lifted the dog back down to the floor.

"My office is right across the hall." He led the way, talking over his shoulder. "We like to think everyone knows how dangerous alcohol is for dogs and cats. But a lot of people don't." He ushered Crystal into a small but tidy room that featured several wall charts about pets, a desk, and three chairs. He gestured for Crystal to take a seat. She accepted the invitation and coiled the slack in Rip's leash around her wrist so he had to sit near her feet. "I have some literature for you and your grandfather. Mostly things I've found online and printed out. Actual alcoholism is, so far as I know, rare in dogs, but it *can* happen. Any time we consume anything daily that has a propensity to become addictive, man or beast can grow dependent."

Crystal told Jack about all the times Rip had run away and come home at three in the morning. "Our friend Tanner believes Rip is going to the Witch's Brew, where patrons buy him beer."

"So Rip is staying for last call." Jack smiled, but no warmth reached his gray eyes. "I can see how upset you are, Crystal. One thing all pet owners need to remember is that as cautious and responsible as you may be, bad things can still happen. Dogs can bolt out a door and be gone in a blink. Most of us *try* to keep them safe at home, but when you have an exceptionally smart dog—and Rip sounds as if he falls into that category— you find your authority challenged often. And looking at it from Rip's side, can we blame him? Your grandfather apparently gave him beer almost every evening. Rip can't verbalize how he feels, but maybe he craves it now, and with you at the helm, he escapes so he can satisfy his needs."

"What can I do to help him?"

Jack spread his hands. "Aside from keeping Rip confined to his own yard, there isn't a lot you can do except keep him away from alcohol. Check the ingredients of all your personal-hygiene products." He named off different things that she should watch for on labels. "I've had dogs brought in with alcohol poisoning from consuming cough syrup, facial cleansing products, and all manner of other things. Keep potentially dangerous things inside a wall cabinet, not in a lower cupboard. Recreational alcohol should be kept in an upper cupboard or in a locked cabinet. If you have a patio party, confine Rip in a safe area or caution your guests never to leave their drinks unattended. Basically, you should use all the same precautions you would for a young child."

"I've never had a child, either."

Jack grinned. "You'll get it down. Just go through your bathroom. Figure out a way to keep Rip at home where he belongs."

"How do you feel about the use of shock collars on dogs?"

"That they are sometimes necessary. If a dog can be controlled without one, fine, but if not, a correction collar does no harm." He turned on the swivel chair to open a file cabinet. "I'll give you some literature for your grandfather to read, and I'll have my receptionist make up some warning signs that I can tack up in bars, preferably in a prominent spot. Ever since the Chesapeake situation, I've been meaning to do an educational campaign." He shrugged. "I got busy. Spring brings with it viruses that remain dormant in the soil all winter. Distemper can be a killer. But Rip's story is a good reminder that I need to do it. There are people who honestly don't realize that pets can be seriously harmed if they're given alcohol."

"My grandfather loves this dog. He'd never do anything to hurt Rip, *never*."

"He'll better understand the consequences after he reads the stuff I'm sending him. And the warnings may carry more weight if they come from a vet."

Jack created a stack of copies and put them in a manila envelope for Crystal to take with her. "I'll call you

Monday with the test results," he told her. "But until then, try not to worry. He appears to be in excellent health. I won't be at all surprised to see a perfect blood panel."

"Did the Chesapeake seem perfectly healthy?"

"No." Jack held her gaze. "I knew when I examined him that something was seriously wrong."

"Did he die?"

Jack sighed. "Yes, but that doesn't mean Rip will. Keep him home. A script for him will be waiting at the front desk, a little something to take the edge off as his alcohol consumption is curtailed. Don't start him on it until I call you with an all clear on his liver, though. If he has issues, we don't want to introduce anything more into his system."

Crystal pinned Jack with a questioning look. "Are you prescribing medication so Rip won't go into alcohol withdrawal?"

"This drug serves the dual purpose of acting as a mild tranquilizer and minimizing the effects of alcohol withdrawal. If Rip has been drinking daily, it certainly can't hurt to keep him relaxed as he's forced to abstain, and it's also a good precaution just in case of withdrawal. He can't tell you how he feels. The medication will provide a safety net."

Crystal bade Jack farewell, paid the bill, and collected a small white sack containing a bottle of pills. She talked to Rip all the way to the car.

"I hope Jack is right and your liver is fine. Imagine that. I'm amazed you've survived, Rip. But don't take that to mean you're a rare canine that can get away with drinking. We must take this very seriously."

Once in the car, Crystal sat behind the steering wheel, thinking something wasn't right. Had she forgotten her purse? No, it was on the floorboard in front of the passenger seat. Rip's script was tucked in a console compartment, and the dog was fine, except that he looked at her expectantly.

And then it came to her. "Oh, dear heaven, Rip! I forgot to give you a biscuit when I got in, and you didn't bite me. Is this a sign from you? Like, maybe you're trying to tell me you're starting to love me?"

The dog snarled. Crystal dived her hand into the door bin to get him a biscuit, but she was still smiling as she handed it over. "You're like a teenage boy, getting all grumpy because you don't like mushy stuff. What blows my mind is that you seem to understand most of what I say." She studied the heeler as he devoured the treat. "Do you know the word *love*, Rip?"

The canine stopped chewing to growl at her. Crystal laughed and started the car.

Given the damage Rip had done to the laundry room, Crystal decided to take the dog with her to the salon for the remainder of the day. Tomorrow was Sunday, and she could stay home. Monday she would take Rip with her to work again while his new collar was charging.

When she called the shop, Shannon answered. "Silver Beach Salon. This is Shannon. How may I help you?"

"Hi, it's me," Crystal said.

"Oops. Sorry. I'm busy and didn't look at caller ID. What's up?"

Crystal explained about the destroyed laundry room and her decision to bring Rip to work. "I need everyone to ditch the salon aprons. Rip doesn't seem to mind the brown slacks and silk blouses we all wear. He sees that outfit at home all the time."

Shannon made an odd sound. "You're bringing the dog from hell to our shop? You come to work with red marks all over your arms. What if he bites somebody?"

"He doesn't bite," Crystal retorted. Then she realized she was starting to sound just like Tuck. "Well, he does bite Tuck, me, and people in uniform, but even then, Shannon, he's never broken the skin. He pinches with his front teeth."

Shannon groaned. "That's comforting."

"He won't do it to any of you. I promise."

Over the next five minutes of driving, Crystal lectured Rip on how she expected him to behave inside the salon. "You were such a good boy at the clinic. I know you can do it."

She parked under the carport at the back of her building, grabbed the end of Rip's leash, opened the driver's door, and started to exit the car. Rip snarled and pinched the back of her right arm.

"Ow!" Crystal gained her feet. The dog nailed her again just above her right wrist. "You little snot! Stop it! I'm getting a biscuit, damn it!"

After appeasing her grandfather's dog, Crystal stuffed at least a dozen biscuits in her purse and pockets just in case she needed them to control the dog inside the salon.

"You'd better behave yourself." Her arm panged where his teeth had bruised her. "I can't believe I was thinking we might be forming a bond."

She bribed the dog at the back door before entering her place of business. Rip, apparently excited by all the strange smells, lunged forward and jerked the leash out of her hand. As Crystal ran up the hall, she heard feminine voices. "Oh, how beautiful!" "Hello, Rip!" "Aw, you're darling." "Oh, what a sweet fellow."

When Crystal reached the front of the building, she stopped and watched the dog go from station to station, grinning at technicians and patrons alike, and charming the socks off every person he encountered. Releasing a taut breath, Crystal relaxed. This could work. She only wondered why she hadn't thought of it before now.

And just then a Federal Express deliveryman opened the front door. Rip saw his uniform and shifted into attack mode. Crystal ran up behind the dog, stepped on his trailing leash to prevent the assault, and dimly registered that the nylon rope had tugged her feet out from under her just before she landed flat on her back. The deliveryman leaped outside and closed the door to protect himself. As Crystal sat up, she saw Rip clawing at the glass.

She struggled to her feet, retrieved her purse from the floor, and got a handful of biscuits. Grabbing Rip's leash, this time winding the rope around her wrist so it wouldn't slip through her fingers, she held the dog back as she opened the door.

"Here," she said, holding the portal ajar with her foot as she handed the man a biscuit. "Just offer him one of these, and he'll let you come in."

Middle-aged with thinning gray hair, the man laughed. "I know the drill. I just didn't expect a dog in here."

He appeased Rip with a biscuit, handed Crystal a parcel, and then paid the dog another toll to leave the shop. Watching him walk away, Crystal realized the salon had gone silent. Not even a hair dryer was running. She turned around and took in the pale faces of everyone who'd just witnessed Rip in terrorist mode.

"He really is a nice dog," she said, feeling foolish. "He's just quirky about uniforms."

Nadine broke the tension. "Well, of course he's a nice dog. All of us met him seconds ago, and he was delightful. I don't like cop uniforms, a hangover from my wild and rebellious teens, so I kind of understand how Rip feels."

An older lady with tinfoil strips layered over her

head said, "My little poodle, Trixie, detests Courier Express, FedEx, and UPS people."

"My spaniel goes crazy when the postwoman rattles the box beside our front door. He thinks she's doing bad things to our house. It gives him a great workout, though. He runs in circles for nearly five minutes."

Crystal was glad to have people visiting again, and she led Rip to her station. She tied his leash to the leg of her styling cabinet. Then she rubbed her back, hoping she wouldn't be bruised in the morning.

Just then Crystal's one o'clock entered the shop. Marietta Adams, a plump blonde with a warm smile that always seemed to light up a room, called hello to people she knew and then gave Crystal a hug.

"Oh, a *dog*. How nice!" She bent to give Rip friendly scratches behind the ears. "Having you here may help with my haircut anxiety. You can be my therapy dog."

Crystal's phone rang and she saw Tanner's name on the screen. "Excuse me, Marietta. I need to take this." Crystal answered the call as she hurried to the rear hallway, where she'd be able to talk in privacy. "Hey, you." It wasn't a particularly romantic way to greet a man who'd made her moan in ecstasy last night. "It seems like a year has passed."

He laughed. "At my end, make it a decade, and not only because I miss you. Although I truly do. I have a bit of an emergency, and I'm wondering if you can help me."

"Of course. What's wrong?"

"My little girl, Tori. A girl at the play park called her 'Kinky.' You know, because her hair is so curly. She's been crying ever since I brought her home. She doesn't want kinky hair, and I, um— Well, I'm probably dreaming, but is there a way to make Tori's hair straight?"

Crystal's heart caught. It bothered her when she encountered cases of girl envy. Why was it that so few females were content with the physical features that they'd been born with? "I'm not sure straightening her hair is wise, Tanner. She's beautiful just as she is." In addition to that, Crystal had reservations about meeting the child of her new lover. She liked kids, but she wasn't very good with them. "Can't you soothe her hurt feelings by telling her how pretty she is and taking her out for ice cream?"

"She wants hair that's straight like yours. After all this time, she still remembers the pretty lady with long red hair. Now, whenever she mentions you, she tosses in *straight* as another adjective."

Crystal said, "My schedule is really tight today, Tanner."

She heard him sigh. "Okay. I understand. If she's still upset next week, maybe I can get her in to see someone after school."

Crystal almost let it go at that. But then she thought of how wrong things could go if a stranger touched the child's hair. Some techs would use a straightening solution, after which Tori's hair might have to grow out before it would be curly again. The harsh chemicals could also do damage. "Hold on." She considered her schedule. "If you can come after six, I can see her."

"Awesome! You're such a sweetheart. But can you make her hair straight?"

Crystal couldn't help but smile. He sounded like a man who was hanging by his fingertips from a sky-scraper ledge. Hearing in his voice how deeply he cared about his daughter's feelings made her admire him even more. "Yes, I can straighten it, Tanner, but it'll be curly again after you wash it."

"That's *perfect*. I don't want it to be permanent. She's too little to make decisions like that. I really appreciate this, Crystal. How about fast food at the park afterward? The kids'll be ravenous by then."

Kids. That meant he planned to bring Michael along. Crystal wasn't ready to meet his family. Alarm bells went off in her mind. "Only if Rip can come." She told him about the laundry room damage. "I brought him to work after taking him to see Jack."

"He's welcome to join us. *Shit.* Tori will fall in love with him and start begging for a puppy. But okay, that's okay. I'll deal with that. So, what did Jack say?"

"I'll tell you about it tonight. I've got the sheriff's wife up front."

"Gotcha. See you at six."

When Crystal's last customer left, she had only fifteen minutes to prepare for her Tori Richards appointment. It hurt her heart to think that beautiful little Tori felt inferior to other girls because her hair was wildly curly. Crystal examined her reflection in the mirror and reached a snap decision. Maybe she could make Tori realize that having curly hair was more of a blessing than a curse.

It was worth a shot, and she had very little time to pull it off. She leaned over the sink in her station and shampooed her hair. Then after fluffing the wet strands, she dried them with a diffuser on the blow-dryer. The curls that she so relentlessly dispensed with every day leaped back to life. Her electric curling irons were already heated. She sat in the chair and made fast work of styling her now-intractable mane. When she was satisfied with the effect, she quickly reapplied her makeup.

Ready. Now maybe Tori will remember me as the lady with the long, red, curly hair and no longer find fault with herself when she studies her own reflection.

As Crystal got up from the chair and went to the

front windows, she saw that she hadn't finished her makeover a second too soon. Tanner's Chevy truck pulled up to the curb. An instant later the kids spilled out onto the sidewalk. Crystal had met Tori that day outside the medical supply store, but she'd never seen Michael. He was a tall boy for eleven. He'd probably gotten his height and sturdy build from his dad. But there all resemblance between father and son ended. He had hair of such dark brown that it was almost black, and his eyes were cobalt, a much deeper blue than his father's or sister's.

Crystal met them at the door, opening it wide to allow them entry. Tori froze on the threshold and stared up at Crystal. "Your hair! It's kinky, just like mine."

Crystal nodded. "Yes. My hair is naturally curly."

"But last time I saw you, it was straight," Tori said.

"Yes," Crystal replied. "I'm *very* lucky. Girls with straight hair often have to get a perm if they want to have curly hair like mine every day, and it takes a long, long time for the artificial curls to grow out. I can let my hair be curly whenever I want or I can straighten it whenever I want with a special iron. Only *very* lucky girls get to have straight hair one day and curly hair the next."

She ushered the Richards family inside. Rip, still tied to the leg of her styling cabinet, trembled and squirmed with excitement. Crystal had never seen the dog interact with kids, and because of Tuck's advanced years, she doubted that Rip had had frequent exposure to them.

She decided to play it safe and kept a firm hold on the leash as she allowed the canine to meet Tanner's children. Michael petted the dog and said hello. Tori chortled and threw her small arms around the blue heeler's neck. Rip returned her exuberant greeting by bathing her face with dog kisses.

Tanner chuckled. "I told you so. Now I'll never hear the last of it." He settled his gaze on Crystal's hair. *"Why?"*

"Why what?"

"Why do you straighten your hair? It looks fabulous this way."

"Thank you. I'll bear that in mind."

As Crystal got Tori situated in the chair and adjusted its height, she ran the child's curls through her fingers and admired their multitone shimmer. She knew women who would happily spend two hundred dollars to have hair like that. "Your curls are absolutely stunning," she told the child.

"I know." An expression of distaste settled over Tori's small face. "When people see me, they almost fall over, just like in the cop shows Michael watches where they stun-gun the bad guys."

Michael groaned. "You just *told*, Tori. You broke our deal! Next time you sneak chocolate chips, I'm telling Dad."

Tanner, who sat in a waiting-area chair, spoke up. "Michael, you know it's against the rules to watch cop shows. Tori isn't old enough to view programs like that."

Watching Michael in the mirror, Crystal saw him shoot a murderous glare at his sister before hanging his head. "I won't do it again, Dad."

"You'd better not," Tanner replied, "or you'll be grounded from all television for a week."

Crystal suppressed a smile. "Actually, Tori, when people say something is stunning, it means it's absolutely *gorgeous*."

"It does?" Tori's eyes, an aquamarine just like her

dad's, met Crystal's in the mirror. "Why does Mandy call me mean names like Kinky, then?"

"I'm only guessing, but I think Mandy is probably envious. I bet she has straight hair."

"Yep. And it goes *swish-swish*, and it's shiny and pretty."

"Yours is shiny and pretty, too." Crystal checked the straightening iron to see if it was up to temp, a gentler heat for Tori's baby-fine curls. She divided the child's mane into sections and held them in place with clips. "Are you ready to have straight hair just like Mandy's?"

Tori giggled. "I'm very ready!"

As Crystal set to work, she realized she might have a bad case of what she called "girl envy" herself. Many young women had straight, silky hair, and she'd chosen to banish curls from her life by straightening them into nonexistence every morning. In a way, she was a grown-up version of Tori, wanting to look like somebody else.

It took only minutes to straighten the girl's hair. Tori squealed with delight as she vacated the styling chair. "Look, Daddy. My hair swishes!" She wagged her head back and forth. "Isn't it pretty?"

"Very pretty," Tanner said. He stood and tipped his head to study his daughter. "You look like a different young lady."

Tori admired her new look in every mirror she could find. "Daddy, do you see? It's not just pretend straight. It's *genuine* straight!"

Tanner smiled. "Yes, it is, and it's very attractive. But I can't help feeling sad. I think your curly hair is so beautiful."

Tori, still gazing at her reflection, touched the stick-straight strands. "Don't be sad, Daddy. If I shampoo tonight, it'll be curly again tomorrow."

"Will you be sad and cry again?" Michael asked, clearly reluctant to go through that drama a second time.

"Nope!" Tori knelt to hug Rip. "I'm very lucky, just like Crystal. I can have straight hair or curly hair, my choice! All I need is a special iron! Nana can help me do my hair for school."

Crystal opened a drawer of her styling cabinet. She kept an extra straightening iron on hand in case her main one went on the blink. She drew it out and approached Tori. "If I give this to you as a gift, do you promise never to use it unless your nana or daddy is helping you?"

Tori nodded and smiled. "I promise!" She held up the iron to show it to her father. "Look, Daddy! Now I have my very own hair straightener!"

Gazing at Crystal, Tanner winked and mouthed a silent *Thank you*.

She felt an odd tug in the center of her chest, followed by a pang. Kids often sat in her styling chair, but none of them had ever touched her heart the way Tori did. She was such a darling child. No wonder Tanner had been frantic over her tears. Those innocent blue eyes grabbed hold of a person's heart and refused to let go.

Chapter Thirteen

Crystal had already fallen for Tori, but it wasn't until the four of them reached Mystic Creek Park that she got to know Michael. He took Rip on several walks, trotting intermittently so the dog could run. He stopped often to pet the animal and give him praise. Then he caught his sister trying to ascend the natural bridge, which could have been dangerous. Tori cried when Michael grabbed her hand and led her back to the picnic area, where Crystal and Tanner sat at a table.

"She went idiot on me," the boy said. "When I wouldn't let her hold the leash, she got mad and tried to go up on the bridge."

Crystal admired the way Tanner handled the situation. He gave Michael a stern look and said, "Don't call your sister an idiot."

"I didn't. I said—"

"That was what you implied, Michael." Tanner settled his gaze on his daughter. "And you, young lady. That was *not* a smart choice. I understand that you're upset because Michael won't let you walk Rip, but going up on that bridge to get even with him was a silly thing to do. You could have been hurt."

"I would've been careful! And Michael's hogging the dog. He won't let me hold the leash. He says I'm too little! And I'm not!"

"Michael is probably afraid you're not strong enough

to hold Rip back if he decides to take off," Tanner said. "And you're making excuses for your behavior, Victoria Ann. The bridge isn't a safe place to play, and you know it. That's why there are signs saying children aren't allowed up there unless they're accompanied by an adult." He drew the girl between his knees and turned her toward the bridge. "Do you see how far you could fall?"

"Yes." Huge tears slid down Tori's cheeks, and her chin quivered.

"What's down below the bridge, Tori?"

"Water and big rocks."

"What would you have landed on if you had fallen?"

"Big rocks, or into water," Tori replied.

"Yes," Tanner agreed. "Would you like me to push you on the swing or merry-go-round? Maybe part of the problem is that you aren't having fun on the playground by yourself."

"But I want to play with Rip!"

"I'm sure Michael will let you play with him while he holds the leash."

"Sure, I'll let her," Michael chimed in. "Come with us, Tori. You can find a stick to throw for him, and when he goes after it, I'll run with him to fetch it."

Tori pouted her bottom lip. "I don't want you to hold the leash. *I* want to."

Michael huffed and led the dog away.

Tanner said, "I understand how much you'd like to take Rip for a walk, but he's a strong dog. What if he got away from you? He likes to run off, you know, and we're right in the middle of town."

"He could get hit by a car, you mean?"

"Possibly, or something else bad could happen."

Tori glared at Michael's departing back, but her expression softened when she looked at the dog. "I guess he might be stronger than me, and I don't want anything to happen to him. He's my new friend."

Tanner gave the little girl a playful bear hug. "There's my girl. Maybe after Rip's new collar comes, Crystal will let you play with him in her yard, where he'll be safe."

At Tanner's questioning look, Crystal felt her stomach clench. She hadn't planned to get involved with his children, and she certainly hadn't expected to feel affection for them. She felt like a hapless hiker who'd stepped into quicksand and was getting sucked under. "Of course," she heard herself say. "On a Sunday, maybe. I can make lunch." Where had that come from? "That way, you can play for as long as you like."

After Tori ran back to the playground, Tanner came around to sit beside Crystal so he could watch his daughter. He sat so close that her shoulder pressed against his upper arm. Heat radiated off him to warm her skin. Memories of the previous night flashed through her mind. That bothered her. It didn't seem right to think about things like that when his kids were present. This was a family outing, not a date.

Forcing herself to focus on something besides her attraction to Tanner, she asked, "Can Tori read well?"

He sighed. "So well that Mom has to hide her romance novels. Some of them contain—well, you know, explicit descriptions of activities I don't want Tori to know about until she's forty."

Crystal tried to suppress a laugh but failed. He slanted her a grin that made her insides go warm. "*Forty?* You sound so *fatherly*—every teenage girl's worst nightmare."

"Trust me. It's only wishful thinking on my part. She's into girlie stuff already, and she'll probably want to wear makeup at twelve. I won't let that happen without a fight."

"I believe it, but you might want to muster up more backbone before she gets that old. She won the war when it came to getting her hair straightened."

Tanner guffawed. "You're so right. I'm doomed, aren't I?" He watched his daughter climb onto a structure composed of crisscrossed bars and hidey-holes. "She's going to be a gorgeous young lady. I'll have boys lined up at my door." He arched an eyebrow. "Why did you ask how well she can read?"

"I thought maybe she didn't understand what the warning signs at each end of the bridge say."

Tanner chuckled. "Do you know how I discovered that she was reading Mom's books? When I tucked her in one night, she asked, 'Daddy, what's *ejaculate* mean?' I hoped she was referring to the word in a conversational sense, but oh, no. She was asking about the physiological phenomenon that occurs when a man is aroused."

"Good grief, what's her reading level?"

"Eighth grade the last time she was tested, over a year ago. Tori's gifted. When she was little, I laid it off on all the attention we gave her. I read to her a lot, and my mom was working with her during the day. She could read the text in her storybooks before she entered preschool."

"Wow. She seems just like any little girl, not that I'm an expert on them."

"We try our best not to push her. She's in a class with children her own age. She gets special tutoring above her grade level to keep her from getting bored."

"Did she get her intelligence from you?"

Tanner laughed. "I'm smart enough, I suppose, but I'm no Einstein. Carolyn's parents say that she was exceptionally bright. Maybe it came from her gene pool."

He resumed watching his children. Tori was hanging from a bar by her knees, and Michael was jogging with

Rip around the baseball diamond. Then he glanced back at Crystal. "Why hasn't the city put safety railings on that bridge?"

Crystal smiled. "That's a topic frequently discussed at town meetings, but because the bridge is a natural feature, people don't want to deface it with man-made materials. Instead, they agreed on warning signs. Residents of Mystic Creek are protective of the stream and bridge."

"Ah, right. The legend about two people falling in love along its banks."

He settled his gaze on hers, and she felt as if she were up to her chin in a delightful blue lagoon. Memories of their lovemaking last night slipped into her mind again. Little pulses of electricity seemed to emanate from his muscular arm, making her shoulder tingle. She resisted the urge to scoot closer to him. This wasn't the time or the place. "You're very good with Tori. If I had a child that tried to sneak up on that bridge, I'd freak out and handle it all wrong."

"Nah. You'd be a great mom."

Everything within Crystal recoiled at the thought. She'd once been left in charge of a little girl Tori's age, and that had ended in a horrible way that would haunt her for the rest of her life.

"Crystal, what is it? You look like you just saw a ghost."

She nearly said, *I'm haunted by one,* but as easy as it was for her to talk to Tanner, she would never share that part of her past with him. Tuck was the only person in Oregon who knew. "We should probably go for fast food," she said, changing the subject. "The kids are having fun now, but at any moment, hunger may strike."

He nodded and smiled, but there was still a thought-ful, questioning expression in his eyes. "I made a delivery to the Cauldron last week. The smells in there made my mouth water. I was thinking it might be fun to eat there."

Sissy Sue Sterling and her mother, Doreen McClain, owned the Cauldron. Crystal had been a regular customer until Tuck's accident. Despite extensive remodeling, the owners had kept their menu prices affordable. "That does sound fun," she agreed, "but I have Rip with me, and he apparently suffers from separation anxiety. I wouldn't dare leave him unattended in my car. He nearly destroyed the laundry room this morning."

"Dang it. I'd like to take you someplace halfway nice, just once."

Michael walked up with Rip just then. "I'm hungry."

Tanner laughed. "Okay, sport. How about you and I walk over to the hamburger joint and buy dinner?" He glanced at Crystal. "Do you mind keeping an eye on Tori?"

Panic surged within Crystal like a sudden volcanic eruption. Tori was eight, the exact same age her little sister had been when she died. *Get a grip,* she told herself. *They'll be gone for only a few minutes.* "Sure," she forced herself to say.

She extended her hand toward Michael to take Rip's leash. The boy tightened his grip on the nylon rope. "Can he go with us? Dad can go in to get the food, and I'll stay outside with him."

Crystal looked at the dog. He wore a happy grin. "I think he'd love to go, if you're certain he won't be a bother."

Michael smiled. "He's no bother." He darted a glance at his father. "Tori is always bugging Dad to get her a dog. I've never really wanted one—until now. Rip is really awesome." Michael turned and dashed away, saying, "Come on, Rip! Let's go!"

Tanner gifted her with a broad grin. "I think I see a puppy in my near future. Piddle on my floors. Stolen socks and destroyed shoes. What a joy."

"That sounds like the voice of experience."

"Oh, yeah. I had a dog. His name was Hoover. He was so christened because he went through our house like a high-powered vacuum, inhaling everything in sight. My folks let me adopt him from the pound. He was six weeks old when I got him." He turned to follow his son at a much slower pace, calling over his shoulder, "Ate my football cleats the first night. Ate my math book the next afternoon. And it was my job to clean up all his messes. Will you please tell Tori we'll be right back?"

"You bet."

Crystal swung her feet over the table bench to get up. Tori saw her father and brother leaving and bounded off the merry-go-round to come running across the grass. "Where's Daddy going?"

"He and Michael are going to get dinner. If you'd like to go, your father is still within hearing distance."

Tori shook her head and beamed a smile. "I'd rather stay with you."

Crystal had expected the child to continue playing on the equipment, but instead she sat across from her at the table. Well, she didn't actually sit. She knelt on the bench and propped her small elbows on the planks. For a moment. Then she turned a full circle, lay on her back to pump her legs as if she were riding a bicycle, and just generally wiggled, clearly so full of energy that holding still was difficult for her.

Fascinated, Crystal watched her, feeling obligated to say something. "So, do you like school?"

"Yep. Lots and lots." Tori put her elbows on the tabletop again and fixed Crystal with a questioning look. "Is my daddy your boyfriend?"

Crystal's mouth went dry. *Brain freeze.* "I, um . . . well, we *are* friends, and he's a boy—sort of a boy, anyway—so I guess it's fair to say he's a boyfriend."

A dimple flashed in the child's rosy cheek. "Do you make love?"

Crystal wanted to catapult off the bench and shout at the top of her lungs for Tanner to come back. She hadn't been around little girls very much, and then only in the controlled environment of her salon. How on earth should she field that question? She decided to deal with Tori as if she were an adult.

"That's an extremely *personal* thing to ask me, Tori, and even though he's your daddy, it's really none of your business."

The child wrinkled her small nose, which sported a smattering of caramel-colored freckles. "I'm sorry. I was rude. Nana says I talk so fast my brain can't keep up."

Crystal thought it was more likely that her brain's processing ability far exceeded her maturity level. "Your father says you like to read your nana's books."

Tori planted her pointy chin on the heels of her hands. "Yes. She hides them from me now, but I can still find them. She keeps switching places. Last time, I found one under her mattress."

Crystal gave Tori a long study. "Have you ever heard of Pandora's box?"

The child nodded. "Only it wasn't really a box. It was a jar, and it was full of bad things."

Mentally, Crystal considered that. How did an eight-year-old child know stuff like that? Until this moment, Crystal hadn't known that the box had actually been a jar. "Yes, bad things, but I think there's a lesson to be learned for all of us from that story. Sometimes things that seem exciting and interesting are actually bad for us."

Tori's gaze sharpened on Crystal's. "You mean Nana's love stories."

It wasn't a question, and Crystal didn't treat it as if it were. "Love stories are written for much older girls and women. At your age, you probably shouldn't be reading about adult relationships. That's not mentally or emotionally healthy for you."

"How come?"

Crystal nearly smiled. "Because you should be reading about things that will help you grow as a person right now."

Tori grimaced. "That sounds boring."

"No, actually. When I was your age, I started reading Nancy Drew mysteries."

With a shrug, Tori said, "I read a whole bunch of them already. I was little then. Now I'm tired of them."

"Oh. Well, there are many other kinds of books that I think you may like. Since you love dogs, maybe you could start reading books about them." *Marley & Me* immediately popped into Crystal's mind, but it had a sad ending. "Have you read any of the Lassie novels?"

"No. Are they good?"

"Oh, they're fabulous!" Aware that Tanner probably couldn't comfortably afford to buy his daughter many books, Crystal quickly tacked on, "Maybe you and I should make a trip to the Crystal Falls library one afternoon, and I could help you find some really awesome dog books—not only novels, but possibly training books. How to raise a puppy."

Tori's face brightened with an eager smile. "Daddy would like me to read how-to books. Maybe then he'd let me get a puppy!"

Crystal wondered where the idea of taking Tori to the library had come from, but it was too late to retract the offer now. "Maybe. But even if you still have to wait for a while, you'll know how to be a good dog owner."

Tanner and Michael reappeared just then. The boy bent to scratch Rip's head as they stopped near the table. "The fast-food joint is closed," Tanner told her.

"You're kidding. On a Saturday night?"

"There's a sign on the door that says the owner has houseguests from out of town."

Crystal couldn't help but laugh. "That's Mystic Creek for you. Most of the businesses are owner operated, and some people have no employees to fill in for them."

"How about we take Rip home and let him finish destroying the laundry room while we eat a proper dinner at the Cauldron? I'll do the repairs as payment for the pleasure of your company."

"That sounds fun. I've been craving Sissy's home-style pot roast."

"That settles it, then."

"If she has beef bourguignon on the menu tonight, I highly recommend it," Crystal told him.

"Yuck!" Michael straightened from rubbing Rip's ears. "When we eat out, I like stuff we never get at home. Do they serve cheeseburgers and French fries there? I can make do with spaghetti and meatballs, too."

Crystal got up. "Sissy's burgers are legendary. Her dinner offerings change daily, though. I don't know if it's a spaghetti-and-meatballs night, but if it is, you're in for a treat."

Crystal hadn't realized how much she'd missed dining at the Cauldron. Not only had she yearned for the wonderful food, but it had also been far too long since she'd seen some of her friends. She introduced Tanner and his kids to Christopher Doyle, one of her favorite people, who had grown so gaunt with age that he resembled a stick figure with skin and saggy clothes draping his frame. After Tanner led them to a table and they were seated, Tim and Lynda VeArd stopped by to say hello before they left the restaurant.

"Early night for us," Lynda, an older redhead, said after the introductions were made. "Our puppy misses us when we're gone and drools all over the car seats."

Crystal remembered that they had recently gotten a dog out of the same sire and dam as Ben Sterling's Australian shepherd, Finnegan. Ben was busing tables for his wife, Sissy, who had learned she was pregnant about two months ago. He seemed to worship the ground she walked on, and tonight he was looking after her with an eagle eye.

"How's that dog working out for you?" His hands laden with dishes, Ben stopped to stand beside Tim. In the overhead light, his burnished hair glistened like varnished oak. "He's what—six months old now?"

Tim, a tall, robust man with a full head of snow-white hair, a friendly countenance, and merry blue eyes, laughed and said, "Five months, and he's sharp as a tack. Sits, lies down, and rolls over on command already."

"And breaks the stay every time Tim turns his head," Lynda inserted.

Ben laughed. Then his gaze sharpened on his wife, who was working behind the counter. "Gotta go. She's lifting a fry bucket again. I've told her a dozen times not to do that."

As Ben rushed away, Crystal exchanged knowing grins with Tim and Lynda. All the regulars at the Cauldron had looked on as Ben and Sissy fell in love, and now they all felt as if they'd been partly responsible for the couple working out their problems and getting married.

"Ben!" they heard Sissy cry in a scolding tone. "It won't hurt me or the baby if I lift a stupid bucket."

"It's filled with five gallons of water and potato wedges," he retorted. He turned to the customers sitting at the bar. Blackie and Ma Thomas, two more of Crystal's favorite people, were in the lineup. "I thought I could trust you guys to watch her."

Tim nodded. "Good man, that Ben. Sissy's no bigger than a minute. I wouldn't want her lifting that much weight, either."

"Tim, we need to run." Lynda held up a doggie bag. "Some people take the leftovers home for themselves," she said with a smile for the kids, "but ours are actually for the dog. He prefers his dinner warm."

"God save me," Tim said with feigned frustration. "She spoils that puppy rotten."

After saying their farewells, the VeArds left. Tanner gazed after them. "They seem like nice people."

"The best," Crystal agreed. "They own the local boat dock and marina."

"When do we get to order?" Michael asked, his tone whiny.

"We just sat down," Tanner reminded his son. "And it's busy. They'll get to us."

As if on cue, Sissy appeared, tablet and pen at the ready. "Hi, Crystal! Long time no see. It's a pot-roast-and-beef-bourguignon night."

"Mmm, the pot roast for me."

Tanner ordered the beef bourguignon. Michael asked for the double cheeseburger with seasoned fries, and Tori wanted the chili dog. While they waited for their meals, Crystal told them about the history of the

Cauldron, how it had been in shabby condition when Sissy inherited it from her aunt.

Michael looked around. "So there didn't used to be a fireplace?"

"No. It's much nicer in here now."

"Where's Ben's dog, Finnegan?" Tori wanted to know.

Tanner fielded the question. "Most places that serve food can't allow dogs to be inside. Finnegan is probably at home, just like Rip is."

"Oh." Tori's shoulders drooped. "I really wanted to meet Finnegan." She cast a sharp glance at her father. "Not that I'll get one like him. I want a blue heeler like Rip. When will I be old enough, Daddy?"

"Soon."

"How soon?" Tori pressed.

Tanner met Crystal's gaze, his own reflecting his angst over feeling pushed to make that decision. Crystal was a complete rookie with kids. She had no sage advice.

Weary though she was, Crystal wasn't ready for the evening to be over when Tanner drove her home and walked her to the door. Darkness edged close, deepening the spring twilight to darker shades of gray. The smells of a spring night in the country drifted on a balmy breeze, and they were surrounded with the mingled scents of wildflowers, new-growth alfalfa, freshly cut grass, and ponderosa pine trees, especially fragrant as they grew new shoots that stood at the tips of their branches like tiny light green crosses.

Tanner's gaze settled on her face, and she knew by his expression that he yearned to kiss her. She wanted that, too, so badly she ached. But his kids sat in the truck watching them, and Rip was barking nonstop in the laundry room. Even from outside Crystal could detect an urgency in the dog's cries.

"No doorstep kissing in front of the kids," she said softly. "Besides, I'd better go rescue Rip before he decides tearing up my clothes isn't enough revenge. The hamper may be next."

Tanner smiled and sent her an air-kiss instead of giving her a real one. Crystal watched as he sprinted out to his vehicle. He tooted the horn as he backed out onto the road. Crystal remained where she was until the dim glow of the taillights vanished around a curve. She sighed, feeling both happy and melancholy at once. Tonight she'd gotten a taste of how it might feel to be married and have a family of her own, and for the first time, she felt as if she were missing out on the best things in life.

Then she turned to open the door, discovered it wasn't latched, and froze. After picking up her car at the salon, she'd followed Tanner to the house, and he'd gone inside with her to put Rip in the laundry room. She distinctly remembered him trying the door to make sure it was latched. Crystal hadn't locked it. In Mystic Creek she never bothered with such things. Crime was almost nonexistent.

She stood well back and nudged the door farther open with her toe. A quick scan of the living room eased her mind. She saw no one, and nothing looked as if it had been disturbed. She stepped cautiously inside. It sounded as if Rip body-slammed the laundry room door when he heard her. Now that she was closer to him, she realized that he wasn't just barking.

He was growling.

Her skin pebbled with goose bumps. She quickly retreated from the house and ran to her car as if the hounds of hell were nipping at her heels. Once inside the Equinox, she locked all the doors, fished her cell phone from her purse, and dialed 911, which connected her with the sheriff's office. A woman named Doreen answered. Crystal didn't know the woman personally, but she remembered the name because Sissy Sue's mother was also a Doreen.

"This is Crystal Malloy."

"Oh, yep, the gal who owns Silver Beach Salon. What's up? You okay?"

The plump woman had been with the sheriff's department for over three years now, but according to gossip, she'd never memorized any of the police codes and was very unprofessional in manner. "I think someone may be in my house. My dog is locked in the laundry room, and he's raising holy heck."

"Where are you? Not inside, I hope."

"I locked myself in the car." Crystal realized her hands were shaking. "I'm a little spooked. What if it's a man?"

"What's the address? I'll send someone right out."

Crystal drew a complete blank. All her mail went to the post office, and she'd never had reason to use this address. "I, um . . ." She squinted to see the number on the mailbox. "The house is on East Sugar Pine. It's getting too dark for me to read the numbers."

"You don't know your own address?"

"I just moved here." Now Crystal understood why this woman had tongues wagging. If it were left up to Doreen, Crystal could have been stabbed to death before a deputy ever got here. "Would you just *do* something? I need help! Just tell the deputy that I'm on East Sugar Pine and a silver Equinox is parked out front."

"Okay. Hold on while I call it out."

Crystal maintained the connection, staring fearfully at the house while she waited. It seemed as if a short eternity passed before Doreen came back on the line. "Done. A deputy is on the way. But stay on the phone with me, Crystal. That way I can call for backup if there's trouble."

"Okay." Silence ensued. "What will we talk about?"

"I don't know. Hair color? I'm a natural blonde, but I've been dyeing my hair red for years. Getting tired of it. Need a new look."

Crystal couldn't quite believe she was discussing hair color while someone might have been ransacking the house.

"I sure hope your burglar isn't that underwear sicko," Doreen observed.

That rang a bell. Crystal remembered the girls at the shop talking about the peeping tom who had started entering houses and stealing lingerie. "He hasn't been caught yet?"

"Nope. They think he lives in another town and comes here where nobody will recognize him. He's not dangerous, I don't think. Just weird."

Crystal preferred not to bet her life on Doreen's hunches. She could have sworn she heard the woman snapping her gum.

Just then a white county truck pulled in beside Crystal's car, and she saw a long-legged, brawny male deputy swing out the driver's side. In the deepening dusk, she glimpsed his golden brown hair before he covered it with a dark brown Stetson. *Barney Sterling.* Crystal wished someone else had taken the call. Barney was a competent law officer, and she liked him, but one night years ago, she'd panicked over a skittering spider that she'd believed to be poisonous, and Barney had entered the flat above her salon to find her standing on the kitchen table in a skimpy camisole. Not many things sent Crystal into full-blown panic, but snakes and spiders did the trick.

"He's here, Doreen. Thanks. Gotta go." Crystal ended the call and climbed out of her car. "Hi, Barney." She quickly explained why she believed someone was inside the house. "On top of the door being unlatched, my grandfather's dog is going ballistic."

Barney nodded. "Just to be on the safe side, please get back in your car and lock the doors."

Crystal turned to do just that and then stopped dead. "Whatever you do, don't open the laundry room door. Rip, my grandfather's dog, is in there, and he hates uniforms."

Barney gave her a thumbs-up. Crystal dived back into her car and watched him go into cop mode. It was surreal, like watching a movie. He drew his weapon before mounting the steps, and then pressed his back to the exterior siding next to the door, barrel of the gun pointed up, elbows tucked against his sides. She jerked when he reached around with his leg and kicked the door all the way open with the side of his boot. He entered the house with the gun at the ready. Sweat broke out all over her body.

A few minutes later, Barney reappeared on the porch and gave her an all-clear signal. Crystal got back out of the car.

"Was somebody in there?" She pushed through the gate and hurried to the steps. "Or did I make a big fuss over nothing?"

"Someone was in there before I got here, and you did exactly what you should have by locking yourself in the car. It appears to me it was the Lingerie Burglar."

"You've given him an actual name?"

"That makes it simpler for us to communicate. When one of us sees a car abandoned along a road, we can use police codes and say only that name. So far he hasn't harmed anyone, but you just never know with a guy like that. Lawmen have a saying: 'Not all voyeurs are rapists, but all rapists were once voyeurs.'"

Crystal gulped. "Did he . . ." Her voice trailed away. "I'm sorry. This is creeping me out. Did he rifle through my dresser drawers?"

"Yes." Barney sat down on the top step. She realized she was quivering like an aspen leaf in a brisk breeze. "Take a load off," he said. "I know it's upsetting. It's understandable to feel violated when things like this happen."

Crystal sank onto the step beside him. She thought about having to spend the night here alone and was tempted to risk a huge confrontation with Patricia Flintlock in order to sleep over at her grandfather's apartment. "Now I don't want to stay here."

"We'll be patrolling your house all night, so you won't really be alone."

"Does that mean you think he'll come back?"

Barney rubbed his nose. "I don't want to unnerve you, but this perp was active at the golf course for a while, and he returned to the same houses repeatedly."

"Marvelous." She could hear Rip inside, still clawing at the door and growling. "Am I wrong to think that means he fixates on certain women?"

"No. That's pretty much my take on him, too."

"What'll I do if he comes back tonight?"

"Just lock up tight. You should be fine." He sighed. "And, actually, Crystal, I'm hoping he will come back. I'd like to get him off the streets. We figure he's from another community and driving here. That means he's ditching his car near his targets so he can walk to them."

"So that's why you'll be watching this area all night. You're hoping to find his car."

"Yes. And we'll be keeping a close eye on your house."

Crystal sighed. "That's good. I won't be quite as nervous knowing that."

"You've also got backup." Barney cocked an ear toward the front door. "Judging by that snarling, I think your grandpa's dog will make hash of anyone who steps foot on this property."

"I can't leave him outside. He runs away. I have to take him out on his leash."

Pushing to his feet, Barney said, "I'll sit in my truck while you take him for a little walk. Just stay within my line of sight. Once you're safely back inside, I'll leave, but I'll come back around ten so you can take him out again."

"Are you afraid of the dog? Is that why you're going to stay in your truck?"

He winked at her. "Actually, I was thinking my uniform might distract him from doing his business. But now that you ask, hell, yes, I'm afraid of him. He sounds like Cujo."

Chapter Fourteen

After taking Rip for his walk around the yard, Crystal waved goodbye to Barney and hurried back into the house. Once off his leash, Rip raced to her bedroom and sniffed all over, emitting a continuous low growl from deep in his throat. She'd heard the dog growl many times, normally at her, but this was different. More menacing. Barney was right; Rip sounded like Cujo, and she had no doubt that he would draw blood for the first time in his life if that awful man returned. The dog's propensity to guard and protect helped to soothe her nerves a bit.

She checked to make sure all the doors were locked. Then she emptied all her drawers and washed every stitch of lingerie that she owned. Rip followed her around the house, something he had never done. Prior to this, he'd been her indifferent roommate, sleeping belly up on his cushion and mostly ignoring her.

Each time she entered the laundry room and saw the damage done to the interior door, she cringed. He'd dug nearly all the way through the panel of solid wood. She didn't know how long that fruitcake had been inside her bedroom, but judging by how deeply the dog had gouged the oak, the man had lingered for a while.

Rip's constant presence near her was comforting. He had been generally destructive yesterday morning, scratching both doors and tearing up clothing, but tonight he'd focused all of his attention on the door that opened into the main part of the home. He'd clearly been intent on doing one thing: attacking the intruder.

Chills ran down her spine when, as she was putting away the lacy garments, she realized that two pairs of her French-cut panties were gone. She was also missing a nightie. And even worse, her bed, made up before she'd left for work that morning, had been disturbed. Only slightly, but being a neat freak, she noticed. Blood began pounding in her temples as she drew back the comforter and saw that her uninvited visitor had ejaculated on her sheets. Bile rose up the back of her throat. She started to strip off the linens to wash them on a sterilizing cycle but then thought better of it.

She called the sheriff's department instead. Doreen was still on shift.

"This is Crystal Malloy again," Crystal told her. "Would it be possible for me to speak with Deputy Sterling?"

"He's out on his route. No can do."

Crystal wanted to reach over the airway and give the woman a good shake. "Can you get in touch and ask him to call me?"

"Sure. What's your number?"

Despite the fact that Crystal knew the department kept a record of all incoming calls, she gave Doreen the information and ended the conversation. Sitting at the table, Crystal waited for her cell phone to ring. Rip sat beside her chair, his gaze fixed on her face. Her heart twisted with gratitude. "You know I'm upset, don't you? And you're worried about me."

The dog whined. Crystal bent to stroke his head. He rarely allowed her to touch him without growling, but this time he endured her attention without protest.

"Will you protect me, Rip?"

He whined again and licked her wrist. That small gesture told her a wealth of things that the dog couldn't express with words. She nearly parted company with her skin when her phone finally rang. It was Barney, and Crystal struggled to explain what she'd found on her sheets without using an explicit description.

"That's *fabulous*," he said. "I mean, I know you don't see it as a good thing, Crystal, but I do. He finally screwed up. We've got a DNA sample. If he's done this stuff before and his DNA is on record, we can ID him. I'll pick up the sheets when I stop by at ten for you to take the dog out. Don't mess with them. I'll wear gloves and bag them as evidence."

An image of the evidence on her mauve sheets leaped back into her mind, and Crystal felt as if she might get sick. She and Tanner had made love on that linen. She felt as if something special and beautiful had been desecrated.

"Do you have any spares?" Barney asked.

Crystal forced herself to focus on the topic of conversation. "Sheets, you mean? Yes. Two more sets."

"Good. You may not see that pair for a while."

"I don't want them back. I never want to see them again."

"I'm sorry this happened, Crystal. Just make sure the doors are locked and the windows are securely fastened." He paused. "Would you like to talk with someone? Serena Paul, one of our deputies, could come out. Sometimes it helps to have a sounding board, and she's a really nice gal."

"Thanks for offering, but I'll be fine."

When the call ended, Crystal went to double-check every exterior door. Then she realized she hadn't checked the windows, which she normally kept closed. While she was going from room to room, it occurred to her that the kitten hadn't made an appearance. She searched the house and found him asleep in a laundry basket.

"Hey, baby. That's a good hiding place." As she petted No Name, she heard coyotes howling in the adjacent woods. The sound made her skin crawl. "I'm sure glad you're not out there," she told the cat. "They'd polish you off in one bite."

Then she heard Rip bark. Carrying the kitten, she followed the sound to the doorway of what would one day be Tuck's bedroom. Snarling, Rip stood in front of the closed and locked slider. The sound he emitted was vicious, indicating that the heeler sensed something dangerous outside. When the dog ran to the living room picture windows and did the same thing, Crystal felt certain he was trying to tell her something.

"Is someone bad out there, Rip, or are you just worried about the coyotes?"

The heeler turned to look at her, snapped his teeth, and jerked his head. Then he barked again. Alarmed but convinced no one was inside the house, Crystal tried to collect her thoughts and reason her way through this. In the surrounding area, coyotes were prevalent, and Rip surely knew that. He had a keen sense of hearing and smell. He'd also covered the surrounding terrain on foot countless times when he ran away. If he hadn't encountered coyotes, then he had undoubtedly heard them and smelled them. Yet he'd never growled at the windows in all the time that he'd lived here with her.

Crystal deposited the purring kitten on the sofa and plucked her cell phone from its case. *Better safe than sorry.* Barney wouldn't be back until ten, and it was now only nine. She looked at her recent call history to find the deputy's number, selected it, and pressed CALL.

Barney answered on the fifth ring. "Hello?"

"Barney, this is Crystal Malloy." She quickly described Rip's odd behavior. "It's as if he's trying to tell me something dangerous is outside."

For just a moment, Barney didn't speak. Then he said, "Blue heelers are incredibly smart dogs and fiercely protective, Crystal. Listen to him and to me. It's been a half hour since I patrolled your house and the parallel roads. That's enough time for that jerk to have parked somewhere and walked to your place."

Crystal turned in a circle. Rip was in her bedroom now, growling at her sliding glass door. Tingles of alarm moved over her scalp.

"Do you have a bathroom door that locks?" Barney asked.

"Yes."

"Good. How about a rolling pin?"

"I, um—yes." She never used it. She was horrible with pie dough. "I've got one."

"Grab it. Lock yourself in the bathroom. I'm calling for backup, and I'm on my way. Any deputy who comes to an exterior door will knock—five knocks, with a pause in between each one. Then they'll wait a moment and do it again until you answer. Do *not* open the door until the person identifies himself."

"You're scaring me."

"I intend to. Garrett Jones, one of our deputies, has desk duty tonight. After you called about your sheets, I contacted him and shared the information. It's a new clue, so to speak, something more that we can run through the database to compare MOs that are on file. Deputy Jones found a match, a perp in Medford, Oregon. The police force there never caught the guy, but his DNA is on file. He repeatedly left a calling card on women's sheets."

"So they know this man's DNA, but they have no clue who he is?"

"Do you have the rolling pin yet?"

Crystal raced to the kitchen and grabbed the implement. "Got it." Trying to calm herself down, she jokingly said, "Now what do I do? Roll him flat and crimp his edges?"

"Now you go to the bathroom and lock the door. If anyone tries to come in, swing that rolling pin at his face with all your strength as he gains entry. Don't hesitate and don't hold anything back. Once you've injured him, keep swinging."

"Okay, I'm in the bathroom." Crystal turned the little knob lock. "You do realize that a nail or hairpin will open this lock. Right?"

"Yes, but you'll hear it disengage. Be ready. Pretend you're standing over home base and want to hit the ball clear out of the park."

"Do you understand what that will do to his face?" She could hear Rip's claws clacking on the barnwood planks as he ran from room to room. His ferocious growls made her nerves leap. "I thought this man was weird but harmless."

"That's what we thought, Crystal. And that may still be true. The calling card left on sheets is the only commonality so far, but—and it's a big but—most men with lingerie fetishes get their jollies by doing that on pieces of sexy underwear, not on bed linens. I think Medford got too risky for him and he chose our town as a safer target."

Crystal tried to imagine destroying a man's face with a rolling pin, and even though she was frightened, her stomach turned at the thought. "I—okay—I'm ready to bonk anyone who comes through the door."

"With all the strength you've got, right in the face,"

he reminded her. "And then don't stop swinging. The DNA collected from sheets in Medford was matched with DNA found on a corpse, Crystal. The woman was raped and strangled."

"Oh, dear God." Crystal's head went swimmy. "How far away are you?"

"Ten minutes, tops. Erin De Laney is closer. If she gets there first, you can trust her. She's a great cop. Is the dog still doing his Cujo thing?"

"Yes. I can hear him growling."

"Stay in that bathroom."

Crystal climbed into the bathtub after Barney hung up. The bathroom was small, and doing so gave her more swinging area with the rolling pin. She could still hear Rip racing from room to room. What if that awful man broke into her house and hurt the dog? Or what if Rip attacked a county deputy? Not everyone understood the blue heeler's hatred of uniforms, and right now the dog was beside himself. He might do a lot more than pinch with his teeth if someone came inside the house.

She stepped out of the bathtub. Rip was out there, ready to protect her with his life. But she didn't want him to pay that price. If he attacked a law officer, a judge might order him to be euthanized.

Palms sweating and hands shaking, she unlocked the door and cracked it open. "Rip! Here, Rip!"

Crystal couldn't recall a single time that Rip had ever come when she called him, but an instant later he appeared outside the door. She drew it back and coaxed him inside the bathroom. Once she had reengaged the lock, she crouched to loop her spare arm around his sturdy neck.

"Good boy. You're such a good dog."

He rumbled at her for hugging him, but even as the

sound came up from his throat, he licked her face. The gesture brought tears to her eyes. Somewhere along the line, he had come to at least like her, and against all her better judgment, she'd come to love him. How had that happened?

Setting all sentiment aside, she stepped back into the tub and assumed a batting stance. A minute passed, only it seemed like ten. Her knees and thigh muscles began to ache. Finally, she sighed and relaxed, but she kept the rolling pin on her shoulder.

Rip lay on the bathroom rug and gazed up at her with a bewildered frown. She couldn't help but smile. "I know. Pretty crazy, huh? If a murderer comes through that door, he'll probably take the rolling pin away from me. Then it will be up to you to save me. Will you do that, Rip?"

He drew his tongue back into his mouth and whined.

"Right. I know you will. Tuck always told me that you'd lay down your life for him. Now I think you'd die for me, too." She heard something and went quiet. Listening, she heard it again, five spaced knocks and then silence. "A deputy," she told the dog. She climbed from the tub. "You need to stay here," she said as she cracked open the door and slipped from the room. "Be good. Don't scratch the door. I'll be back."

As Crystal crossed the main living area, she heard the knock again and determined that it came from the front door. Her heart was pounding and she was still holding the rolling pin on her shoulder as she stepped closer. "Who's there?" she called.

A woman replied, "Deputy De Laney, Mystic County Sheriff's Department."

Crystal hurried to open the door. De Laney stood on the porch, holding out her ID so Crystal could verify who she was. She needn't have bothered. Crystal had seen the deputy around town and recognized her. A slender brunette with blue eyes, she filled out the county-issue khaki uniform in a way no man ever could. A chocolate brown Stetson sat on her head, the brim tipped slightly forward. She wore her shoulder-length hair pulled back with a clip.

"Have they caught him?" Crystal asked.

"May I come in?"

"Oh, of course." Crystal stepped back. "I'm sorry. Where are my manners?"

The deputy came inside and immediately turned to relock the door. "No, they haven't caught him. But I saw a man looking in one of your side windows when I pulled up. He ran. I called it in. Deputy Sterling and Deputy Tanger are hoping to find his vehicle parked on a parallel road and intercept him."

Crystal realized she still had a death grip on the rolling pin. Compared to the composed and self-confident woman who had just entered the house, she felt ridiculous. As she went to put the baking tool on the breakfast bar, she could hear Rip clawing at the bathroom door. "So you didn't chase him. Wise decision. If he's the Medford guy, he's killed a woman."

A slight smile curved the deputy's lips. "I'm perfectly capable of holding my own with a man," she said. "But my assignment is to protect you while the guys do the fun stuff."

"Thank you." Crystal gestured toward the sofa. "Even if protecting me isn't as exciting, I'm relieved you're here. Please, have a seat."

"No, thanks. With your permission, I'd like to check all the doors and windows."

"Permission granted. I've already checked them, but I guess you just never know."

"Right. Unless you have high-grade locks, they may

be easy to pick. Even dead bolts can be compromised by an experienced burglar."

Crystal shivered as the female officer toured the house to make sure all points of ingress were secure. When the deputy returned, her posture seemed more relaxed. "We're good." She extended her right arm and gave Crystal a full smile. "My first name's Erin."

Crystal shook hands with her. "What a crazy evening. Do you think there's any chance this is the guy from Medford?"

"Possibly. It's not that far to drive." She walked to the dining table. "Mind if I sit here?"

"Not at all. May I get you something to drink?"

Erin sent her a grateful look. "I'm dying for a glass of water. I forgot my bottle at home, and I didn't get an evening break."

Crystal deduced that the deputy had missed getting a break on her account. "I'm sorry. I may have overreacted when I realized someone had been in the house, but I've always been told never to try dealing with a situation like that by myself."

"Good advice." Erin's blue eyes sparkled and emanated kindness. "And I'm very glad you followed it. Even though I've been trained, I wouldn't go in my house if I suspected someone was inside. I'd call for help, too. Someone who's broken into a home is on the alert for trouble. You can't know where he may hide to jump out at you, and he could be armed."

Crystal sighed. "I was frightened. I'll admit it. And that was before I learned that this guy might be a killer."

"Any intruder might be a killer. They have a lot to lose if they get caught."

A voice blasted over the hand unit Erin carried on her hip. The sound startled Crystal so badly that she slopped water from the glass that she'd just filled. Erin listened to what was said. Crystal recognized Barney Sterling's voice coming over the channel, but she didn't understand much of the cop jargon.

When the transmission ended, Erin sighed. "Well, they've found his car, or think they have. Tanger called in the plate number. Now they're getting in position to watch the vehicle. With any luck, he'll think he's gotten away and try to reach it."

Crystal delivered the glass of water and an optional cup of ice. Erin tipped the tumbler back and drank all sixteen ounces without taking a breath. "Ah," she said, then wiped her mouth with the back of her hand. "Sorry. I was really parched." She got up from the chair. "Mind if I get more?"

A moment later she returned to the table. This time she dropped a few cubes of ice into the water and only sipped. Crystal wanted to scold Rip for scratching at the bathroom door, but given that she knew it would do no good, she took a seat across from the deputy instead.

Erin inclined her head. "Is that the dog that sounds like Cujo?"

"Yes. I'm surprised he isn't doing his most ferocious growl."

The deputy's cheek dimpled in a half smile. "Thanks for locking him up. A lot of dogs detest uniforms."

Tuck knew it was silly, but he was worried about Crystal. Normally, she tried to drop by and see him at least once a day, and failing in that, she almost always called. But he hadn't heard from her today. Busy, he supposed. Sometimes he forgot the hectic pace you kept when work and daily necessities pulled you in different directions. It was ten past nine. She'd probably gone to bed, thinking she'd have plenty of time to visit with him tomorrow, her only free day of the week.

He clicked off the TV and pushed farther back in the recliner. Beside him on the table sat a cold beer. The faint scent of hops drifted to his nose as the effervescence released its fragrance. His floor lamp cast a circular spot of light on the ceiling, giving him something to stare at. He liked Essie's living room better than his own. Even though half of hers was taken up by office furniture, she'd still managed to create a cozy and attractive sitting area, and he appreciated the little touches—the fancy lampshade with flowers on it and the small throw pillows barely large enough to support someone's head. Useless things, but he admired them because she did.

A knock came at his door. He swore under his breath. These days he kept the damned thing locked. He wanted no women in his apartment unless he invited them. Since Crystal had hired that lawyer, Tuck no longer had to hide his indulgences, but he still didn't appreciate feminine yammering or snooping.

"Comin'," he called.

He'd get his brace off on Monday, and he couldn't wait. The doc called it a cast, but to Tuck it was a newfangled excuse for one. Still, it was lightweight and had done the job. It might take him a few days to work his arm muscles back up to full strength, but at least he'd be able to move freely and bend his wrist again. He struggled to his feet and crossed the floor with what he felt were strong strides. *Almost recovered,* he thought. *I'll be able to go home soon.* What a fine kettle of fish that was, because now that he'd met Essie, he wasn't sure he wanted to leave.

"Who is it?" he called out.

"Me," a soft voice replied.

A smile sprang to Tuck's mouth. "Hot damn." He disengaged the door chain and opened the portal. Essie looked so pretty standing in the hall. She was all gussied up in a straight brown skirt and matching jacket over a silky blouse the same color as pearls. "Come on in, beautiful."

She smiled and accepted the invitation, running the palm of a slender hand over his chest as she moved past him. With only that little touch, she made him feel forty years old again and hornier than a three-pronged billy goat. "What brings you so late? I figured you'd be in your nightie and reading a good book by now."

She turned to face him as she reached the sofa. "I came to stay over if you don't mind having me."

Tuck's heart skipped a beat. "Stay over?"

A mysterious smile curved her mouth. A bewitching twinkle warmed her eyes. She peeled off the brown jacket to reveal a long-sleeve red cardigan underneath it.

"You cold? I can turn the heat on."

Essie giggled. "No, silly. The sweater is my getaway garment. Patricia the Horrible watches the camera footage. She allows no intimate fraternization between unmarried residents. But she can't watch every second of footage, so if she sees me enter your apartment wearing one thing and leaving in something else come morning, she may think she missed some frames."

"Uh-*huh*." That was Tuck's standby response when he couldn't think of anything else to say. *Over, she's staying over.* Did that mean what he hoped it meant? "Can I get you something?"

She slowly drew off the cardigan. Hussy red, it was, and the color made his blood hum through his veins. "Just you," she said as she tossed the sweater on the table.

Tuck didn't need to hear that invitation twice. "The bed or the sofa?"

"Sit in your chair first. I want to set the mood."

He was already in the mood. But when a woman was slowly unfastening her blouse and a black lace bra played peekaboo with a man, he didn't argue the fine points. He sat in his recliner.

Essie twirled to look at him. It seemed to him that she went into slow motion, taking so long to get that dad-blamed blouse off that he wanted to get up and help her. Only then he realized she was performing an elegant striptease. He couldn't for the life of him relax on the recliner. He sat forward on the edge of the seat like an offensive line center who was about to snap the football. All his muscles went taut. His attention was riveted entirely on her and what those slender fingers might uncover next.

Holy smokin' Jehoshaphat. As she unveiled the bra, he saw that it was like no other he'd ever seen, possibly because it wasn't lace after all, but more like doily crochet with dainty black flowers and just as many holes. Parts of her breasts showed through, and as all-over beautiful as they were, his gaze snapped to those erect nipples that posed for him like harlots on a street corner. He started to get up.

"Ach!" Essie held up a hand. "You stay right there, mister. I'm not done yet."

Tuck feared if he waited for her to be done, he might be finished before he got started. "Essie." His voice sounded like somebody had both hands wrapped around his throat. "This ain't necessary."

She unfastened her skirt, turned partly away from him, and began inching the waistband down over one bare hip—only then he saw that it wasn't totally bare. A thin band of black elastic pressed against her soft, creamy flesh. A *thong*? He'd only ever seen them in girlie magazines.

He was up off the chair so fast that he felt like his

new hip joint had been lubricated with WD-40. He looped his good arm around Essie's waist and drew her back against his chest. Her shoulder blades poked against his ribs.

"I'm not finished," she protested.

Tuck hated that his right hand was partly covered by fiberglass. But he made do with what he had and slowly moved his left palm over her body until he reached her breasts. She gasped and arched, welcoming his touch. He was pleased she wasn't quarreling with him about it now.

She'd come here to seduce him, and he was plumb seduced. He wished he could sweep her off her feet, but he wasn't strong enough yet. Instead he led her to his bedroom, jerked back the comforter, removed the rest of her clothes, and nestled her on the mattress. She still wore her brown heels, but unless he decided to kiss the undersides of her toes, a sensation he knew drove some women wild, he didn't give a shit about her footwear.

She tried to unfasten his shirt as he lowered himself over her, but her hands went still when he drew one of her nipples into his mouth. Tuck's last conscious thought was that she liked this. Well, his brain did resurface once when he brought her to a climax and she screamed. For a split second, he worried that her cries might echo up and down the hall to disturb the peace, and he knew Flintlock would be all over that. Otherwise Tuck just lost himself in this sweet, wonderful woman who gave so generously of herself to him. She made him feel as virile as a young man again, and he used every last store of strength he had to make her scream twice.

Not for the first time, Tanner wondered why drug researchers hadn't developed a safe sleeping pill for kids. Tori sat in the tub with bubbles pillowing around her shoulders, a new requisite for bathing when Daddy had to help. She was beginning to feel modest, and Tanner, not wishing to discourage that in any way, had started investing in a physician-approved bubble-bath liquid that helped keep his daughter covered while he assisted during hair washing. Right now she was chattering like a windup doll. Rip, of course, was her main topic of discussion. Tori wanted a blue heeler, amen. Now that Tanner had seen how wonderful Rip was with kids, he wasn't quite as predisposed to avoid that breed when he went puppy shopping.

With a weary sigh, he sat on the toilet. His daughter slithered around like a cartoon mermaid in sea froth, one side of her hair wet and springing back into curls, the other side as straight as an arrow and moist only at the ends. Tanner glanced at his watch. He'd allow her five more minutes. Then it would be time to give her a quick shampoo and rinse, wrap her in a towel, and leave the room so she could put on her pj's in privacy.

"How come Nana is coming over to sleep on the futon in our study?" she asked for at least the sixth time. "I thought it was her night out."

"It was, but she came home early and offered to come over so I can go somewhere." Tanner planned to pay Crystal a surprise visit and turn that lame air-kiss he'd given her earlier into a full-blown one that would curl her toes. "Nana's bringing movies. You get to stay up late because there's no school tomorrow. She's going to make her super-fast caramel corn. Just remember to brush your teeth before bed."

Tori's brow furrowed in concentration. "You're going to see Crystal, aren't you?"

Tanner tried never to lie to his kids. "I might. Do you object to that?" He'd also learned not to dumb down any conversation with his daughter. "If you don't like her, I'll stop seeing her." *Really, Tanner? Don't make promises that'll be hard to keep.* "You and Michael always come first, no matter what."

"I like her. She's taking me to the library to find dog books. She says reading Nana's romances at my age is like opening Pandora's box. I don't think she knew the box was actually a jar, but that's okay. Not everyone thinks Greek mythology is fun to read."

"What do you find interesting about it?" Tanner could remember struggling to stay awake while he studied that stuff at university.

"It's like fairy tales, Daddy, only for grown-ups. What's a girdle? I looked it up, but none of the definitions explained why Hippopotamus would have one."

Tanner was so relieved that Tori had just referred to Hippolyta as a huge amphibious mammal. It made her seem more like the eight-year-old she actually was. "A girdle is— Well, it can be anything from a belt to an elasticized body garment for women that trims their figures and flattens their stomachs. Hippolyta's was made of gold. I think it was probably a really wide belt."

"And it was magic. Heracles killed her to get it."

Tanner wondered which reading material was worse for the development of his daughter's character, Greek mythology or his mom's romances. At least in love stories the main protagonists didn't typically murder people to possess prized treasures.

"Okay, Princess, it's time to shampoo."

"Aw." Tori's voice went whiny. "Why can't I keep my hair straight for tomorrow?"

"Because one side is already wet and going curly." When he glimpsed tears welling, he quickly added, "Crystal gave you a straightening tool. If you want no curls tomorrow, I can do your hair in the morning." As he said that, Tanner wondered how he'd pull that off. "I may not be quite as good at it as Crystal is, though."

Crystal lay on her bed, covered by only a clean sheet. After apprehending the Lingerie Burglar, Barney Sterling had come to bag her soiled linen as evidence, and Erin had helped her remake the bed. Wanting to be sure all her bedding was sterile, Crystal had thrown her blankets and comforter in the front loader. Then she'd put them in the dryer, which would finish its cycle in a few minutes.

She had no reason to feel nervous now. Whether harmless or dangerous, the burglar was in custody. Only a match of his DNA with that of the Medford killer would finger him for murder, and the laboratory process might take weeks. Regardless, Barney had assured her that Thomas McVoyer would be kept in jail until the authorities could verify that he'd harmed no one. Even then he would do jail time for breaking and entering.

Tom McVoyer. With a first and last name like that, I might turn out weird, too, Crystal thought. It was strange how names sometimes seemed to predict people's destinies. She'd never forget the Idaho dentist named Dr. Pang, or the meat cutter named Floyd Butcher. *Voyer* was spelled differently than *voyeur*, but the pronunciation was almost the same. Had the Lingerie Burglar been teased as a youngster by other kids who called him a "Peeping Tom" or "voyeur"?

She heard a noise outside and jerked around to stare at the sliding glass door. Rip whined and stood on his hind legs to put his paws on the edge of the mattress. He cocked his head and studied her. "I'm okay, Rip. I just have trouble calming down after a bad scare."

The dog jumped on the bed and lay down about a

foot away. He'd never offered to sleep with her, and Crystal knew the only reason he did tonight stemmed from his desire to comfort her.

"You know I'm uneasy, and you're trying to make me feel safe. Thank you, Rip. You're becoming one of my best friends."

No Name suddenly joined them.

"What is this? Has my bed become a community area?" She couldn't help but smile as she fingered the kitten's fur. "What a night."

No Name meowed, the sound plaintive.

"Oh, dear heaven, I totally forgot to feed you guys! You're probably starving."

Crystal swung out of bed and rushed to the kitchen. She put kibble and fresh water in the cat bowls first, and then she started to feed Rip his usual fare. Only when she glanced down at his face, which was becoming dearer to her by the moment, she remembered a steak in the fridge that she had thawed for her dinner tonight. Since she'd already eaten at the Cauldron, even if it did seem like forever ago, she decided to cook the meat for Rip instead.

"A hero should dine on steak," she said. "You protected me tonight. If not for you, I wouldn't have known that creep was outside and he wouldn't have been brought into police custody."

After heating a skillet, she added a tiny dollop of oil. The steak sizzled when it hit the pan. She seasoned it lightly with only salt, vaguely recalling that either garlic or onion powder, both her favorites, was bad for canines.

"Rare, medium rare, medium, or well-done?" she asked the heeler.

He barked and pranced, clacking his nails on the wood. Crystal couldn't determine what his vote was, but she could see that he was eager, so she decided on rare. When the steak was done, she put it on a plate and cut it into bite-size pieces. As soon as she set the meal on the floor, Rip devoured it.

After licking the plate clean, he appealed to her for more with one of those happy grins. "That's all I've got that's special, Rip. But I'll fill your bowl with regular dog food, just in case you're still hungry."

After measuring out some kibble, Crystal returned to her room, leaving the lights on at the front of the house. She couldn't bring herself to turn them off, not tonight. Barney believed that he had caught the culprit. The registration of the man's vehicle linked him to a Medford address. But what if Thomas McVoyer was just another tourist who had been taking a walk along the road? In Mystic Creek, a lot of people, even women, did that late in the evening. It was one of the perks of living in a small, rural community where the crime rate was low. No evidence was found in McVoyer's car to connect him to the burglaries, which troubled Crystal. If he was the man who was in her house today, where had he stashed her lingerie?

Another noise from outside gave her a start. This time it was a loud thump. Rip jumped up on her bed again, but this time, instead of staring at the window, he pricked his ears and looked at the east wall, which divided her room off from the front of the house.

"What was that?" Her skin felt like she was being turned inside out.

The dog nudged her arm with his cold nose. Then he sat erect and whined. Crystal's body jerked when a heavy knock came at the front door. Who would be showing up here this late at night? It was half past ten.

She slipped out of bed, grabbed a cotton kimono she used as a cover-up, and crept from the bedroom. Rip leaped down to flank her left leg. She felt his warm fur grazing her calf.

"Who is it?" she yelled.

"It's me, Tanner."

Crystal knew that voice, deep yet silky. Last night she'd felt the vibration of it in his chest as she lay in his arms. She threw the door open. The porch light bathed him in gold, making his honey-colored streaks shimmer. She looked into his eyes and could barely restrain herself from seeking the safety of his embrace. Rip gave a happy bark.

"I've never been so glad to see anyone in my whole life!" she cried. And then she followed her instincts, pressing her body against his and hugging his neck. "Oh, Tanner."

"Hey? What's wrong?"

"The Lingerie Burglar was inside the house when you brought me home!"

"The *what*?" He released her and bent to pet Rip, who bounced excitedly at his feet. "The *who*?"

"That's what they call him. At first he was only a Peeping Tom, but he escalated to burglary. He rifled through my underwear drawers, stole some of my lingerie, and left a disgusting calling card on my sheets! And everyone at the sheriff's department thinks he may have raped and strangled a woman in Medford."

"Dear Lord." Tanner looped his arms around her waist again. "Why in the world didn't you call me?"

"I knew you had the kids. They couldn't be here with all that going on."

He pushed the door closed, engaged the dead bolt, and led her to the sofa. "I'm glad I came. You shouldn't be alone, not tonight of all nights."

When he sat beside Crystal on the sofa, she leaned

against him, feeling absolutely safe for the first time since she'd found the front door ajar. Then, seeing Rip sitting near his outstretched legs, she felt a stab of guilt. The heeler had made her feel safe, too, and if he could read her mind, she didn't want him to be offended. She felt as if she were falling in love with two different guys simultaneously, only one of them had four legs.

"Rip protected me through all of it. Didn't you, Rip?"

"Good job, Rip!" Taking Crystal with him, Tanner leaned sideways to ruffle the canine's fur. "No, *awesome* job, man. I'm so proud of you." Then to Crystal, he said, "Tell me everything. I'm dying to know why the rolling pin is on the bar. Did you make a pie while all that was happening?"

Crystal giggled. It sounded a little hysterical, even to her. "No. That was my weapon."

"Dear God."

"I'm so glad you came back. Why? Did you sense that I needed you?"

"Um, I wish I could say yes. But the truth is— Well, remember that air-kiss I gave you as I left? My mom got home early, and I wanted to come back to give you a real one that would knock your socks off."

Crystal couldn't think of anything she needed more right then. "I'm not wearing socks, but I can pretend. Please, kiss me and knock them off."

Chapter Fifteen

Crystal couldn't imagine Tanner being able to top the wondrous feelings he'd gifted her with last night, but somehow he did. With the only light coming from a fixture over the kitchen sink, her bedroom lay mostly in dimness, making him seem real one moment and more like a shadow the next, every titillating touch of his hands on her body airy, every brush of his lips on her skin whisper soft. He built the anticipation and need within her until she could barely stand it.

After a crinkling of foil, he rose over her, his muscular body limned in a golden shimmer. As he pushed into her, she grabbed his defined upper arms and lifted her hips to meet his. Then she found his cadence, which echoed the violent hammering of her heart. Desire and urgent need edged out sanity.

Since young adulthood she'd imagined how it might feel to ride a gigantic wave on a surfboard to its crest, only to lose balance and succumb to its indescribable power. Now she knew that it was a beautiful but devastating sensation, becoming like flotsam, surfacing and then getting sucked under, being tossed to incredible heights and then pulled down into a crushing depth where her lungs ached for breath and her whole body clamored for release. When the climax finally came, it was like an explosion of brightness, splintering through darkness until she rode a gentle wave of absolute pleasure to a sun-warmed shore of bone-melting contentment.

Limbs intertwined, skin damp, they lay in each other's arms like exhausted children who'd run and played too hard all day. Crystal could barely muster the strength to tell him, "Oh, Tanner, that was beyond incredible."

She felt his lips curve into a smile against her hair. "It's called spontaneous combustion."

Crystal sighed. "If I live to be a hundred, I'll never experience the equal of that."

"Oh, yeah? Give me thirty minutes."

He'd taken her words as a challenge. Obviously. She smiled and snuggled closer to him. "I need at least an hour, and you've got to go home."

"Nope. I already texted Mom. Told her about the underwear murderer."

"That makes him sound as if he goes around killing panties."

"Don't change the subject by trying to make a joke. I'm not leaving you here alone." When she started to protest, he tightened his hand over her hip. "Period. End of discussion. Mom can handle the kids. I care about you. Don't ask me to walk away when you may be in danger. That guy they arrested, with a car registration showing a Medford address? Medford's not that far away. If I'm from there, and that guy in jail is from there, how many other Medford men could possibly be in town? No offense to Sterling, but right now his case hangs on circumstantial evidence. He found nothing in the vehicle. Where did the dude put your underwear? Unless he has a residence here or found somewhere to stash his souvenirs, he didn't take your things. They could have the wrong man."

"You're scaring me."

"I don't mean to. I'm just saying that until we know for sure he's the man who entered your house, I'm not leaving you alone." Just then, Crystal felt Rip jump up on the bed behind her. "And hello. Rip says I'm right. He wants to protect you, too."

"Or he just knows I'm upset and is trying to comfort me."

"I'll double down on that. Protect, comfort. Kind of the same thing."

Crystal thought of the long night that would lie ahead if Tanner bailed on her. She would have Rip, of course, and she'd probably be fine, but she would feel twice as safe if Tanner stayed. Then she'd have two bodyguards, and she had a feeling both of them would do whatever it took to protect her.

"Thank you," she said.

"Thank *you*," he whispered. "You've made me feel really alive again. Not that my kids and mom don't. Please don't get me wrong. But meeting you, coming to care for you—well, it's a totally different kind of feeling."

Crystal almost reminded him she wasn't looking for a permanent relationship, but she let the moment slip by. Being with him and his kids had given her a glimpse of everything she was missing, and for the first time in her adult life, she wanted to take a chance on love.

She drifted off to sleep in the strong circle of his arms, aware of Rip lying just behind her, also guarding her safety.

The dream came softly, just as it always did. She was a young girl, straining with all her might to draw back the bow far enough to put power into her shot. Sweat broke out all over her body. She trembled with the effort. Daddy would be proud of her if she did it right. Maybe, if she did it perfectly and hit her target, he'd even say he loved her. A hunger to hear those words created a raw, empty place inside her, and that ached far worse than her arms and back as she overtaxed her muscles.

"Come on, Crystal. You're a tall, strong girl. Pull it back, steady and sure. Your arms are jumping all over the place."

Because I'm not strong enough, she wanted to scream. Only, she didn't, because then he'd never say he loved her.

"Sight in. Take a deep breath and let it out. Aim for the heart."

Crystal squinted at the target. Daddy bought big paper pictures of bull elk, and the heart was painted on its body, a red ball surrounded with black rings. He tacked the targets on stacked hay bales. The outlined dot at the center of the red area was the bull's-eye. If her arrow didn't hit there, he'd cuss, light a cigarette, and blame her for being such a disappointment to him that she'd made him smoke behind her mom's back again. Then he'd tell her she had just put another nail in his coffin.

It was then that the dream always changed. Crystal struggled to awaken. Somewhere in her subconscious, she knew this was the nightmare. A recurring one she had experienced so many times that all she wanted was to open her eyes. Only, they seemed to be glued shut.

The bull's-eye remained the same, but the antlered elk vanished, and just as she released the arrow, the target became her little sister, Mary Ann. She was *beautiful*—not tall and skinny like Crystal with sharp features, but little with an oval face, a button nose, strawberry blond curls, and huge blue eyes. She looked like a church angel.

The arrow hit home, and Mary Ann jerked, her arms flying out at each side of her body as the impact knocked her backward. Crystal felt as if the arrow had plowed into her own chest instead. She couldn't breathe. *Running, running.* She had to reach Mary Ann. If she pulled the arrow out, it would be okay. It was archery practice, not real life. Nothing got hurt. It was just pretend.

Only when she reached the little girl lying on the grass, she *was* real. Not made of paper. And blood came away on Crystal's fingers. She held up her hands. The crimson dripped from her palms and went down her wrists. *No!* The scream echoed on the air, bouncing back at her. *No!*

Gasping for breath, Crystal jolted awake, barely managing to stop herself from screaming that word aloud. She jackknifed to a sitting position. Sweat from her skin dampened the sheets. With a sick lurch of her stomach, she recognized the muscular length lying beside her as Tanner's body. Thank God she hadn't woken him. The dream was something she shared with no one.

Okay. Okay. She gulped for breath. *Just a dream. Wake up. Focus on something real.* What Crystal's searching gaze landed on was Rip, who was wide-awake and sitting beside her on the mattress. She wrapped both arms around him, grateful when he didn't growl.

She grabbed the kimono that lay crumpled near her pillow and tugged it on. After picking up the dog, who still felt as heavy as a boulder, she swung out of bed. Once in the living room, she sank to the floor and braced her back against the wall, her arms still locked around the heeler. He licked at the tears streaming down her cheeks.

"I didn't mean to kill her," she told him in a whisper.

"I truly didn't, Rip." Her voice sounded little and choked, like that of the horrified child she'd once been. "Mama left to go grocery shopping during my practice hour. I was supposed to watch Mary Ann. My baby sister wanted me to stop shooting at targets and play with her." Crystal drew the dog closer and pressed her wet face against his fur. "Only, I wanted Daddy to love me. I knew he never would if I didn't practice."

Rip whined and twisted on her lap to lick her face again.

"Mary Ann wanted to play dolls and started pestering me. Every time I got my arrow nocked and was in a position to shoot, she'd dart out and make me lower the bow. I kept telling her I only had to practice a few more minutes. Finally, I bribed her to stop interfering by telling her I'd play with her for a whole hour if she'd be good. She agreed to the deal."

Crystal's mind tumbled back through the years, and she was eleven years old again, reliving those few moments. She'd resumed position and focused on the target. This time she knew she would hit the bull's-eye. Her shoulders and arms didn't ache, because Mary Ann's interruptions had given her several chances to rest. Daddy wasn't there. When she showed him her targets, he'd never know she'd cheated to hit the center.

"Okay, Mary Ann," she yelled. "I'm going to shoot now! Stay back out of my line of fire. Okay?"

"Okay!" Mary Ann called back.

Crystal took a bracing breath and drew a bead. And then, just as she let the arrow fly, Mary Ann cried, "Ha, ha! Fooled you!"

Those were the last words Crystal's baby sister ever spoke.

Crystal hugged the dog tighter. "I didn't mean to

hurt her, Rip. I was frustrated with her, but I truly didn't mean to hurt her. Why wouldn't anyone but Tuck believe that?"

Rip whined and bathed her face again. The rasp of his warm tongue soothed her. When the dream finally lost its hold on her, she took measured breaths until she felt drowsy again. Tanner stirred awake when she slipped back into bed. She scooted close and found the safe haven of his arms. The hollow of his well-padded shoulder provided her with a perfect pillow for her head.

"Where'd you go?" he asked.

"I just sat in the living room with Rip for a while. Bad dream."

"Need to talk about it?"

"No, I'm good." She had just talked about it with Rip, and oddly enough she felt better. Not good, but better. "I'd rather experience incredible again."

He rose on an elbow and bent his head to trail his silken lips over hers. "I think I can deliver on that request," he whispered.

And he did.

Tuck awakened at dawn in bed with Essie. He smiled with contentment. Their lovemaking the previous night had been beautiful, and there was no question in his mind that he'd fallen in love with her. At his age, what did a man do with feelings that ran so deep? He couldn't go down on bended knee yet, not even on a good day. And he sure as hell couldn't promise her forever. He couldn't even guarantee her six months.

As if she sensed the tension in him, she stirred awake and fixed him with that gorgeous brown gaze that always made him feel besotted. "Uh-oh. Morning-after regrets?"

He kissed her forehead. "Never that, Essie. I just realized I'm in love with you, and I'm not sure what to do about that."

She smiled. "I think you made a fabulous start last night. I'll be content with repeat, repeat, and *repeat*."

Tuck sighed. "This isn't only about sex for me."

She giggled and toyed with the silver hair on his chest. "At our age, it *can't* be only about sex. We'd both die of overexertion." Her hand cupped his breast muscle. "Has any woman told you that you've got the body of a much younger man?"

"Marge used to, but she died twenty-three years ago, when I was only fifty-seven. It's much nicer to hear that now."

"I'll tell you often, then."

Tuck couldn't help but laugh. "Are you deliberately tryin' to avoid talkin' about our feelin's for each other?"

Essie sighed and locked gazes with him. "Tucker Malloy, are you thinking that you need to make an honest woman of me? I didn't come here last night to make you feel obligated to me in any way."

"You're already an honest woman, one of the finest I've ever met. But I've gone and fallen in love with you, Essie. For me, that's really somethin', and I want a whole lot more than just sex from you. Bein' able to hold you in my arms. Wakin' up with you in the mornin'. Maybe havin' breakfast in bed together. And I sure as hell don't wanna sneak around to do it."

"Are you asking me to marry you?"

"I reckon I am."

"At our age? I'm seventy-eight."

"You don't have to wear white for the ceremony."

She giggled. "That's a mercy. God might strike me dead with a lightning bolt."

"Be serious, please. I ain't a player, Essie."

That brought her up on her elbow. "A *player*? Have you been reading the Urban Dictionary?"

"Nope. I got a granddaughter that uses young-folk language. And you're still laughing this off. If I'm alone in my feelin's, then just tell me so."

Her brown eyes went shimmery with tears. She traced his whiskery jaw with a fingertip. "You aren't alone. I have deep feelings for you, too. I just— Well, if you want the bald truth, my kids would have conniptions if I got married. Garth, especially, although Rebecca's no slouch in the greed department. They'd be afraid I might kick the bucket before you do and put their inheritance at risk in a community property state."

"We can sign one of them agreements. I don't want your money, darlin'. Hell, if I live to be a hundred, which ain't likely, I probably won't spend all of my own unless I go wild and buy a fleet of sports cars."

"Prenups are so *mercenary*. I hate the thought of that."

Tuck chuckled. "If it keeps your kids happy, nothin' else matters. All I want is you. So far as I'm concerned, you can give every dime to your kids right now, and we can live on my money. I'm not your kind of rich, but I sure as hell ain't poor."

"But I want to transform this facility. If I give my money away, I can't do that. And quite honestly, Tuck, I think I'd lose some of my drive if I stopped trying to build my holdings. I've been acquiring wealth since I was wet behind the ears. It's not the money that matters, but the challenge of keeping what's there and adding to it."

Tuck relaxed on his pillow with her in the circle of one arm. "I hear you. Givin' up my ranch in Idaho was hard for me. It was my reason for gettin' up in the mornin'."

"Did you notice a difference in your activity level once you sold it?"

"Damn straight. I bought me a twenty-acre hobby farm in Crystal Falls, and I kept my gelding, Bolt. No real money to make, and nothin' to lose if I just lazed around. I'm a rancher. If I'd had the capital, I would've stayed in Idaho and hired cowboys to do the work. That way, I could've supervised and stayed in the game. But I wasn't that rich, so I had to let it go."

"So you understand where I'm coming from."

"I do." Tuck understood better than she could know. "So keep doin' what you love. I'm supportive of it. But it brings us back to—what did you call that agreement?"

"A prenup. Only, I'm torn, Tuck. I'd like to believe my kids deserve to be my heirs, but blood alone doesn't afford them that privilege."

"Well, cut 'em out of your will, then. Give everything to charity. Just make sure, if we get married, that not a dime comes to me. I'll do the same on my side. Since you don't need it, I think all my money and assets oughta go to Crystal."

"I agree. I like that girl. She loves you, and she shows you that she does."

"Yep. And she sure as hell won't get a nickel from her parents."

"What happened, Tuck? I understood before when you hesitated to tell me about her past, but things have changed between us now."

Tuck closed his eyes. Essie was right; loving each other as they did, it didn't seem right to keep secrets from each other. He told her Crystal's story, leaving nothing out.

"Oh, dear," Essie said. "Poor Crystal. How could her parents turn on her like that? A girl that age shouldn't be left alone for target practice, much less be in charge of a younger child. What was her mother thinking?"

Tuck had traveled the same paths of reasoning so many times that doing it again only made him feel tired. "My daughter and her husband accused Crystal of murder. She was even taken in for questionin'. The cops figured out she was innocent of any wrongdoin', but by then the damage was done. My daughter and her husband were arrested and faced all kinds of charges. Lisa left the kids alone to go grocery shoppin'. Her husband put a lethal weapon in Crystal's hands and demanded that she target practice unsupervised. They had endangered both their children. Their reputations were destroyed, and that only made 'em madder at Crystal." He swallowed. "And there was somethin' more. I've never even told Crystal this, so you're on your honor. I never want her to know. She's had enough heartbreak."

Essie nodded. "You can trust me, Tuck."

"When I drove to Washington to get Crystal, I confronted her father. I knew my daughter wasn't blameless, but I held him to be more responsible for what happened. He was the one who forced Crystal to take up archery, the one who insisted that she practice daily, whether he was there or not. As I was lacin' into him, he turned to me and said, 'She's not mine. Your daughter was knocked up when I married her, and she never told me until just before Crystal was born three months early.' I was plumb speechless. But then it all started to make sense, how Mary Ann was the apple of her daddy's eye, while Crystal always seemed to be on the outside, lookin' in.

"What really broke my heart, though, was that Crystal wanted so bad to please that man. How she pandered to him. How hard she tried to make him notice her and feel proud. It was a hopeless situation for Crystal, a battle for his affection that she could never win. He adored his own daughter and had little attention to spare for some other man's child. With the exception of archery, of course. Only, he set the bar so high for Crystal that she could never please him by doin' that, either."

Essie patted his chest. "I'm so glad you took her away from them."

"Me, too. What really eats at me to this day is that my daughter went along with her husband, treatin' Crystal like she was the odd one out. You can't tell it now. Crystal's all grown up and seems okay. But they scarred her in places we can't see. They sure enough did."

After Essie got dressed and put on her getaway cardigan, Tuck saw her to the door and agreed to meet her for breakfast in the dining hall. Sunday was the official day for family members to drop by and the only time all week when the cooking was halfway decent. Every resident in the place looked forward to it. *Real* bacon. Tuck salivated as he took a quick shower, protecting his cast with a plastic bag. Afterward he took special care as he shaved and combed his hair. Essie was so beautiful. He wanted to look extra nice today. He finished off his grooming with a second splash of cologne. *Not too bad,* he decided, taking a final look in the mirror. Not for his age, at least.

He arrived at the dining hall, carrying Essie's brown jacket in a paper sack. He set it by her chair before he sat across from her. On Sundays they got menus, and that was a special treat.

"Uh-oh, I have to decide what I want again," Tuck

said with a laugh. "I get so used to not havin' a choice that seein' a menu gives me anxiety."

She sighed and said, "Just you wait. When I own this place, we'll have breakfast, lunch, and dinner menus, and they'll change daily. And the food will be prepared by an actual chef, not a grade-school cafeteria cook."

Tuck nodded. "Hurry it up, darlin'. Bacon every morning." He peered at the meat selection. "Holy smokes. Chicken-fried steak! With gravy. I think I've died and gone to heaven."

Essie decided on eggs Benedict with a short stack of pancakes on the side. "I won't be able to eat all of it," she said. "But I do miss my flapjacks."

They'd finished eating and were walking toward Tuck's apartment when Crystal and Tanner entered the building with Rip on a leash. The dog gave a joyful yip and lunged toward Tuck, jerking the leash from Crystal's hand. Tuck bent and spread his arms. The heeler jumped at his chest, and Tuck caught him in a hug.

"How's my boy?" Tuck pressed his face against the dog's fur. "I missed you so much."

Rip planted a paw on each of his shoulders and licked his face as if it were a rapidly melting ice-cream cone. Tuck couldn't help but laugh.

Just then Patricia Flintlock appeared. In Tuck's opinion, she looked like a drill sergeant with an attitude problem. He wondered why she hadn't joined the marines so she could tongue-lash people and receive merits for her nastiness.

"Get that *mongrel* out of the common area *now*," she said.

Tuck sorely wished Essie already owned this joint. But for now, Flintlock was in charge and could still throw her weight around. "You bet," Tuck told her. "It's startin' to smell like spoiled fish in here."

As they walked to his apartment, Tuck noticed that Crystal looked a little tired. He also noticed that Tanner held her hand, which made him hide a grin. *Hoorah,* he wanted to shout. His granddaughter couldn't do better than Tanner Richards. He was a stand-up guy.

Once inside Tuck's suite, Rip was allowed to run free. He was so excited to see Tuck that most of his attention was centered on him, but in between master-and-dog love sessions, the heeler circled back to Crystal. It touched Tuck that the dog had grown to love his granddaughter. And rightly so, in Tuck's opinion. She tried to hold herself apart and keep her feelings under tight rein, but she had a heart of pure gold.

Once the initial excitement died down, Crystal regaled Tuck and Essie with an account of everything that had happened last night. Now Tuck understood why she hadn't called or dropped by to see him.

"The Lingerie Burglar?" Essie repeated. "And people at the sheriff's department think he may have murdered a woman? Dear heavens. You should have spent the night with us." Essie's face turned scarlet. "Well, with Tuck, I mean."

Crystal didn't appear to have caught the slip, but Tuck saw Tanner's gaze sharpen. The younger man studied Essie for a moment and then flashed Tuck a knowing grin. Tuck winked.

"I was fine," Crystal assured them. "Rip protected me. And then Tanner came to spend the night."

Tuck watched his granddaughter's face turn as red as Essie's had seconds earlier. It was an aha moment, confirming what he had suspected when he saw Tanner holding Crystal's hand. The kids had a thing going. Tuck couldn't have been more pleased. He just hoped Crystal wouldn't bail out this time. In her younger years she'd been in relationships, but she'd always ended them without offering Tuck a clear explanation of why. That was how he'd learned the term *player*, because that was what she'd often told him when she was done with a guy and ready to move on. "He's a player, Tuck." Well, if there was anything Tuck could attest to, it was that Tanner Richards wasn't.

He decided to set aside his concerns about Crystal's inability to remain in a relationship. He didn't like what he'd just heard about someone entering his granddaughter's house, and he was even more worried about the possibility that the man had raped and strangled a Medford woman.

"Hearin' about that panty burglar makes me realize I need to share a secret with you, Crystal, and with Tanner, too, if he may be around when trouble occurs."

"I'm all ears," Crystal said with a smile.

"Me, too," Tanner inserted. "If that creep comes around again, I can use all the advice I can get."

"Well, this here is a secret about Rip. I trained him from a pup. Did a lot of readin' on how to do it. I wanted a dog I could count on in a life-or-death situation, a dog who'd go against impossible odds if I gave the command, or another man if it was ever necessary." Tuck fondled the dog's ears. "You gotta be careful when you train a dog to attack. The commands can't be easy to guess. You gotta be certain nobody, and I do mean nobody, will ever be able to tell your dog to attack or guess the command to call him off."

"Gotcha." Tanner winked at Crystal. "Although I have to say, Tuck, I don't think Rip needs much encouragement to attack someone."

"Oh, he'll pretend to attack." Tuck looked down at his dog. No one in the room knew just how well trained

Rip was. "But he don't mean to hurt nobody, and he's never drawn blood. If he's given the attack command, though, he'll go in for a kill."

Tuck felt the mood in the room change. Crystal had lost the color in her cheeks; Tanner had a solemn, thoughtful look on his face; and Essie sat forward as if she couldn't wait to hear what Tuck said next.

"Isn't that a little extreme, Tuck?" Crystal questioned him with her gaze.

Tuck looked her directly in the eye. "When you face a huge grizzly and all you got is a pistol that'll piss him off, you come talk to me about extreme. I love my dog, but when it comes to sacrificing Rip's life or my own, it don't take a whole lot of thinkin' for me to make the choice. I hope you never get into a pickle like that. But if it ever happens, you'll be glad you've got a dog that'll die to protect you or someone you love."

Crystal nodded. "I understand."

Tanner said, "I'm still stuck on the grizzly. Did that really happen, Tuck?"

Tuck chuckled. "Oh, yeah. And Rip saved my life. He's fast on his feet, that dog. He came out of it without a scratch. But he kept the bear so focused on him that I could get away. That old grizz didn't know what hit him. Rip went after the backs of his feet, just like any good heeler will. Old boar kept whippin' around, tryin' to whack him. One swipe would've been Rip's waterloo. But he never stayed in one place long enough to take a hit."

"So Rip didn't really attack the grizzly," Crystal said. "He only distracted it."

Tuck couldn't help it; he laughed. "Honey, you know how tall an old male grizz is when it's standin' on its hind legs? On average, ten feet. Now take measure of Rip. He attacked, but all he could bite was ankle and lower leg. Last time I dared to look back—I was runnin' for my life—I saw the bear go down on all fours, but Rip was managing to avoid the swipes. Don't know what happened after that. I only know Rip came back to the truck grinnin' like no tomorrow. We had us a couple of cold ones to celebrate."

Tanner shook his head. "That's a story I want to hear from beginning to end."

"Sounds like a plan." Tuck sat back in the recliner and patted his leg, inviting Rip to jump up. "But for now, with that burglar possibly still on the loose, it's more important to tell you the attack command. Never share it with your kids, Tanner. Youngsters don't understand the seriousness."

"I won't," Tanner assured him.

"Some trainers choose words in a foreign language that they figure nobody'll ever guess," Tuck explained. "I have enough trouble talkin' plain English, so I decided on a command I knew I'd remember even if I was scared half-senseless. Listen up, and don't forget it. It's *spring forward*. I can say it just talkin', and it don't mean squat to Rip." He ruffled the dog's fur. "But if I yell it, he goes for broke." Understanding his granddaughter's kind heart, Tuck smiled at her. "And if you decide that burglar has had enough, I chose your grandma's name, Margie, to call him off."

A bewildered frown pleated Crystal's forehead. "Spring forward. How on earth did you come up with that?"

Sad memories swamped Tuck. "The day I picked you up in Washington and took you home to Idaho, I was still grievin' for your grandmother. And there I was, saddled with a child to raise, all of a sudden like." Tuck remembered how panicky he'd felt. He'd tried so hard to regroup and get over losing Marge, but it had been easier said than done. "People had told me I needed to move forward with my life. That I couldn't feel sad forever. I knew that was true, but I was makin' progress at a snail's pace. And in a blink I knew I had to hurry myself up. All the way home to the ranch, I kept thinkin', *You gotta* spring *forward, Tuck. No more lollygaggin' allowed.* And in all the days that followed, when I started to feel sad and depressed, I'd tell myself, *Get a grip. Think of that child. Spring forward.* Those words came to mean a lot to me, because I did spring forward. I made a new life for you and myself. So when it came time to choose a command for Rip, I chose that. I knew I'd never forget those words, *never.*"

He saw tears in Crystal's eyes. "And neither will I now that you've shared that story. I had no idea you were so sad when you took me to live with you."

"That was as it should've been. You were just a girl, and havin' you to raise saved my life. You gave me a reason to be again. Your grandma would have cheered me on."

"So, in a dangerous moment, all I have to do is yell those words, and Rip will go into attack mode?"

"There's a little more to it than that." Tuck pushed Rip off his lap and went to the closet. He opened the louvered doors and rummaged through the coats hanging from the rod. "Here's one I don't care about. Got holes in the pockets."

He closed the closet doors and hung the old parka from the knob. "You all just stay seated, and Crystal, you watch me. You, too, Tanner, just in case."

Tuck wrestled playfully with his dog for a moment, making sure his audience saw that Rip was relaxed and in a frisky mood. Then he straightened, pointed at the parka, and yelled, "Spring forward!"

Rip, in the process of jumping up on Tuck's leg, almost turned a somersault and hit the carpet at a dead run. When he leaped at the jacket, both closet doors bent inward under the impact. Rip jerked the coat and hanger off the knob and tore into the fabric, shaking the garment with unleashed ferocity. Tuck let him go until feathers started to fly.

"Margie!" he called.

Rip immediately stopped and backed away from the coat, still snarling. Tuck slapped his knee. "Good dog. Come!"

Rip came directly to him.

Crystal said, "Huh. That'll work."

Tanner grinned. "Oh, yeah."

Crystal smiled at Tuck. "He's only ever come to me once, and that was last night."

"Is that right?" Tuck studied his dog, who was back to wanting to play again. "How do you call him?"

"I say, 'Here, Rip,' or 'Come here, Rip.'"

"Well, that's the problem, honey. You say one word in a stern voice. *Come.*"

Tuck waved his granddaughter to her feet. "Now you do it. Play with him for a second so he forgets about the coat. Then hang it back on the closet knob, point at it, and give him the attack command."

Tuck resumed his seat in the recliner. He could tell Crystal felt silly and didn't want to do this. But he had every confidence in his dog. Crystal hung the coat back up; bounced around on the living room rug for a minute, playing with Rip; and then pointed at the parka and yelled, "Spring forward!"

Rip tore into the parka again. Feathers flew until Crystal yelled, "Margie!"

"Now praise him," Tuck reminded her. "He did good."

Crystal went down on her knees and said, "Come!"

Rip ran to her. She gathered his wriggling body in her arms. Tuck watched the heeler lick her face. Rip had clearly come to adore her. Tuck waited until the canine had gotten his reward of praise and fondling.

Then he said, "Damn it, Crystal, you stole my dog!"

Chapter Sixteen

Crystal had scheduled time in her appointment book to take Tuck to the doctor's office on Monday to get his cast removed, so the following day at one, she loaded Rip into her car and drove to pick up her grandfather. She'd been mulling over the fact ever since yesterday that Tuck and Essie were sleeping together, and she wasn't quite sure how to compartmentalize that. She was even less sure how she felt about it. It wasn't her business, though, was it?

She arrived at the facility with a knot in the pit of her stomach. Should she acknowledge to Tuck that she'd caught Essie's slip of the tongue? She reminded herself that she'd also spoken without thinking yesterday, and Tuck probably knew that she and Tanner were engaging in physical intimacy, too. How would she feel if he got in the car and said, "Oh, by the way, I know you and Tanner are having sex"? Crystal knew she would be mortified, so she decided to keep her mouth shut about her grandfather's relationship with Essie.

After parking in the shade of a pine tree, she cut the engine and stared out the windshield at nothing. Recognizing where they were, Rip squirmed with excitement on the passenger seat, eager to see her grandfather. A tap came on the front passenger window, and Crystal nearly jumped out of her skin. Tuck leaned down to grin at her through the glass. Essie stood behind him.

Crystal hit the button to unlock the door, and Tuck drew it open, saying, "Toss me a biscuit, would you? I don't wanna get pinched when I get in the back with Essie."

Crystal dug in the door pocket for treats and deposited them in her grandfather's outstretched hand. *He brought Essie.* Crystal had planned to stop by a deli and get them an assortment of food for a picnic to celebrate the removal of his cast. She'd envisioned parking somewhere along the creek, and she had even put a blanket in the trunk of her car. It would have been special one-on-one time with her grandfather. She couldn't help but resent that he'd brought his girlfriend without at least asking if she minded.

While the oldsters got in the back of the Equinox, Rip sailed over the console to greet Tuck. Crystal was almost pleased when she heard the dog growl at Essie. *Take that,* she thought. *Good for you, Rip. Let her know she's horning in where she isn't wanted.*

The thoughts no sooner went through Crystal's mind than she felt ashamed of herself. She wasn't a jealous eleven-year-old girl. She was a grown woman who looked back on her life and felt grateful to her grandfather for all the sacrifices he had made to finish raising her.

Essie leaned forward to touch Crystal's shoulder. "I hope you don't mind that I came. I rarely get to leave this place, so when Tuck invited me, I just couldn't say no."

Crystal smiled at her and noted as she did that Essie was beautiful. Was it any wonder that Tuck had fallen for her? "I don't mind in the slightest." And as she said those words, Crystal realized they were sincere. "With you along, it'll be more fun. It's a gorgeous day. After Tuck gets his cast off, I thought we might celebrate by having a picnic."

Essie's crinkly face broke into a smile. "Tuck, did you hear that? We're going on a picnic!" To Crystal she said, "Did you bring the food?"

"No. I didn't have time to make anything. I thought we'd stop at a deli and pick out whatever looks good."

"Oh, how fun! We never get to do stuff like that. Just going for a car ride is a treat."

"It sure is," Tuck seconded. "I want potato salad with extra mayo!"

Both Crystal and Essie laughed. Crystal said, "I'll buy a squeeze bottle of mayonnaise so you can mix in as much as you want."

The appointment went smoothly. Crystal sat with Essie in the waiting room while Tuck went in to see the doctor, a man with the surname Payne. It reminded Crystal of the Lingerie Burglar and her theory that one's name could sometimes direct one's footsteps in life.

When Tuck emerged from the back room, he wore a broad grin and had a spring in his step. "The X-ray looked great. The fracture has mended. I'm on the road to recovery."

Essie linked arms with him as they left the building. Crystal walked behind them. They behaved like two excited teenagers who'd skipped school.

For Rip's comfort, she'd parked in the shade, which made it a longer walk to the car. When they reached the Equinox, Crystal's heart plunged to what felt like her knees. Through the partially open driver's window, she saw that Rip had clawed the passenger door. "Oh, dear!"

When Tuck saw the damage, his smile vanished. "You got insurance. Right? And I'll pay for anything it don't cover."

Crystal composed herself. "It's my fault, not yours.

Rip can't stand to be locked up and left alone. I should have known better than to leave him out here by himself."

"Damn dog."

"He's a wonderful dog," she corrected. "He just has some quirks."

An instant later when Essie got in the back of the car to sit beside Tuck, the dog snarled at her again. Essie met the animal's glare and placed her hand on Tuck's knee. "Bring it on, Rip, or behave yourself. We can be friends or enemies. I don't give a shit which, but either way, I'm not backing down."

Crystal was shocked by the older woman's language. In appearance she was a genteel lady, but under that veneer, she was tougher than a pine knot. Crystal wasn't sure how she felt about that. Rip, on the other hand, seemed to have gotten Essie's message. He understood tone of voice and manner if not actual words. Essie showed no fear of him, she had challenged his claim on Tuck, and the dog seemed to accept that.

Essie met Crystal's gaze in the rearview mirror and smiled. "I'm a dog lover, and I've never met one I didn't like. I think they sense that."

Crystal searched the woman's eyes and saw only goodness in their depths. She smiled her approval at her grandfather. Tuck nodded slightly and grinned.

The heeler whined at Tuck as if seeking advice. "You heard the lady," Tuck said. "Friends or enemies, your choice, but I think you'll be happier if you choose friendship. She don't scare so easy, and I sure as hell ain't gettin' rid of her on your account."

Crystal started the car, amazed to see Rip surrender to the older woman. She remembered the times when she had allowed the dog to get his bluff in on her. Maybe she should have challenged him from the start.

Crystal stayed in the car with Rip while Essie and Tuck went into Flagg's for the picnic items. "Don't forget eating utensils!" she called after them.

A half hour later, the older couple finally emerged from the market. They carried five plastic bags that were stuffed full. Crystal opened the cargo door from inside so they could stow the groceries in back. "Good grief, we could survive for a week on all that food!" she exclaimed with a laugh.

Essie said, "It's a rare occasion for us! And everything looked so good! We went a little crazy."

Crystal found a picnic spot along Mystic Creek. A grassy knoll overlooked the sparkling waterway. A short way upstream, a waterfall spilled over rocks, creating a musical sound. A pine tree cast some shade, so she spread the blanket there. Essie displayed the agility of a much younger woman as she lowered herself to the ground. Tuck joined her with a grunt.

"Damned hip."

"We need to start taking walks," Essie observed. "And maybe do some exercising together. That would be fun."

Tuck groaned again, but Crystal saw a twinkle in his eyes. She decided Essie just might be good for him.

Their late lunch was divine. They dined on a trimmed rotisserie chicken, an assortment of salads, and lemon meringue pie for dessert. Crystal had driven a stick into the ground and tied Rip's leash to it so he could lie on the blanket and partake of the meal.

"Why does food taste so much better on a picnic?" she asked.

Essie grinned. "The tiny gnats add flavor."

Crystal laughed and helped herself to more pie. Tuck had remembered that lemon meringue was a favorite of hers.

Essie told Crystal about her childhood in Alaska and how she had started having sex with men for money as a young teen. Crystal couldn't judge Essie for her path to success. She had been loyal to her siblings and given them opportunities. How she had accomplished that didn't seem important now. If not for Tuck, where might Crystal have ended up as a teenager? She felt certain her parents would have kicked her out the moment they could find an excuse.

Crystal had never volunteered to tell anyone about the death of her baby sister, but there was something about Essie that compelled her to tell that story now. Tears sparkled in the older woman's eyes as Crystal told her how Tuck had rescued her, taken her to his ranch, and given her a fresh start.

"Almost everyone could use a fresh start at some point," Essie observed. "You appear to have it all figured out now, and that's what matters."

Crystal wasn't sure she had anything figured out or whether she ever would, but she nodded in agreement. She settled a thoughtful gaze on her grandfather, wondering where his relationship with Essie might take him. Seeing the two oldsters together brought her to understand that they truly were still fit and mentally sharp. She had seen couples their age in Mystic Creek, sightseeing in motor homes. When Tuck was finished with his physical therapy, maybe they'd decide to do something like that. She vowed to herself that she would be supportive. Why shouldn't they take a road trip? Life wasn't over until the heart stopped beating.

To her surprise, she enjoyed the outing so much that she hated to see it end. After dropping the older couple off at the center, she drove home. Rip resumed his seat beside her and hung his head out the open window to enjoy the rush of wind in his face.

"So, what do you think of Essie?" Crystal asked.

Rip responded with a growl, which made her laugh. "I think you've met your match in her, buddy."

Just as she pulled up in front of the gate at home, her cell phone rang. She saw Barney Sterling's name on the screen. "Hello?"

"Hi, Crystal," he said. "I just wanted to let you know we tracked down where McVoyer was staying when he came to town. He rented a kitchenette by the week at the Dew Drop Inn."

Crystal tightened her grip on the cellular device. "And?"

"We found his stash of lingerie. I'm sure some of it's yours, but we've got to keep it as evidence. The good news is, we've already got him behind bars. You can feel safe in your home now."

"Thanks for letting me know, Barney. I'll rest easier tonight."

"That was my aim. When we get results on the DNA, I'll be back in touch."

Crystal sighed as they ended the conversation. She was relieved to know that the sheriff's department had apprehended the right man, but she was also disappointed, because Tanner had made arrangements to stay over at her place again tonight. Now she had no real reason to let him do that. She was tempted not to call him so he'd come anyway. Making love with him at night was so . . . *everything*, the perfect way to end a day. Only that wouldn't be fair to him or his mother.

Tanner answered on the fourth ring. Crystal envisioned him pulling off onto the shoulder of a gravel road in order to talk. "Hey, you," he said, his voice as smooth as honey on warm toast. "I can't wait to see you. If I didn't have to return the company vehicle, I'd drive straight there."

"That's why I called, Tanner. You don't need to come. Barney just gave me an update." She quickly related to him the conversation she'd had with the deputy. "I'll be as safe as can be tonight."

"I'll get home so late, anyway, that it really won't make much difference to Mom. By the time I roll in, she'll have all the actual work done."

"Why will you get home late if you don't come here?"

"You forgot," he said with a laugh. "Remember those collars I delivered to the salon this morning? I hope you thought to charge one of them."

Crystal groaned. "I did, but then I totally spaced out. Now I have to drive all the way back to town." She paused. "It really isn't necessary for you to be here for the trial run, Tanner. I know how to do everything."

"But I *want* to be there, especially if it doesn't work. Rip may sail over the fence and make a run for the tavern. I don't want you going into the Witch's Brew alone. JJ seems like a pretty nice guy, but his patrons are rowdy. And they've grown fond of Rip, so they aren't going to like it when he's snatched off a barstool and taken home."

Crystal considered arguing the point. But by relenting, she would get to enjoy Tanner's company all night. "What sounds good for dinner?"

"You. And I'll have seconds for dessert."

She laughed. "I'll go get the collar and see you when you get here," she told him. She could almost feel the heat of his strong arms around her. "Drive safely."

Rip pushed the limits with the new collar and tried his best to withstand the shocks until he could get over the fence, but the strength of the signals proved to be more than even he could handle. Tanner slipped an arm around Crystal's waist as they watched the blue heeler back away from the danger zone and turn in circles, chasing his nearly nonexistent tail.

"Mission accomplished," Tanner said. "Now he can run free on the ten acres and enjoy being a normal dog. No more drinking sprees."

Crystal stiffened. "Oh, *dang* it. Jack was supposed to call me today about the blood panel he ran, but he never did."

As if on cue, her phone suddenly rang. Her stomach bunched into knots of anxiety when she saw it was someone from the clinic. "Hello?"

"Hi, Crystal. Jack Palmer. Sorry I didn't call earlier, but I had two emergencies. I know you're worried about Rip, so I'll cut right to the chase. His blood work came back completely normal. No liver damage."

Her shoulders sagged with relief. "I can scarcely believe it, but that's wonderful news. Is it okay to start him on his medication, then?"

"Absolutely. Just follow the directions on the bottle. The stuff may make him sleepy, but I doubt it. It'll probably just mellow him out and help prevent any negative effects from the sudden cessation of alcohol consumption."

Crystal gave Tanner a thumbs-up so he would know the news was good. "I just tried a new collar on Rip. He can't go under or over the fence now."

"Good," Jack replied. "The shocks won't harm him. Drinking alcohol will. Keep the collar on him, and maybe you'll have the problem solved."

After Crystal returned her phone to its case, Tanner swept her off her feet and into his arms. She let loose with a startled cry, and Rip came charging across the yard, snarling and baring his teeth.

"It's okay, Rip," Crystal said, aiming for a soothing tone even though Tanner's embrace made her nerves leap to attention. When the dog continued to threaten him, she yelled, "Margie!"

Rip whined and sat, apparently still convinced Tanner had done something to hurt her. With a laugh, Tanner carried her to the porch while she tossed biscuits to the blue heeler to afford them both safe passage into the house.

When Rip tried to follow them inside, Tanner blocked his way. "Oh, no. If that one little cry set you off, you'll really go nuts in a few minutes. When she climaxes, she shrieks."

"I don't, either," Crystal protested.

"Wanna bet?" he challenged.

After a lovemaking session that Crystal was sure she would never forget, she had to face the fact that she'd never felt this way about a man, and she sensed that Tanner was falling for her, too. The realization frightened her. Love didn't factor into her life plans. Forming bonds didn't, either. She'd learned that the only way to avoid heartbreak was to never be vulnerable in the first place.

Tanner held her close, trailing his fingers over the small of her back in circles that delighted her nerve endings. "Do you mind if we talk?"

That was a danger signal. Men who felt nothing for a woman didn't want to engage in pillow talk after having sex. "What about?"

"Us. Where we're going with this."

A lump formed in her throat. To any other man, she would have said, *Nowhere. I made that clear from the start.* But with Tanner, she'd already stepped over an invisible line and started to care for him. She couldn't hurt him with a flippant reply. "Okay, let's talk."

"I've been giving our relationship a lot of thought."

He nuzzled her hair. "Your business is here in Mystic Creek. I work out of Crystal Falls. On the surface, it appears impossible for us to be together as a couple. But I spoke to my boss this morning before I left to cover my route."

"What did you speak to him about?"

"I asked if I could possibly keep the Mystic Creek route. He agreed to let me make the switch. He even said I can keep the company van here at night, drive in early to the distribution center, and get it loaded before I come back here to make deliveries. It would work perfectly, Crystal. My workdays would start an hour earlier, but I'd get home earlier in the afternoon to spend quality time with the kids. My mom and I could sell our homes and move here. My boss has agreed to the plan."

She'd been sure he wanted to talk about a long-term relationship, but this went beyond her wildest imaginings. "You're going to uproot your kids? Sell your houses?" She raised herself on one elbow.

"Why not? Don't look so astonished. I love this little town, and so do they. I think it would be a fabulous place for them to grow up. There's hardly any crime, the schools are good, and when there's a threat to the community, the sheriff's department acts quickly."

Crystal could think of a dozen reasons why not, none of which would make the slightest bit of sense to him. And they suddenly didn't make a whole lot of sense to her, either. Only, he needed to understand she wasn't the prize he believed her to be. "Tanner, I know this all seems like a reasonable next step to you, but there are some serious pitfalls. I'm awful with kids. You have no idea just how awful."

"I don't see how you can possibly be sure of that. You haven't been around children often enough to know, and you were great with Tori and Michael that one evening."

"That was only one visit."

"During which you convinced Tori not to read my mom's books again. Instead she asks Nana to help her find online sites that teach her about training a puppy. I'd like to bring the kids and my mom here for a picnic. I want you to meet my mother. You'll love her, guaranteed. She's an awesome lady, and I know she's going to think the world of you." He tightened his arm around her. "I don't expect you to be a mother to my kids. I'll never ask you to give up your profession to be with me. My mom will continue to help out with my children. I talked with her, and she not only agreed but insisted on it. So it's not as if you'd be stepping in as a mother figure. My kids like you. All you'd need to do is be their friend."

Since meeting Tanner, Crystal had often wondered what it might be like to get married and have a family. Now she allowed herself to actually envision it. The kids sometimes coming to her salon after school when Libby had an afternoon off. Her taking one or both of them to buy shoes or go clothes shopping. Taking them home to cook Michael's favorite dinner, spaghetti and meatballs, or Tori's beef ravioli. Not being expected to be an actual mother figure suited her perfectly. She could be a fabulous friend to Tanner's kids.

Just then No Name jumped up on the bed and came to snuggle on the pillow above their heads. He turned his purr to full volume and began kneading her hair as if it were bread dough. Outside Rip was probably lying on the porch, fretting because he'd heard her cry out. Two months ago, she couldn't have imagined herself having a dog and a cat or, even more amazing, allowing herself to love them. And so far, nothing horrible had happened.

Was she truly jinxed when it came to loving things, as she'd come to believe after her sister's death? Could she have and love a ready-made family without raining misfortune upon their heads? Though she and Tuck rarely spoke of Mary Ann's death, her grandfather swore to this day that Crystal hadn't been responsible. Maybe Tuck was right and it was time for Crystal to stop blaming herself for all the tragic things that had happened.

Tanner could see that Crystal was unsettled by his suggestion that they become a couple, and he didn't know why. It wasn't as if he was asking her to marry him, although with his feelings for her running so strong, he couldn't discount that possibility in the future.

"Can you honestly say you don't feel that something truly special has developed between us?" When he saw the corners of her mouth tip up in a smile, he added, "I never expected to meet anyone who'd make me want to get married again." He felt her stiffen, and continued. "But from the first instant I saw you outside that store, I was wildly attracted to you. Haven't you ever wondered if our relationship is meant to be? Just think about it. We might never have seen each other again. I lived and worked in Crystal Falls, and your world was here. But I met Tuck and we became good friends. Then Tuck was relocated. You filed a complaint against me, and now, as punishment, my route covers Mystic Creek. We're developing a serious relationship. Don't you see a guiding hand in all this?"

Leaning her head back, she gazed up at him. In the deepening dusk outside the bedroom windows, her eyes looked as green as clover leaves and luminous with wonder. "I'm amazed that we ever ran into each other again. When I met you, I felt entranced. I wanted to ask for your number, but I didn't have the guts."

"I didn't expect us to meet again, either. When I became friends with Tuck, I learned that he had a granddaughter, but you were just a faceless someone who didn't factor into my relationship with him."

"Until I filed the complaint." She sighed and fell quiet for a moment. "I see what you mean, Tanner. Maybe there was a guiding hand, moving us step-by-step toward each other. It boggles my mind that God may have used Patricia as a tool to help orchestrate his plan."

Tanner laughed. "God sometimes works in strange ways." He pressed a lingering kiss on her forehead. "Let's not blow it, then. Please agree to a picnic so you can meet my mom."

Crystal nodded. "Let's do it."

After making love with Tanner a second time, Crystal convinced him to go home. With McVoyer behind bars, Crystal no longer felt uneasy about staying alone at night. She and Tanner had enjoyed the best part of the evening together, and it made no sense for him to clutter up his schedule tomorrow by sleeping at her place.

They kissed each other goodbye on the front porch. Then, shivering in the lightweight kimono, Crystal hugged her waist and watched until his taillights were swallowed by country darkness.

Pensive, she went back into the house to write Tanner a note. Using her cell phone as a flashlight, she went out to the oak and placed the piece of paper just behind the bag of dog treats where Tanner would see it. Then she bribed her way past Rip to reenter the yard and go up the steps to gaze out at the moon-silvered darkness again. She didn't know when Tanner would find her message, but if it took a few days, she'd be fine with that. Choosing to write it had been a huge decision for her, and it would be good if she had some time to let it simmer in her mind and let herself grow relaxed about having done it.

She glanced down at the heeler sitting beside her.

"Well, Rip, shall we go to bed?"

The dog barked and ran into the house. Crystal, holding a dog biscuit in one hand, couldn't help but smile. In his excitement to race her to the bedroom, he'd forgotten to charge his toll. She closed and locked the front door, the latter of which was a newly acquired habit. Since McVoyer's invasion of the house, she would never again leave her doors unlocked. Though it was true that Mystic Creek had an extremely low crime rate, other towns weren't far away, and there was no guarantee that nefarious individuals wouldn't visit this peaceful mountain community, bringing their evil ways with them.

Crystal grinned when she reached the bedroom doorway. Rip was already on her bed, looking comfortable atop the tangled bedding. "Aha! So you think you're my bedmate now, do you?"

Just then her phone, sitting on the nightstand, emitted its loud and startling ringtone. Considering that it was late evening, nine thirty the last time she'd checked, Crystal suspected it was Tanner calling. Instead it was Marsha from the assisted living facility.

"You need to get out here!" she cried. "Tuck's in trouble, and this time it's really bad."

Medical. It had to be medical. Crystal whirled and ran for her purse to grab her car keys. In midstride, she demanded, "Is he being taken to the hospital?"

"Not that kind of trouble. Essie's son showed up. Essie locks her door, but the son got a key from Patricia. I guess he wanted to surprise Essie, and he sure did. He walked in and caught her having sex with Tuck in her bedroom."

Little black dots swam in Crystal's vision. She blinked and braced a hand on the kitchen counter. "So? Isn't that what people do when they're in love?"

Marsha made an odd sound. "Yes, and I think this is nuts, Crystal. But her son is raising holy hell! He's accusing Tuck of raping his mother. He claims she isn't of sound mind. Patricia is all over it and has already called the cops. Tuck may be arrested!"

Crystal remembered the loving look in Tuck's eyes when he turned his gaze on Essie. "That's the craziest thing I've ever heard! My grandfather would never do such a thing!"

"I totally agree. But come out here and tell that insane son of hers that!"

Crystal hung up and dashed to her closet. She almost grabbed jeans and a sweatshirt, but then an image of Essie in her chic clothing pushed into her mind. The woman's son was probably a flashy dresser, too, and Crystal decided she might need to wear a power outfit that would make a statement.

She went for black, which set off her red hair. Straight skirt, cut short at midthigh. A suit jacket sporting a flared waist that created a balance between edgy and feminine with dainty chain trim and pleats. Matching over-the-knee boots with sturdy four-inch heels completed the outfit. Once dressed, she sat at her vanity to hurriedly address her face and hair. When she walked into that building, she wanted Essie's son to know the instant he saw her that she meant business and wouldn't be easily intimidated.

Armed with dog biscuits, she led Rip from the house, locked the front door, and gave the dog a final treat as she went out the gate. "Hold down the fort, sweet boy. I'll be home as soon as I can."

On the way to the center, Crystal called Pete Ramsey

to let him know Tuck was in trouble. Then she dialed Tanner. When she told him Tuck might be arrested for molesting Essie, he said, *"What?"*

"You heard me. Her son says she isn't of sound mind."

"That's *nuts*. She has a mind like a steel trap. You want me to drive back?"

Crystal appreciated his willingness to be at her side. If she ever got married, she'd choose Tanner as her mate, because he'd always be there when she needed him. "Let me assess the situation first. If it's a shit show, I'll call you."

Normally, the facility lights were dimmed in the community areas at ten, but tonight the large building was lighted up like the White House Christmas tree. When Crystal entered the building, she saw Marsha talking with three elderly women who appeared to be upset. While crossing the room toward Flintlock's office, she heard Marsha say, "No, no, dear. No one was raped."

Rape? The very thought of Tuck being accused of doing such a thing made her blood boil. At Flintlock's door, Crystal didn't bother knocking. Instead she walked right in. She would *not* be a mouse. Deputies Barney Sterling and Mark Tanger stood in front of Patricia's desk. Tuck stood off to the left, looking alone and unnerved. Essie, off to the right, was flanked by a dark-haired, well-dressed man whom Crystal guessed to be in his early forties. He held Essie's left arm in what appeared to be a firm and possibly biting grip. Essie met Crystal's gaze, her brown eyes smoldering with what could only have been anger.

Crystal walked over to hug her grandfather.

"I'm in serious trouble," Tuck said. "Essie's boy wants them cops to arrest me."

Crystal rubbed his arm and gave him a pat. "That

isn't going to happen, Tuck. I've called your lawyer. You've done nothing wrong."

Crystal turned to the deputies, who were now talking to Patricia. She sat behind her desk like a queen on her throne, and judging by her smug expression, she believed all hell was about to rain down on Tuck's head. Crystal's palm itched to smack her a good one.

"Deputy Sterling, Deputy Tanger," Crystal said by way of greeting. "What exactly is going on?"

Barney settled his gold-flecked hazel gaze on Crystal, and she saw a flicker of sympathy in its depths. "Mr. Childers claims that his mother has dementia and your grandfather molested her. Actually, he wishes to press rape charges against Mr. Malloy. He says your grandfather got his mom drunk and then took advantage of her. There is a bottle of cognac sitting out in her living room, and two snifters still smell of the alcohol, so I am fairly certain Mrs. Childers and your grandfather were drinking."

"They enjoy an occasional drink, Barney. That isn't a crime. You're a cop. Do they look or act drunk? And they were inside a private residence. Even if they were drunk, it's no one's business but theirs."

"If she's of sound mind, I agree," Barney conceded. "But when I've got the woman's son here, swearing she's got dementia, I'm caught between a rock and a hard place."

Pete Ramsey walked in just then. He wore jeans and a T-shirt. Crystal suspected she'd interrupted his sleep. Saying nothing, he stood with his back against the wall.

Crystal straightened her shoulders. "I've spent time with Mrs. Childers. She and my grandfather have been keeping company, and today I even took them out for a picnic. She's never exhibited any signs of dementia when I've been around her."

Barney frowned. "She is seventy-eight. In the early stages, I believe people have long periods of mental clarity interspersed with confusion."

"That's absurd," Crystal replied. "Have you talked with Essie? You can tell when a person isn't tracking well. I'm sure you've had training and can spot that better than most of us."

"Her son says she's upset, and he's reluctant to let me question her."

"Because he knows she'll blow what he's told you clear out of the water." Crystal strove to keep her temper. "I don't question his sincerity. I'm sure it was upsetting for him to walk into his mother's residence and find her in bed with a strange man. But for him to suggest that her mental acuity is compromised has to be either a lie or the result of overprotectiveness. Essie is a delightful conversationalist, she forgets nothing, and she's intelligent enough to think circles around most of the people in this room. Ask *her* if she feels able to talk with you."

Essie stood only a few feet away. "I'm perfectly capable of answering your questions, Deputy." She met Barney's gaze and the blazing anger in hers was apparent. "My son has taken my cellular device and removed my portable phones from my apartment. He's trying to make it impossible for me to call my legal representatives. Mrs. Flintlock has put my devices in a safe. I demand that my property be returned."

Barney adjusted his Stetson. "I'll see to it, Mrs. Childers." He directed a glance at Patricia. "What harm can it do if the lady has her communication devices?"

"She's addled. I don't want a bunch of lawyers breathing fire down my neck because she calls and tells them outrageous stories."

"Outrageous *stories*?" Essie echoed. "What's outrageous is that I'm standing here. My son entered my residence with a key you gave him and without knocking. He invaded my privacy. You and your sidekicks did as well. Then my son put his own spin on what he saw! *That*, Patricia, is the *outrage*."

"Mother," her son said, giving her arm a shake.

"Don't interrupt me, Garth. And from this moment forward, do not address me by that title. No son worth having does this to his mother."

Garth gave Barney an appealing look. "Unreasonable anger is one of the symptoms." A flush reddened his tanned face. He pointed at Tuck. "Arrest that man! He raped my mother."

Pete stepped forward, but before he could speak, Barney held up his hand. "I can't handcuff an old man and remove him from a facility where he's receiving care." He looked at Essie. "Mrs. Childers appears to be physically unharmed. I suggest that her phones be returned to her and that everyone should retreat to their own corners. A time-out, if you will, for tempers to cool. We can reconvene in the morning to discuss this."

Garth Childers' face drew into rigid lines of rage. "I *refuse* to leave my mother in a building where a lecherous old pervert is on the loose!"

Barney sent Crystal a look that said, *Help*.

"I'll stay the night in my grandfather's unit to make sure he goes nowhere near Essie," Crystal offered. "That should eliminate any concerns you may have for your mother's safety."

Garth, although visibly reluctant, accepted Crystal's solution, but he pointed an accusing finger at Tuck, saying, "This isn't over yet. In the morning, I'll have my lawyer present, and I *will* press rape charges against you." Then, releasing his hold on Essie's arm, he rounded on Patricia. "I'm also going to sue this facility for taking such deplorable care of my mother." He strode to the door, paused, and glanced back at Essie. "I'm leaving to find a motel room for the night, but rest assured, I'll be back in the morning."

"All bad pennies keep turning up," Essie said with a saccharin-sweet smile.

Patricia still hadn't moved from her chair. Barney leveled a stare at her until she finally lifted her hands and said, *"What?"*

"The phones? No matter who Mrs. Childers may call, you had no right to confiscate them. It's theft."

Chapter Seventeen

After watching Crystal lead her grandfather across the common area toward his apartment, Essie returned to her own residence. She slammed the door so hard she hoped she woke every resident in the place. Tears stung her eyes when she looked in her bedroom, where the bed coverings were still rumpled from her and Tuck's lovemaking. What had happened between them had been beautiful, and it nearly broke her heart that Garth had tried to make it seem ugly and criminal. She hoped that Tuck had no regrets and realized she didn't. Her son was a greedy, self-serving pain in the ass.

She poured herself another brandy and set herself to the task of returning her portable phones to their charging bases. Then she plucked her cellular device from her pocket and called Tuck's number.

"Hello, darlin'," he said. "You doin' okay?"

Essie smiled through tears. "I'm fine. Furious with my son, of course. I just want you to know there's nothing to worry about. He blustered and made threats, but I'll see to it that he can't carry through with any of them. You won't be arrested and put in jail."

Tuck chuckled. "My own attorney was here, and he'll be back in the mornin'. But I figured you might be up to somethin' like that. You callin' in the troops?"

"Yes. Garth has overstepped his bounds this time. I'm finished with him, and by morning, he'll comprehend the full extent of my anger. So will Patricia Flint-lock. She made a bad mistake by siding with my son against me and giving him a key to my place. Stupid of her. She's always resented that I stand up for myself. I think she wanted a small measure of revenge, which she is going to regret."

"Don't get all worked up, honey."

Essie wiped her cheeks. "I don't get worked up, Tuck. I get even."

After telling him good night, Essie sat at her desk to place some calls. Though it was late and she would wake people up, her employees were paid handsomely to be at her beck and call 24-7.

Tanner found no one at home when he drove by Crystal's house, so he headed to the assisted living facility. When he walked to the front doors, he discovered that they were locked. Marsha sat at the front desk. He guessed that her shift ended at midnight. He rapped his knuckles against the glass. She glanced up and smiled. Moments later, she had disarmed the security system and opened the door to let him in.

"Crystal is staying the night with Tuck," she said with a roll of her eyes. "Essie's son doesn't want him at large in the building for fear he may rape his mother again."

Tanner shook his head. "Rape? That's a pretty serious charge."

"It's a ridiculous charge." She waved Tanner toward the hall. "Hurry along. I'm sure Crystal will be glad to see you. But, please, be back at my desk by midnight so we can leave the building together. If I arm the system and leave without you, you won't be able to get out—unless, of course, you want to roust Patricia from her bed to assist you."

Tanner grinned. "I'll be quick. I dislike dealing with

Flintlock at the best of times, and I have a feeling she had a bad evening."

"I think what morning brings may be far worse. Essie's nobody to mess with."

Tanner lengthened his stride to cover the distance to Tuck's apartment quickly. When he knocked on the door, Crystal asked, "Who is it?"

"Tanner."

She opened the portal and stepped into his arms. "Oh, Tanner. Tuck is so upset, and even though I'm certain this will iron itself out, so am I."

Tanner hugged her close. Then he drew away to go to the living room. Tuck sat in his recliner with a can of beer in his hand. Tension had drawn his wrinkled cheeks taut over his cheekbones. Tanner suspected the old man was worried about being put in jail, but he had undoubtedly weathered worse storms.

"Crying in your beer, Tuck?" He hoped to inject some levity into the situation. "That's not like you."

"I'd never dilute good beer with tears," he said. "I'm just ruminatin' on the fact that Essie's son wants to send me up for rape. My attorney says he's got my back, and he'll be here early to argue on my behalf."

Tanner grabbed a kitchen chair and dragged it across the carpet to sit in front of his friend. "Essie's son doesn't have a leg to stand on. This will all come out in the wash. You did nothing wrong. Having consensual sex with a woman isn't a crime."

"He's sayin' Essie has dementia."

Tanner laughed. "He'll have a devil of a time proving that. Have you ever once seen Essie confused or muddled?"

"No, can't say that I have. But it could take time for her to be evaluated by professionals. In the meanwhile, I could land in jail."

"I don't think it'll come to that. I know it must have been an unnerving evening, though."

Tuck harrumphed. "*Unnervin'* don't say it by half. Without warnin', Garth stormed into her bedroom, jerked the covers off us, and started threatenin' to kill me. Next thing I knew, Flintlock and two female aides was in there, with both me and Essie sittin' there on the bed, as naked as two plucked birds on a spit."

Tanner tried to imagine the indignity of that and couldn't. Tuck and Essie deserved to be treated with more respect. Glancing at his watch, he saw that it was nearly midnight. "Well, Tuck, if I mean to get out of here as Marsha leaves, I need to hustle." He pushed to his feet and turned to Crystal. "I can stay the night at your place and take care of the animals."

"I hate to ask that," she told him. "But Rip is outside, and I know coyotes frequent the woods close to the house. With no people around, they might challenge the fence. Rip is a fighter, but he wouldn't stand a chance against a whole pack."

She grabbed her purse and gave Tanner the house key. "Remember to get dog biscuits out of the tree. Otherwise you'll be stranded just inside the gate and have to call me for help."

Tanner leaned over to kiss her cheek. "Get a good rest. Keep me updated on what happens in the morning." He waved at his friend. "Good night, Tuck. See you tomorrow evening."

Tanner made the short drive to the farmhouse in record time. In his truck's headlights, he saw Rip racing in circles inside the front gate. As he cut the engine, he heard the dog's barks, shrill with excitement. Though he wore civilian clothes and doubted he would need them, he walked to the oak tree to take several biscuits from the plastic bag. As he fumbled in the dark, he felt a slip of paper brush against his knuckles, and a smile touched his mouth. He drew his cell phone from its case, switched it to a flashlight app, and read the note Crystal had written.

I love you, Tanner. That's really difficult for me to confess, but it's true. Knowing you and coming to love you has given me the courage to take chances I never dreamed I might. I'm excited about our future. Much love, Crystal.

Smiling, Tanner put the note in his shirt pocket and grabbed a large handful of dog treats. He loved Crystal, too, and was glad she felt ready to roll the dice. She had so much to offer, and it would have been such a waste if she never took a chance on love. Though he was weary after such a long day, he now felt revitalized. He'd meant what he told her about believing their relationship was destined to be, and no matter what happened, he'd never regret taking this particular gamble with his heart.

At first light the next morning, Crystal got a text from Tanner. Rip's collar was still working to keep him in the yard, and Tanner had put out food and fresh water for him. No Name was inside the house and also fine. Tanner ended the text with *"Oh, and by the way, did I mention that I love you? Keep in touch. Tell Tuck I'm cheering for him."*

Crystal held the phone over her heart for a moment. It felt surreal to read in a message that a man loved her. But it also felt absolutely right.

She heard Tuck taking a shower. She went to the kitchen and rummaged through his cupboards to find the coffee. When Tuck wandered out a few minutes later, she greeted him with a filled mug. He sniffed the rising steam. "The *real* thing. With a cast, I didn't make any, and I plumb forgot I had beans. The stuff in the dining hall is awful. I could make stronger coffee if I shoved a bean up a duck's ass and ran downstream to dip a cup of water."

Crystal forced a smile. She'd heard that one a gazillion times. "Pete Ramsey said he would be here by eight. Just in case you don't remember, he doesn't want you to speak with anyone until he's present."

"I remember. I ain't senile yet."

"I didn't mean to imply that you are, Tuck."

Crystal sat on the sofa and crossed her legs. Last night she'd slept there in an old T-shirt of Tuck's, preserving her black outfit so she would look presentable today. For her morning ablutions, she'd used the half bath off the living room, making do with the brush and what little makeup she carried in her purse. She was so frightened for Tuck that she searched frantically for something else to think about.

"Does Essie really have a team of lawyers?"

"She says she does. I think she's richer than we can imagine."

Crystal puzzled over that. "Do you think her son wants control of her assets?"

"That's her story, and after what I witnessed last night, I don't doubt it for a second. He'll be lucky if she don't cut him out of her will."

"Garth Childers doesn't strike me as the type of man who'd trouble himself unless a veritable fortune was at stake."

Tuck sighed. "Well, all I care about is one thing, honey: that he leaves Essie enough to enjoy her little comforts and be happy."

*   *   *

Pete knocked on Tuck's door at five before eight. Crystal went to invite him in. Tall and lean, he had the look of a Ramsey with his dark brown hair and blue eyes. Members of his family had lived in Mystic Creek since the town had been founded. This morning he'd dressed professionally in a brown suit over an ocher shirt. His warm grin displayed even, white teeth. After shaking Crystal's hand, he slipped by her to find his client. Crystal joined the two men in the small living area.

"Basically, Tuck, let me do the talking," Pete was saying. "If you're asked a question and I give you a nod, you can answer, but be as brief as possible, keeping your responses limited to yes or no whenever you can."

"Okay."

"So, in your own words, tell me exactly what happened between you and Essie last night."

"She made me supper in her apartment. We visited. Had two snifters of brandy. Afterward we went to bed." Tuck's eyes went glittery. "If you want details about that, you ain't gettin' 'em."

Pete smiled. "I'm fine without details. So, whose idea was it to go to her bedroom?"

Tuck studied the attorney as if he were a species of bug he'd never seen. "Son, I know nothin' about your sex life, but if you've been with gals who expect a long discussion before makin' love, you need to chat with me over a couple of cold ones some afternoon."

Pete threw back his head and laughed. "I walked right into that one, I guess. What I should have asked was, did both of you want to have sex?"

"Yep. Well, Essie never said that in so many words, but she was sendin' out all the right signals."

Pete nodded. Then he rested his elbows on his spread

knees and folded his hands. "Was last night the first time you'd been intimate?"

"No. We've been together that way for a spell. Mostly we meet at night. A couple of times in the mornin'."

"So her willingness to engage with you in sexual congress had been established prior to last night." Pete braced his hands on his knees to push up. "That's all I need to know. I'm ready to go a few rounds with Mr. Childers' attorney."

Thirty minutes later, Crystal stood beside Tuck against the left wall of Patricia's office. The small enclosure was so packed with bodies that the scents of perfume, men's cologne, and perspiration made her feel light-headed. From various locations, cell phone notifications chimed, the different tones reminding her of a child's xylophone. She wondered why on earth Patricia hadn't set up a meeting area in the dining hall, where everyone could have sat down. But, no, everyone but the administrator had to stand. Maybe, Crystal mused, this was the only way Patricia knew to showcase her position of authority.

Barney Sterling had taken center stage in front of Patricia's desk. Garth, looking dark and foreboding, stood along the opposite wall beside an older man in a tailored gray suit who looked as if he'd traveled cross-country on a red-eye flight. He had the edgy look of a combatant who faced a showdown he feared he couldn't win. He held a black satchel in one hand and a sheaf of notes in the other. Forehead creased in a frown, he kept glancing down at a bulleted list as if to refresh his memory.

This morning Essie stood apart from her son in the back corner of the room. She was flanked on each side by individuals Crystal assumed were attorneys, two fortysomething men who wore slacks and dress shirts, and two thirtysomething women, a blonde and a brunette. Both ladies had opted to travel casually dressed, wearing silk blouses and designer jeans.

Garth's legal counsel looked more professional in his pricey suit, but Essie's companions emanated a subtle air of confidence. All of them had parked identical briefcases at their feet, each made of hand-tooled leather.

Garth's attorney didn't wait for Barney to speak. Instead of showing deference to the lawman, he began the meeting by saying, "I'm George Staff, attorney at law, and I represent Garth Childers. Let me start this off by informing all of you that I called Adult Protective Services this morning, and on behalf of my client, I've filed for emergency custody of his mother, Essie Maxwell Childers, so she can be removed from this facility immediately and placed where she will receive more supervision."

One of Essie's flank men, the older and more robust of the two males, stepped forward to shake hands with Garth's lawyer. His graying brown hair was buzz-cut, and his eyes, a silvery blue, looked as sharp as a well-honed chisel. "Stan Mercer," he said. "My team and I represent Ms. Childers. You should be informed that she took legal action years ago to protect herself from attempts by her children to gain control of her assets and/or to have her deemed legally incompetent. In order for her trustees to make decisions regarding her care or her business interests, she must be evaluated by three court-appointed medical professionals and deemed by them to be mentally impaired. She was evaluated two months ago, found to be of sound mind and body, and shouldn't need to address the issue again for another ten months unless something unforeseen occurs that seems to have affected her mental acuity."

"Bullshit!" Garth cried.

Garth's attorney placed a hand on his arm. "Please, Mr. Childers, allow me to handle this. That's why you hired me."

"Well, a fine job you're doing so far!" Garth said with a sneer. "She's my mother! I have every right to step in and make decisions regarding her welfare when it's obvious she's incapable of doing so herself. The very fact that she's chosen to reside in this remote one-horse town proves that."

Essie interrupted. "I live here in order to limit the frequency of your visits, Garth. They're always unpleasant and they upset me."

"If you're upset because your son is trying to protect you, it's only another sign of how muddled your thinking is."

"I don't need protection, Garth. I have trusted and well-qualified professionals on board to watch out for me now. Since I am of sound mind and choose to remain at this facility, I will do so. My legal team assures me that there's absolutely nothing you can do about that."

"This is utterly absurd." He swung his hand toward her lawyers. "These people are here for one reason and only one reason: the money."

"They work hard for every dollar they make. You should try it." Essie released a weary sigh. "You stepped over the line last night, and I'm finished with you. As of this morning, I revised my will. It's already signed, witnessed, notarized, and electronically filed. When I die, neither you nor your sister will get a dime."

"You can't do that!" Garth cried. "We're your children, your legal heirs."

"It's already done," Essie replied, her voice calm and without much inflection. "I've been extremely generous, and both of you have lived well as a result. All you had to do was bide your time. Instead you've been trying to take over ever since your father died."

"We were only trying to protect the company. Dad was the mastermind, not you. We were afraid you'd make stupid investments and lose everything. We have a vested interest in the holdings our father acquired!"

Essie bent her head. When she looked back up at her son, her expression had gone stony. "If you'd ever bothered to review the archived ledgers, you would know that I went into the marriage with as many businesses and as much money as your father did. You'd also know that my investments, a fair half of them made prior to the nuptials, have maintained a large percentage of annual profit while many of your father's took sharp downturns prior to liquidation. He made his fortune following trends. I made mine by investing in commodities that might go through cyclical downturns but were predicted to maintain their worth. I take nothing away from your father by saying that. He knew when to buy and when to sell. He was a brilliant man. Your mistake, and Rebecca's as well, was to underestimate and underappreciate my business savvy."

Garth turned his palms toward the ceiling in a pleading way. "Mother, I meant no slight to you. Rebecca and I both admire you and—"

Essie cut him off. "I no longer care what you think of me. You can try to get my revised will overturned, but I strongly advise against it. You'll spend your last penny trying to wage a battle you can't win." She smiled stiffly and lifted her shoulders. "But, of course, you won't listen to me. You never have. So give it your best shot."

Garth paled under his tropical tan. "I only wanted

to surprise you when I arrived unannounced last night."
His voice had turned wheedling.

"And you succeeded. You unlocked the door of my
apartment with a key I didn't give you." She glanced at
Patricia. "You entered my residence without warning
or permission and proceeded to invade my personal
privacy in the worst possible way. You humiliated and
embarrassed me. Then you made vile accusations
against Tucker Malloy, a man for whom I have the ut-
most respect, and you called in law enforcement, trying
to get him arrested—not because you believed he'd done
anything wrong, but to further your own cause. Your
behavior was despicable."

"Don't start a war you can't finish, Mother. Cutting
us out of your will is a mistake. Rebecca and I at least
deserve our father's half of the assets, and we'll hire the
best attorneys in the country to fight you."

"You can't, Garth. I've already retained them. That's
all it takes, you know, a retainer, and they're sewn up."

A vein in Garth's temple began to pulsate. "Half of
everything you have was left to you by our father. No
court in the land will disregard our birthright. We've
waited over twenty years to get what's coming to us."

"Correction. Over the last twenty years, I've doubled
what assets we had when your father died." Essie ran a
sad, assessing gaze over her son. "I owe you and Rebecca nothing. Neither of you has done an honest day's
work in your life. Let me suggest to you that the most
successful gold diggers are the ones with blisters on
their hands from using a shovel. I am requesting that
you leave now, and let this matter rest. If you persist,
I'm prepared to file criminal charges against you."

"For *what*?" Garth looked like a startled goldfish.

"Would you like a list?"

Garth shot a burning glare at Tuck. "You'll take his side against your own flesh and blood?"

"In a heartbeat. He's a wonderful man, my friend, and my lover. I look forward to residing here and enjoying his company for however many years I can."

Patricia cleared her throat. "In regard to Mr. Malloy and his residency here. Out of necessity, I have reached a difficult decision."

All eyes turned toward Patricia. In Crystal's opinion the woman had abysmally poor timing.

"Given Mr. Childers' accusations against Mr. Malloy last night, many of the elderly women here no longer feel safe," she said. "It's my responsibility to provide a worry-free environment for them, and that's impossible when a man of questionable moral rectitude is living here. By noon, Mr. Malloy will be given a notice of eviction."

"Oh, *really*!" Essie sighed. "Thank you for making this easy for me, Patricia. As of right now, you are relieved of your duties as administrator."

Patricia stared at Essie as if now firmly convinced the woman had lost her mind. "You can't fire me. You have no authority here."

Stan Mercer intervened. "Actually, Ms. Childers now has absolute authority here. Early this morning I contacted the corporation that owns this facility and made a purchase offer on her behalf that was too attractive to be refused. Her people are hard at work as we speak to finalize a cash transaction. Until you and a few other key individuals can be replaced, my employer will be overseeing operations here and filling any vacated positions with temporary employees."

Patricia's mouth dropped open. Crystal wondered if hers had as well. Garth looked ready to pass out. Patricia managed a faint gurgle. "I don't believe a word of it. No one has notified me. Besides, there are all kinds of permits and licenses to acquire! That isn't to mention the training of personnel. You can't just hire people off the street to care for the elderly. And a change of ownership can't be accomplished in a day! Even with the purchase of a house, a closing takes longer than that!"

The attorney replied, "The elderly at this facility will be in good hands. We've got all the bases covered, both practically and legally."

Patricia folded her arms over her ample bosom. "I'm not abandoning my post until I receive notice from the corporate office."

Stan cupped Essie's elbow in his hand. "How long has it been since you checked your email, Ms. Flintlock?" He turned to escort his employer from the room but paused to address Tuck. "Essie is hosting a catered luncheon in the dining room today. Social hour starts at eleven, and Ms. Childers has invited you and your granddaughter to honor her with your presence at the head table."

"Mom!" Garth nearly knocked his attorney over in his haste to follow his mother. "Please. Let's not be impulsive. I'm your *son*. Just give me a moment and hear me out! At least give me a chance to apologize."

Essie hugged Stan's brawny arm and kept walking. Garth's attorney grabbed his satchel and followed his frantic client from the room. Patricia had already opened her laptop to check her emails, and she didn't even glance up. A moment later, she leaped up from her chair, clamped a hand over her heart, and cried, "Oh, my God, it's true! Essie bought the place!"

Crystal had no choice but to decline Essie's invitation to lunch. She'd already abandoned several clients that morning, and she needed to run home, check on the animals, and dress for work. She could only hope Essie would understand. Surely she would, Crystal reasoned. Essie hadn't gotten where she was today without putting in some long hours. As Crystal drove to the farmhouse, she called Tanner and updated him on the outcome of the meeting.

"Holy smokes!" he exclaimed. "I had Essie pegged as a smart cookie, but I never dreamed she could be *that* rich."

Crystal laughed. "Me, either. On our picnic she was so down-to-earth, and I've never seen her put on airs. It's sad about her kids. I think she's come to accept it now, but at some point their betrayal must have broken her heart."

By ten Crystal was at the salon, her nostrils filled with the rotten-egg odor of permanent-wave solution coming from Shannon's station, the varying baritones of blow-dryers humming all around her. Tonya Lucas, her ten-fifteen appointment, seemed less focused on her hair than usual.

"Is everything going okay for you and Troy?" Crystal asked. The couple had met on the Mystic Creek Natural Bridge, had fallen wildly in love, and had been happily married for almost ten years. Right now they were remodeling an older home at the Bearberry Loop Golf Course. "How's the house coming along?"

Tonya sighed. "One step forward and two back, pretty much like all remodels. Usually I roll with it, but my little granddaughter is having a sleepover Friday night." Her eyes filled with warmth. "It's the most important party *ever* in her estimation, and my kitchen is torn apart. Troy has volunteered to barbecue and supervise a marshmallow roast. Otherwise I'll be winging it."

Tonya's granddaughter, Macy, was an adorable child. *Not as cute as Tori, though,* Crystal thought. And then, as she swabbed color on sections of Tonya's hair, she allowed herself to imagine a sleepover for Tori at the farmhouse. She pictured herself supervising games, serving treats little girls that age would love, and enjoying every second of the chaos.

After Tonya left, Crystal texted Tanner. *I promised to take Tori to the Crystal Falls library to look for books. Would tomorrow after school be a good time?*

Tanner texted back saying Tori's schedule was clear as far as he knew, but he'd check with his mom. Excitement fluttered in the pit of her stomach. With Libby on the sidelines to help, Crystal didn't feel quite so intimidated by the thought of coparenting two kids with Tanner. Libby had already raised a wonderful son, and she was doing a great job with her grandchildren. The safety of Tori and Michael wouldn't be solely Crystal's responsibility unless she took them out to do something fun.

Realistically, what could go wrong at a library?

After the luncheon, Tuck got to be alone with Essie for the first time since all hell had broken loose last night. Offering him a smile, she looped arms with him and suggested they take a tour of the building to discuss changes they could make to the facility. Now that Tuck knew just how wealthy she was, he could really enjoy dreaming with her.

They took measure of the kitchen first, which Essie deemed to be sufficient as it was. "The first order of business will be to hire at least three chefs," she told him. "I want first-class dining available seven days a week, three meals a day."

"Some of these old folks have never eaten fancy food," Tuck reminded her.

"We'll have choices for everyone. Ordinary things

and gourmet delights." She gifted him with a saucy grin. "But I'm willing to bet people will soon develop a taste for finer offerings."

When they reentered the common area, Essie waved her free hand. "Just look at the space out here. And most of it's wasted. Few people gather in these conversation areas. What do you think about leaving only a small visiting area and partitioning off the rest into rooms?"

"What kind of rooms?"

"Definitely a card room, only we'd call it something else."

Tuck laughed. "You gonna allow us old farts to gamble?"

"Hell, yes. Otherwise why bother to play?"

"Maybe we can call it the High Roller Room."

"There you go." She pressed her cheek against his arm. "And we need a lounge, a place where people can socialize and order mixed drinks. They'll need scripts from a doctor to consume alcohol, of course. Some will have a daily drink limit. But we'll hire bartenders who can create fabulous virgin cocktails for those who can't imbibe."

Tuck let out a blissful sigh. "It'll be amazin'."

"We'll add a new wing for people with pets, too. Some individuals really are allergic to cats or dogs, but if we keep the animals in only one section, we'll be able to make it work. Courtyards off each patio with gates so a dog can go outside or be taken for a walk. You'll be able to have Rip with you full-time again, and I'd enjoy having a lapdog. I also want an equine center. Not a huge one, but large enough for old-timers who have horses to be able to keep them here."

Tuck's heart caught. "Bolt?"

She grinned. "As I came up with that idea, I was

thinking of him, I must admit. And I think we should create a temporary shelter and pasture for him right away. It's ridiculous for him to be boarded elsewhere."

"This sounds like a place I won't be able to afford," he said with a laugh.

"Oh, no. Everyone will be able to afford this. Well, not everyone will be able to keep horses, but they'll be able to enjoy everything else. They'll be charged on a sliding scale according to income. Those on government assistance will enjoy all the same perks as everyone else."

"You'll go broke doin' that, honey."

She laughed. "It'll all even out, with wealthier people making up the difference. If I have to invest a little myself, my accountants will use it as a tax write-off. I can always use one of those."

Tuck gazed down at her, feeling like the luckiest man alive. "Why me, Essie? With your looks and money, you could have your pick of men. What do you find attractive about a common, broken-down old rancher like me?"

She stopped and turned her lovely face up to his. Tears shimmered in her eyes. "Everything, Tuck. Absolutely everything."

Chapter Eighteen

Over the next two weeks, Crystal forged friendships with Tanner's children. Her trip to the library with Tori was delightful. The child went home carrying a tote filled with books: several dog-training tomes and three novels about canines. Crystal met Tanner's mom, Libby, and accepted her invitation to stay for tea and cookies after they returned from the library. Crystal found Libby to have a casual, low-key personality with a ready smile and a soft laugh. Her home was bright with sunshine coming through the windows, and the decor reflected Libby's lifestyle, that of an older woman who pursued her own interests—such as jewelry-making and ceramics classes—and a grandmother who spent much of her time focused on her son's motherless children. Her kitchen was a comfortable gathering place with a refrigerator lurking somewhere beneath countless magnets, school assignments, and pieces of artwork. A stand mixer sheathed in a cheerful hand-quilted cover sat on the counter near a slow cooker that emitted mouthwatering smells. A step stool stood in one corner to elevate Tori to counter height so she could help Nana in the kitchen.

Toward the end of the visit, Crystal asked, "Does Tori enjoy baking?"

"Oh, yes." Libby's blue eyes danced with merriment. "And it's very interesting. Tori has an inquisitive mind. She doesn't just accept that baking powder is a rising agent. She wants to know *how* it makes things rise. I'm the opposite. If it works, I don't feel compelled to know why. Whenever we use a new ingredient, she looks it up afterward."

Crystal smiled. "Tanner told me she's exceptionally bright. It's a shame Michael wasn't interested in visiting the library with us. We had a lot of fun."

"Michael is a physically active child. If it's wet enough to drown a duck, he'll watch television or read, but when it's nice, he's outside exercising."

"I'd like to do something special with him."

"Given Michael's age, you're better off to just go with his flow. He'd love to have you attend one of his baseball games. His team plays on Wednesday afternoons. It would be fun if you came and sat with me. Tanner can't always be there, because of work."

"I'd love to see Michael play. I'll have to juggle some appointments, though."

"This Wednesday? Just come here, and we'll drive together."

"Perfect."

As Crystal drove to Libby's house the following Wednesday, she realized she hadn't been this nervous even on her first date as a teenager. She'd definitely spent less time choosing an outfit. She hadn't a clue what a twelve-year-old boy might think was appropriate for a ball game. She finally settled on jeans, white running shoes, and a red top. Then she drew her hair through the open back of a green ball cap. Examining her reflection, she decided she was good to go. She needed to take Rip along, of course. The thought made her smile. If the dog saw balls being thrown, he'd want to chase them.

Having played baseball in high school, Crystal wasn't out of her element in the stands with Libby and Tori.

The little girl spent much of her time petting Rip instead of watching the game. At one point, a boy hit a grounder, and Rip lunged so hard against the leash that Crystal lost her grip. The dog shot down the bleacher steps, dashed across the diamond, and got the ball before the left fielder could reach it.

"Rip!" Michael yelled. His face turned as red as Crystal's shirt.

The other boys joined in to yell at the dog, and the chase began. Tori clapped her hands in delight. Rip had the time of his life while the batter walked the bases. Crystal ran onto the field. Remembering what Tuck had told her, she pointed at her feet and used a stern tone to yell, "Rip! Come!"

To her amazement Rip obeyed and dropped the coveted ball at her feet. She collected the end of his leash and led him back to the bleachers. The coaches had a conversation and called for a replay. The same batter had to step up to the plate again.

Crystal enjoyed every aspect of the game even though Michael's team lost. What really enchanted her, though, was how Libby handled the team's defeat.

"Who wants to have a pizza party to celebrate?" she asked the glum-faced boys.

"What are we celebrating?" Michael asked. He held Rip's leash and had bent forward to fondle his ears. "I don't know if we're in the mood."

"The amazing performance shown by each and every one of you!" Libby grinned at one of the pitchers, a freckled redhead, and said, "You've got a dynamite arm on you, Jimmy! I won't be surprised to see you play for a pro team one day." Then Libby went on to praise all the boys individually and soon had them grinning with sheepish pride. "So what do you say? I think a pizza party at my house sounds fun."

Crystal had imagined that Libby would have the party at a parlor where the pizzas and cleanup would be provided. She was startled when she realized that the older woman intended to make that many pizzas from scratch.

"I can help," she heard herself say. "To attend the game, I took the rest of the day off."

One of the mothers, a freckled redhead who greatly resembled Jimmy, offered to chauffeur the boys to Libby's house in her van and then help with the party. In Libby's kitchen, Crystal donned an apron to slice toppings and grate cheese while the hostess rolled out rounds of dough like a pro. The double ovens accommodated eight pizzas, and Libby baked sixteen in all. The boys set up folding tables in the fenced backyard, where Rip had been turned out to play. Tori was in charge of setting out paper plates, napkins, cups, and plastic eating utensils.

A few of the parents showed up. Tanner trailed in behind them. He grinned when he saw Crystal topping rounds of dough with assembly-line swiftness. Her cheeks went hot when she saw him. He'd opened the front of his uniform shirt because of the heat, and even through the cotton tee he wore as a cover-up, she could see the contours of his chest. He strode up behind her and snatched pieces of pepperoni from the platter, which earned him a playful slap on the hand.

"Seeing you makes me hungry," he whispered near her ear as he stole more meat.

"Shh!" she hissed, glancing around. "Someone might hear you!"

Tanner looked injured, though his twinkling eyes gave him away. "Just because I'm hungry for . . . pizza?"

Later, as Crystal drove home, she couldn't stop smiling. *I did it.* For the first time in her adult life, she felt as if she had cracked through the wall of fear that had governed her world for so long. This week she'd taken her first steps toward being a normal woman. She had entered into a *serious* relationship with a man. She was participating in his children's activities. She'd helped make pizza for a game party. How fabulous was that?

On Sunday, Crystal's only day off, she invited Tanner and his children for a playdate with Rip and a barbecue. Libby came for the outdoor meal and brought side dishes. Crystal supplied the meat, a German potato casserole, and a tossed green salad. Tanner manned the grill.

The month of June had brought with it warm evenings, and in a few days the solstice would officially bring in summer, which had always been Crystal's favorite season. Prior to eating, she tossed a baseball with Michael, painted Tori's toenails, and chatted with Libby over a glass of white wine at the patio table. Rip, of course, was the main act. The children spent most of their time playing with him, their primary activity being to throw sticks into the pond for the heeler to fetch. Rip was in his element, and he did his best to shake water over everyone.

"I'm sure glad you got waterproof collars." Tanner basted steaks on the barbecue shelf with a homemade sauce. "We'll need to test it later to make sure it survived the dunking."

"Good idea," Crystal agreed.

Tanner sent her a steamy look that made her stomach do flip-flops. She'd heard of men with bedroom eyes. His brown lashes shadowed his and made her wish he were making love to her.

As the sunlight faded, Crystal lighted the fire, which she'd laid earlier in a rock fire pit built into the paver patio. The dancing flames added just the right touch, sending out warmth, lending golden light, and scenting the air with smoke from lengths of lodgepole pine.

The dinner turned out perfect, the steaks done to a turn. The kids preferred hot dogs, but each of them took a small piece of beef, which they fed to Rip on the sly. Crystal's German potato casserole was a hit. Libby had brought dessert, a delightful peach crisp that everyone enjoyed with a dollop of vanilla ice cream.

After the mess was cleared away, Crystal brought out a surprise, a bag of marshmallows and four roasting sticks. The kids were excited. Both of them loved s'mores and were over the moon when they learned she'd also gotten graham crackers and milk chocolate. Tanner added to the fun by asking if Crystal had peanut butter. The spread added a special twist to the unexpected treat.

Soon growing full, Tori said, "This one's for you, Rip!"

"Tori," Libby said gently, "Rip can't have chocolate. It's poison to dogs."

The little girl got a stricken expression on her face. "Oh, *no*! I already gave him a little bite." Then she burst into tears and hugged the dog's neck. "I'm sorry, Rip. I'm so sorry. I've killed you."

Crystal ran over and crouched by the child. "No, you haven't killed him, sweetie. You didn't give him that much. Unless Rip ate a lot of chocolate, he should be fine." Crystal had owned only one dog, a pup when she was twelve, and she would always blame herself for his death. Even if Rip got sick, she didn't want this little girl to feel guilty. "Years ago people didn't know chocolate was bad for dogs, and they gave it to them all the time. Not all of those dogs died, and Rip won't, either. He probably won't even have an upset tummy. One smidgeon of chocolate? He'll be okay."

Tori sat back on her heels and wiped away her tears with chocolate-smeared fists. "He looks happy, not sick."

"Exactly. And you can still make him his own s'more with the crackers and only a marshmallow. He'll love that."

Tanner added, "Nah. He should get peanut butter, too. I don't think it's bad for dogs." He arched an eyebrow at his daughter. "You want the s'more specialist to help you make it for him?"

Tori's face was now smeared with melted Hershey bars. "Yes, Daddy. I want Rip's s'more to be the best one tonight."

Michael joined in the fun, making a s'more for the dog, too.

Tori wore a pink top with spaghetti straps and an elasticized midriff. While hugging the child, Crystal had felt goose bumps on her skin. "Did you bring a jacket for Tori?"

"It's in the truck, Tanner," Libby said. "It doesn't feel cold to me, but Tori doesn't have much insulation."

"I'll run and get it," Tanner said. "Michael, are you getting chilly?"

"Nope. I'm good."

Crystal took over for Tanner in supervising the children as they roasted their last marshmallows. She complimented each kid on technique, saying that their finished products would be browned perfectly.

Michael said, "Watch the master!"

He moved his stick in a figure eight, trying to mimic the dashing lunge of a fencer. On the apex of the second swing, his marshmallow went airborne. From where she stood beside Tori, Crystal felt as if the melted confection cannoned through the air at the speed of light before landing on Tori's shoulder. Tori screamed, dropped her stick, and spun in a circle, stamping her feet.

Crystal's only thought was to pluck the gooey substance off the child's shoulder. In her peripheral vision, she saw Libby dashing toward them. With her bare hand, Crystal grabbed the marshmallow. Some of Tori's skin came away with it. The child screamed again.

Libby grabbed a pitcher from the table, held Tori's arm so she couldn't run, and drizzled ice water over the goo-flecked burn. "It's okay, darling. I know it hurts, but this will make it feel better."

Tanner appeared with the jacket, which he tossed aside when he realized his daughter was hurt. He saw the patch of raw skin on her shoulder. "What happened? I was gone for only a minute!"

As Libby explained the mishap, Crystal felt sick to her stomach. *I happened,* she thought. Libby had been sitting in a lawn chair away from the fire. Tanner had gone to the truck. Crystal had been the adult in charge.

"Why on earth would you fling a stick around, playing swords, with a hot marshmallow on the tip?" Tanner asked his son.

Michael's eyes filled with tears. "I didn't know it would come off and hurt anyone."

"Well, now you know, Michael. I understand it was an accident. But don't ever do that again. Okay?"

Tanner flew into action, fetching a large first aid kit from his vehicle. Then he carried both Tori and the plastic case inside. He set the child on the counter by the sink. Everyone else gathered behind him.

He turned on the faucet and adjusted the temperature. "Cool water should help with the burn."

"I used ice water," Libby said. "The hot marshmallow was still partly stuck to her, and I didn't want the burn to go deeper."

"You did the right thing, Mom. Running cool water over a burn minimizes the damage."

Crystal couldn't help but think that she'd done very little. "I'm so glad you were there, Libby."

Within twenty minutes, Tori was bandaged and playing outside with Rip again. Crystal stood near the fire, arms locked around her waist. "Are you sure she doesn't need to see a doctor, Tanner?"

"We'll change the dressing tomorrow and have a look, but I'm pretty sure she'll be fine."

Crystal still felt nauseated. She was standing in the same place she had been earlier, and Libby had been sitting at the table, her view of Michael blocked. Crystal should have known that roasted marshmallows could become burning projectiles. If Michael had been under proper supervision, the accident might never have happened.

"Excuse me for a moment," she said to no one in particular. Moments later, she knelt by the toilet in the bathroom adjoined to her bedroom and purged her stomach.

Tanner sensed that Crystal was upset and followed her into the house. When he heard her vomiting, he set aside polite protocol and went in to check on her. She folded her arms around the commode seat to hide her face as she retched. He found a cloth and ran it under water. Then he crouched to press the cold terry cloth against her throat.

"Sometimes this helps. Do you think it was something you ate?"

She straightened and used the cloth to wipe her mouth. "No," she said, her voice tremulous. "A fright response, I guess. When I pulled that marshmallow off and her skin came away, I nearly fainted." Eyes filled with shadows, she met his gaze. "I'm sorry. I know you thought I'd watch the kids, and I totally blew it. You may as well have left Michael in charge."

"You're not blaming yourself for what happened, surely?"

"I blocked your mom's view where I was standing, so I was the only adult supervising. If I'd told Michael not to swing the stick, Tori wouldn't have gotten burned."

"Okay." He studied her face. Hers was not a symmetrically beautiful countenance, but he thought it was perfect. "You know what I've learned from being a father?" When she shook her head, he answered, "That if anything can go wrong, it *will* go wrong. My kids and I have roasted so many marshmallows I've lost count, and when Michael started playing around, I might not have said anything, either. I learn from my mistakes and hope I'll do better next time. That's all anyone can do."

"What if something *horrible* happens? What then, Tanner?"

"That's not how it usually goes. With kids, tragic things can occur, but mostly it's cuts, scrapes, and bruises. You're fabulous with my children. They like you—a lot. Just relax and enjoy them. Shit happens. When it does, you do the best damage control you can and move on. You know what I did once?"

Her lips finally curved up at the corners. "No, what?"

"Tori finally had her balance on her bike, so I removed the training wheels. She'd been riding it on the sidewalk for weeks. That required steering. Or so I assumed. But apparently training wheels also help a child steer, because right after I took them off Tori's bike, she started wobbling and veered off the sidewalk, went over the grass median, and hit a parked car. Did I see that coming? No. Was my daughter hurt? Yes. She flew onto the hood of the vehicle and fell on the asphalt. She was scraped and bruised. Her head was bleeding. When I got her to the ER, the physician said she had a concussion. It was a mess."

"Oh, no. You must have felt *awful*."

"I did. And then my mother reminded me of the day my dad said I was a good enough swimmer to no longer wear a life jacket at the river. There was a nice swimming hole there. Only, I choked on water and sank like a rock. The current caught me, and when my father dived in after me, he couldn't find me. By the time he did, I wasn't breathing. My mom called for paramedics, Dad started CPR, and I was fine before help arrived. But my father said I could never go swimming again without a flotation device. I was sixteen before he finally relented."

She emitted a weary sigh. "You've made me feel better. Supervising kids is trial and error."

"Sometimes it feels as if it's a series of mistakes. Want to go back out and get a little food back in your stomach?"

She nodded and took his hand.

A few evenings later, Tanner and his children came to Crystal's for dinner again. She had prepared a kid-friendly meal: hamburgers and homemade fries with ice cream sundaes for dessert. They ate on the patio, and everyone devoured so much food that it was decided the sundaes could wait until later. Yelling and laughing, the kids raced around the property to play with Rip. Crystal and Tanner sat across from each other at the table, holding hands.

"I'm disappointed that your mom couldn't come."

"She went out with some friends. That'll be good for her."

Crystal gazed at the kids. "I could get used to this."

"That's my plan, to get you addicted."

She smiled. "I never allowed myself to dream about

having a family. But I love having your kids around. Just listen."

It was growing dark, and he tipped his head. Tori was angry with Michael because he wouldn't give her a turn throwing a stick. Michael retorted, "Go find your own stick!"

Tanner chuckled. "All I hear is trouble and *more* trouble."

She laughed. "I hear life happening. It makes me realize how empty mine has been. Children fill it up."

"What am I, chopped liver?"

"You fill it up, too."

The kids came to the patio, both red cheeked from exertion. "It's too dark to see, and we're ready for ice cream!" Michael said.

"Me, too!" Crystal got up from the chair. "I want a banana split with a little of all three syrups and whipped cream on top!"

"Yum. I love banana splits!" Tori shouted.

Everyone adjourned to the house, and Crystal began pulling bowls from the cupboard and bananas from the fruit bowl. "Michael, would you get the ice cream out so it'll soften a bit?"

Michael opened the freezer door. "I don't see it."

"It should be there on the top shelf."

"I still don't see it."

Crystal went to look herself. There was no vanilla ice cream. "Uh-oh. I had it on my list. I thought for sure I got some. I must have been so absorbed in choosing toppings that I forgot the most important thing."

Tanner intervened. "Not a big deal. I can drive to Flagg's and get some in only a few minutes, and it'll be just the right softness for scooping when I get back."

"Can I go?" Michael asked.

"Sure. Tori, would you like to come?"

The girl bounced around the kitchen. "I'll stay and help Crystal."

After the guys left, Tori asked, "What can I do? I'm really good at slicing bananas the long way. Nana lets me do it with a table knife."

"I'd prefer to slice them just before we're going to eat them. I don't want them to turn brown."

Tori nodded. "Do you know what makes that happen? It's oxidization."

Crystal studied the child's face. "Did you look that up?"

She nodded. "On the computer. Only that's a big word. Did you know you can make a computer say words for you? That's how I learn."

Crystal wondered why an eight-year-old would care what caused fruit to turn brown. "That's interesting. And it's great that you remember things you've looked up."

"My teacher says my brain takes pictures." Tori sighed. "If I can't slice bananas yet, can I go outside to play with Rip?"

Crystal glanced at the windows. "It's way too dark."

"We can play in the front yard with the porch light on. Daddy lets us do that at home."

Crystal decided that would be safe. "Only if you leave the front door open so I can hear you and you promise you won't leave the lighted area. There are coyotes in the woods."

"They normally don't hurt humans."

"True," Crystal agreed. "But you're small, and I don't want to take any chances."

Crystal followed the child to the front door to make sure she left it open and turned on the porch light. "Okay, be sure not to leave the lighted area. And if you need me, just yell."

"I will!"

Tori bounced down the steps to play with the dog. Crystal decided to quickly put the dinner leftovers in the fridge before she joined Tori and Rip in the front yard.

She kept her ears pricked for Tori's voice. She heard the child consistently, either calling to Rip or telling him to fetch. Then, as she straightened a shelf, she realized she heard nothing coming from the yard.

Crystal ran to the front door and grabbed the flashlight that she kept sitting by the mopboard. "Tori?" She stepped out onto the porch. Both the child and the dog were gone, and with a leap of her heart, Crystal saw that the front gate yawned open. "Tori!" she called. "Where are you?"

Just then Crystal heard coyotes. And straight out of a nightmare, she heard Tori scream. She bolted off the porch and hit the ground at a dead run. "Tori!"

She heard coyotes keening and snarling. Then Tori's shrill voice rent the night. "No! *Stop it! Help, Crystal!* Help!"

Flipping on the flashlight, Crystal followed the sounds. Then she heard Rip bark, and a cacophony of snarls and battle cries ensued. Half the time, she ran blind, the flashlight beam bouncing over pine trees one moment and the ground ahead of her the next. She caught her toe on something and fell, smacking her face against the dirt and knocking the breath from her lungs. Staggering back to her feet, she forced her legs to scissor forward again, knowing that if she stopped Tori might be killed.

She burst into a small clearing. In the splashes of light, she saw Tori backed against a pine tree with No Name clutched against her narrow chest. A group of coyotes, shimmering in the illumination like a writhing mass of gray fur, was lunging at the child. All that held them at bay was Rip, who danced back and forth, snarling and slashing with his teeth at any wild creature that dared to get too close.

"Get!" Crystal yelled at the coyotes. "Get out of here!"

But it was as if she made no sound. The cacophony rising from the pack of wolflike animals filled the night. Rip was outnumbered and barely managing to hold them at bay. One predator circled out and around while the others held Rip's attention. Crystal, in a full-out run, realized that the pack wanted the kitten and the dog, not the little girl. But Tori's presence wasn't enough to frighten them away.

"Turn No Name loose!" Crystal screamed.

"No! They'll kill him!"

Crystal felt as if she were in one of those dreams where she tried to run and went nowhere. She estimated that she was about thirty or forty feet from the child, and just as that settled into her brain, the lone coyote darted in behind Rip and leaped at Tori. The little girl whirled to face the tree and hunched forward to protect the kitten. The attacking animal collided with her back. If not for being slammed against the tree, Tori would have been knocked down. Rip whirled at the sound of her cries.

Twenty feet. Crystal knew she wouldn't get there in time.

"Rip!" Still running, she pointed at the pack. "Spring forward! Spring *forward*!"

Rip had already sent the lone marauder fleeing. Now the heeler whirled around and went after the pack. No hesitation. No more trying to merely hold his ground. He dived into the midst of the predators, tearing viciously at fur and flesh. And then he vanished under an undulating wave of gray.

Crystal, deafened by the snarls and whines of several coyotes in a killing frenzy, reached the pine tree, tossed down her flashlight, and grabbed Tori. "In the tree!" Lifting the little girl as high as she could, she yelled, "Grab the limb! Grab it, Tori, and swing up!" She'd seen the little girl on monkey bars. She was as agile as a gymnast. But before Tori did as Crystal told her, she set the kitten on the limb. "Forget No Name! Get in the tree!"

Finally, the child grabbed the limb. With a twist of her body, she soon straddled the barky appendage. "Rip!" she screamed. "They're killing him!"

Now that Crystal had Tori lifted to safety, she retrieved the heavy flashlight. Without stopping to think about the danger, she waded into the fray, swinging the torch as if it were a battle club. *Rip.* He'd gone down. They would tear him apart.

"Get out of here!" The heavy end of the flashlight cracked against something hard. A coyote squealed in pain and ran off. Crystal kept swinging. She had only one thought: that she'd commanded Rip to go after the pack, and now she had to save him. He'd offered the ultimate sacrifice to protect Tori, and she couldn't allow these bloodthirsty killers to take his life. She waded deeper into the pack and kept swinging. Her makeshift weapon connected again and again with bodies. The thudding sound of heavy metal impacting with flesh resounded against her eardrums.

Finally, after what seemed an eternity but was probably only seconds, the last of the coyotes fled with their tails tucked between their legs. Gasping for breath, Crystal dropped to her knees beside the dog. With one play of light over his ravaged body, she wanted to turn her face to the sky and scream. Only, she heard Tori sobbing. This was no time to lose it in front of the little girl.

"Is he okay?"

In the dance of light, Crystal saw more blood than fur. Rip didn't move. She couldn't tell if he was breathing. She feared he was dead.

"He's badly hurt, sweetie." In some sluggish part of her brain, she realized she needed to soften her delivery and give Tori some hope. "I have to get him to the vet. Jack Palmer can fix him." *Maybe.* His injuries looked grave. Crystal doubted that Rip could be pieced back together again.

"Can I get down?"

"No, honey, stay in the tree. The coyotes may come back." A moment of clarity struck, and Crystal didn't want the little girl to become terrified of the wild creatures. "They're hungry. It's not that they're mean. Their tummies are empty, and they need food. To them, Rip and No Name are food, not our little friends."

"Oh," Tori squeaked. "Am I food, too?"

"No." Crystal laid her palm over Rip's torn shoulder and thought she felt a pulse. "But right now you may smell like Rip and No Name, so please stay in the tree."

"Okay."

Crystal's brain felt like congealed mush. "Tori, will you stay in the tree while I go get my car? We need to take Rip to the clinic."

"Yes."

The child sounded sincere, but it occurred to Crystal that she'd also agreed to stay in the yard earlier. If Crystal left and the coyotes returned to feed on Rip, the little girl might shinny down the tree trunk. Coyotes weren't given to attacking kids, but they were predators, and these animals were clearly hungry. The immediate area was splattered with blood, which would excite their primal instincts. She couldn't gamble with the life of a child. Only what else could she do? Just kneeling here while Rip bled to death wasn't an option.

"Okay, Tori. You can get out of the tree and go with me to get the car." Crystal hated to leave Rip here alone, but just as Tuck had recently tried to explain, sometimes a dog's life took second seat to a human's. She didn't like that reasoning. As she looked down at Rip, her reluctance to abandon him rose up in her throat like bile.

"But who'll protect Rip?"

Crystal said the first thing that came to her mind. "God's angels, sweetie. We'll hurry and get back with the car really fast."

"*No!* I've read about coyotes! They know he's hurt, and they'll come back to eat him. He got hurt saving me! I can't leave him!"

Tears burned in Crystal's eyes. She understood the child's feelings. Oh, did she ever understand. "Get down," Crystal ordered. "Now."

Tori drew up her feet to perch on the limb. "You can't make me. I'm higher than you can reach."

Crystal's shoulders slumped. "All right. Stay in the tree. I can't leave you here to go get the car. It's too dangerous. So I'll stay, and Rip won't go to the hospital."

"No!" Tori cried. "Then he'll die for sure!"

Just then it seemed to Crystal that it suddenly turned daylight. Confused and blinded, she turned to locate the source of the glare.

"Crystal? Dear God, what happened? I saw the light and figured it had to be you this close to the house."

"Tanner?"

"Daddy, we have to save Rip!" Tori screamed.

Resembling a shadow dancer cast against a white wall created by headlights, Tanner moved toward them. It wasn't until he was only a few feet away that Crystal could make out his face. He knelt beside Rip. "Oh, Lord, what happened?"

"No Name ran away!" Tori cried. "And then the coyotes tried to get him. Rip saved him . . . and *me!*"

Tanner yelled, "Michael, bring me my jacket!"

Seconds later Michael appeared. Tanner jerked the garment from the boy's hand and spread it on the ground. Then he carefully lifted Rip onto the denim. "Crystal, can you grab that end? It's the only way to carry him without moving him too much. We've got to get him to the vet before he bleeds out."

Chapter Nineteen

For Crystal the rest of the night was like a bad dream. Jack Palmer met her and Tanner in front of the clinic. He said two techs were on their way to assist him during surgery. She and Tanner carried Rip between them to the operating room. Jack was already in scrubs and washing up before Tanner led Crystal back toward the front of the clinic.

Once in the waiting room, Crystal collapsed on a metal-frame chair. With every beat of her heart, she heard the rush of her blood. Did Rip even have any left? She looked down at her crimson-streaked hands. Tanner sat beside her. At first he didn't speak, and she was relieved. Any exchange would have required brain function she momentarily lacked.

She felt Tanner touching her lower leg. "Oh, dear God. You've been bitten."

Crystal tried to focus on that. Before she could make sense of the words, he'd scooped her up in his arms. He carried her to an examining room and set her on the counter, jerked off her sandals, and lifted her feet into the sink.

"What're you doing?"

"Washing out these punctures. When a person's bitten by possibly rabid animals, thorough cleansing of the wounds minimizes the chance of contracting rabies."

She endured his ministrations for a moment, too

numb to worry overmuch about getting rabies. Only then she remembered the coyote leaping on Tori. "Oh, God, Tanner. Go check Tori."

"She's fine. I got out blankets for both kids. Michael's going to sleep up front. She's going to snuggle with No Name on the backseat."

Crystal grabbed his broad wrist. "I can cleanse my own wounds. Go check on your daughter. A coyote got past Rip and leaped on her back."

Tanner's face lost color. "Was she bitten or scratched?"

"There wasn't time to check. That's why she was in the tree. I was afraid the coyotes might go after her."

Tanner found a bite on Tori's back and a scrape on her upper arm. He put Michael in charge of the kitten before, heart pounding, he ran back to the clinic, took Tori to another examining room, and began washing her broken skin.

"It hurts," Tori complained.

"I know, but these punctures have to be flushed out." Tanner used paper towels to dry her off and then carried her to the waiting room, where Crystal was once again sitting. "I need to take her to the ER. You should be seen, too."

"I can't leave Rip," she said. "I just can't."

"I don't want to leave *you*," he told her. "You can't help Rip by sitting out here. Please come with us to see a doctor."

She shook her head. "I'll go later." She glanced at Tori. "Focus on her, Tanner. I'll go in for treatment later—after I know how he's doing."

Tanner truly didn't want to leave her. But it was his duty as a father to seek medical treatment for his child. "I'll be back as soon as I can."

"Take her to St. Matthew's in Crystal Falls. The emergency care here is limited."

Tanner carried his daughter from the building, but he left part of his heart in that waiting room. In Crystal's eyes, there was a blank, distant expression that worried him. He sensed that she shouldn't be alone right now.

The minutes crept forward as slowly as ants trying to crawl over tacky lacquer. Crystal glanced at her phone countless times to see how long Rip had been in surgery. One hour turned into two, and she was alone with her thoughts every second. Each time she glanced down at her hands, she remembered the blood that had been caked on them before she washed them, and she was swept back in time to the afternoon she killed her sister. Although twenty-one years had passed, Crystal still felt as if it had happened yesterday. For her, there was no escaping those memories or the devastating sense of guilt.

Another hour slogged by, and finally Jack Palmer appeared. He wore a rumpled shirt and faded jeans. His hair was tousled. A shadow of whiskers darkened the lower part of his face. He pulled over a chair to sit across from her.

"He's still alive," he said. "As long as we can keep him that way, he may make it through this. He lost a lot of blood. We transfused him to keep him stable during surgery. The coyotes tore him up badly. I've never seen the like."

Crystal still felt numb. "So you're not sure he'll make it."

Jack slumped his shoulders. "It's up to God now. I've done all I can for him. I know how much you love him. I wish I could offer you more hope."

She nodded. "It's not your fault, Jack." She paused to search his weary gaze. "I'd like to stay with him. Can you arrange that? Call me silly, but I think he'll sense that I'm here."

"I have cots and bedding in the back. If you'd like, you can bunk near his cage. You can't get much closer than that."

Crystal nodded. "I'd like that. Thank you, Jack."

"I'll ask the ladies to get things set up for you. I've used a cot plenty of nights. They're fairly comfortable."

Crystal doubted that she would be able to sleep. "That's good to know."

Tori received an injection of rabies immune globulin, which would start to protect her from contracting rabies right away. Tanner was given a follow-up schedule for a series of four more shots, and the ER nurse stressed to him that Tori had to get the injections on the specified dates. After sticking a list of possible side effects in his shirt pocket, Tanner led Michael from the hospital while carrying his drowsy daughter. When they reached the truck, he saw No Name peering out at them over the edge of the blanket.

Acutely aware that he'd left Crystal stranded at the vet's, Tanner took his kids to his mother's house. Hair mussed from her pillow and still half-asleep, she met him at the door, took one look at his face, and came wide-awake.

"Tanner, what happened?"

He gave her the briefest version of the story possible, helped get the kids settled in the extra bedrooms, and then went over the common side effects of the RIG injection. "If any of these things happen, call the ER. If you need to take Tori back in, please call me. I'll meet you at St. Matthew's."

"You're leaving?"

"I left Crystal at the vet's without a car. She was also bitten. More times than Tori. The ER doctor said I should get her in as soon as I can. Even though cases of rabies in this area are rare right now, he can't rule out that those coyotes have lost their natural fear of people because they're rabid."

"Playing it safe was the right decision, Tanner." She followed him to the door. "And antirabies shots aren't that bad anymore. Just get Crystal in for an injection."

"I'll try. Right now she won't leave the dog."

"He saved Tori's life. All of us owe him a debt of gratitude. Please tell Crystal I'll keep Rip in my prayers."

Tanner was too upset to feel drowsy as he drove back to Mystic Creek. When he reached the clinic, he found Crystal sitting in the waiting area. He sank onto a chair beside her and reached for her hand. She jerked at his touch and drew away. "You need to go," she told him in a flat voice. "I stayed out here to tell you that. You need to go."

"Where?"

"Anywhere that's away from me. Everything I've ever loved, except for Tuck, has died. I have a gift for making stupid decisions and putting those I love in danger. Protect yourself. Protect your children. You need to stay away from me."

Tanner couldn't quite believe his ears. "*What?* How can you blame yourself for what happened tonight?"

"Why wouldn't I? I'm the one who let Tori play outside with Rip after dark."

"With the porch light on and the door wide-open. You were only a few feet away. I do that all the time in the summer. It's a safe neighborhood."

"My neighbors are coyotes. I wasn't worried about

them jumping the fence. They've never gotten that brave. But I didn't take into account that No Name might go outside if the door was left open, and I didn't think about Tori leaving the yard to go after him." She rested her clenched fists on her knees. "That's a clear case of me not considering all the possibilities and making unsafe decisions for a child in my care."

"Tori should have called for you. According to what she said, that was the agreement. Instead she took off after the kitten alone. I plan to have a talk with her about that tomorrow."

Crystal sent him a withering look. "Tori is eight years old. I'm thirty-two. I should have known not to take her at her word. Children don't consider the possible consequences of their actions. It's up to the adult in charge to do that for them."

"Please don't beat yourself up about this. Tori's going to be just fine."

"Rip isn't. When that one coyote got around Rip and jumped on Tori, I realized that the animals were in a frenzy. They were between me and your child. I gave Rip the command to attack, Tanner. I sent him to his death."

"To save my daughter."

"Yes. But was it really necessary? In the end, I used the flashlight as a club and chased off the coyotes without Rip's help."

"For the love of God, Crystal, my daughter had just been bitten by a wild animal, and now you're questioning your decision to sic Rip on the pack to keep Tori safe. No offense intended, but it's almost as if you *want* to blame yourself."

She looked as if he'd just slapped her, and Tanner wished he'd chosen his words more carefully. There was a look in her eyes that he could only describe as haunted.

Maybe, to satisfy some twisted need within herself, she actually was searching for reasons to blame herself, but it sure as hell wasn't his place to tell her that. "I'm sorry. I didn't mean that."

"I think you did."

"Let me just say that I consider my daughter's life to be far more important than a dog's. I'm glad you commanded Rip to attack the pack. He created a distraction that allowed you to reach Tori and get her up in the tree where she was safe. I think you made the only decision you could under the circumstances, and I'll always be grateful you did."

"But was it really necessary?"

Tanner knew he shouldn't feel frustrated, but he had an awful feeling Crystal intended to end their relationship over this. If he didn't get through to her now, she might never give him another chance. "You can second-guess every decision you made tonight, but I'm looking at the end result. My daughter lived through it. Why can't you pat yourself on the back for that instead of finding reasons to eat yourself up with guilt?"

"Because, in the end, I have to go back to the decision I made to let Tori play in the yard in the first place. If I hadn't done that, Tori wouldn't have been in the woods. Rip wouldn't have been out there, either. It was a domino effect, starting with me. As a result, the last domino has yet to fall. Rip may die."

"And you've convinced yourself it's all your fault. Well, that's just great."

She shook her head. "There are things about me that you don't know, Tanner. It's true, what I said. Anything I've ever loved has ended up dying, and each death was caused by stupid decisions I made."

Tanner looked deeply into her eyes, and all he saw was pain. She began to talk, telling him in stark detail about her sister's death. He sat there in shock, listening and wondering how an eleven-year-old girl could survive such a thing.

"Tuck got me away from my parents and took me to his ranch. Right away he bought me a horse. I fell in love with her. She had a registered name, but I just called her Beauty. She ran like the wind. Then Tuck got me a puppy. Beauty's former owner didn't warn Tuck that she didn't like dogs in her stall. Tuck always took his dog Tabasco into the stables with him, but Tabasco was old and horse smart. He didn't get within hoof reach of equines he didn't know. I named my pup Lucky. I took him everywhere with me, just as Tuck did Tabasco. One afternoon Beauty kicked Lucky in the head and killed him. He wasn't so lucky. He got me for an owner."

Tanner's heart twisted. "Oh, Crystal."

She fixed him with a tear-filled gaze. "Tuck said it wasn't my fault. Beauty's former owners should have warned him. But the truth is that any horse may kick. A responsible dog owner trains a puppy to stay back and respect a horse's personal space."

"You were just a kid," he protested, but it was as if she hadn't heard him.

"About two months later, I was exercising Beauty. I didn't hold her to blame for killing my puppy. I knew it had been my fault. It's important for you to know I wasn't angry with her. I was just riding her around the pasture. I wasn't even running her. She stepped in a chuckhole and broke her front leg. Tuck had to put her down. Again, he said it wasn't my fault, but I hadn't walked that area to check for holes before I rode Beauty there. Good horsemen check." Her mouth quivered at the corners. "Since that day, with the exception of Tuck, I've never let myself love anyone or anything. Until I met you." One of her eyelids started to twitch, and she looked away. "That's not turning out well. Tell me I'm not the key factor in these situations, Tanner. Tell me it wasn't due to my decision that Tori was out in the woods tonight."

Tanner felt like he'd fallen down an elevator shaft and left his stomach several floors up. How the hell could he deal with this? He groped for something reassuring to say. "Crystal, you made the best decision you could in the moment."

"And it was the *wrong* one. Rip may die before morning." She held up her hands in silent appeal. Then she said, "If Tori has No Name, please let her keep him. I don't want him anywhere near me."

"No Name loves *you*, not Tori."

"He'll grow to love Tori. She's a precious little girl, and No Name will be safe with her."

"That's nuts. In fact, every word you've said since I got back is nuts."

"No, Tanner, it's all fact. Why can't you see how dangerous it is for me to love you and your kids? You need to stay far, *far* away from me." She stood and looked down at him for a long moment as if she were memorizing his face. "Cassidy has offered to drive me to the farm tomorrow so I can get my car. You need to go home and be with your family."

"And not come back." Tanner didn't phrase it as a question. He saw the answer in her eyes. Keeping his gaze fixed on her, he stood. "You're breaking my heart."

"Broken hearts heal, Tanner."

She turned and walked away. Tanner stayed where he was until she opened a door and vanished into the back rooms. He sank down on the chair and held his head in his hands. In a way, he understood Crystal's reasoning. He didn't believe she was jinxed in love, but he could see how she might think that. In her mind all the horrible events of her life had been results of bad choices she'd made. And the most awful part was, he couldn't argue that point. She'd chosen to obey her father and continue with archery practice, which had resulted in her sister's death. She'd thought it was safe to take her puppy into the stable, which had resulted in its death. She'd exercised her horse in a pasture that she hadn't checked for gopher holes, which had resulted in its death. He couldn't look her in the eye and say that those deaths hadn't been a direct consequence of decisions she'd made.

Only it was such a messed-up way of thinking. Everyone made mistakes. Tanner couldn't count how many times he'd decided this or that and regretted it later. It had been Crystal's misfortune that her mistakes had led to tragedy. He had no doubt that she needed counseling to help her look at her past more logically. As it stood, she was trapped in a web of misconceptions and irrational fear.

He considered staying until she returned to the waiting area. Everything within him yearned to wrap his arms around her, pooh-pooh her foolish notions, and try to heal her with his love. Only that would never work. Crystal alone had the power to heal herself, but until she realized how messed-up her thinking was, she'd probably never seek help.

Crystal lay on the cot to rest her body if not her mind. Tanner wasn't the only one whose heart was breaking. She longed to call him and tell him she hadn't meant a word she'd said. But that would be a lie. She didn't know why her love rode double with heartbreak, but ever since Mary Ann's death, that had been the case. Maybe it was God's way of punishing her for what she'd done to her sister.

Rip whined. Crystal jumped to her feet so fast that her head spun. She stepped over to his cage, and sure enough his eyes were half-open. She called for Cassidy, who'd stayed awake to watch over Rip while the other tech slept. Cassidy emerged from the lab office, where she'd been working on a computer.

"He's awake!"

Cassidy walked over to look at the dog. Then she smiled. "That's a good sign. He's not out of the woods yet, but it's encouraging. He may be in pain, so I'll put a little something in his IV to ease him up."

Crystal watched as the tech administered the medication. Rip drifted back to sleep; then Cassidy washed her hands. Just as she grabbed paper towels, the other technician entered the room. "Your turn to snooze, Cass. I got my four."

Cassidy laughed. "You don't need to tell me twice. I'm off to see the sandman."

After the brunette left, the other tech looked at Rip's chart and then opened the door of his cage to check his heart. "Strong and steady. He's a fighter, for sure. We almost lost him on the table."

She closed the door and latched it. Turning toward Crystal, she flashed a warm smile. Her scrub jacket was wrinkled. Her amber hair, glossy and straight, fell to her shoulders in a tousled bob. "You want some coffee? I could use a double shot straight into a vein."

Crystal shrugged. "I can't sleep. Why not?"

Rip lived through the night. Jack came in the next morning, examined the heeler, and smiled at Crystal. "He's one hell of a dog. I figured him to be a goner, but he's going to prove me wrong. His vitals are good. I think he's going to make it."

Crystal cupped a hand over her eyes and burst into tears. Jack curled an arm around her. She pressed her face against his scrubs. When her spigots ran dry, she drew back. "I'm sorry. I'm not normally so emotional."

"You're exhausted. Last night was a frightening ordeal. Then you were afraid Rip might die. I'd tell you to get a ride home with Cassidy and go straight to bed, but you have bites on both calves. Once you have your car, you should head straight for the ER at St. Matthew's to start antirabies treatment. Some or all of those coyotes could be rabid. Go. Do it. The world will keep turning without you for a day."

Crystal knew he was right. Once she got back to her car, she needed to drive to Crystal Falls. But first she needed to see Tuck.

After picking up her car, Crystal drove to the assisted living center. She found Tuck sitting at a table with Burt and a pink-haired older lady. Burt called the woman sweetie, and she kept batting her false eyelashes at him.

Tuck glanced up, smiled, and invited Crystal to sit down. "I'm sorry Essie ain't here," he said. "She's twice as busy now that she bought this place."

Crystal didn't take a seat. "I need to talk to you in private."

"Uh-oh." He pushed back in the chair and got up. His eyes narrowed on her face. "You look like hell. How's about we sit out back? It's nice out there this time of day."

Crystal followed him to the patio. A sun-touched breeze wafted over them as they sat beside each other in plastic chairs.

"What's up? The way you look, it ain't good."

Crystal told him about the string of events that had occurred last night. "Jack thinks Rip will make it. I just wanted you to know he's in a bad way and needs to have visitors. You're well enough now to drive again. I can take you by the farm so you can pick up your truck."

Tuck's gaze grew so intent on her face that Crystal struggled not to fidget. "Why can't you visit him? I can drive now, but tryin' to crawl up into that truck won't be easy."

She gestured at her legs. "I was bitten by coyotes last night. The wounds aren't serious, but I have to start a series of antirabies shots. And when I get back, I've got to get some sleep. I was up all night."

"How's everything goin' at the salon while you're gone?"

The question came at her from left field. She had expected a string of questions about Rip or at least a show of concern about her bites. "I don't know. I haven't called to check."

"That ain't like you."

Tuck left that observation hanging in the air between them. Finally, Crystal asked, "Where are you going with this, Tuck?"

"You've got that look."

"What look?"

"I've come to think of it as the Mary Ann look. You're pullin' away from Rip and from me. I see it in your eyes."

"Don't be silly."

"Have you sent Tanner packin' yet?"

Crystal hated that her grandfather could read her so easily. "That's my business."

"That means it's done. Poor sap. He loves you, Crystal. And I don't peg him as a man who falls in love easy."

Crystal sprang to her feet. "Your dog needs you. That's all I came to say."

"And now you're runnin'. How long you gonna keep runnin', Crystal?"

Tears burned in her eyes. "It's not like you to be cruel, Tuck."

"Am I bein' cruel or just shovin' the truth under your nose? Sit back down."

Crystal remained standing.

Her whole body jerked when Tuck jabbed a finger at the vacated chair and roared, *"Sit—back—down!"*

She sat, but every muscle in her body was taut with her urge to escape.

"I screwed up, Crystal. The minute I got you to the ranch and had sole custody, I should have taken you to counselin'."

"I went to counseling in Washington!" Crystal had never told him that, and she wished she'd kept the information to herself now. But words were like toothpaste: once you squeezed it from a tube, you couldn't push it back in. "The authorities made my parents take me in. But every word I said during a session was recorded, and every word was held against me. Twice a week, they ranted and raved all evening at me for saying bad things about them."

"Why in the hell would any counselor betray the confidence of a child who needed help like you did?"

"Because my parents told her I was emotionally damaged," Crystal blurted. "That I was jealous of Mary Ann and wanted her out of the picture so I'd be the only child in the family for them to love." She felt the bite of her nails digging into her palms. "There was a smidgeon of truth in that, Tuck. I loved my baby sister, but I envied her, too. She was so cute, and I wasn't. Our father loved her so much that sometimes I felt invisible.

There were times when I wondered if anyone would miss me if I disappeared."

"You never would have harmed Mary Ann."

Crystal squeezed her eyes closed. "Are you *sure* about that, Tuck? During those sessions, the doctor almost had me convinced a few times that I had subconsciously *wanted* my sister gone. Now I can't be certain that my jealousy of Mary Ann didn't influence the decisions I made that afternoon. Becoming excellent at archery was the only way I knew to make Daddy feel proud of me, to make him love me. Practicing and showing him my targets at night was important to me. I knew Mary Ann wasn't allowed to be anywhere near my practice range. I knew it could be dangerous. I also knew she was spoiled and didn't always mind our parents. Was there some part of me that hoped Mary Ann would dart into the path of my arrow so I could be the only little girl my father could love?"

"Oh, Jesus." Tuck leaned forward and held his head in his hands. "Oh, sweet Jesus."

Crystal pushed unsteadily to her feet. "I loved my sister. As an adult, looking back at the child I once was, I don't believe I intended for Mary Ann to be harmed in any way. But there's no denying that my choices that afternoon were not about keeping her safe. They were about *me* and what *I* wanted. Daddy got upset if I didn't practice. I *always* disappointed him. And that hurt, Tuck. Way deep inside me, it hurt so much. Maybe that counselor was right. Maybe she saw an evilness within me that I couldn't acknowledge then and still can't now."

Crystal turned to walk away. Behind her, she heard her grandfather say, "You don't have an evil bone in your whole body."

"Maybe not!" she retorted. "All I know is that everyone and everything around me always gets hurt.

It wasn't just Mary Ann. Remember Lucky and Beauty? And last night I added Tori and Rip to the list."

On the way back from Crystal Falls, Crystal got a text notification on her cell and pulled over to see that Tanner had sent her a message. She didn't know if she had the strength to read it, but some perverse part of her nature pressed her to open it.

"I love you," he wrote. *"I hope and pray you can work your way through whatever is tormenting you and find your way back to me. I believe we're meant to be together, and you once said you believe that, too. Don't give up on us. Please don't. Love always, Tanner."*

Crystal closed the message and pulled back onto the two-lane highway. She wanted nothing more than to call him. Only if she got back together with him, it would be disastrous for him and his kids. While talking with Tuck, she had faced the fact that she had emotional issues, really serious emotional issues. She wasn't sure what to do with that knowledge. Tuck wanted her to get counseling, and she could see why he encouraged that, but her last experience with a psychiatrist had nearly destroyed her. To this day, even though she would have happily died in Mary Ann's place, she wondered if some sick, blackened part of her had actually wanted her sister gone.

She knew she should call the salon and at least let Nadine know what had happened, but she didn't think she could talk with anyone right now. Besides, just as Jack had said this morning, the world would keep turning without her for one day, and at the moment, her business and the livelihood it provided didn't seem important. Nothing did. She felt as if a brutal hand had hollowed her out with a metal scoop, leaving only an awful, horrible ache that radiated from her center to make even her arms and legs throb.

When she got to the house, she stepped inside and stood listening to the silence. *This is my future,* she thought. *I'm going to be alone for the rest of my life.*

For a short while, she had allowed herself to envision her life being different. Sleepovers for Tori. Attending Michael's games. Cooking special meals for a family. She'd had a man who loved her. She had even had a dog and cat. Now the walls of the farmhouse seemed to mock her. Every room she entered would be empty.

Essie had been so busy all day she'd barely found time to eat, so she'd looked forward to a quiet dinner in her apartment with Tuck. By seven she had gotten the imagined dinner, but she wasn't working her way toward the bedroom with the man she loved. Instead she was sitting in the backseat of a taxi on her way to see Crystal. Tuck knew that she was going. After talking to Crystal that afternoon, he believed his granddaughter needed a stern shake-up, and he didn't have it in him to do it.

As the cab pulled up beside Crystal's Equinox, Essie saw that there were still lights on inside the house. *Here goes nothing.* Whether Crystal wished to receive advice or not, she was about to get some.

Essie climbed out of the vehicle and told the driver, "Please wait for me."

"I can't do that unless I charge for the time, and that can get really pricey."

Essie opened her purse and handed him a twenty. "I'm good for it. While you wait, take a nap. You look as if you need one."

Once inside the gate, Essie crossed the lawn to the

porch, thinking a nice walkway was in order. Big holes could hide under grass, and she had no desire to lose her balance and fall. She wanted to enjoy life with Tuck. He'd promised to take her dancing soon. And he also hoped to move his truck to the facility so he could take her for rides into the surrounding mountains for sight-seeing adventures. His hip needed only a bit more time to heal, and then he'd be back up to speed. Essie didn't want to get hurt and delay their plans to have fun.

She took a deep breath and knocked on the door. Before she could focus on her life with Tuck, she needed to help Crystal move forward with her own. Sometimes before festering wounds could heal, they had to be lanced so the infection drained out. Essie didn't like the thought of being the scalpel that sliced through the protective walls Crystal had erected around herself. She never enjoyed causing anyone pain, especially when that person had already endured enough. *Nasty business, this.* But Essie was determined to do what needed to be done, because Tuck was counting on her.

Crystal had just taken a shower, and her towel-dried hair hung in damp ropes over her shoulders. She wore only a blue nightshirt. When she heard a rap on the front door, she glimpsed Essie through one of the picture windows. The last thing she wanted right now was company, and at the moment, Essie ranked high on her list of people she least wanted to see. Oh, how she regretted telling Tuck about the counseling sessions she had endured years ago. Crystal had no doubt that her grandfather had shared details about the conversation with Essie, and now the older woman was probably here at Tuck's behest to talk with her.

The antirabies shot was starting to make Crystal feel a bit feverish, and she had a headache. She'd been told at the hospital that both side effects might occur and that she shouldn't be alarmed unless she ran a fever of a hundred and four degrees. She hadn't used an oral thermometer yet. So far, she just felt icky, which was a small price to pay to avoid getting hydrophobia.

Crystal thought about evading Essie by ducking into her bedroom and pretending she was asleep, but she suspected the other woman had seen her through the glass. *Great.* She was stuck with answering the door. And then another thought struck her like a thunderclap. Oh, God, what if something had happened to Tuck, and Essie had come to break the news in person?

Crystal ran barefoot across the room and yanked open the door. Essie, smartly attired in a forest green jacket and skirt with matching pumps, stood on the welcome mat. She smiled slightly. "Oh, honey, you look like death warmed over."

Crystal ignored that. "Is Tuck all right?"

Essie blinked. "He was when I left, yes. You're the one who looks like she's been hit by a truck."

"I'm feeling pretty rough." Crystal glanced beyond the older woman and saw a black cab parked beside her car. "I don't want to be rude, but maybe you should signal that driver not to leave. I had my first antirabies injection this afternoon, and I'm experiencing a headache and low-grade fever. All I want to do is go to bed and sleep."

"I already asked him to wait. I'm sorry you're not feeling well, dear, but this won't take long."

Crystal sighed and stepped back to let Essie enter. "You look lovely, as always."

"Thank you."

Essie strode past Crystal to the dining table, where she deposited her purse and drew back a chair. Crystal suspected that, for the first time, she was seeing Essie

Maxwell Childers, the businesswoman, in action. With an air of absolute confidence, she made herself comfortable and said, "Please, won't you join me?"

Reluctant, Crystal moved toward the dining area. "Why are you here, Essie? Let's cut right to the chase, shall we? I'm really not feeling well."

"I always cut right to the chase," Essie said with a smile. "I asked the cab driver to wait because I anticipate that you'll kick me out after you've heard what I've come to say."

Crystal sank onto a chair across the table from her. "Essie, I won't venture a guess as to what you intend to say, but I will ask you to postpone this until I'm feeling better. I've had a trying twenty-four hours."

"This won't keep, dear. I came to tell you that you are, hands down, the biggest coward I've ever met."

Chapter Twenty

Essie's voice cut through Crystal like a knife, and being called a coward hurt. She felt as if she'd just been punched in the solar plexus. *"What?"*

"You heard me. You're a coward." Essie leaned forward to brace her arms on the table. "You try to hide that, even from yourself, by pretending that you somehow endanger all the people you care about. But that is such bullshit, I almost need hip waders to trudge through it."

"It isn't bullshit." Anger surged within Crystal, creating molten heat in her chest and the base of her throat. "And how dare you say such a thing to me when you know next to nothing about my reasons for feeling that way?"

"I don't need to know your reasons. The actual truth is clear to see. As a child, you went through some horrible things, and I can't blame you for not wanting to endure anything more. But I can't stand on the sidelines and watch you self-destruct without saying something. You tell yourself that you've ended your relationship with Tanner to protect *him*. You tell yourself that you always manage to harm the people or things you love, so to prevent that from happening, your answer is to not let yourself care. But you're not protecting Rip by abandoning him, Crystal. You're not protecting Tanner or his children by ending your relationship. The truth is that you're actually protecting yourself."

"That's preposterous!" Crystal shot up from the chair. "For the time being, this is my home. I don't have to put up with you coming here and flinging insults at me."

"Not insults, dear. Only truths that you are too confused to see. Think about it, Crystal. What's the most surefire way for you to avoid ever feeling heartbroken again? I'll tell you. If you don't allow yourself to love anyone or anything, you believe you can't get hurt. But that isn't true. The greatest heartbreak of all for you will be in running from life instead of embracing it." She patted the table, and in a gentler tone, she said, "Sit back down. Just hear me out, and then I'll leave."

Crystal's headache had morphed into what felt like a full-fledged migraine, and she was afraid anger alone had not caused the sensation of fiery heat she felt in her body. She sat, not because she wanted to hear another word Essie said, but because she didn't have the strength to walk away.

"Tuck told me about your horrible experience with a counselor when you were a child," Essie said. "It's unconscionable that a medical professional betrayed your trust and shared everything you said with your parents. And it's absolutely despicable that the doctor suggested to you in any way that you may have subconsciously wanted to get rid of your sister."

Feeling drained and weak, Crystal said, "There's nothing that can be done about that now, and there's no good that can come from our discussing it."

"I think you're dead wrong. Have you done any reading at all about the research that has been done on the power of suggestion?"

"I barely have time for pleasure reading."

"Well, I'm at the helm of a corporate ship, and that was necessary reading for me. I've also hired professionals to train my employees to use the power of suggestion to positively impact subordinates in the workplace." Essie's gaze suddenly seemed like a powerful magnet, and Crystal's eyes felt like metal chips that were inexorably drawn to it. "If I tell a person that a dental procedure he is about to undergo is nightmarishly painful, he is more likely than not to have a very negative experience. If I tell someone that an upcoming test is almost impossible to pass, that person will probably pull a low score. It's a proven fact that negative power of suggestion sets people up to fail, Crystal.

"That doctor used the power of suggestion on you in the most harmful of ways. I'm guessing your parents convinced her that there was good reason to believe you had deliberately harmed your sister, and her aim was to pry a confession out of you, but it was *wrong*. You were a grief-stricken child with parents who had turned on her. And you were at an impressionable age when kids develop a sense of self-esteem and identity. It's during the years from age six to fourteen that children internalize their expectations of themselves, whether they will succeed or fail at certain things. Somehow, dear heart, you developed an expectation not only that you will fail at love, but that your love will also cause harm."

Essie's words arrowed straight into Crystal's heart, and she began to shake with violent tremors that ran through her entire body. Essie jumped up from her chair and circled the table.

"Oh, honey." Crystal felt the older woman's arms tighten around her. "You're burning up. I thought you were just trying to get rid of me when you said you were sick."

"I w-wanted you t-to leave. I d-didn't w-want to h-hear this."

"I'm so sorry. But those things had to be said. You

can't live your life like this. You'll never be happy, and you *deserve* to be."

"D-do I? M-my own f-father hates m-me."

Essie's arms cinched tighter. "He isn't your father. Your mother was pregnant by another man when she married him. Tuck found out after Mary Ann passed away. He never told you. He felt you had endured too much already. Now he regrets that decision."

Crystal went still, and as she did, she felt as if a missing piece of the puzzle that had been her childhood suddenly fell into place. "Oh, G-God, that's why he d-didn't l-love m-me. No matter how h-hard I tried, n-no matter what I d-did, he never l-loved me."

"I don't know the man, but I suspect he felt your mother tricked him, and he resented you. It was cruel and selfish of him, but for whatever reason, he punished you for your mother's betrayal. Not fair, but a lot of things in life aren't."

Crystal awakened with a start to darkness that was broken only by a light coming from the kitchen. She sat up, wondering how she had gotten into bed. The last thing she readily recalled was sobbing her heart out in Essie's arms.

She reached to turn on her bedside lamp. A note lay on the oak nightstand. With a shaky hand, she picked it up, rubbed the sleep from her eyes, and focused on the elegant handwriting, which reflected the grace and beauty of the woman who'd held the pen.

Dear Crystal:

I know I said horrible things to you, and whether you believe it or not, it was as painful for me as it was for you. You're such a good person, so loyal

*to and considerate of your grandfather. I admire
you. But I couldn't stand by and let you ruin the
one chance you may have for happiness. Please
contact Tanner and tell him you'll go for counseling. He's a wonderful man, and I doubt you'll ever
find another one like him. Give him at least some
hope that the two of you can build a future together. I've asked around. The following psychiatrist has a practice right here in town. He's young,
not a stodgy old man, and he's reputed to be a
respectable counselor. Please follow through on
your promise. Call him. See him at least once to
find out if you're comfortable with him. If not, I'll
help you search for someone else.*

Crystal stared at the contact information. Jonas Sterling. He was Ben Sterling's younger brother. He'd set
up his practice in Mystic Creek a few months ago, and
Crystal had heard good things about him. Only, she
couldn't remember promising Essie that she'd see anyone. She frowned and rubbed her aching forehead. A
vague recollection formed in her mind. *"Yes, I'll go,
Essie. I promise I'll go."*

She set the note aside. Stepping into the bathroom,
she opened a vanity drawer and fished through the
contents to find her thermometer. It was one of those
instant gadgets, and moments later she squinted to see
the digital readout. Her body temperature was one
hundred and two degrees. *Crap.* Wasn't it just her luck
to be one of the people who had a reaction to a RIG
injection? She stumbled back into the bedroom. *Tanner.
A wonderful man*, Essie had called him. And she was
right. Tanner was one of the greatest guys Crystal had
ever met.

And I love him with all my heart.

Her cell phone lay on the nightstand. Crystal went to her messages and found at least a dozen from Tanner. As she read them, tears filled her eyes and kept making the letters blur. He said how much he loved her. How much he wanted to have a future with her. How concerned his kids were because she hadn't been in touch. He'd had to call the veterinary clinic to learn that Rip had survived the night. Tori was especially worried, because she had disobeyed Crystal by leaving the yard. She was afraid Crystal was mad at her.

That last bit hit Crystal dead center in her chest. The child had disobeyed, but in that moment when No Name left the yard, she'd probably not anticipated that he would run from her and go into the woods. She was only eight. When Mary Ann had yelled, "Ha-ha! Fooled you!" had she realized that her actions would result in her death?

Crystal's mind closed in on itself, just as it always did when she recalled that moment, and the haunting question she could never answer resounded inside her head. *As you released that arrow, did you know it would result in Mary Ann's death? Was there an unacknowledged wish within you to have her gone so your father would love only you?*

Crystal tapped her fingertip on the reply line of the message thread and typed, *"Please tell Tori I am NOT mad at her. I don't want her thinking that. Tell her that I love her and I'm very glad she's taking such good care of No Name."*

Tanner jerked awake at the musical bing of a text notification. Lying on his side in bed, he reared up on one elbow to check the time. *Three o'clock in the morning.* It had to be a message from Crystal. He almost fell off the edge of the mattress trying to grab his phone. As he read her missive, she texted again.

"*I miss you so much. Essie talked to me, and I've decided to go to counseling. Will you give me a little time to get my head on straight?*"

He almost leaped to his feet and delivered a victory punch in the air. He texted back, "*I love you, Crystal, and you can take all the time you need. You're worth the wait.*"

She wrote back, "*Will you give my message to Tori?*"

"*First thing in the morning when I wake her up to go to Mom's. I love you.*"

"*Ditto, ditto, ditto, to the nth degree.*"

By morning Crystal felt better. Her temperature was back to normal, and the fierce headache was gone. She showered and dressed for work, feeling cautiously hopeful about her future. Even though she had put Tanner's daughter in peril, he still loved her. Everyone around her seemed to think she needed counseling, and though she had avoided seeking any help because of her first experience, she was now willing to give it one more try.

Nadine greeted Crystal with a hug when she arrived at the salon. Expecting to be asked to explain her absence, Crystal was pleased to learn that the Mystic Creek gossip mill was still in fine working order. Everyone knew about the coyote attack, Rip's consequent injuries, and the necessity of antirabies treatment for both Tori and Crystal.

Crystal went straight to work. Her first customer of the day was Charlie Bogart, who owned Charlie's Sporting Goods. A large man with a trim build, he had light brown hair and grayish blue eyes. He regaled Crystal with jokes as she gave him a trim. Her second client was Catherine Scott, an attractive natural blonde in her early forties who wore her hair nearly to the waist and preferred a wardrobe with a homespun look. She talked nonstop about her summer vegetable garden as Crystal snipped away her split ends.

By noon Crystal had lost track of how many people she'd serviced and she was weak with hunger. For lunch she went across the street to the Jake 'n' Bake for a beef calzone with a side salad. Jake had small tables in the display area of his bakery. Needing a break from all the salon's chemical smells, Crystal sat near a window to eat and entertain herself by watching people come and go along East Main. She nearly choked on a cherry tomato when the bell over the entrance door jangled and Jonas Sterling walked in.

"Hi, Crystal." A tall, attractive man with burnished skin, hazel eyes, and golden brown hair sorely in need of a trim, he flashed a dazzling grin. "I don't think I've seen you since Barney and Taffy's wedding. How are you?"

Crystal was wondering if the hand of God was at work. During her lunch hour, she had planned to call Jonas' office to make an appointment with him. Now here he was. "I'm all right. It's been a crazy couple of days."

"I heard." He shrugged his broad shoulders. "Our small-town grapevine is better than a daily newspaper. Are those antirabies vaccines as horrible as they used to be?"

"No. I had a mild reaction last night, but I'm fine today."

He ordered a calzone and salad, too, and then sat at her table. "Hope you don't mind. I always feel conspicuous when I sit by myself."

"Me, too."

"Good. I've solved the problem for both of us." He unfolded a napkin and placed it on his lap. "How much do you charge for a haircut? My practice is just taking off, and I'm living on a shoestring. But if I don't get in to see someone soon, my mother will come after me with clippers."

Crystal liked Kate Sterling, a small, dark-haired woman with an outgoing personality. "I normally charge fifteen. But given the fact that I meant to call your office today to make an appointment, maybe I can offer you free haircuts in exchange for a discount on your usual hourly fee."

He had just taken a bite of his calzone, which he tucked into his cheek. "That sounds great. I tried getting a really short cut so I wouldn't need a trim again soon, but I *hate* the white-sidewall look. Makes me want to wear a skullcap."

Crystal smiled. She could see why Jonas was good at what he did. He had a way of making people relax, and he wasn't afraid to reveal who he really was. "Well, no more short cuts, then. You can see me for a trim as often as you like."

"How soon do you want an appointment?"

"Yesterday."

His cheek creased in a grin. "Can't do yesterday, but I'm wide-open this afternoon."

"I work until six. I'll juggle appointments and arrange for a time later."

"Six would be *great*, actually. I'll order in a pizza, and we can talk over a simple dinner. What's your favorite topping?"

Crystal couldn't imagine herself baring her soul over pizza, but at the same time, it sounded better than a clinical environment. "I like everything but anchovies."

Jonas' office was located in the living space above the Straw Hat on West Main. The restaurant owner, José Hayden, resided in his childhood home, once owned by his deceased mother, so he had used the upstairs flat for storage until recently, when he'd started leasing it out. Crystal finished with her clients fifteen minutes early, so she decided to walk. She hoped the exercise would help her relax for her first meeting with Jonas. Choosing him as her counselor had seemed like a good idea at first, but now she was having second thoughts. He was a local and came from a large family. If he told anyone what she shared with him, everyone in town would know about her past.

She all but ran through the busy restaurant to reach the stairway that led up to his flat and was relieved when none of the diners seemed to notice her. Jonas answered her knock and ushered her inside. "Sorry about the in-home office. It's all I can afford right now."

Crystal glanced around what had originally been a living room but was now an office–living area combo. A painting of a fawn held court over his sofa. She glimpsed another oil, of a mountain stream lined with clusters of aspen. His decorator had aimed for a soothing atmosphere.

"This is fine, Jonas. I know how hard it is to get a business on its feet."

"Boy howdy, you can say that again." He drew open a trifold privacy screen in front of his desk and gestured for her to sit in a cushiony leather armchair with her back to it. "José will have our pizza delivered. The screen will block you from view. Having a shrink is a status symbol only in Hollywood."

Crystal couldn't help but laugh. She liked this man more by the minute. She guessed him to be in his late twenties, probably two or three years younger than she was. "Actually, I am a bit worried, not so much about people knowing I need counseling, but more about what I reveal to you being bandied around town."

"That won't happen. Anything you tell me will never be shared with anyone."

Crystal relaxed. The firm tone of his voice reassured her. "I saw a psychiatrist when I was eleven. She told my parents every word I said."

"*That* was cruel. Who was this gal?"

"I don't recall her name. She practiced in the state of Washington."

Jonas sighed. "Well, I'm sorry she did that, and I'm surprised you found the courage to see me." He sat across from her and leaned back in his chair. His stomach growled, and he placed a large hand over his midriff. "Excuse me. My lunch wore off hours ago." He winked at her. "You can trust me. Whether I can help you remains to be seen, but I can promise you absolute confidentiality. So, to get the ball rolling, what brings you here? Is it the same issue after all these years?"

"Yes." An ache took up residence at the base of her throat. "When I was eleven, I killed my little sister. I shot her with an arrow, straight in the heart."

His gaze locked on hers. "Pardon me for asking this, but I really need to know. Was it an accident, or did you do it deliberately?"

Crystal swallowed. "I hope that's what you'll eventually be able to tell me, Jonas. I don't think I did it on purpose, but the doctor I saw back then suggested that I subconsciously wanted to get rid of my sister. That left me"—she gestured limply with her hand—"confused and no longer absolutely sure it was really an accident."

Just then someone knocked on the door. "There's our pizza." He got up and skirted his desk. "Maybe I should order a bottle of Rolaids for dessert."

Crystal left Jonas' flat two hours later, feeling as if she'd just chatted with a good friend. He was as down-to-earth as leather boot soles, and he was delightfully direct. After only one session, she felt as if a thousand pounds had been lifted off her heart. He had asked her, point-blank, if she'd ever had dreams about Mary Ann dying prior to the accident that took her life. Crystal couldn't recall ever having a single dream like that, but she did confess to sometimes feeling frustrated or angry with Mary Ann, and envious of her church-angel cuteness.

Jonas had laughed and said, "Anybody who says he never felt angry with a sibling is either abnormal or a liar. There were times when I wanted to punch one of my brothers in the face, and my little sisters drove me nuts. I felt frustrated and angry a lot. As for feeling jealous? My dad had four boys, one right after another, and then he got two adorable girls. Adriel and Sarah were masters at manipulating him. All of us boys felt a little jealous now and again. It's perfectly normal."

"So feeling a little jealous isn't a prelude to murder?"

"Of course not, and you should put that concern out of your mind. You've told me about feeling frustrated and angry, but you haven't talked about moments of mindless rage. Typically, a kid will commit acts of lesser violence prior to totally losing it and taking someone's life. I'll also point out that while our subconscious minds *can* induce us to behave in certain ways, they cannot compel us to do anything we wouldn't do while fully conscious. Proven fact. Since you never *consciously* wanted Mary Ann dead, the psychiatrist who suggested that you might have killed her because of subconscious urges was absolutely wrong."

"So it was definitely an accident?"

"You tell me. Did you ever once consciously wish that Mary Ann was dead?"

"No. Never. I didn't even wish that she'd get hurt."

"Then it's extremely unlikely that you deliberately

harmed her. That psychiatrist should have lost her license. I can only hope she's retired now and no longer practices. People like her do more harm than good."

"What about my decision to continue shooting at targets when my sister wanted me to play with her instead? Could my subconscious have pushed me to keep going so that she might run into my line of fire? Was there some part of me that wanted her gone even though I couldn't deliberately take her life?"

A sad smile touched Jonas' firm mouth. "Crystal, that doctor really did a number on you. The power of suggestion can be a fabulous tool to effect positive change, but when misused, the tactics can plant seeds of doubt, set people up for failure, and make them horribly self-conscious of physical flaws they don't even have. If that psychiatrist had suggested to you repeatedly that your nose looked like an eagle's beak, you probably would have spent a fortune on rhinoplasty by now." He held up a hand. "You have a beautiful nose. Get your fingers off it." He laughed. "Damn. You're an easy mark. We need to work on that once you get everything else figured out."

Remembering that, Crystal smiled. Her father, whom she now knew was *not* her father, had told her she had a straight-edged nose, and he hadn't meant it as a compliment. Even though Nadine and Shannon now said that her nose was a near duplicate of Kate Middleton's, Crystal still felt self-conscious. Jonas had her pegged right: she was vulnerable to the power of suggestion.

As she drove home a few minutes later, she almost called Tanner to tell him about her first session with Jonas. But she decided it would be easier to share the details in writing. It was oddly exhilarating to have put to rest that one troubling concern and feel free of it after so many years. She had *not* deliberately killed her sister. Feeling so much better gave her hope that Jonas could eventually help her to let go of everything that had governed her life for so long.

Crystal had been too tense during the talk with Jonas to eat, so he had sent her home with four slices of pizza wrapped in foil. Once in the house, she kicked off her shoes, reheated the food, and poured herself a glass of wine. Then while she nibbled and sipped, she penned a letter to Tanner, describing in detail her conversation with Jonas and how each exchange had made her feel.

When the missive was finished, she texted Tanner. *"I wrote you a letter. You'll find it in the tree. XXXOOO."*

Tanner left for Mystic Creek early the next morning. He wanted to pick up the letter from Crystal and park somewhere along a road to read it before he began his route. When he drew the envelope out of the old oak, he was surprised by how thick it felt. He had expected a short letter. Instead she'd written what felt like the chapter of a book.

Since her car was gone, he read the letter parked in front of the farmhouse. Some of her revelations made his heart ache. Others made him smile, albeit a bit sadly. After reading to the end, he sighed. It appeared to him that she'd taken the first step forward, and he couldn't help but hope that Jonas Sterling could help her find her way to a sense of peace. Even if she couldn't be with Tanner again, he wanted her to be happy.

That afternoon Tanner went to the veterinary clinic during his break to visit Rip. The dog lifted his head and wagged his snub tail. Tanner took a picture of him for Tori. The little girl had expressed feelings of guilt over Rip's injuries. The heeler wouldn't have been hurt if she hadn't disobeyed Crystal by leaving the yard. Tanner wondered if anyone had bothered to comfort Crystal after her sister's death. He doubted it, and he didn't want to make that mistake with his daughter. It was a fine line to walk as a parent, though. Tori needed to understand that adults made rules for a reason, mostly to ensure a child's safety, and there could be serious consequences if she disobeyed. On the other hand, he didn't want to instill within her a lifelong sense of responsibility for what had happened to Rip.

He had decided not to make light of Tori's disobedience or deny that she had led Rip into a dangerous situation. Instead he focused on life being a series of important lessons that everyone had to learn. As an example, he had used the mistake he'd made by driving the company van for personal reasons and drawn a comparison between that and Tori's disobeying Crystal to keep No Name safe. They had each broken a rule to help a friend. Neither of them had intended any harm, but in the end, rules existed for good reasons, and breaking them often resulted in unpleasant and sometimes awful consequences.

After finishing his route, Tanner decided to drive back to the farmhouse and write a letter to Crystal about Tori. He found a piece of paper in the van and wrote a single-spaced letter, explaining his thoughts about Tori's feelings of guilt, his reluctance to gloss over her disobedience, and how he was trying to handle it. Given Crystal's experience with guilt, he asked for her opinion and guidance on how to deal with his daughter. He also praised Crystal for her courage in seeking help from Jonas Sterling and told her that he prayed with almost every breath he took that her counseling journey into the past would lead her forward into a beautiful future with him.

Before driving back to Crystal Falls, he texted Crystal and told her to look in the tree for a letter from him when she got home. As he drove away, he decided he really liked communicating with her this way. When a person put feelings into words, he had plenty of time to think, back up and reword, or scratch out sentences that didn't properly express them. Verbal exchanges demanded quick thinking and didn't always allow for soul-searching.

Crystal couldn't wait to get home to read Tanner's letter, but after her session with Jonas last night, she needed to visit Rip first. It wasn't that she no longer felt guilty for giving him the attack command or that she had stopped questioning the necessity of doing so. It was more that she already had too many regrets and didn't want any more. Rip needed to see her. And she needed to let the dog know how much she still loved him, just in case he died. Jack believed the heeler was on his way to recovery, but he'd also made it clear that this period of time was fraught with dangers. The dog could still develop complications. He wasn't out of the woods yet.

When Crystal approached Rip's cage, he lifted his head, wagged his stump tail, and growled. She laughed even as tears streamed down her cheeks. "Will you always be impossible?"

His bark was a ghost of the sound he'd once made, revealing how weak he still was, but at least his spirit was strong. Crystal opened the cage door to pet him. It was difficult to find a place where her touch wouldn't hurt him.

"I love you, Rip."

He growled.

"And I know you love me."

Another growl.

"All that aside, Mr. Tough Guy, I just want to tell you that Tori and No Name wouldn't be alive if not for you. And you also need to know that little girl will never forgive herself if you give up and die." She leaned inside the cage, pressing her shoulders against the doorframe as she whispered, "Neither will I, Rip. Please don't leave me with that sadness. Get well. Spring forward. Live life to its fullest for at least another seven years. We wouldn't know what to do without you."

The dog lifted his head and licked the tears from her cheeks. Crystal closed her eyes. Then she took a bracing breath and drew back. "When you're released, you'll be going home with Tuck. It doesn't mean I don't love you. Okay? You'll be happier with him and Essie."

"That ain't true, but I'm sure glad to see you here visitin' him."

She almost jumped out of her skin. She turned to find Tuck standing behind her. "You scared me out of ten years' growth."

"Didn't mean to. Just pleased as punch to see you." Tuck spread his arms, stepped forward, and gave her one of his fabulous hugs. "How you feelin'?" he asked as he released her. "Essie told me you weren't doin' so good after that rabies shot."

"I had a reaction, but I was much better by morning."

"I'm glad." Tuck looked past her at the dog. "Hey, you, Rip. You're lookin' better today."

"You came yesterday?"

Tuck stepped in close to cautiously pet his dog. "Sure did. Hired a cab. Not quite ready for that truck yet. I'm thinkin' about gettin' some runnin' boards for it."

"That's a good idea."

"Yep." He smiled over his shoulder at her. "Make it

easier for Essie, too. We don't got as much bounce as we used to."

Crystal was glad that she'd had time alone with Rip to speak from her heart. She figured maybe Tuck needed some one-on-one time, too. "I should go. I have a load of laundry to do tonight. Been a long day."

"Not quite yet," Tuck said. "Give me a minute, and I'll meet you in the waiting room to walk you out."

Crystal nodded. "Bye, Rip. I'll be back tomorrow."

When she reached the waiting room, she kept going until she'd exited through the front doors and could stand outside to enjoy the heat of the setting sun and the fabulous smells of an early-summer evening. At the center of the front lawn, a silver maple grew, its mottled white bark striking a contrast to the backdrop of green. In only minutes Tuck joined her. They stood in silence for a moment.

Then Tuck said, "I want to say I'm sorry for never tellin' you the truth about the man you believed was your father. I should've, but you were still just a girl, and I wasn't sure if you even knew how babies got made."

Crystal thought back. "Hmm. I'm not sure, either, Tuck. If you'd told me right away, I might have been confused. Maybe saying nothing was the better choice."

"Maybe. But at some point you grew up. I could've told you then, and I didn't. You weren't with him and your mama anymore. I kind of felt like I'd be diggin' up old garbage."

"True. By then I had moved on." Crystal looped her arm through his and leaned her head against his shoulder. "I didn't need my father by then. I had you to love me."

"And I loved you a powerful lot. Still do."

"I love you, too, Tuck. And, please, don't worry about things you didn't do back then. What you did do was more than enough."

When Crystal got home, she ran to the oak tree. She found Tanner's letter, a neatly folded piece of paper with writing on both sides that she couldn't wait to read. Moments later she sat at the dining room table, savoring every word he'd written and feeling connected to him by his masculine scrawl in a way she wouldn't have while reading a text or email. She approved of his decisions about how to handle Tori. She could only wish that she'd had a father like him: someone who looked at all the angles, made careful judgments, and loved her without condition. Even though Tori had lost her mother at so early an age, she was still a lucky little girl.

After heating a can of soup for dinner, Crystal fetched some paper and a pen to reply to Tanner's letter. First she told him that she believed he was right on target with how he was dealing with Tori. As she moved on to share more personal thoughts about herself, she chewed as much on the end of the writing implement as she did on the bits of beef in the bowl. It was cathartic to describe her feelings and the events that had led her to have them. While attempting to explain everything to Tanner, she was, in a weird way, learning to understand all of it herself.

She was to meet again with Jonas tomorrow evening. She had a feeling he would approve of this letter-writing business. It helped her recall moments in her life and analyze them dispassionately, as if the child she wrote about had been someone else.

She felt sorry for the little girl she described to Tanner: a tall child with bushy bright red hair, sharp features, toothpick appendages, and a yearning to be loved that had been bigger than she was. While composing those descriptions, she felt as if she were seeing snapshots of her past in a different and unforgiving light, and as she purged her heart with a pen, she was able to see her parents as the individuals they'd actually been. Not even Mary Ann, the adorably cute daughter, had gotten a fair shake. They'd showered her with attention one moment and been self-absorbed the next, leaving Mary Ann to depend on Crystal for the stability every child needed.

Crystal wished that she could create a copy of this letter for Jonas to read, but because she'd written it to Tanner, the man she loved, there were personal mentions that she couldn't share. When she finished writing, she texted Tanner and told him she had left him a message in the tree. He texted back almost instantly, which told her he anxiously awaited any contact from her.

I'll pick it up first thing in the morning. I wish I could hear your voice, though. When you feel ready, maybe you can call me. I love you. Always will. Don't forget that.

Crystal knew she would never forget. The problem for her was learning to love him back without feeling terrified.

Chapter Twenty-one

A month and a half passed, and August heat had descended upon Mystic Creek. Rip had been released from the clinic last week and was now staying with Tuck and Essie at the facility. Crystal had been going to see him there as often as she could. His limp wasn't pronounced, and Tuck predicted it would go away entirely over time. Fur had grown in around his incisions to help hide the scars. Eventually he would look almost like his old self again.

Barney Sterling had called to tell Crystal that the results of the DNA had finally been sent in. There was a positive match with specimens taken from the Medford murder scene. The man who'd entered Crystal's bedroom and rifled her lingerie drawers was a killer. Crystal's skin crawled when she got that news. That night when she'd stood in the bathtub ready to swing a rolling pin, her life could have been in danger. And Rip, bless his heart, had somehow sensed that and been ready to protect her with his own.

Crystal had always loved summer, but she could find no pleasure in it this year. She longed to be with Tanner and his kids, enjoying the sultry evenings and hearing the children's voices as they ran and played. Only, she wasn't sure she was ready. If she rushed back into a relationship with Tanner and then started having misgivings again, it would be disastrous, not only for her, but also for Tanner and his family.

She finally decided to discuss the situation with Jonas during one of her counseling sessions. When he learned that she had put a wonderful relationship on hold, he asked, "What are you thinking, Crystal? If you're sure he's Mr. Right, doing this could put your future with him in jeopardy."

Crystal already knew that. Tanner loved her. Of that, she felt certain. But she couldn't expect him to wait forever while she waffled. "I feel ready now to move on. Mostly. But isn't it better to risk losing him than to jump back into a relationship too soon and possibly hurt him again?"

Jonas folded his arms and gave her a thoughtful study. "What are you afraid of, exactly?"

"Making bad choices. Not thinking of every possibility and letting his kids do something potentially dangerous. Discovering that I can't be all that he needs me to be. Breaking his heart again. Getting mine broken again. Maybe I should make a list."

"I get the picture. You want to be sure nothing will go wrong. But the problem with that is, there are no guarantees. Not for any of us. This is life. It's a trial run. There'll be ups, and there'll be downs. You're bound to make mistakes as a parent. All of us do. Does that mean we can't be wonderful parents? No. We learn lessons as we go along, and eventually, when the kids are about thirty, we think we know it all. Then we turn right around and make mistakes with our grandkids. We're human. None of us is perfect."

"Not everyone is terrified, though."

He sighed. "That's true, and you shouldn't be, either. You're a good person. You'll do your best. That's all any of us can do."

"My best is never quite good enough."

"I don't doubt it. My best is never quite good enough, either."

"I was hoping for some advice, Jonas."

He chuckled. "You aren't here for advice. The whole point is for you to come up with your own answers. What do you think you should do?"

"All I know for sure is that I don't want to lose Tanner and his kids."

"Then make sure you don't."

"Part of me wants to jump back in with both feet. Another part of me is afraid I'll crash and burn. And what if something bad happens to him or one of his kids because of me?"

"Ah, so we're back to the boogeyman in the closet, are we? How do you defeat him, Crystal?"

"Open the door and face him."

"You have to do the same thing with your fears. If you crash and burn, I'll be here to listen. My hair grows half an inch a month."

The next afternoon, Crystal texted Tanner and asked him to meet her that evening by the old oak tree where they still hid notes for each other. For the rest of her shift, she agonized over what she should say. She hadn't engaged in an actual conversation with him in so long. What if it was uncomfortable to talk with him again? That was why she hadn't invited him into the house. If the meeting didn't go well, it would be easier to end it out by the tree.

Crystal left in plenty of time to get home before Tanner arrived, or so she thought. When she reached the farmhouse, his delivery van was already parked out front. She saw Tanner leaning against the old oak, looking so wonderful that tears sprang to her eyes. At this time of year, he wore brown uniform shorts, which show-cased his well-muscled legs. She climbed out of the Equinox and walked slowly toward him. She stopped about three feet away.

"I know I've hurt you, Tanner. I'm so sorry about that."

Tanner said nothing. He just closed the space between them and drew her into his arms. Never had anything felt so perfect. "I've missed you so much," she confessed. "I'm still seeing Jonas. It's mostly like talking to myself, voicing all the things I feel and already know. I've learned a lot about myself, but some things will always remain a mystery. There's one thing I'm absolutely certain of, though: I don't want to lose you and your children."

He tightened his embrace and swayed from side to side. "One thing I'm absolutely certain of is that you won't. In order for me to be happy, I need you in my life. And so do my kids."

He bent his head to nuzzle her neck. "You feel so good. I'd almost forgotten how fabulous it is to have you in my arms. And I see one really positive sign that the sessions with Jonas are helping. You took a step in the right direction, toward me. I love you, Crystal. I don't expect you to be perfect."

"That's good, because I'm not. I never will be. I've come to understand that none of us come with a mistake-proof label." She looked up into his expressive blue eyes and wondered how she'd managed to stay away from him so long. "Will you come sit on the porch with me?"

He grasped her hand and walked with her to the veranda. When they were seated next to each other, he started to put his arm around her. "Please, don't. I can't think clearly when you're touching me."

"Maybe I don't want you to think. Maybe I hope you'll just follow your heart."

"That would be easy. Making wise decisions isn't, and I want to be sure you're making wise ones."

She reached over for his hand. He turned his wrist to encompass her fingers with his longer and stronger ones. She stared at the sky. "Can we just talk for a while? Not about anything in particular."

He ran his thumb over her skin, lighting up her nerve endings in a way no other man ever had. "How's Rip doing?" he asked. "I try to stop and see him during my lunch breaks, but most days I cram down a sandwich and get back to work so I can get home earlier."

"He's doing great. Jack kept him on the alcohol-withdrawal medication at the clinic, and he is now officially on the wagon. He loves being with Tuck and Essie. You should take Tori and Michael to visit him. I doubt he's strong enough to fetch sticks yet, but he would love to go for a walk. He adores those kids."

"Maybe we can do that together soon."

"Yeah. I miss him so much. I'd like that."

He sighed. "I, um, have some news. Quite a lot, actually. While we weren't seeing each other, I was busy."

"Doing what?"

"Well, on the Rip front, I bought his son for Tori and Michael."

For an instant, Crystal thought she'd misunderstood him. "You what?"

"I delivered a package three days ago and walked into a yard where I encountered an eight-week-old blue heeler pup that has all Rip's quirks. He's got the same blaze on his forehead, and he has the toll-cookie game down pat. His mama is a purebred. The woman who owns her described Rip right down to the curry-colored toe on his left rear foot. Said he came calling one afternoon when the female was in heat."

"Are you *serious*? Rip fathered puppies?"

"Yep. And years ago, Tuck somehow got Rip registered with the AKC, and he dug up the paperwork for me. That made the woman happy. She can sell the pups for a lot more. She gave me a discount because I gave her a copy of his registration."

"You paid good money to get the kids a dog that will probably be a total pain for the next fourteen years?"

Tanner chuckled. "Yep. I already asked Tuck to teach him obedience. He'll be a train wreck in some ways, but I think he'll be wonderful with the kids." He gave her a questioning look. "If you hate the idea, I'll forfeit the money, and we can get some other kind of dog. A nice, easy kind of breed."

Crystal envisioned Rip. His face. How he'd dived into that pack of coyotes to save Tori's life with no thought for himself. "No. If I raise a dog, I want one that will take on a grizzly to protect our children."

Tanner nodded. "My thoughts exactly."

Crystal smiled. "A baby Rip. What do the kids want to name him?"

"Hercules."

"Oh, I *like* that."

"Me, too. Tori wanted to name him Heracles, the actual Greek name, but Michael threw a fit."

Crystal smiled. "That child is going to think circles around both of us."

"Probably. But there's one other thing I need to bring up. Tuck says he'll never leave the facility now that Essie owns it, so I asked him if he'd sell us this house. He said yes. I think it's a perfect place to raise a family. What do you think?"

"So you knew all along?" She studied his face, which had become so dear. "You knew I'd reach this point."

"No. Sometimes you roll the dice and spring forward, Crystal. Just like Tuck did. Just like Rip did. I love you. Win or lose, what choice was there for me to make?"

She stared at him through tears. "I love you, too, and once that happens, there isn't a choice, is there?"

His eyes delved deeply into hers. "Oh, yeah. We still have decisions to make, and I need a forever house here before I move my kids. I think this place is it."

Crystal imagined a fire on the patio on a warm summer night. And the farmhouse would create a postcard-perfect setting for white Christmases. It was a home originally designed for a large family, and Crystal had become acutely aware of that while living here alone.

"I agree," she said. "It's a perfect place to raise kids. And Rip's son."

He sighed. "I've enjoyed all your letters. I've gotten to know you so much better. I understand now how people can fall in love with each other online. They can reveal all the important things about themselves before they ever meet."

"Do you honestly still love me now that you've read all that and know how screwed up I am?"

His gaze held hers. "I love you even more. And you're not screwed up. You're amazing."

Silence fell between them. Finally, he asked, "Where are we going, Crystal? We've discussed a family dog, and we agree that we should buy this house. But what's the next real step for you and me?"

She stared at the sky. "Do you ever wish God would write answers up there?"

He joined her in studying the blue expanse above

them. "If He did, all of us would know exactly what to do, and life wouldn't be such an adventure. Instead He allows us to make our own decisions and mistakes."

"I make more mistakes than most people."

"No, you don't. Not really. Tori has said things to me about that night in the woods. One evening I popped off to my mom about those coyotes being vicious, and Tori chimed in to tell me you said they weren't really mean, only hungry. That they saw Rip and No Name as food, not as our little friends."

"So?"

He cast her a sidelong glance. "I was blown away. You'd lifted my little girl up into a tree to keep her safe. You'd been bitten by possibly rabid coyotes. Rip was torn to pieces and bleeding to death. But you still had the presence of mind to prevent my child from being terrified of coyotes for the rest of her life."

"I know firsthand how bad experiences can affect kids."

"The point is that you kept a level head."

Crystal fell quiet to assimilate that. "Okay, I suppose that's true. Yay. I did one thing right."

"You did a lot of things right. If a hundred women were lined up in front of me and I had to choose only one to be with my daughter in a wilderness area, it would be you." He leaned over to kiss her forehead. "You'd protect her with your life, and you'd do your best not to let the frightening stuff scar her emotionally."

"I made one huge mistake that night."

"No. Tori did when she disobeyed you. You did damage control, and as I see it, you did a damned good job of it. Not every woman would wade into a pack of coyotes in a killing frenzy with only a flashlight as a weapon. Don't you realize how astounding that was?"

"I've never really looked at it that way. I'm not brave, Tanner. I guess I was running on pure adrenaline."

"You're brave, and that night you were extremely brave."

She searched his sun-burnished countenance. "I was afraid to love you. I was afraid to love your kids. I'm not brave. I'm a coward."

"You allowed yourself to love us, anyway. Even though you were afraid. Even though you had every reason to run the other direction. You loved us, anyway. Spring forward with me, Crystal."

"What?"

"You heard me. Life isn't a destination. It's a journey. Sometimes we have to spring forward and take it on just like Tuck and Rip did. Did Tuck hesitate when he took you home? Hell, no. And did Rip hesitate when you yelled, 'Spring forward'? Hell, no. Rip knew Tori's life was at stake. He just dived in. He recognized the odds. That dog isn't stupid. But he loved her so much it didn't matter. He sprang forward, because in the end, what else really counts except giving it our best shot? Maybe we'll get the shit kicked out of us. Maybe we'll win most of the battles and lose a few along the way, but if we stand together, we'll make it."

Crystal had already decided that she wanted to make a life with this man and his children, but still buried within her was that boogeyman in the closet. "What if I make awful mistakes?"

"What if I do? It's not the mistakes that matter. What matters is making enough good decisions to make it to the finish line." He shifted closer to her. "I love you. Do you love me?"

"Yes."

"Then spring forward with me. Love me with every-

thing you've got for as long as you can. Let's take on
the challenges together and be as brave as Rip. If he'd
hesitated that night, Tori could have been killed. We
shouldn't hesitate, either. I don't know about you, but
if I can't be with you, a part of me will die."

Crystal felt as if she stood on a precipice and someone was about to push her over the edge. Only if she
fell, it would be straight into Tanner Richards' arms.
How could that end badly?

He tipped his head and kissed her lightly on the lips.
That single brush of their mouths made her heart
pound. "I can't guarantee bad things won't happen,"
he told her. "I'll make mistakes. You'll make mistakes.
Life and everything it dishes out can be both brutal and
wonderful. But if people love each other, the wonderful
stuff outweighs all the bad."

"And without the wonderful, what do any of us really
have?" she asked.

He looped an arm around her shoulders and pressed
his cheek against hers. "Does that mean you'll spring
forward with me?"

She hugged his neck. "Yes. You're my taste of wonderful, Tanner. So are your kids."

Before she could anticipate what he meant to do, he
scooped her up in his arms, stood, and carried her into
the house.

"For richer or poorer. For better or worse. In sick-
ness and in health." He stopped outside her bedroom
door. "Even wedding vows allow for the fact that our
life together won't be perfect."

"No, life is never perfect," she agreed. "But in between the moments of chaos or despair, maybe we can
aim for almost perfect."

"Now you're talking. Almost perfect works for me."

As Tanner carried her toward the bed, she knew he

was the only man in the world for her. And as he began making love to her moments later, every touch of his hands on her body told her that she was the only woman in the world for him. No matter what challenges the future held in store, they would face them together.

And together they would be a winning team.

Don't miss

THE CHRISTMAS ROOM,

a heartwarming contemporary romance filled with
homespun good cheer, available now!

As Kirstin Conacher led the way to her table, she was acutely aware of the man behind her. He'd caught her attention the moment he entered the building—muscular, six feet of handsome, with tousled hair that gleamed like the well-varnished knotty pine bar. His eyes were a radiant sky blue, and he had a burnished tone to his skin that pegged him as an outdoor enthusiast. She could tell with only a look that he was no stranger to physical labor, and she'd been impressed by the easy, warm way he conversed with Trish. No fake charm, no canned lines. She found the sense of authenticity that he gave off very refreshing. There was also something vaguely familiar about him, but she couldn't recall ever having met him.

Oh, Kirstin, she mentally scolded herself, *what on earth were you thinking to hit on him like that?* Her cheeks burned with embarrassment. So what if she'd been searching for the right guy for six years and could hear her biological clock ticking? That was no excuse for her to be so forward. Normally she waited for a man to hit on *her,* not the other way around.

She resumed her seat, where a martini, extra dirty and straight up, still awaited her. In Kirstin's opinion, Trish made the best one in the valley. Only she hadn't come here for an afternoon drink. The martini was merely one of her stage props. She'd learned over time that men in bars tended to steer clear of a lone woman having a soda. A recognizable mixed drink seemed to spur on conversation.

Cam took a stool across from her. "Have you already ordered?"

She met his gaze, and a tingling sensation moved up her spine. That surprised her. She'd met dozens of handsome men, but she'd never felt like this. "Yes. The cook seems to be dragging his feet today."

"Come here often?"

"Not that often." *Liar, liar, boots on fire.* She came to the Cowboy Tree as often as she was able to escape from her dad's ranch for a couple of hours. The male patrons tended to be landowners who put in an honest day's work. She knew most of them, and unfortunately, they also knew her. Local men didn't mess with Sam Conacher's daughter. She kept hoping for a stranger to drop in, someone wonderful who wouldn't know about her dad. "Are you new to the valley?"

"Oh, yeah." He flashed a dazzling grin that creased his lean cheeks and displayed straight white teeth. "Anyone whose family hasn't been in the valley for three generations is a newcomer, or so I'm told. It'll be years before I earn the privilege of being recognized as a Bitterrooter."

She bent her head and toyed with her olive pick. Her cheeks went warm again. When she looked up, she said, "I hope I didn't give you the wrong impression. I don't habitually hit on guys."

A twinkle danced in his eyes. "Did you hit on me? It went over my head. I guess I need to get out more."

"My name's Kirstin."

"Cam."

"I know. I heard Trish talking with you after you came in. Short for Cameron?"

"Yep. Cameron McLendon."

Her fingers tightened on the olive pick. "Scottish?"

"Only half. My mom's Irish."

Kirstin's father was a Scot, and he was the most stubborn, irascible man she'd ever known. He hadn't always been that way, though. The death of her mother six years earlier had changed him. "Well, half Scottish or not, you seem nice."

He chuckled. "I take it you have a low opinion of Scots."

"Not really. Just a difficult experience with one in particular." She took a sip of her drink. "So, Cameron McLendon, tell me about yourself."

He smiled. "Boring story."

"So is mine, I'm afraid, but to get acquainted, we have to start somewhere, and I asked first."

He chuckled. "Want me to get two toothpicks so you can prop your eyelids open?" He followed the question with a sigh. "Okay, here goes. I got a job opportunity with Long Barrel Ranches, and I've wanted to live here or in northern Idaho most of my adult life. It was finally my chance to chase my dreams, so I took the position."

"I'm not bored yet. Keep talking."

He shrugged. "For a long time, my dreams took second seat to my responsibilities, and I got stuck in Northern California. It's not that I dislike California, but after a couple of trips to this area, I fell in love. I kept hoping I might settle here, but life kept throwing me curveballs."

"Still interesting. What kind of curveballs?"

"It's kind of personal to share with a stranger."

Kirstin huffed. "Oh, boy. You haven't been in the valley long enough. No one can keep a secret here. You may as well spill your guts."

"I guess it's not *that* personal." He shrugged. "I got my girlfriend pregnant in high school."

"Uh-oh. I'm not sure that qualifies as a curveball. More like a demolition ball."

He paused to search her gaze, his expression conveying a mixture of surprise and appreciation. "Most people just say 'tough luck' and then move on to more interesting subjects."

Kirstin had met individuals who skimmed only the surface with her in conversations. When she told people about a life-altering event and they barely acknowledged her comment, she felt unimportant if not invisible. It also hinted that the other person had little emotional depth. "It *was* tough luck, I suppose, but the ramifications go well beyond that and probably lasted for years."

His cheek creased again in a suppressed smile. "Voice of experience?"

She shook her head. "No. I lived a very sheltered life in high school." She wanted to add that she still lived a sheltered experience, but that would shift the conversation to her, and her own life bored her to tears. "I did have a friend who got pregnant, though. She kept the baby, and her future was totally steered off course." She popped a green olive in her mouth. "So what happened? After you learned of the pregnancy, I mean."

He took a sip of his drink. "Well, it didn't demolish my life, but it did drastically alter it. My dad insisted that I marry her."

"At seventeen?" If Kirstin ever had kids, which seemed more unlikely with each passing year, she'd never force her son or daughter to get married that young. "That must have been a recipe for disaster."

"Pretty much. Our feelings for each other—or at least hers—weren't strong enough to withstand the trials of a teen pregnancy, and she filed for divorce before the baby was born. I think it was the shortest marriage on record." He shrugged. "Not all her fault, not entirely mine, either. She wanted to put our child up for adoption, but my parents helped me get custody. Right after she had the baby, she faded from the picture completely. No phone calls, no visitations. But even so, she refused to give up her parental rights. That ended up being a mess when I tried to get authorization from her to move my son out of state. She wouldn't cooperate. I think that, for whatever reason, she still holds a grudge against me. I'm not sure for what. Both of us were just kids."

Kirstin nodded. "At that point she should have turned loose of it. But apparently she didn't, and without her authorization to relocate, you were screwed."

"Pretty much stuck in California, for sure. And then, about five years ago, my dad was diagnosed with stage-four colon cancer."

She glimpsed a shimmer of moisture in his eyes and felt a burn in her own. She knew how devastating it was to lose a beloved parent to cancer. Kirstin would never forget the day her mother had been diagnosed. "That must have been rough."

"Three years of rough. He was stubborn and didn't give up easily. My mother, God bless her, stood by him and cared for him until the end. All during his illness, I lived and worked an hour and a half away. They had a gorgeous home in snow country, and when a storm came during the winter, my first call of the day was to my folks to see how deep the white stuff was. Anything over three inches had me hauling ass north so I could clear their driveway, a necessity in case Mom had to call for an ambulance." He shook his head. "As Dad's illness worsened, her burdens increased, and my father needed moral support. What kind of son would have left them?"

Kirstin's heart squeezed. Though his story differed

from hers, she *completely* understood how he must have felt back then. "No siblings to help you out?"

"I've got an awesome older sister." His eyes warmed with fondness. "She loves our parents as much as I do. But she'd gotten married before Dad got sick, has a family, lives on the East Coast, and has a challenging career. It was really hard on her when things got bad. She couldn't come home for every rough spot in the road. Airline fares alone made that impossible. Our folks helped with her travel costs, but mostly she tried to come when she could spend quality time with them."

"When her visits really counted." Kirstin remembered how her own life had become centered on her parents during her mom's illness. When she wasn't needed to care for her mother, she'd been trying to comfort her father. "That must have been so awful for her, wanting to be there all the time and unable to be."

"Exactly. She couldn't just abandon her family and career to be around constantly. She did what she could. And at the end, even though she couldn't catch a flight to get there before he died, she was there when it mattered most, to support me and Mom afterward." He took a sip of his drink. "It was difficult for me. I won't say it wasn't, or that I didn't feel resentful sometimes. I know she felt awful about it. But, hey, I'd chosen my path, mistake driven though it was, and that left me being the only kid on the ground to take care of our folks."

Trish delivered their meals. Kirstin smiled when she saw that they'd both ordered wings. "Great minds think alike." She eyed her basket of food and cringed. Eating chicken wings was messy and required no fewer than ten napkins to keep the sauce off her hands and face. For reasons she had no time to analyze right now, she wanted to be at her best as she got to know this guy. "This isn't what I would have ordered if I'd known I'd be eating with you."

He seemed to welcome the distraction, and Kirstin understood that. When she recalled her mother's painful death, she felt as if her heart was being pushed through a meat grinder.

"Chow down," he said. "If you smear sauce all over your face, I won't hold it against you. Just do me the same favor."

Kirstin grabbed a pile of table napkins and set it between them. "We have a deal. But don't let good table manners take precedence over telling me the rest of your story."

Around a bite of food, he said, "Only if you play fair and tell me yours."

"I can do that."

He frowned as if trying to remember what he'd been saying. "Anyway, my dad passed away almost two years ago. I think Mom was in shock the first year. Me too, I suppose. And my son took it really hard. Dad was our patriarch, the hub of our lives." He took two of the napkins. "Last spring, when I got a chance to work for Long Barrel Ranches, selling exclusive agricultural or recreational properties, I really wanted to grab the opportunity. Only I couldn't leave my mother behind in Northern California. What family she has there is spread out over the state and up into Oregon. She had some friends, of course, but that isn't the same as people who love you."

"So she agreed to move here with you?" Kirstin guessed, dabbing the corners of her mouth.

"She said she was ready for a change so she wouldn't constantly be reminded of Dad—their favorite restaurants, the trails they loved to walk, things like that. So I took my son before a judge. He was nearly sixteen. Caleb told the judge that he had never heard from his mom, that she had never even sent him a birthday card, and he didn't think it was fair that he couldn't move to Montana with me. The judge deemed Caleb to be old enough and mature enough to make that choice for himself. In a little over a week, I had permission to relocate my son. I put my farm on the market and came to the Bitterroot Valley to find a piece of land. Now we're here on our property, essentially camping out while our residences are being built."

Kirstin nearly choked as she swallowed. "Is your property on the river?"

He wiped his mouth. "Oh, yeah. We got so lucky. A large chunk of property with a lot of river frontage. Gorgeous piece of land. As rough as our living conditions are right now, even my mother loves it. Incredible three-hundred-and-sixty-degree views of the mountains. Fairly private. Good soil for alfalfa. The only problem is that Murphy's Law reigned supreme this summer, slowing things down as far as construction went. We had to get septic system approval, and the county is especially careful about granting that on river property. The builder hasn't even broken ground yet. He will soon, though."

Kirstin collected her composure. "I think we're neighbors. You're the people with the—um—huge camp."

Cam looked startled for a moment and then smiled. "Everyone who drives along Fox Hollow Road probably sees it. I think it's become a conversation piece, with people speculating about what crazy thing I might do next. When you're trying to create comfort for your family out in an alfalfa field, you have to be inventive. I've nicknamed it the Hillbilly Village."

"I'm glad you have a sense of humor about it. My father says we've been invaded by the Clampetts."

He threw back his tawny head and barked with laughter. She loved his broad smile. "Fair enough. I got everything in our camp functional, but I couldn't make it pretty. We tried to rent a house, but no landlord would accept us. We have three dogs and six cats, not to mention horses."

"We drive by your place going to and from town." She fiddled with a crumpled napkin. "When I first saw you walk in, something about you seemed familiar. Now I know why. At a distance, I see you all the time. My father owns the ranch behind your property."

Cam stared at her. "You're Kirstin *Conacher*? Sam Conacher's daughter?" He thumped himself on the forehead with the heel of his hand, leaving a smear of red sauce above his left eyebrow. "Oh, shit!"

Kirstin realized that he was already aware of her father's reputation. "My dad isn't as bad as rumor makes him out to be." The moment she spoke, she knew she needed to make a retraction. "Well, he actually *is* pretty bad, but I've learned ways around him."